The Never Ending QUEST

Susan Corey

Copyright © 2013 by Susan Corey
First Edition – October 2013

ISBN
978-1-4602-2582-0 (Hardcover)
978-1-4602-2583-7 (Paperback)
978-1-4602-2584-4 (eBook)

All rights reserved.

No part of this publication may be reproduced in any form, or by any means, electronic or mechanical, including photocopying, recording, or any information browsing, storage, or retrieval system, without permission in writing from the publisher.

Produced by:

FriesenPress

Suite 300 – 852 Fort Street
Victoria, BC, Canada V8W 1H8

www.friesenpress.com

Distributed to the trade by The Ingram Book Company

SUSAN COREY

For all those who believe we can save Earth.

ACKNOWLEDGEMENTS

The Never Ending Quest would never been written if it was not for my dear friend Sandra Murley who awakened my spirituality and gave me the courage to explore it. By providing insights and ideas, she has been a vital part through the writing and typing of The Never Ending Quest. The whale tail concept for the cover is her idea. She has been my 'rock' throughout the process. Her support and encouragement were unwavering. Thank you, Sandra for being there from the moment the book was a spark of an idea to its completion.

Thanks to my brothers Peter and Lez, who are always there for me, even when I was distracted or unavailable from time to time.

I'm indebted to Andrea Kelter of Nova Scotia, a fellow fan of watching the gentle majestic giants in the Bay of Fundy, for allowing me to use her description of the day she gazed into a right whale's eye, a rare and incredible experience.

My gratitude to Cindy for her never ending support and enthusiasm.

Thanks to Sarah and the crew of the sailboat on which I have spent many an hour watching the whales in the Bay of Fundy.

It takes a lot of people to take a manuscript and transform it into a book. I thank everyone and their editor at Friesen Press for helping to make my dream come true.

FOREWORD

During the four summers I was studying for my Honours Biology degree, I worked as a summer technician at the Federal Research Station in St. Andrews N.B. It was here that I fell in love with the ocean and marine biology. My love and respect for the sea grew stronger and stronger while working on and receiving my Ph.D. from the University of Glasgow. During my career at Guelph University, my research on the Bay of Fundy brought me full circle back to St. Andrews and Grand Manan Island where I currently spend my summers writing and whale watching.

In the year 2000, a dear friend of mine moved into a retirement home where I met Sandra Murley who reawakened my long dormant spirituality which had been buried due to my scientific background.

At first I felt very conflicted because I had been taught that 'if it can't be proven, then it does not exist.' Through my awakened spirituality, I have learned to focus, listen and believe in my intuition which in turn has confirmed the many truths I have experienced in my lifetime.

By combining science and metaphysics in a fictional story to show how and why we have abused Earth to the virtual point of no return and why our oceans are the key. As a reader, you will learn about many truths which are intertwined in this story.

PART ONE
1990 – 1991

"Matthew:

My name is Chris Renfrew, a microbiologist you met at last winter's conference in California. We had several interesting discussions about your upcoming promotion. I was diagnosed with advanced cancer in early April; I have only a few weeks to live. I hope you remember me!"

"Indeed I do," Matt said out loud.

Matt had met Renfrew a couple of times. They worked in the same field and in the same building in Boston—but they might as well have been working on opposite sides of the globe. This lab complex consisted of ten floors: six above ground, and four below it. Matt worked on the second underground level, whereas Chris worked in the lowest two levels, which were off-limits to all but a few scientists and their technicians. It was here that top secret research was located. They had their own entrance, elevator, separate sets of labs and offices, and a private cafeteria. Matt sometimes wondered what went on there, but had never really questioned it. He continued to read the letter:

> I remembered how very important integrity was to you. I'm sending you this material, as I didn't know where else to turn; I'm running short of time.
>
> About three months ago, I became apprehensive. We were put on a high-security alert without being told why. Several scientists arrived over the course of a week, and some very high-level discussions were held. I recognized some of them as top bacteriologists, and was aware that two or three of them were working on communicable diseases and their cures. There was one man in particular whom I recognized; we had previously worked together for a while. I did not like him, as he had questionable integrity; he was let go by a certain university for that very reason. I started to do some research and quietly kept track of their comings and goings—dates, times, that sort of thing. Because of the communicable disease aspect, I kept alert for unusual disease outbreaks, their locations, etc.
>
> Matt, I have no proof—no smoking gun, so to speak—but I suspect that something illegal is going on in our research facility. Maybe I feel this way because I'm old and unwell, but I don't think that's the case. Due to my condition, I cannot do much more. Please read over my notes and findings to decide whether or not it's necessary to do something.

In trust, your colleague,

Chris Renfrew.

An hour ago, Matt had been watching the ten pm news. His doorbell rang, which caught him unawares; he wasn't expecting anyone. When he opened the door, he was mystified—no one was there. As he closed the door, he noticed a package sitting on the porch immediately to his right. He picked it up, and as he did so, he was aware of a dark-coloured car pulling away from across the street. Shutting the door, he checked the address on the two-inch-thick yellow envelope. It was indeed addressed to him.

Full of curiosity, he opened it and dumped the contents on the kitchen table. There was a small brown journal, a cover letter, and sheets of paper which were separated into three sets; the handwriting on them was identical to that of the cover letter. It was almost eleven pm by the time he began to read the journal and papers—and the more he read, the more he wondered, *Are these the ramblings of an old, ill scientist, or is there some truth to it all?*

Matt realized that, no matter what he thought at the moment, he was too tired to do anything more; he placed the material back in the envelope. As he was climbing the stairs to make his way to bed, he was struck with a frightening premonition; when he reached the top of the stairs, he immediately turned and went back down to the kitchen. Compelled by a sudden sense of urgency and fear, he picked up the package, took it to the basement, and hid it.

After a very restless night, he made himself a strong pot of coffee, retrieved the package from the basement, and placed it on the table.

What am I going to do with all this? he thought.

By his second cup, his mind was much clearer. *First of all, I must make a couple of copies; I'll have to find a secure hiding place for each one of them.* He wrote down some of the thoughts which were swirling around in his head; he topped up his coffee, and went to his study.

Matt reread each page before he photocopied it, and the more he read, the more he began to realize that Renfrew was on to something. He picked up the phone to call Renfrew, but the housekeeper answered instead.

"I'm sorry," said the housekeeper, "Dr. Renfrew died early yesterday morning in hospital."

"I...I'm very sorry. Are there funeral arrangements?"

"He has no family. He made all his own arrangements."

Stunned, Matt slowly placed the phone back in the receiver; looking at the material again, he was struck anew with the implications. If Renfrew's observations were true—and if Chris's superiors had even a hint of what he had done—then Matt would have to be extremely careful.

Thankful that it was Saturday—giving him time to strategize—he hid the original documents in the basement, at the bottom of a box containing old papers. As he was placing the other copies into separate envelopes, he had a flash of inspiration: he'd recently received some mint stamps from Gibbons; he would put Renfrew's notes in the British Commonwealth folder and lock it in his large safety-deposit box at the bank. Once that was done, he would pack a box of food, along with some beer, and go out to his cabin for the remainder of the weekend for some fishing.

Matt was pleased with himself; the idea of fishing over the weekend—a pastime he frequently enjoyed—was especially appealing. He knew he had a lot to think about, and he needed a quiet place to do it.

As he drove down the lane that led to his retreat, his imagination wandered to the rustic, thousand-square-foot cabin that his grandfather had built in the 1940s. It stood on a hill, about twenty feet above the lake's edge, and occupied the middle of five lots. Walker Lake was not large; it was nestled right in the centre of a chain of three lakes.

The lane was bordered by large old spruce trees, and it curved gently as it led to a small parking lot. He stopped, parked the car, and got out. Matt breathed in deeply. The fresh, rich air was filled with the clean smell of the thick woods surrounding him, and as he exhaled, he heard the laugh of a loon in the distance; he had always loved the sound of their call.

While unlocking the door to the cabin, he contemplated what to do next: would he relax inside, go outside on the deck, or would he go fishing? After closing the door behind him, he placed his computer, notepad, and other personal effects on the large antique oak dining-room table which sat against the wall that separated the kitchen, two bedrooms, and a bathroom from the large, open space. At one end of this expansive area was the big old cast-iron fireplace, standing on a platform raised six inches off the floor by ornamental claw feet.

The front of the cabin was all windows, offering a clear view of the ten-foot-wide deck which ran the entire length of the cabin and around the corner to the door. Matt's attention was drawn to the wall behind the table; it was covered with a series of family photographs, along with a large topographic map of the area. Hearing yet another call of the loon, he turned and looked out at the lake. *Yes,* he decided. *Fishing.*

Matt gathered his fishing gear together with the bait he had purchased, made himself a sandwich, and grabbed a cold beer. Placing this in his cooler bag, he picked up the envelope containing his own notes and the material Renfrew had sent him;

these he slid into a large zip-lock bag. He wanted it with him to keep it safe.

He got into his rowboat and decided to go up to the head of the lake. He never really cared whether or not he caught anything—the peace, quiet, and solitude were enough for him. Here he was by himself, with nothing but a few fish and the odd Mallard or Merganser duck floating by. Half-watching the Belted Kingfisher sitting on a branch of an old dead spruce tree, he baited his hook and cast into an area of thinly-spaced weeds. This was his little piece of heaven.

Still, he could not relax his mind. He knew he had to come up with a plan before he went back to work on Monday. He was quite satisfied with what he had done so far, but what was he going to do next? Again, concerns regarding the security at the lab became paramount in his mind. *What if Security was suspicious of Renfrew? Would they not be keeping an eye on him? If so, did they know that Renfrew sent me this package? If so, are they watching me?*

After a time, he decided to quit fishing; it looked like rain was coming, and he got back to the cabin just as it started to pour. Once inside, he checked the weather forecast: rain was expected for the rest of the day and overnight. *Perfect*, Matt thought. *I can spend the time doing some research on my computer.* He grabbed a sandwich, cracked open a beer, and sat down at the table. He began several hours of research, specifically looking for any unusual outbreaks of disease or poisoning that occurred anywhere in the world. If his suspicions were correct, such outbreaks would probably be in remote areas, which would be relatively easy to control. After two hours of online searching, he decided to bring up news releases from all over the world. As he keyed in certain words, a list of reports, news articles, and medical releases flooded his screen. To narrow it down, he went country by country in alphabetical order.

Australia was the first country that showed anything of interest. In an area somewhere in the outback, eleven people in three days had died of an unknown disease or poison. Officials were still investigating, but there were no conclusions. Matt made a note of it and continued searching.

Later, just as he was getting tired and hungry, he found a report dated three months earlier: in the Canary Islands, several people had died on a remote island. A small group of nine people who had gone to fish and snorkel had perished from what was said to be poison from fish they had consumed. *Two separate incidents, and I'm only up to the letter c. Coincidence?* he wondered. After reading the rest of the report, he put his computer on sleep mode, and went and got himself something to eat.

Finally, at one am, he reached the end of the alphabetical list; he had discovered five more incidents similar to the first two, and all were in different countries. The number of individuals who died in each incident varied from six to fourteen. All cases were in relatively remote areas, and were caused by mysterious diseases or poison.

Matt was now certain that Renfrew was on to something. All seven cases had occurred over a period of three months; the last one occurred in Russia within the previous month.

Several questions troubled him as he stumbled to bed. When he finally succumbed to a shallow sleep, his dreams were fitful.

Early the next morning, he woke up with a monster headache. He usually welcomed the sunrise coming over the mountain and the haunting call of the loon, but on this day he could barely stand it. His head was throbbing and his mouth tasted awful. After brushing his teeth and gargling, he brewed a pot of exceptionally strong coffee and took two Advil. He went out to the deck to have breakfast; he needed fresh air.

The two loons who had earlier beckoned him had apparently decided to go fishing in the upper lake; all became quiet. Matt tried to think, but he just couldn't concentrate. It was only after his second cup of thick black coffee that the headache started to recede, and he was able to think clearly again. He had made up his mind that the cases he'd found were related to the three of Renfrew's. The ten cases were *not* random. One or two of them could be explained away, but the other eight or nine? Highly unlikely.

He sat quietly for a few minutes when a thought broke through: *Why didn't I think of this before?* he asked himself. Leafing through Renfrew's material, he compared it with his notes from the previous night. He quickly discovered that some of the scientists on Renfrew's list were from or had worked in the same countries he'd listed the previous night; he could see the correlation. The scientists' names lined up with eight of the ten countries where the mysterious deaths had occurred. *Renfrew, you really were on to something!*

During his third cup of coffee, it hit him: *What if these ten incidents are, in fact, controlled experiments by the company I work for? Are they testing new drugs—or something much, much worse? Is this a part of some covert research into biological warfare? If so, who are the ultimate targets?*

"Matt—you're over-caffeinated and paranoid. Stop!" he said out loud. His voice echoed in the empty room.

It was Sunday evening, and he could not put the whole business out of his mind. The more he thought about it, the more he realized he had to tell someone—but who?

Who would ever believe that our governments, our military, or civilians would do such a thing—and why? he wondered.

After a couple of hours, Matt made a decision: he would leak the information. There were two people he knew he could trust: Mary, the woman he loved and had lived with while they were studying for their postgraduate degrees in microbiology. He would have to be very careful in how he communicated with her. Writing in code was the answer. Mary had taught him this; it was a game she and her father played when Mary was a child.

This made him think of Megan, his daughter. *Will you ever forgive me, Megan?* he thought, as he often did when she came to mind.

The other person he knew he could reach out to was Gwen Ross, a former girlfriend who was an investigative reporter.

Later that night, he sat down and wrote to Mary, using more than one of their simpler codes. It had taken three attempts and two and a half hours to write it. It looked like a letter from an old fling. It was an apology for the way he had left Mary and Megan three years ago. More importantly, it contained vital information as to where Mary would find the data he had gathered. He wanted her to know this in case, for whatever reason, he was unable to convince Gwen of the potential importance of what he had already found.

On Monday at work, everything went as usual. No one seemed unduly interested in him, so he was feeling fairly certain that nobody was aware of what he had discovered.

* * *

"Sir, I'm afraid we may have a leak or a mole," said Patrick O'Brian, head of security for Bio Tech.

"Where, and in which section?" A voice, sharp with authority and concern, came booming forth from behind a very large and ornate hand-carved oak desk. Earlier, he had been pacing around his office, which was located on the lowest underground level of a very unobtrusive-looking building. He turned around to glare at Patrick while straightening the name plaque on his desk, which read *Dr. Marshall Sandforth III*.

He pressed the intercom button. "Hold all calls," he barked, and released the button. This was not what he wanted to hear first thing on a Monday morning. "Now Patrick—what is this all about?"

"We don't have absolute proof yet. You said to report anything—even the slightest indication that there may be a problem."

"Yes, yes—go on."

"Security on underground level three think that Renfrew was up to something just before he became ill, right around the time he stopped working. He died in hospital Saturday morning. Security noted Renfrew was taking an unusual interest in the comings and goings of several scientists who visited here a few weeks ago."

Sandforth stood up and moved to another chair. He didn't want any sign—even the slightest—to reveal how concerned he was.

"You must have more on this, O'Brian, or you wouldn't be here talking to me."

"True, sir. When Renfrew asked if there was a special conference going on, we got curious and entered his office at night; we checked his computer, and found he had been researching two of the scientists and had placed question marks beside their names. We also took the top page from a notepad he had been writing on; it showed pen impressions. It was a list of many of the scientists who were here, along with the dates, and the countries they came from. Beside one of the names—Dr. Smyth—he had placed a large, heavy question mark, along with the name of a small and rather isolated community: Black's Hill, Australia."

"Anything else?"

"Yes. We had our girl at the hospital keep an eye on Renfrew and note any phone calls he made, and any visitors he had. He had one visitor: an apparent grandson, to whom he gave a large yellow envelope. By the time our girl had reported this to us,

Renfrew had died. We searched his room and found nothing, and there was nothing in his apartment that was suspicious."

"What about the grandson?"

"Renfrew did not have a grandson, as it turns out."

"I see. Does he have other relatives?"

"None. There is one other thing: I don't necessarily think it's related, but there's an investigative reporter requesting an interview with you. Her name's Gwen Ross—and she will not be easy to put off."

"I know who she is. She's won several awards and is known to be a very hard-nosed reporter. Do the very best you can to put her off for a while."

"I'll do my best."

"Thanks, O'Brian. See if Renfrew has had any connection with anyone working here."

Within the hour, Sandforth had his answer.

"Renfrew and a bacteriologist, a Matthew Stone, who also works here on the second subterranean level, have attended a few conferences at the same time," reported O'Brian. "The most recent conference was last winter. There have been no phone calls between them."

"Have your people search Stone's place," said Sandforth. "Be sure he doesn't leave town, and put him under surveillance."

* * *

After work, Matt stopped by the house to pick up part of the package he had hidden in the basement. He left Renfrew's journal, as it contained nothing of immediate value. He knew Gwen's habits; if she was not working on a story, she would be at her favourite watering hole—so he found himself there, at Morgan's Bar.

He scanned the room, but he didn't see her right away. *She must be on a story,* he thought. Just then, he saw her come in. She was still as beautiful as ever, standing at about six feet tall, with long, curly blonde hair and the greenest eyes he'd ever seen. She was looking around before their eyes met.

"Matt! What are you doing here?"

They had been lovers; after they split up, they remained friends and bumped into one another every once in a while.

"Just thought I'd pop in for a drink and see if you were here."

He ordered two double scotches on the rocks and sat at a place that backed against the wall.

"You remember this spot?" he asked, sitting down beside her.

Gwen smiled. "I sure do."

When they were lovers, this was their favourite spot. She cleared her throat; she knew Matt very well—seeing him here was no coincidence. "What's up, Matt?" she asked.

"What do you mean, 'what's up?' Nothing really; can't a guy buy his former gal a drink once in a while?" he asked her as he winked.

She took another sip. Matt had not touched his drink.

"Matt, seriously...what is it? There's something bothering you. I can tell."

They had started out as friends, which quickly turned into an intense emotionally and sexually-charged relationship. They talked a lot and trusted one another completely. Then Gwen had been offered a job in New York. He had to stay where he was, as he was under a fifteen-year contract with his employer. They simply grew apart. A couple of years earlier she had returned to Boston as a very successful and well-known investigative freelance reporter.

"Okay, Matt—out with it," she demanded softly.

He took a deep breath, hesitated, and sighed.

"Well...I really don't know if this is something or not..." he began. He told her about the package, but did not say when he'd received it or who he got it from. He explained how he had done a fair bit of research and what he had found.

Gwen appeared only mildly interested at first—that is, until he told her that in each case, the name of a certain scientist and the name of the country coincided with where these suspicious deaths had occurred. On hearing that information, she lit up and became very inquisitive.

"Can you give me something more to go on?"

"I can't give you a list of names until I'm more certain; I *can* tell you where to look on Usenet, but that's about it."

"Matt, several investigative reporters, including myself, have formed a worldwide coalition. We've been looking into something that may be related to what you found. Our government and military are not only withholding important secrets from the general public—they are also doing a great deal of top secret research, which in and of itself isn't an issue; the problem, though, is that most of their findings appear to be kept for their own profit. We've discovered that these covert facilities are located throughout the US and also around the world. From what we can gather, they are both military and civilian, and are funded by various governments through the Black Budgets. There is good evidence that members of certain wealthy civilian families are involved and have funded some of the projects. We have nicknamed this combination 'The World Power Elite,' but we cannot quite figure out their motivations or plans for the immediate and distant future." Gwen took another swallow of whiskey. "Matt, if you can help us in any way, we would really appreciate it." She did not tell him she'd already asked for an interview with Sandforth and was refused.

"I will do what I can Gwen, but I can't promise you anything at this point."

That evening, Matt made his will leaving everything to his daughter Megan. He had an appointment with a lawyer in the morning. He would drop it off as he went to work, and on his way home he would sign it.

* * *

While Matt was talking to Gwen, three individuals dressed in appliance repair uniforms quickly and neatly swept through Matt's house, floor by floor, room by room, square foot by square foot. The layout of the upstairs and main floor was basically the same. On top of the old upright piano was a series of photos of people. The basement was relatively messy—just what one would expect of a bachelor. They'd just about finished their search when someone spotted a nondescript cardboard box in the corner containing a couple of old books, newspapers, and old notebooks from Matt's university days.

"I think I've got it!" one of the searchers said, carefully removing a small journal. Flipping through the contents, he confirmed it with the others. "This belonged to Renfrew!" he said. They quickly photographed everything and departed, making sure they left the house the way they found it.

Back at the lab's security office, everything was given to O'Brian. He noted the journal contained some sensitive material and was written in a shaky hand. He put everything in a large folder and dialled a four-digit extension.

"Sir, we've found something—I'm on my way with it."

As Sandforth and O'Brian carefully examined all the material, Sandforth's mouth went dry.

"Keep searching, and keep the tail on Stone. I want to know his every move," he ordered.

"Yes, sir."

This was Sandforth's worst fear: somehow, someone was going to start to figure things out. The fact that someone in his own lab complex may have done so worried him. Although the evidence against Stone was not strong, he knew he had to call his superior and report it. Taking a moment to calm himself, he picked up the phone and dialled. Someone on the other end answered; Sandforth bypassed standard greetings and got straight to the point.

"We have a problem—a leak. I recommend we hold all tests until we are sure it is safe to go ahead."

He listened very carefully to the reply, and answered, "Consider it done."

He summoned O'Brian.

"It's time to call in the cleanup crew," he told him. "We need to scrub the situation—*now*."

* * *

On Wednesday morning, Matt went to work as usual. By four o'clock that afternoon, his assistant found him on the floor of his lab. He was dead. The company doctor had been called. The next morning, it was announced that Matthew Stone had accidentally cut himself on a broken petri dish containing a deadly virus. How a carefully-trained scientist had such an accident was never explained. The local coroner had double-checked their findings and had ruled Matt's death an accident.

* * *

Gwen listened to the news at eight on Thursday morning. Every neuron in her body fired up. She grasped the edge of the kitchen counter to steady herself. She listened very carefully. Then all her instincts and intuition kicked in.

No way was it an accident! she thought. *It's far too coincidental. I don't believe it!*

Grief and shock quickly gave way to steely resolve; she made up her mind then and there that she would not rest until she got to the bottom of this.

She called Mary Teal, the woman Matt had lived with at university. He'd frequently talked to her about Mary and his daughter Megan.

"Mary, this is Gwen Ross, calling from Boston. I'm afraid I've some bad news."

Mary intuitively knew what Gwen was about to tell her. Nonetheless, she was shaken, and she sank down into the little chair that was set beside the telephone.

"I'm very sorry to tell you this, but Matt died as a result a lab accident yesterday afternoon."

"What? A lab accident!"

"Yes...it's true, Mary. I don't know any of the finer details of how this happened or what will happen next. There will, of course, be an investigation—of that I am certain."

Mary was in shock. Yes, they had split up, but they had remained friends and had kept in touch. Matt had always remembered Megan's birthdays. They also had met up at a couple of conferences over the past four years.

"Mary, Matt often spoke of you and Megan with love. I knew you would need to know as soon as possible."

"Thank you, Gwen."

"If there is anything I can do at this end, please let me know."

"I will," said Mary. She put down the phone.

A lab accident—No. There's no way! He was always so careful and meticulous...almost to a fault, she thought.

* * *

"Good work, O'Brian," said Sandforth after being updated. "Did you collect everything from Stone's lab?"

"Yes, we did. We left it clean."

The phone on the massive oak desk gave a shrill ring, punctuating the tension in the room. O'Brian turned to leave Sandforth's office after a brief, terse nod from his superior. As he was closing the door, Sandforth answered his phone.

"I agree—all aspects of those tests must be halted for now," Sandforth said. "Stone's death is officially an accident."

* * *

Mary was having a great deal of trouble concentrating. She just couldn't believe that Matt's death was an accident. Her intuition kept telling her that she was right—it was *not* an accident. As she was thinking about this, her phone rang.

"Hello, Mary Teal speaking."

"Dr. Teal, this is Allison Campbell calling you from the law offices of Williams, Campbell, and Horace in Boston, Massachusetts. May I please take a moment of your time?"

"Certainly."

"I have Dr. Matthew Stone's will. He is the biological father of Megan Teal, correct?"

"Yes."

"First, please let me extend my condolences to you and your daughter."

"Thank you."

"There are a few matters of his estate which are a bit complicated. Would it be possible for you to come here to Boston in the near future to meet with me?"

Mary knew this was important. Looking at her calendar, she answered, "Yes, of course—I'll try to get a flight and will aim to be there tomorrow by around noon."

"Excellent. I'll have one of my staff meet you at the airport and bring you directly to the office. Just let me know the details of your flight times, and we'll make the arrangements."

As soon as Mary ended the call, she called her mother, Nona, who lived on the Island of Grand Manan, New Brunswick.

"Mom, have you heard about Matt?"

"No, Mary—what's happened?"

Mary explained and told Nona all she knew about Matt's death.

"I have to fly to Boston tomorrow," she said. "Do you think you can get a flight here in time to take care of Megan?"

"Of course, dear; I'll leave now and catch the next ferry; I'll be at your place in Halifax this evening. Let's talk more then."

"Thanks so much, Mom."

* * *

On Thursday, Gwen was starting her search for answers.

I wish Matt had given me more to go on, she thought. *I'll get to the bottom of this if it's the last thing I do. I swear to you, Matt—I'll find the truth.*

She brought out a fresh pad of paper, and at the top of the page wrote the words The Truth.

At eleven am on Friday, Mary was entering the lawyer's office in Boston.

An attractive woman with straight, pitch-black hair extended her hand in greeting.

"I'm Allison Campbell. Please accept my deepest sympathy on the loss of your friend, Matthew Stone."

"Thank you," Mary said. She appreciated the greeting and the firm handshake that went with it. "Please call me Mary."

The office was tastefully decorated with a small sofa and two matching deep red leather chairs, and a beautiful round drop-leaf cherry table with a tray of coffee, tea, and water.

She was curious about the three envelopes sitting beside the tray. She knew one of them would contain the will—but what was in the other two? Before she could share her thoughts, Allison said, "You know that Matthew had you as next of kin, along with Megan."

Mary fought back tears. "Yes, we lived together when we were both at university, and Megan is his daughter. Did you know Matt?"

"I met him for the first time when he came in to do his will earlier this week," Allison replied. "He seemed worried."

"Earlier this week!" exclaimed Mary.

Allison nodded. "Before I show you the will, I must explain something to you," she said. Mary looked at the two envelopes left on the table. Allison had put the one with the will aside. "Matt asked me if he could trust me with a package. He showed me this yellow envelope and opened it so I could see some handwritten notes. He explained he had been doing some research and wanted this to be sealed. I was to tell no one I had it. I was to give it only to you, and to give you this message: 'This could be very important, Mary—it's for your eyes only.'"

"This was earlier this week?" asked Mary.

"That is correct. Here it is."

There was a message in code which said *Read this now.* Then, in Matt's handwriting, which was not in code: *If you don't wish to follow through, please give it to Allison, and have it destroyed in front of you. Love, Matt.*

"I'll leave this with you. Take as long as you need," said Allison. She stood up and left Mary alone in the office.

Mary took out the top few pages and noted they had been photocopied. The handwriting was not Matt's. She leafed through some of the pages and found a note from Matt which read *These were given to me upon the death of Dr. Chris Renfrew.* Stapled to this note was Renfrew's letter. She gasped, noticing the note was dated only last Saturday. She called Allison back into the office.

"Did Matt give you anything else?" she asked. She carefully slid the documents back into the big envelope.

"As a matter of fact, he did." Allison picked up the other small envelope and gave it to Mary. On the outside it merely said *My dearest Mary.* This immediately signalled to her that whatever was inside it would be in code. She held back tears as she remembered the fun they'd had with these codes. His words also meant *Be careful.* As she opened it, she thought, *Oh, Matt...what have you done?*

Mary took the letter and put it in her purse. She would read it later, when she was alone. Allison opened the will. "This will is very straightforward," she explained. "Matt basically split his estate between you and Megan, fifty-fifty; as Megan is a legal minor, her half will go into a trust fund that we can set up for you. You will be the trustee until Megan is eighteen years of age; then it will be all hers. I gather he had a house and a cabin. These are both yours to do with as you wish. If you wish to sell one or both of them, we can help you with that." Allison passed the will and the sheet of assets over to Mary.

Mary glanced at it; Megan would be free of financial worry for the rest of her life. "Oh, Matt...*thank you*," she whispered. Then she looked at Allison and asked, "What about all his research papers?"

"We checked on that. They belong to the lab he worked for."

Mary nodded. "Can you recommend a good hotel?"

"Yes. I'll have my secretary get you a reservation and a cab. Are you staying in Boston long?"

"Just for a night or two. Can you please arrange to have Matt's house sold for me? Also, can we reseal this large envelope? May I leave it with you?"

"Yes to all of your questions. I will get somebody on the sale of the house as quickly as possible. As for the envelope, I'll keep it secure. Only you and I know that it's here. When you wish to have it, just call me."

As Mary got out of her chair, she took Allison's hand. "Thank you for all you've done," she said.

* * *

O'Brian was in Sandforth's office updating his findings.

"Mary Teal arrived this morning, and we followed her to the lawyer's office. Allison William's background check came back clean; however, this is the same lawyer who Matt Stone went to see earlier this week. One of the people in the main office owed us a favour, so we had an inside contact. She assured us that Matt only had a will made; our source noted that when Teal left, she just had a copy of the will with no other large envelopes. Teal's visit seemed unusually lengthy, but our contact explained why the meeting took so long: her secretary told her she would have to work late in order to draw up papers for a trust fund for Teal's daughter. We're still keeping an eye on her—she's staying at the Dorchester Hotel for at least one night."

"Hm. Okay. Is there anything new on Ross?"

"Not really. We're keeping an eye on her also."

Sandforth's phone rang; he paused to answer it. He listened for a moment before his face blanched.

"Shit!" he said. "How the *hell* did that happen? Well, find her, and fast!"

He ended the call and glared at O'Brian.

"Ross gave our man the slip," he said.

"We'll find her," said O'Brian.

Sandforth had a stony expression. "You had better—and fast. I want to know every move that woman makes."

* * *

Mary was settled in her hotel room and called Nona.

"How are you and Megan getting along?" she asked.

"Very well. Andrew's playing cards with her. How did everything go at the lawyer's office?"

Mary told her about the contents of Matt's will, but did not tell her mother about the envelope with the notes regarding Renfrew. "I inquired about Matt's remains and was told the city coroner was in charge," she continued. "He's being cremated. Other than that, I don't have much else to report."

"How long will you be there?" Nona asked.

"I'm staying here until at least Sunday. I want to arrange to have his house cleaned out and put up for sale. For now, I'll keep the cabin."

"Okay dear; please be careful."

When she hung up, she received notification that there was a message; it was Gwen. Mary called her back immediately.

"Gwen; it's Mary. You left me a message, and it sounded urgent."

"I really want to talk to you about Matt. Are you at home?"

"Actually, I'm here in Boston. Matt's lawyer asked me if I could come here to meet with her as she had his will and some other papers." She wanted to say more, but thought better of it.

"Are you staying here for a bit? I would really like to meet you and talk to you."

"Yes. I have some more papers to sign at the lawyers tomorrow, and I want to get Matt's house up for sale. I'll be very busy tomorrow; how about tonight?"

"That would be great. Would you like to go out for dinner?"

"Sure—do you have a place in mind?"

"Yes, I know of a quiet little Italian restaurant. I'm going to give you some rather strange directions: at about five o'clock, go for a walk and hail a cab. Go to the railway station; it will be extremely busy at that time with commuters. Switch cabs quickly and come to the address I'm about to give you. I wish I could explain this to you, but I'm sure that I was being followed earlier today. I will explain as best I can when I see you."

"Okay Gwen; I'll see you soon," said Mary, once Gwen had given her the address.

As she hung up the phone, her intuition told her to be very careful. The more she thought about the events of the day, the stranger things seemed—and the more questions she had.

* * *

"We've got Teal, O'Brian. She's getting into a cab; we'll follow her."

"Does she have any parcels or large envelopes with her?"

"I doubt it—she's only carrying a very small purse."

"Okay. Keep her in sight at all times, and let me know where she goes and who she meets."

Twenty minutes later, O'Brian's phone rang.

"What is it?" he answered.

"You won't believe it—we lost her. Her cab stopped briefly at the train station. I let John out to follow her, but the crowd was huge. It's rush hour, and this place is crazy tonight. There must be a game or something."

"Alright. Go back to the hotel, and wait for her there."

* * *

Mary paid the cabbie and walked the last block to the restaurant. It was a small family-owned business. A dozen tables filled the main section, and only three of these were occupied by more than one person. Mary, figuring Gwen wasn't there yet, started to walk towards a table when a busboy intercepted her.

"Mary...Mary Teal?" he asked quietly.

"Yes."

"Please come with me. Gwen is expecting you."

They walked through a large archway into a smaller room. There were only three tables there. As they entered, Gwen rose; nodding to the busboy to dismiss him, she took Mary's hand.

"I'm so very sorry, Mary." She paused a moment, and added, "Matt was a wonderful person."

"Thank you, Gwen. We'll both miss him greatly."

Gwen nodded; in that one short sentence, Mary told her that she knew about her and Matt. They paused as a server approached the table, and they placed their orders, starting with drinks.

"There is no easy way to say this, Mary: I'm certain Matt's death was not an accident."

Mary remembered Matt saying something about Gwen being a reporter. *I may have to be careful here,* she thought.

"You *are* a reporter, aren't you?"

"Yes, I am—but at this moment I'm not. I loved Matt, and right now his friendship means more to me than anything. I know it also does to you."

"Sorry, Gwen. With everything that has happened the last few days, I just don't seem to be myself."

"I know. I understand."

Relaxing a bit, Mary began to talk.

"I have very strong intuitive abilities. At the time Matt died, I knew it, but I didn't want to believe it. It was too painful, and I was in a meeting, so I pushed the feeling away. Then I got your phone call."

"When you had that feeling, was it a vision? Or...sorry, Mary. I'm beginning to sound like a reporter."

"You know about visions?"

"Yes. A dear friend of mine gets them now and then. Don't worry, Mary—I believe that certain people do have this ability."

"It really wasn't a vision; it was more like a strong feeling." Wanting to change the subject, Mary asked, "Gwen, you were saying you're certain it was not an accident. Why? You obviously know something. This is more than your reporter's sixth sense, isn't it?"

Gwen smiled to herself and thought, *Watch it, Gwen—Mary is very sensitive and intuitive.* "Matt arranged a meeting with me the Sunday night before he died," she said. "He'd come across information regarding the people he worked for. Matt had done more research and was sure he was on to something. He wouldn't tell me more until he'd confirmed a couple of things."

"And did he?"

"No, Mary, he didn't. He must've found out about something or someone—I think that's why he's dead. I gave you that evasive route to get here because I suspect you're also being followed."

"I wondered. Have you been able to find out anything more?"

"He gave me a couple of leads which I've checked. I haven't made much progress."

"You're still actively pursuing this?"

"Definitely. I made a promise to Matt that I would."

Mary locked eyes with Gwen and smiled. She raised her glass and said, "To the truth."

"To truth," Gwen answered, and they clicked their glasses.

"Mary, there is something else I must tell you," Gwen said as she put her glass down. She explained about the worldwide group of reporters with whom she was affiliated. "There is so much circumstantial evidence coming out about governments and military branches—not just here in the US, but elsewhere; it's coming out that they are covertly spending millions and millions of tax dollars on secret projects."

"Didn't the media announce recently that more than nine trillion dollars of US government spending is unaccounted for?" Mary asked.

"True. The US government tried to cover it up."

"So you think these missing funds are being used by various agencies under the guise of top secret research and Homeland Security initiatives?"

"Yes. There are many such agencies under that umbrella which makes it extremely difficult for our group to get any information."

"And you think the company and lab that Matt worked for may be connected somehow."

"I do. It's not only government agencies worldwide and their militaries that are involved. There is growing evidence that they're also being funded by private corporations and some of the very wealthiest families around the world."

They hesitated briefly as their meals arrived. When the server left, Gwen asked Mary if she'd had any contact with Matt over the past few weeks.

"I received a small sealed envelope with my name in Matt's handwriting. Instead of writing Stone, he had written *Seton*, which told me that what was inside was in code."

"Have you read it yet?"

"I only had time to glance at it. He has written it in two codes and mixed them up, so it will take a while for me to decipher it."

"In codes? How did he come up with that idea?"

"It was one of my favourite games which I played with my father when I was growing up. When Matt and I were living together, I taught him some of these codes. We used them to send messages back and forth."

Gwen nodded. "Good," she said. "Keep it safe, and don't let anyone see it—in fact, don't even let anyone know that you have it."

"Once I've deciphered it, I'll let you know," Mary said. She had taken the letter she'd received at home out of her briefcase; it was folded up in her purse along with the other one. She wanted to see for herself what these two letters contained before she said anything more. "What do you suspect these governments and other agencies are doing that has to be kept so secret?"

"It could be anything, but we do have evidence which tells us that the military is definitely working on several projects, such as antigravity propulsion and even biological weapons."

"What? That's illegal—and it sounds like science fiction!"

"Well, we have good reason to think that the secret areas—such as Area 51—have really developed some of these things."

"You mean the US actually has a vehicle capable of significant space travel—one which is superior to the shuttle fleet?"

"We believe so, Mary. Did you ever question why they haven't developed a craft to replace the shuttle fleet? We suspect they have, and are not telling the public about it."

"Why would they do that?"

"Some of us feel they're using a type of antigravity means of propulsion; with that technology, there is no need for fossil fuel any longer."

"Wait—you're talking about free energy! Wow! You mean to tell me they've this technology and it's being kept from us?"

"Yes. Can you imagine if the government announced tomorrow that, within a year or so, we would no longer require the oil and gas we currently use? So much of our infrastructure is based on oil and gas; the US economy would crash. Think of the amount of tax revenue the government would lose. I don't even think Medicare and Old Age Security would survive."

"Is it just the military, or is NASA involved?"

"It's a huge business all across the board. Governments, militaries, and private concerns are all involved. It's sometimes called 'The Shadow' or 'Secret Government' which uses a vast amount of our tax dollars while they hide what they've discovered, developed, or constructed."

"How did you find out about all this?"

"There are bits and pieces of information which are constantly being revealed—especially by some of the senior military personnel who were formerly in this group. Many of them are now in their eighties; now that they're older, they are beginning to come forward to tell the truth."

"Clearing their consciences, I guess," Mary remarked as she finished her meal. "So is the lab that Matt worked for involved?"

"We have our suspicions. A lot of the research is being done, not just by the Boston lab, but by several others which are being funded by the Black Budgets. They are either under the direct control of what are called Secret Governments—sometimes referred to as 'SGs'—or through contracts to civilians. Most of their research is never published, and yet untold millions of our tax dollars go to these establishments every year." Gwen knew a lot more than this, and decided at this point that she'd said enough.

Mary sat up straight. "Could Matt's death have happened because he discovered something they've developed which, if it got out to the public, would reveal what these 'SGs' are really up to?"

"I believe so. It'll be almost impossible to prove, but I'm damn well going to try."

Having finished their dinner and drinks, they paid their bills. As they left the restaurant, Mary turned to Gwen.

"I'm going to help you, Gwen, if it's the last thing I do!" she promised.

* * *

O'Brian made his report to Sandforth at about nine pm.

"Both Ross and Teal are back," he said. "Teal arrived back at the hotel at around eight-twenty pm. She was walking—from where we don't know. Ross was at her place at ten pm. It's impossible to determine if they were together or not."

"Keep an eye on *both* of them from now on. Do you understand?"

"Yes, sir."

O'Brian was annoyed, and not just because his people had lost track of these two women. He also felt that Sandforth was being paranoid. *Why had they killed Stone? Was it really necessary?* he thought. Then again, he didn't know everything about the situation—nor did he wish to.

* * *

Mary entered her hotel room, and instantly knew that someone other than the maid had been there. A cold shiver swept over her. She quickly and quietly moved about the room. No one was there. She checked her briefcase, and she turned over some papers. The one which was on top was now at the bottom. Was someone careless, or was this a warning?

She was upset by all that had happened that day. She poured herself a stiff drink and tried to relax, but she simply could not unwind. She made sure all the security locks were on her door. She wrote down the key points about Secret Governments that Gwen had told her. *If world-renowned investigative reporters are taking this seriously, then there must be something to it,* she thought.

She turned her attention to Matt's letter—the one she'd received prior to coming to Boston:

Dearest Mary O'Teal,

Mary remembered when he used her full name when writing in code; it meant that the subsequent text was of a serious nature.

> I've been thinking of you and Megan a lot lately, and would love to have you come to visit for a weekend at the cabin. How does the 18th and 19th, the 25th and 26th of next month sound? It would be great. I was looking at that photo of the two of us when you were here last. It is so unfortunate that Megan got a bacterial infection in her ear. She did recover quite quickly. By the way, I got rid of all that poison ivy.
>
> I was up there on the weekend and fished a bit, but the rain started. I was reading a mystery book about some strange poison or whatever. I didn't like it, so I didn't finish it.
>
> I think your idea of the trip to Australia is a great one. I put a deposit towards it.
>
> Anyway, we'll talk more about this when you come to Boston. I'll tell you about the changes I'm planning to make to the house. I'm going to get rid of that big box of old sports equipment that I stored so safely in the basement.
>
> Looking forward to seeing you both. Travel safely.

Love you,

Matt.

She realized he'd used a couple of different codes and had mixed them up. She picked up her pen and a small pad of paper. After rereading the letter two more times, she jotted down the following list:

O'Teal—the spelling of my name means the message is serious.

Bacteria—Megan had actually been fine that weekend.

Poison—Matt always finished a mystery when he started it.

Australia—I wasn't planning a trip.

The words *deposit* and *safely*—he had not deposited anything into my account.

Safely—he had used the word twice.

Big box—he'd already thrown it out.

She also noted that there were two sets of numbers: 18 and 19; 25 and 26 were significant. They had already discussed a visit for the following month. She tried these four numbers in various combinations by adding them together; for example: 18+19 = 37; 25+26 = 51. She took this one step further by adding 3+7 = 10 and 5+1 = 6. The numbers 37, 51, 10, and 6 appeared to be important.

Next, she put the words together. Her first attempt resulted in a series of sets of words: *bacteria, poison, big, deposit, box,*

Australia, and *Boston.* She thought that there might be some connection between Australia and a big safety deposit box. The words *poison* and *bacteria* didn't seem to fit.

She picked up the letter the lawyer had given her:

> By now you've read the material in the yellow envelope. I should have taken your advice; instead, I left and came here. You were right and I was wrong.

Mary remembered that they actually *hadn't* fought. She didn't want him to leave—for Megan's sake—but he was ambitious. And she'd had a gut feeling something was wrong with the way the lab was run.

> I want you to know I'm very sorry. Don't let Megan forget me. She's a very special little girl. There is so much more I want to say; I cannot seem to find the words.
>
> Take whatever you want from the house—any photos, books etc., especially those you gave me last year on my birthday.

She stopped. She had given him those books at *Christmas,* not his birthday. They must be important.

> Sell the house if you wish—but I would like you and Megan to keep the cabin and share it. It has so many special memories. Dad's stamp collection belongs to Megan.
>
> You were my one and only true love, Mary.
>
> Love,

Matthew.

* * *

Mary was up early Saturday morning. Allison's secretary was making arrangements for a real estate agent to meet her at Matt's place. Mary wanted it on the market immediately, but she wondered what she was going to do with all the furniture. She looked up movers and storage facilities and listed several numbers. She would spend a good part of the day at his house and would sort out what she felt she should keep and have it shipped home, such as the books he mentioned; Mary would take those with her, along with his laptop and photographs.

By nine-thirty am, she had talked to Allison's secretary. She was to meet the real estate agent at eleven am. He would have the papers with him for her to sign. By ten am she had booked a mover who also had storage facilities. It would give her time in the future to sort out his things. She then took a cab to the bank and opened Matt's large safety deposit box.

Mary noted the stamps were organized in alphabetical order by country. She pulled out the envelope marked *Australia*, and very carefully went through the stamps, sheet after sheet. In about the middle, she came across a small piece of paper; on it was scribbled *This should be in the British Commonwealth*. She took out the British Commonwealth envelope and came across another torn piece of paper. It matched like a jigsaw puzzle to the one in with the Australian stamps. Written on this piece of paper were columns of numbers. Could this be another code? She put it in her pocket. Returning the box, she made arrangements to transfer it into her name. Then she caught a cab to Matt's house.

Mary arrived before the real estate agent, which gave her a chance to look around before the real estate agent arrived. She found the books and placed them in her briefcase. She added some CDs and videos he'd put aside, along with three or four of the photos she liked. Then the doorbell rang.

An hour later, the price was set and the papers were signed. The moving representatives arrived as the real estate agent was pounding the for sale sign into the front lawn.

The storage was going to be costly, but it would be worth it. Mary had far too much on her mind to even think about moving the stuff herself. She would take care of it later. She had made arrangements with the real estate agent to be there at the house when the contents were being packed up.

She was about to leave when she thought, *Matt's laptop is missing. He probably left it at the lab. If that is the case, I will never see it.*

* * *

Mary showered and had dinner in her room. She looked at the piece of paper with all the code numbers on it, and picked up one of the books and started to work on it. After twenty minutes, she quit; her mind was starting to go in circles. She was totally exhausted.

Before going to bed, she made an exact copy of the list of numbers, tore up the original, and flushed it down the toilet. It was a precaution; if somebody found the list of numbers, they would not connect it directly to Matt.

She slept with her bra on and had tucked the letter and the list into it; after a few hours, she was restless. She got up at four-thirty am, showered, ordered her breakfast, and was at the airport before six am. While waiting, she made a quick call to Gwen. There was no answer, so she left a message; she would call her from home.

Once she had landed in Halifax, she saw her mother and her daughter Megan waiting for her. Megan started singing and babbling in her own peculiar language. Hugging her mother, Mary couldn't hold the tears back.

"It's okay, sweetheart; you're home now. You've been through a lot in the last few days," said Nona.

Mom, you don't know the half of it! Mary thought.

Nona drove them back from the airport. Mary was in the front seat, sound asleep, and Megan was babbling away behind her in her car seat. They pulled into the parking lot at the ferry terminal in Blacks Harbour.

The crew of the car ferry, *The Adventure*, gave Mary big hugs of sympathy. An island is an island, and everyone knew about her loss.

Driving to her home in North Head, Nona asked, "You're staying with us for a while, I hope?"

"Yes, Mom. I would really like that."

As they pulled into the driveway, Andrew came out to meet them. He hugged Mary.

"You're home now, Mary. You're safe."

Once inside, Mary made a phone call to her lab to say she'd be back in a week. Then she turned to Nona, who was behind her.

"Oh, Mom," she cried as she reached out. Nona hugged her. Tears began to flow. "Mom, it was exhausting."

"It's okay, dear. We'll talk about all this after dinner, when Megan is in bed."

"Has she been a good girl?"

"Yes, she's been an angel. When she's on the boat and we come upon some whales or dolphins, she becomes ecstatic; she dances and sings to them. Mary, there's something special between her and those whales. I can't explain it."

True to her word, nothing was said about Matt or Boston until later that evening.

"Mom, it's so good to be home."

"Do you want to talk about it?" Nona asked.

Mary told them most of the story, but purposely left out the bit about her hotel room being searched, the letters he wrote, and the times she was being followed.

"So you're certain it wasn't an accident?" Andrew asked.

"Several things point to that," Mary said. She explained about the large envelope which she'd left at the lawyer's office in Boston, and Matt's two letters in code. "I feel very strongly that Matt was murdered."

"Why, in heaven's name? He was a scientist!" Andrew said.

"True, but Gwen and I think he discovered something his company was doing that was covert and illegal." Mary explained who Gwen was and that she belonged to a group of international investigative reporters. When they came to the question as to how these labs were funded, Andrew piped up.

"Where do you think the trillions of dollars that the US government cannot account for ended up? Apparently, it's not just the government that's involved! I'm sure their military's involved—along with heaven knows which other countries, companies, and individuals!"

"But why?" Nona asked. "Why the secrecy?"

Mary gave her the same explanation Gwen had offered.

"It's the tip of the iceberg," Andrew added. "It basically all started with Roswell. There is so much coming out about how the United States military and government have tried desperately to cover it up. So much time has passed; if they came out with the truth now, it would cause them to lose face. They would have to reveal all the information and inventions, plus all the other advancements in technology. They have probably even found a free replacement energy source!"

"Mary, you said you received a couple of letters from Matthew which were in code. Could you decipher them? Does it give you any clues as to why Matt was killed?"

"Actually, Andrew, I only had time to work on the one I received before I left for Boston. He had used a combination of a word and a number code. It really doesn't make much sense. The second letter, along with a list of numbers I found, I haven't looked at yet."

"Mary, please be very careful—if this is what Matt was killed for..."

"I know, Mom. If this helps to put away whoever was involved, I must do it. Whatever I find, I'm turning it over to Gwen; she'll take it from there. I will no longer be involved at that point. I'm going to decipher the letters, and that is it."

Nona changed the subject. "If it's a good day tomorrow, would you like to go whale-watching? The humpbacks are here, along with some of the finback whales."

"Mom, I'd love to. I need to get out on the ocean again to totally relax. Besides, I want to see Megan do her thing."

* * *

"As far as we can tell, sir, things have calmed down in the Stone case," O'Brian reported. "Teal flew home and has not gone back to work yet. She's staying with her mother and her three-year-old daughter on Grand Manan. We have a man on the island, but he has to be extremely careful—it's a small, closely-knit community. We're acquiring her mother's phone log."

"And Gwen Ross?" asked Sandforth.

"Nothing out of the ordinary."

"So...it may all have blown over. Keep an eye on them and let me know if they make any contact."

* * *

Mary spent the next two days going out on the boat whale-watching, but she actually spent more time Megan-watching when the whales were around.

"See what I mean, dear?" Nona said as they watched Megan do her song-and-dance routine. "There is one particular humpback which comes closer to the boat than any of the others."

"Which one?" Mary asked; she was still watching Megan entertain the whales.

Nona could see the unique white pattern on the underside of its tail as it dove. "Oh, that's Lacuna; she's four years old."

"I *swear* they're communicating with one another in some way," Mary commented.

"Yes, I know. I wonder if she has inherited your ability of being able to mentally communicate like you and your father used to do."

It wasn't until the third night, after a wonderful, fresh scallop dinner, that Mary took out the list of numbers and the books she had taken from Matt's place. She worked on it for about an hour to no avail. She wondered if Matt reversed each set of numbers: 243 would become 342. She tried it and, getting excited, she worked past midnight. She found all the words. Now she had to mix and match them until something made sense. She decided she'd get back to it in the morning.

"Did you get the code figured out yet?" Nona asked as she poured Mary a cup of coffee.

"I think so, Mom. I've a lot of words, but they don't make sense yet. There's a thick fog out there; I'll spend the morning working on them."

"Were they from the books you brought home?"

"They were from two books."

Mary took a couple of pieces of homemade bread and jam, a cup of coffee, her books, a pad of paper, and went out to the sun porch. Nona had offered to take Megan for the morning so that

Mary would have some peace and quiet. She looked at her list and began to mix and match the words she'd found the previous night.

Matt had used a very simple and straightforward code of a series of numbers arranged in two or three columns which related to two books. The numbers in the columns gave the book, page, and the word. For example, the number 1246 was in the first column, and 18 in the second column; this told her to go to book one, page 246 and pick out the eighteenth word.

After doing this, she began to group certain words together. These were *small groups, several isolated regions, bacteria, past eight weeks, poison, dead, laboratory, company, people*. She reassembled these words and got *Several small groups of people in isolated regions, found dead, poison or bacteria. Company laboratories are involved.* Then, using the third column, she deciphered the following: *Further details, cabin, Uncle Bill's Place.* This last part told her there was more information hidden in Uncle Bill's Place, which was the name of a secret hiding place Matt used as a child.

How was she safely going to get this information to Gwen? She doubted Gwen even knew about Uncle Bill's Place. As she was contemplating the variables, her mother called her.

"Mary, phone—it's the Boston lawyer's office."

Mary picked up the phone.

"Hello Mary; Allison here. How are you?"

"Allison, it's good to hear from you so soon. I'm getting rested and I'm planning to head back to work on Monday. How are things there?"

"Things are going well; we've had a couple of offers on Matthew's house. One is for $20,000 less than the asking price, with a few conditions and a sixty-day closing date. The second offer is for the asking price. There are no conditions and they wish to close as soon as possible."

"The last one sounds unbelievable."

"Would you like me to fax them both to you?"

"No, just the last one." Mary hesitated a moment. "Could you please send any other papers which will be required? I'll probably be accepting the second offer."

"I thought you might. Give me your mother's fax number. I'll send it to you right away."

"Thank you, Allison. This is good news. Oh, about the yellow envelope I left with you: is there any way you can release it to a specific person without me coming back to Boston?"

"Certainly; I'll send you a release form along with the house papers. Just fill in the person's name and add any special instructions you wish, and send it back to me."

"Thanks so much, Allison, for everything."

"My pleasure, Mary."

Mary hung up and exclaimed, "Mom, you won't believe it! I think I've sold Matt's house for the asking price with immediate possession and no conditions!"

"It's almost too good to be true," said Nona.

Andrew joined the conversation.

"When are the papers due to be signed?"

Before Mary could answer, a fax came through. "That's probably them now."

Mary went and picked up the pages, placing them in order. She took out the letter regarding the transfer of the yellow envelope and placed it with the lawyer's covering letter. She couldn't believe her eyes when she saw the buyer's name. "I should have known," she said with a smile.

"What's that, dear?" Nona said, carrying a tray with coffee and some homemade date squares.

"It's Gwen—Gwen Ross. She wants to buy Matt's house. I knew she loved it, but I never dreamt she would buy it."

She read the documents thoroughly and signed them. Andrew witnessed it. Within an hour, Allison called Gwen, and three hours later, the deal was done. Mary picked up the phone to call her, and offered her congratulations.

"Thank you, Mary. This was a golden opportunity for me."

"It is a win-win situation," Mary said. She was so pleased. "Did you get the—"

Gwen cut in. "Yes, I got the extra keys with the yellow tag. When you come to Boston, you can stay with me."

In all the excitement about the house, Mary had briefly forgotten about the message that she had deciphered.

"Gwen, I found a note for you in Matt's house about a book you'd left there. I brought it home with me, but you should have it. When I find it, I'll send it to you." Mary was hoping Gwen got the real message.

"Really, Mary? I can't think of what it could be."

She knew Gwen understood. "I'll let you know more later," she said.

The code which they'd worked out in Boston had worked. Mary's message told Gwen two things: Mary had solved the code and wanted to get it to Gwen as soon as possible.

* * *

"You have something for me, O'Brian?"

"Nothing concrete, but I'll start with Teal. According to Nona's phone records, someone received a twelve-minute phone call from the lawyer in Boston. We contacted our source in the lawyer's office. Apparently Gwen Ross has purchased Stone's house."

"Now *that* is very interesting," said Sandforth. "Anything else?"

"Yes. Gwen Ross went to the same office to sign some papers and came out with an envelope."

"Was it the yellow one?"

"No sir—it was a small, thin envelope…probably the papers regarding the sale of the house."

"Okay. Continue to keep a very close eye on both women. I don't like the relationship that is developing between the two of them."

"Fine, sir."

O'Brian had learned a long time ago to never question Sandforth.

* * *

On Thursday morning, Nona, Mary, and Megan all went out on the boat. When they awoke, the fog had crept in silently overnight and hugged the island. As they ate their breakfast, they watched the fog play its typically coy game of receding to reveal the water's edge, only to roll in and hide it again. As a child, Mary had referred to this spectacle as a game of "Now you see it, now you don't."

Mary took a sip of her hot coffee and sighed with contentment.

"You know, Mom, I never get tired of watching the fog," she said. She knew that, after an hour or so, the fog would ebb out into the Bay of Fundy and linger near the Grand Manan Basin—or it would disappear altogether. Today it was the former.

Reluctantly pulling herself from her peaceful contemplation, Mary turned her thoughts back to the matters at hand. She picked up the phone and made reservations for a flight to Boston the next morning, then called Gwen to arrange for them to go to Matt's house together as soon as she arrived. Mary felt an increasing sense of urgency to get the decoded message to Gwen; it was troubling her greatly, and she knew that Gwen would know what to do. She decided to tell Gwen about "Uncle Bill's Place" later on.

The next day, Gwen met Mary at the airport as planned. They went to Matt's place—now Gwen's—and walked through the empty house so that Gwen could refresh her memory as to its layout; this would make it easier for her to decide which pieces of furniture she wanted. She knew that she wanted the dining table and chairs; half an hour later, they drove to the storage facility.

"Gwen," Mary said nervously, "are we being followed?"

"I do believe we are. Not to worry."

Once they arrived at the storage facility, Gwen signalled to Mary that the building was possibly bugged.

"Let's see if we can find the table and chairs," she said casually.

They chit-chatted as they rummaged through the contents of the storage unit. After about an hour, Gwen had tagged the items she wanted. Mary was going to refuse payment, but then she realized: *this is the opportunity I've been waiting for*. She wrote a figure on the back of a piece of paper with the decoded message. She folded it in such a way that Gwen would see there was some writing on it when she handed it to her.

Gwen nodded and turned it over to see what price Mary had written.

No charge, it said. *Make it look like you are making out a check*.

"Mary—this isn't enough," Gwen said for the benefit of anyone listening.

Mary picked up on what Gwen was doing. "Okay, but I'd rather—"

Before Mary could finish, Gwen wrote it out to Megan for $500; at the bottom was written, *For your education*.

Mary looked at it; she smiled and nodded. "Thank you, Gwen. Thank you."

Driving back through the city, they reminisced and traded stories about Matt. They had several good laughs and shared a few tears. After they had lunch together, Gwen drove Mary back to the airport.

* * *

Sandforth was pacing back and forth with his hands clasped behind his back when O'Brian entered the office.
"You're late," he said. His voice was slightly raised.
"Yes sir, I am."
"Well, this had better be important."
"I believe it to be so," said O'Brian.
He gave a detailed report on the movements of Ross and Teal—what they did, where they went, and even what they had for lunch.
"Did you pick up any of their conversation?"
"Not much; they were talking about things that one would expect to hear between two friends."
"Did any envelopes or paper pass between them?"
"Yes, at the storage facility; Teal appears to have made a list of items of furniture Ross wanted and handed it to her. Ross promptly wrote out a check and gave it to Teal."
"Is there any way that they may be communicating other information between the two of them?"
"They could be, sir, but there was nothing to indicate they were."
"With the material you found written by Renfrew, plus the fact that Ross and Teal seem to be spending a lot of time together, I can't believe they're not onto something. I think now is the time to scare Teal off. Arrange it, O'Brian. I don't think we have to do anything with Ross—if she had something, she would be all over it by now."

"I agree, sir. As far as Teal is concerned, it may be difficult, because she's back in Canada already."

"I know—but I want to put a stop to the relationship between Teal and Ross. Put a really good scare into her, along with a threatening message."

"I'll take care of it."

* * *

Mary spent the weekend on Grand Manan. On Sunday afternoon, she flew home to Nova Scotia with her daughter. By nine pm she'd settled Megan, and the house was quiet.

What am I going to do with the information about Uncle Bill's Place? she thought. *I can't send it to Gwen without an explanation, and I can't go to the cabin myself; I'll be followed.* After some contemplation, she decided to store the meaning of the phrase in her safety deposit box, along with instructions for delivery to Gwen.

The next two weeks were extremely busy; she got caught up on her lab work, and finished a research paper, along with an application for research funds which was due in three weeks.

Mid-afternoon on a Friday, she picked up Megan after her doctor's appointment, and chose her favourite route for the drive home. It was a beautiful, quiet back road which ran through hills covered in forests of mixed trees dominated by the rich shades of evergreens; many of them were old, tall, and stately. She felt they were watching over her, protecting her year-round. A few deciduous trees were scattered amongst them. Birch trees were her favourite; their stark white trunks were so striking against the sea of green. To her, white represented peace, solitude, and strength. Oak and maple trees dotted some of the hillsides; she found the solitary, mighty oak trees so silent and dependable. Trees and their meanings were a solace to her. No matter what the season, or what was going on in the rest of her life, Mary found peace driving home. She'd arrive home in a gentle, quiet, peaceful mood.

Mary loved her brand-new white Tucson. She felt secure in the way it took the hills and the corners. They were approaching a section with some rather sharp curves, and part of it ran along the edge of a steep ravine. She glanced in her rear-view mirror and noticed a half-ton truck coming up behind her.

Boy, he's going too fast for this section of this road, Mary thought.

She slowed the car, knowing there was a fairly sharp curve coming up. She'd been listening to the radio, and had turned on her tape recorder to make a list of groceries. Glancing again in her rear-view mirror, she noticed the truck had backed off a bit. A few moments later, she glanced in the mirror and was immediately alarmed—the truck was now picking up speed.

"What does he think he's doing?" she exclaimed out loud.

Suddenly, Mary realized he was trying to run them off the road, or at least sandwich them against the guard rail. Trying to remain calm and clear, she attempted to drift towards the centre of the road in order to prevent him from passing her. The truck came up beside her and began to force her back over towards the guard rail.

Remembering that her audio recorder was still on, she exclaimed, "A black half-ton truck is running me off the road! Oh please, God, *please!*"

The truck inched closer and struck, causing Mary's car to begin to careen out of control. With dream-like clarity, she noticed that the guardrail was badly damaged in places. Before Mary could get the car back under full control, the truck was on her rear bumper, pushing her towards the guardrail. Her car hit and bounced back—then she was hit hard again on the left rear end of her car. She started to spin, but the right front bumper caught the damaged guardrail. Her car started to move to the centre of the road, but the black truck hit her one final time, crashing the car through the damaged guardrail and catapulting it over the steep ravine.

The driver of the truck glanced in his side mirror. They had just come through a small hairpin curve when he saw a tractor-trailer truck coming up behind him. He knew he had to get out of there fast. Mary's car had come to a rest, but it was in plain view. The driver of the black truck could not stick around to observe any longer without being discovered, so he sped away.

Mary was unconscious; the driver's window was down and her airbags had deployed. The impact had wrenched her neck very badly and she had a terrible nosebleed.

Miraculously, Megan was not badly injured.

"Mommy, *Mommy!*" she screamed, sobbing.

Mary groaned; she was coming to, but the pain was excruciating. In a state of profound shock, Mary tried to undo her seatbelt. She could not.

"*Megan!* Megan—I'm trying to reach you, but I *can't!*"

She desperately tried once again to twist herself around to check on Megan, but was immediately blinded by a white-hot jolt of agony; before she could stop herself, she let out a horrifying scream of pain.

Mary realized with an odd sense of detachment that she was bleeding badly—and suddenly, she was unable to move altogether.

"Mommy is trying, Megan…I…can't move," she cried.

Through a haze of diminishing consciousness, she realized she was getting weaker and weaker; she knew that she was not going to make it.

"Oh, Megan…" she gasped, "I'm so…sorry…I love you…"

She slipped into unconsciousness; the last sound she heard was that of Megan crying.

"*Help,* Mommy! *Please!* Help!" Megan screamed over and over, until she no longer could. Soon she was exhausted, lapsing into deep, guttural sobs as she gasped for air.

Joe had stopped earlier to check his map on the way to his destination; he needed additional directions to an address, and those directions had taken him along the same road as Mary. Within minutes of starting up his enormous eighteen-wheeler again, he came upon the scene of Mary's accident; he knew right away that it had just happened. He quickly parked about fifty feet back on a straight piece of the road and called for help on his CB radio. He jumped out of the truck, placed a flare in front and behind his truck, and ran towards the wreckage of Mary's car.

Oh God, I hope I'm in time! Please God, let them be okay, he thought.

He slipped and, almost falling, slid his way down to the car. When he got closer, he could hear sounds.

Thank God! Someone is alive!

About eight feet from the car, he fell forward; he stumbled, but managed to keep his balance.

No smell of gas—that's good, he noted.

He ended up on the driver's side of the vehicle, and immediately gasped at what he saw.

"No God, *no!*" he cried aloud; he saw a woman slumped lifelessly over the wheel.

His heart was beating so fast and hard that he felt sick. He felt for a pulse; he could not find one. Then he tried to open the car door. It was jammed. He could not open it, no matter how hard he tried. He felt for a pulse once more—nothing. His training as a medic told him the woman was dead.

His attention turned immediately to a very young child in the backseat; with relief, he could see that she was not in a critical state, but he was still deeply concerned. He knew he couldn't move her; he'd have to wait for help. Nonetheless, he got the left back door open, and with professional hands, he quickly examined her. He couldn't believe it—she appeared to be okay.

She was moving her arms and legs, desperately trying to get to her mother as she continued to call, "Mommy, Mommy!" By now, her voice was hoarse. Her tears were all dried up, and the sound of her words broke his heart.

Joe took his leather jacket—emblazoned with a Harley-Davidson insignia on the back—and very carefully tucked it around her to keep her warm, as he knew she must be in shock. As he did so, he knelt down beside her, and in his deep, gravelly voice, he began to speak to her softly.

"Sweetie, you're okay. Help will be here soon," he said, his voice full of emotion.

He leaned across her and picked up a well-worn, stuffed black and white humpback whale. Carefully, he placed it in front of the young child.

She immediately grabbed it and began to rock it back and forth. She became much calmer and quieter, and fixed her eyes on this big, rough, unshaven man. He had the bluest eyes she had ever seen. She went silent and still; as their eyes locked, he could swear she already knew she would never hear her mother's voice again.

As tough as Joe was, tears ran down his unshaven cheeks. He tried to calm her with his deep, bass voice, but inside he thought, *she knows...she knows.*

Fire trucks, an ambulance, and police arrived, followed by a car driven by a young female medical doctor. She joined the paramedics at Mary's car and quickly confirmed that she was dead—thus Megan immediately became their primary focus. As the police, doctor, and paramedics came around to the far side of the car, they were struck by the sight of the big, husky middle-aged man—who was well over 200 pounds of pure muscle and tattoos—as he gently sang to this young, silent child. The police asked him to move, but he continued to kneel there, humming and whispering to the child as tears kept flowing from his eyes.

"Sir—please move and let the doctor examine the child," said a second police officer. His tone was authoritative and insistent.

Joe paid no attention.

The police officer stepped forward to pull him away, but the doctor intervened.

"Please, leave him be," she said. "He appears to have her calmed down. It'll make it a lot easier for me to examine her if she stays calm."

The police officer relented, and stepped back.

The doctor moved closer and checked Megan, being ever so careful and gentle with her.

"What's your name, sweetie?" she asked.

There was no answer. The young child could not take her eyes off this giant of a man who was continuing to hum.

"Sir, we need to remove the car seat, with her in it." Noticing a tattoo on his right arm, she recognized he was a trained medic. "Sir, would you like to help us get this little one out? She seems to be totally focused on you, and she's in shock."

"My name is Joe...Joe White. And yes, I would like to help. I can't seem to take my eyes off of her. She's like a wee angel. May I stay with her until we get her to the hospital?" he said, carefully lifting Megan and her car seat free of the car.

"But what about your truck?"

"Right after I called 911, I radioed my boss and told him the situation; they'll take care of it. Let's get this little one out of here."

"This may not have been a single-car accident," said one of the officers.

"There *was* another vehicle on the road ahead of me," said Joe.

The policeman edged closer. "What? Can you describe it?" he asked.

"I really don't remember. I think it was a dark-coloured pickup."

The doctor, acting with a sense of urgency, interrupted. "Joe—you ride with her in the ambulance, and I'll meet you at the hospital."

All the way to the hospital, the child and Joe were inseparable. She clung to her stuffed whale and never said a word. She just kept looking at Joe, with her eyes silently pleading, *Why?*

Joe in turn was thinking, *A little one her age could not possibly understand—or could she?* Her eyes were begging for an answer. Joe had none. He decided he would stay with her until a relative could be found, regardless of how long that may be.

They were met at the hospital by a hearty, robust nurse. "Hi, I'm Nurse Brody," she said, introducing herself in a broad Scottish accent. "I'm going to get her clothes off and put her in a gown. We'll be conducting an initial examination to assess the extent of her injuries."

"All right—I'll just wait here," said Joe. As he stepped back, Megan began to cry.

"It's okay, little one," Joe called to her. "I'll be right here. I won't leave you." He stood on the other side of the curtain and reassured her as the nurse and aides worked.

Once behind the curtain in the emergency room, Nurse Brody gently removed Megan's jeans and top, along with her pink and white socks and shoes.

The doctor joined the nurse as she worked; he pressed his stethoscope against her skin, and cast a seasoned eye over her from head to toe. When he was done, he shook his head in disbelief; Megan was physically fine, though she had a few bruises and was in a state of shock.

"Lord, I can't understand it," said Nurse Brody. "In all my life, I've never seen so little trauma under the circumstances. It's a miracle—a beautiful miracle!"

"It's as if there were an angel there protecting her," a nurse's aide added. "I tell you—this one is special. She was meant to live!"

Once Megan was in her gown, and after the staff had conducted their initial examination, they opened the curtain so she could see Joe. At the sight of him, her crying immediately ceased. Nurse Brody smiled at him warmly and beckoned him over to Megan's side.

With the initial medical examination complete, a young woman with short, sandy hair approached them. She walked and spoke with confidence as she introduced herself.

"I'm Constable Holly Summers with the RCMP—Forensic Science and Identification Services."

Joe nodded and shook her hand. "Joe White,' he said.

"How is Megan doing?"

"You know her name?" Joe asked.

"We found her name on some papers in the car."

"Megan," said Joe, looking back at the little girl. She kept her eyes fixed on him as he said her name.

"She's doing very well," said Nurse Brody. "Aside from a few minor bruises, the only problem seems to be that she isn't speaking."

"She's in shock," said the doctor. "so we'll have to maintain close observation. We administered a sedative to help calm her."

Holly turned to Joe. "I'll need to ask you a few questions, if you don't mind."

Joe looked at Megan; she was beginning to doze off.

"Sure, but let's wait a minute or two first to see if she will drop off to sleep," he said.

They sat very quietly for a few minutes. With the stuffed whale tucked under her arm, Megan soon fell asleep.

The poor child must be exhausted, Joe thought.

"Megan is three years old," said Holly in a very quiet voice, once it was safe to talk without disturbing the child. "Her mother's name was Dr. Mary Teal."

"A medical doctor?" asked Joe.

"No, she was a researcher at a marine lab near Halifax."

"Oh," he said. "Any information on relatives?"

"We did get the name of the next of kin—Dr. Nona Teal, Mary's mother. She lives on the island of Grand Manan, New Brunswick. We're attempting to get in touch with her."

Joe nodded. "Good. If it's all right, I'd like to stay with Megan until the next of kin gets here."

"I don't see why not. You certainly seem to have made quite a connection with her. Can you share with me what you know about the accident?"

Joe described what he'd witnessed and how he'd responded. It all came flooding back to him. When he related how she was crying and calling "Mommy" over and over, his throat and chest tightened, and tears began to well up in his eyes.

"Joe," Holly asked gently, "You say she was talking? Megan was saying words?"

"Constable Summers, she was *definitely* talking," Joe said. He paused as the significance of that detail sunk in. "Then she suddenly stopped," he added.

"She never said a word after that?"

"No. She sobbed for a while—but no, not another spoken word." Joe paused, frowning, then said, "Although...just before she went to sleep, she made a sound. It wasn't a word—it was more like...like a brief *hummmm*."

Holly had a pensive look on her face; at that moment, she was contacted on the portable radio that hung on her hip.

"Sorry Joe, I have to take this," she said. She wandered a few feet away while she conducted her call. She turned her back for privacy, and spoke on the radio briefly before using the phone at the nurse's station for a few minutes. She came back when she was done, and had a grim expression on her face.

"We've contacted Mary's mother, Nona, who is out of country," she told him. "She'll be here tomorrow. We may need to talk to you some more."

"No problem; I live close by and I plan to stay with Megan until her grandmother arrives."

"She'll be so thankful; she'll have lots of questions for you, I'm sure."

After Holly departed, Joe sat beside Megan's bed, thinking, *God, she's so tiny. What was the sound Megan made? Was it just a hum—or was it something else?*

* * *

Nona had just finished giving the most important paper of her career at a meeting in Glasgow, Scotland. She was feeling quite pleased with herself: the paper had been positively received. She was typing up some follow-up notes on her computer in her hotel room when the phone rang.

"Hello...Yes, this is Nona Teal."

"I'm Constable Holly Summers with the RCMP. I understand you have a daughter whose name is Mary. Is that correct?"

Nona immediately knew something was very wrong. "What's happened?" she asked. She was beginning to feel nauseated, faint, and dizzy. "Is she all right?"

"I'm afraid it is bad news."

"No...no!" Nona gasped.

"I'm terribly sorry to have to deliver this news, Dr. Teal, but your daughter Mary was killed in a car accident about two hours ago. I'm so very sorry for your loss."

Nona was stunned and afraid. Then she thought, *Megan*.

"She has a young daughter," she said. "Was she in the car?"

"Yes she was, but she's safe. Megan is in hospital and has been thoroughly examined; she appears to be fine other than a few bruises, and is being treated for shock."

"I'll be there as soon as I can," Nona answered.

Andrew came into the room. He'd overheard the last part of the conversation and knew that something was terribly wrong. Nona was pale and appeared to have had the breath knocked out of her.

"Andrew, it's the RCMP—Mary has been killed in a car accident!" she cried out at the sight of him. Her voice was shaking. Trembling, she released the phone into Andrew's hands.

Andrew picked up the phone and pressed it to his ear. His heart was pounding.

"Hello...Ma'am...are you still there?" asked Holly.

"Sorry, hello—this is Andrew, Nona's partner. I don't think Nona can talk just now. Is...is it true?"

"Yes, sir. Mary Teal was killed in a car accident earlier today."

Andrew took a deep breath and quickly pulled himself together. "What can I do?"

"Megan was in the car; she's okay and is being treated for shock here in hospital. She's awaiting your arrival."

"I will get Nona there as quickly as I can. Can you please give me all the necessary details and your contact information? I'll need to write this down."

"Of course," answered Holly.

After gathering the information and ending the call, he went straight to Nona.

"I'm here, sweetheart," he said. He put his arms around her.

She was devastated. She sat on the sofa with her head in her hands, slowly rocking back and forth as she sobbed.

"Mary...oh, Mary, *why?*" she whispered through her sobs, repeating this over and over.

After a time, she became quiet and still, and looked up at Andrew. More tears began to well up, but she tried to gather herself. She took Andrew's hand.

"Please—I *must* get there as soon as possible," she said.

"I've all the information," he said, giving her a gentle hug. "I'll have the conference centre make all the arrangements."

"Please...hurry."

He loved Nona so much that his heart was breaking. He wanted to just hold her, comfort her, and protect her.

Her mind seemed to be spinning; it felt like she was thinking about a hundred things at once. "I have to let the conference leaders know; I was supposed to chair a couple of sessions tomorrow," she said. Then she fell unusually silent.

Andrew picked up the phone and contacted a conference representative named Anne; he informed her of the tragic news. After requesting assistance in making urgent travel arrangements, he hung up the phone and looked at Nona; he could see that she really wasn't there.

What must Nona be thinking—or is she thinking at all? he wondered. *Is she so overwhelmed with emotion that she simply can't think? She's just come from the highest point in her career to the lowest, most awful point in her personal life. Her only child—her daughter—is gone.*

He had often observed that Mary and Nona were so close that sometimes it seemed as if they were communicating by telepathy. As he was thinking this, Nona spoke.

"Andrew—I knew...I felt...I just *knew* something was wrong. It was during the question session after my paper; I suddenly felt very strange. I had to really work to concentrate on those around me, so I pushed the sensation aside. Oh, Mary...I'm so sorry...and...there was something else. I know it was very important, but it's gone."

She went over to the desk and started sorting and packing her papers.

"Darling, you've so much on your mind right now. You'll remember," he said.

The phone rang. Andrew answered the phone while keeping an eye on Nona.

"It's Anne at the conference desk," said a sympathetic but professional voice on the other end of the line. "We reserved the first flight we could get, but there is unfortunately no direct flight to Halifax. You'll be flying to St. John's, Newfoundland. After a three-hour wait, you'll fly to Halifax. I'm sending someone up to your room to deliver the tickets and a printout of your travel itinerary."

"That's wonderful, Anne. Thank you so much for all you've done for us."

"You're very welcome. We've notified the head of the conference. He, on behalf of everyone, sends his deepest condolences and sympathy. Is there anything more we can do?"

"Actually, there is. Could you please have all the notes and any other relevant material gathered together for Nona?"

"We're already on that."

"Thank you. I'll let her know."

He turned to Nona and told her of the arrangements. He was not sure if she'd heard him, but she had.

"Andrew, that doesn't give us much time; we'd better get ourselves organized," she said. She was exhausted and anxious, and though she was edgy, she knew that everyone was doing their best to get her to Megan as quickly as possible.

Andrew, being a strong and supportive partner, leapt into action. He took over all the phone calls and arrangements, and had called the hotel doctor to acquire sedatives for Nona. At first she refused to take any.

"I know you hate taking medicine, but please listen to me," he said gently but firmly. "There is nothing you can do to help Megan from here. We know she's safe and cared for. When we get there, you'll need to be well-rested; Megan is going to depend on you, Nona. You and I are all she has now. You must get some rest."

After a few moments, Nona gently squeezed his hand in agreement.

Andrew went to get her a glass of water, and was thankful for a brief moment of privacy; he didn't want her to see his own tears as they slowly made their way to his chin. He ran cold water for her and quickly wiped his eyes with his sleeve. His thoughts drifted back to when he and Nona had come together.

He had known her for many years, and had been good friends with her husband, Michael. After Michael died of a massive heart attack, Andrew and Nona became close friends. When Mary went off to university, Nona was lonely, so Andrew and Nona would go for long walks on one of the many beaches on the island. Sometimes they would just walk in a comfortable silence. At other times, they would have great discussions and even enjoyed some silly chats.

One day she'd turned to him as they were sitting on a big old log on the beach; the tides had played with these logs over the years, pushing them to their permanent home well above the high-tide mark. She'd taken his hand in both of hers and said, "Andrew, I love you. Please come and live with me and be my partner. I need you."

He'd almost fallen off the log.

"Oh, Nona—my dearest Nona—I have loved you from the first day I saw you," he'd answered. "Yes, I'll..."

He hadn't been able to finish the sentence; she was gently stroking his face, and their lips met. Just as suddenly, they were interrupted by a puppy that had run up to Nona, jumping on her lap. They laughed as the pup ignored the calls of its owner; it crawled higher and began to lick her face.

"I'm so sorry!" the puppy's owner called out. "Willie, come here!"

But Willie still paid no attention.

"Dogs seem to know when people are happy and in love," Nona had said with a laugh.

"...Andrew, are you okay?"

Nona was calling him, jolting him out of his reverie and bringing him back to the present moment. He finished filling the glass of water and took it to her.

By the time the bellhop arrived and took their luggage, Nona was beginning to feel the effects of the sedatives. Andrew would give her a stronger dose once they were on the plane; hopefully she'd get some rest during the flight home. The earliest flight only offered availability in business class, but he was glad as it would offer more comfort and quiet for Nona.

They had no sooner arrived at Glasgow airport when Nona and Andrew were paged. They went to the customer service desk and used the phone. It was Constable Summers.

"Is Megan okay?" Andrew immediately asked.

"Yes, she's sleeping a lot."

"That's good to hear. We'll be there soon," he said.

"Before you get here, you should know that it was not a single-car accident," Holly added. "It was a hit-and-run. Confidentially speaking, we are treating it as a suspicious incident. Because you'll be focussing primarily on Megan's wellbeing when you arrive, I wanted to give you this information sooner than later."

Andrew took the information in and stored it away for further reference; he'd have to consider the timing and manner in which to deliver this news to Nona.

"That's greatly appreciated, Constable Summers. Thank you."

"I also want you to be prepared before you get here: Megan appears to be unable to speak. The doctors feel it's because she's in shock. Also, she's hugging a stuffed whale; does it have a name?"

"That's Lacuna. Megan is crazy about it. It goes everywhere she goes."

"Thanks. We felt if we knew its name, we might get her to talk through it."

* * *

Megan was awake again. Joe called the nurse. "Well, well! You're awake again, sweetie," Joe said very softly.

Megan rolled over and reached for Joe's hand.

My God, she is so tiny! Joe thought. He looked at her tiny hand in his own thick-fingered mitt of a hand. *How could you have survived such a terrible accident? You look so fragile, and yet...*

"Here we are, Joe," said the nurse. "Would you like to see if you get her to eat? She really needs to have something in her stomach."

Joe took the tray. He offered Megan a drink, but she shook her head. He then tried to offer her some of the solid food. Megan again shook her head. Then he thought, *I'll try with some ice cream.* Once again, the response was negative. He tried everything he could think of to get her to eat, but she continued to refuse.

"Megan, sweetheart—you really must try to eat something. Your grandmother is on her way to see you and you don't want her to think that we are not taking very good care of you, do you?"

Megan very slowly shook her head *no*.

He tried once more. It was no go. Then he realized she was still hugging her stuffed whale, and he got an idea.

"Lacuna, you look hungry. Would you like to share Megan's snack?"

Megan moved Lacuna's head up and down to indicate *yes*.

Joe picked up a tiny bit of food on the tip of the spoon. "Lacuna, you must be starving," he said. "Here, have some of Megan's food. I'm sure she won't mind."

Megan reached up and took the spoon from Joe and looked at Lacuna then back to Joe. He nodded. Megan offered the spoon to Lacuna, but she made Lacuna shake her head *no*. Megan then pointed the spoon and the whale's head towards herself.

Joe held his breath, thinking, *Is this really going to work?* but he said nothing; he just sat there and smiled.

Megan smiled back and put the spoon in her mouth and nodded *yes*.

Joe began to hum ever so softly as he watched Megan eat.

"You sure have a way with this wee one, Joe," Nurse Brody said. She was smiling ear to ear as she began tidying up.

After Megan had eaten a bit more, she said, "Megan, my darling, time for a bath and change of your gown—if Mr. Joe says it's okay. And it looks like that whale of yours could do with a bit of a cleanup."

Megan looked at Joe for reassurance.

"Go ahead, sweetie. I'm here; I'm not going anywhere."

The nursing staff was abuzz with how well Megan was doing, and with how great Joe was with her.

"Why, he's even gotten her to eat," they said. "Maybe he'll be the one to get her to talk."

* * *

The plane was on time. Nona was sitting quietly at the flight gate with Andrew beside her for support. This was one of the aspects of Andrew she loved most: he knew when she needed her space and when she needed to be by herself. She always had been that way, even as a child. She loved to play outside with friends, but she also loved being on her own, doing her own thing, her own way.

Nature was her best friend. She spent hours and hours playing or walking in the bush or on a beach. Andrew instinctively knew when she felt this way and would just let her be. This was one of those times. She needed to think. The pills had dulled her mind a bit—enough to keep her calm so she could begin to sort things out.

She took out some paper and a pen. She always thought better with a pen in her hand. Andrew gently squeezed her hand, and she turned to look into those deep ocean-blue eyes.

"I love you," she whispered.

Soon afterwards, their flight was called.

It's strange how time moves so slowly when one is in a hurry to get somewhere, Nona thought. Once on the plane, she took more sedatives and dozed for a while.

As she slept, she had a very strange dream; when she awoke, she could not remember it all. The more she tried to remember, the more elusive the memory seemed. She quickly picked up her pen and wrote down what she could recall.

The dream was about either Mary or Megan; she couldn't remember which. There was a whale—a humpback, she thought—and it was trying to tell her something. She knew it was an important message of some sort, but she couldn't remember.

Her meal arrived, and she put pen and paper away. She only nibbled at her food. Her mind was spinning, so she stopped eating and began to write. She knew she had to do so—and right away.

> My dearest, gentle Mary, my love, my daughter—
>
> You are, have been, and always will be the love of my life. Wherever I go, wherever I am, or whatever I do, you are and forever will be with me. This I know. You are my strength. When your father died, you were just a young woman. You were mature beyond your years—an old soul—and you instinctively understood life so well. You always, always marched to your own drummer, danced your own dance and to your own rhythm. You were always in tune with everyone and everything around you. Your smile lit your way, with your eyes always twinkling, as if there was an imp or sprite behind them. I know there always was. Compassion and kindness were your constant companions. I will miss you terribly.

Nona could no longer hold back her tears. Her heart was pounding as she put her pen down and pushed the pad away, but not before a couple of tears had fallen on the letter. Her tears came in a flood.

Andrew immediately took her in his arms and held her firmly but gently; softly caressing the top of her head, he whispered, "Let it out, my angel, let it all go."

Tears began to well up in his own eyes as he felt the deep rolling sobs that racked her body. His heart broke to see her in such despair.

"Is there a problem, sir? May I get you anything?" asked a flight attendant.

Andrew nodded. "Yes," he answered, and his voice broke. He cleared his throat. "Sorry. May we have a couple of glasses of ice water, please?"

The flight attendant quickly produced two glasses of ice water, along with a blanket and a pillow. The attendant put her hand on his shoulder. Andrew looked up and thanked her. "We just lost our daughter."

"I know—your friend over there told me. I'm so sorry. Please don't hesitate to ask for anything." She quietly turned, nodded to the man sitting one row behind on the opposite side of the plane, and gave him a friendly wink. He winked back.

Andrew turned around to look. He recognized his close friend, Rance, and caught his eye.

"Rance, what are you doing here?" he asked.

Rance motioned to Andrew to be quiet and then mouthed to him, "It's okay. Talk to you later."

Typical Rance—he always shows up when I need him. How did he know? Andrew thought.

By this time, Nona's tears were spent, but she was still catching her breath. Andrew offered her the pills and a glass of water. She nodded in thanks, and with shaking hands she took them. She looked at the pad and paper again and knew that she had to keep writing and finish the letter she'd started. She sat up straight and took another sip of water. She pulled the pad closer, picked up the pen, and tried to calm herself. Then she turned to Andrew and kissed him.

"Andrew, what am I going to do without Mary? A large part of my life has died with her. I will miss her so. The pain is unbearable! Hold me, please—never let me go."

Another wave of grief washed over her, and she began to weep again as Andrew held her.

"Sweetheart, I'll always be here. I love you," he said.

Suddenly, Nona sat up straight as if she felt a jolt of energy. "Oh, Andrew—poor Megan!" she exclaimed. She paused for a moment, and firmly said, "Megan is going to come and live with us. I will love her and care for her like I did Mary."

Andrew knew what was coming next. "It's okay; I'll be a good father—the one Megan never had," he said. "I'll love her as my own. We'll raise her together."

He could tell by the look in her eyes that this was the way it was going to be. It was going to be a rough time for both of them. He would have to be her rock.

Nona's tears were spent for the time being. She took a deep breath, picked up the pen, and continued her letter to Mary.

> Mary, my heart is breaking. I will be strong for Megan's sake. I want you to know that Megan is okay; she survived the accident. I know you know this. We are on our way to see her and hopefully take her home. You know that Andrew and I will love her and raise her. I love her as I love you. She will come and live with us, and I will raise her as I did you. I will also follow your wishes, as I know you have written them down. We both know that there is something very special about our Megan. I see it in her eyes. They are your eyes. I cannot really explain it, but I know it's good. I'll watch over her as I know you will from heaven. She will be fine.

Nona's writing was interrupted with the announcement that they were beginning their approach to St. John's, Newfoundland. She tucked the letter into her briefcase.

Andrew leaned over. "Darling, Rance is here," he told her.

"Where? Is he on this plane?"

"One row back."

She glanced back, and sure enough, there he was. "How? When?"

"I don't know, but I feel that he's here to help us."

As they were departing the plane, Nona turned around and saw their friend.

"Rance—how did you know?" she asked in amazement.

"I got a phone message from a mutual friend who was at the conference in Glasgow. I was in the area on business. He told me what had happened. Nona, I'm so very sorry. My private jet is here to take us to Halifax immediately. There'll be a cab waiting to take you to the hospital."

"But what are about our luggage?"

"Not to worry. I've spoken with the airline; all of that has been taken care of. Let's go. Follow me."

Nona was stunned and overwhelmed with gratitude. "This means we'll get to Megan sooner than we thought," she said.

* * *

In conducting research on all involved parties, Holly discovered that Joe lived in the area. He had served for twelve years in the US Navy Medical Corps in the Gulf War, in Afghanistan, and in Iraq. He was honourably discharged three years previously, at which time he'd moved to Canada. He'd married when he was twenty while he was serving his second year in the Navy. He had a daughter.

No wonder he's so good with Megan, Holly thought as she read on.

He and his wife were divorced. The mother had kept the child and moved out west. The little girl was about four at the time.

As she mulled over these details, her phone rang. It was Sergeant Tom Randall, her superior.

"Summers, I just received word that Dr. Nona Teal and her partner will be arriving earlier than anticipated; can you be there on time to talk to them?"

"Certainly, sir."

She had no sooner hung up when her phone rang again; Forensics had found something when examining Mary's car.

* * *

Upon their arrival at the hospital, Nona and Andrew were met by Dr. Williams, Nurse Brody, and Constable Summers.

"I would like to see my granddaughter, please," Nona asked. She was very pale and was clearly working hard to maintain her composure. "Then I would like to see my daughter."

"We understand, Dr. Teal," Holly answered quietly.

"Please—call me Nona."

"Nona...Megan is sleeping, so it's a good time for us to speak with you a bit more comprehensively," said Dr. Williams.

"Is she not doing well?"

"On the contrary—with what she's been through, she's doing exceptionally well."

Dr. Williams filled them in on all the test results of Megan's various examinations.

"You're aware Megan has not said a word since she arrived here," he said. "We think it's shock-related. We'd like to evaluate this and discuss this with you again after you've seen Megan."

"When will I be able to see Mary?" Nona asked. She looked extremely tired.

"Soon, I assure you. For now, I shall leave you in the capable hands of Nurse Brody who has been Megan's nurse since she came to us."

Nurse Brody turned to Nona. She paused, wondering where to begin.

"Joe White, who was the first person on the scene of the accident, has not left Megan's side since the accident. He arrived only moments after Mary's car crashed. Joe was a medic in the US Navy, and when he got to the car, he determined that Mary was gone. That's when he heard Megan calling to her mother."

"I thought you said Megan wasn't talking," Andrew interrupted.

"Actually, Megan *was* talking at first, for a minute or so. From what I've heard from the paramedics, when the emergency crew and police arrived, they were astonished to find this big, strong man kneeling beside the back door of the car. Megan was still fastened in her car seat, hugging her stuffed whale. Apparently she was totally focused on Joe, and he was humming in a very low-key tone. They said it looked like they were communicating with one another without speaking. Because he assured them that he had medical training, they let him carry Megan—after a preliminary examination—to the ambulance. He rode with her to the hospital and has not left her side since. He said he would stay with her until you got here, Nona." She paused to allow Nona and Andrew some time to process what she'd just divulged. After a few moments she asked, "Now, would you like to go see your granddaughter and meet Joe?"

"Please," Nona said; her voice was trembling with emotion.

Hand in hand, Nona and Andrew followed Nurse Brody to Megan's room, where they came upon a very tender scene.

Joe was sitting beside Megan's bed, humming softly. Nona's first impression was that of a very large teddy bear of a man with the voice of an angel. The three of them just stood quietly and let the ambience in the room flow over them. Nona said later that it felt extremely calm, almost sacred. Andrew was spellbound. No one wanted to be the one to break the spell. Joe, sensing their presence, turned his head. When he saw them, he smiled warmly.

"She's still asleep," he whispered. He slowly rose from the chair and walked over to Nona and Andrew. Nona was transfixed by his deep blue eyes; he took her hand gently and firmly.

"You're Nona?" he asked.

She nodded.

Tears began to well up in his eyes. "I'm Joe," he said.

Nona reached up and gave him a hug. "Thank you, thank you, *thank you,*" she whispered in his ear.

Joe whispered to her, "I'm so sorry."

The two clung to one another for support. As they separated, he held her gently by the shoulders. "You have her eyes...I mean, *Megan* has *your* eyes," he said. "There is something extremely special about your granddaughter."

Megan was beginning to stir. Joe turned and started to go to her and then stopped.

"Sorry, Nona. I'm already just so accustomed to—"

"Joe, it's okay," said Nona. "We'll both go and sit beside her as she wakes up. Nurse Brody tells me that you and Megan and you have formed a bond; it would be best if you stayed. Come, Andrew, and sit with us. Joe, please do whatever you've been doing when she wakes."

Joe nodded, and softly he began to hum the same notes and phrases he'd used from the start. A shiver went up Nona's spine. Slowly, Megan awoke, and as she did so, she turned to listen to Joe as always. Her eyes fluttered and closed a few times, and then she was awake. She grasped Lacuna and gazed into Joe's eyes. She didn't cry or make a sound. Then she saw Nona beside him. Her eyes slowly moved back and forth a few times. Nona immediately moved closer to Joe. Megan moved Lacuna so that it appeared that she nodded, and then Megan gave a wee smile.

"Megan, sweetheart, we all love you so," Nona said; it felt as though her heart was breaking. As she spoke, Joe was humming ever so softly and sliding gently over, allowing Nona to move even closer.

Joe started to move further away, but Nona put her hand on his and whispered, "Not yet, please, not yet."

He squeezed her hand, letting her know he would stay as long as was necessary.

* * *

Jerry—the head of the Forensics lab—was in his mid-fifties; he had closely-cropped salt and pepper hair, was very tall and thin, and had steel-grey eyes. He was one of the best scientists in the field, and Holly had tremendous respect for him.

"What have you found?" Holly asked as she walked briskly into Jerry's office. He was focused on his computer as he input data using forensic mapping software. Sergeant Tom Randall was standing at his side, peering at the screen.

"Come with me," he said, getting up from behind his desk. "You'll find this interesting."

They moved from his office area into a huge garage where they worked on several vehicles at any one time. Holly saw the car, and in spite of all her training and experience, a cold shiver consumed her being. On the rear of the vehicle, she could see three distinct areas of black paint and some very large dents. Two of them looked similar, and the direction of the scrapes and scratches were different on the largest dent.

"She was hit at least twice," she said.

"We took photos from all angles and with a variety of lighting. Holly, this car was not only hit twice—it was hit many times by the same vehicle, and she was pushed at least once."

"What? Are you sure?"

"Yes—I'll show you the results of one of our newer software programs."

As he led Holly and Tom into an adjacent lab, Jerry explained: "This program can separate the various layers of paint; each layer has unique scrapes and scratches which show directionality." He brought up a grid of six photos on a large monitor.

"The first photo is of the largest area of black paint. The other five are individual layers of paint making up that spot. The top layer represents the most recent hit and is the thickest of the five. The smudging indicates the car was also being pushed. The next two represent relatively minor bumps. The fourth is the first hard bump. This program tells us she was hit or bumped at least four times and was pushed once from the left rear corner of the car. She was also bumped two or three times behind the driver's side passenger door."

"This was definitely no accident. It was intentional." Tom vocalized what everyone around him was thinking.

"But why so many times? It's as if someone was bumping and pushing her in a specific manner for a specific purpose," Holly added.

"We sent our cameramen out to photograph the actual spot where the car left the road and had them start shooting several feet before it," said Jerry. He showed the video. "I'll slow it down so you can view it frame by frame. Here are some skid marks, and again, more—now keep your eyes on the dents in the guardrail. This particular one dent has white paint on it. Watch as I slow it down more. There's the dent with white paint on it where her car made contact; this impact caused her car to go into the ravine.

"The technicians just noticed this," he continued. "They found a personal recording device—a micro-cassette recorder that would be commonly-used by professionals in her field. They believe it was turned on at the time of the accident. They are currently dismantling the car and will send you the results."

Tom turned to Jerry and Holly. "This is now to be investigated as a homicide," he said. "I want that vehicle stripped and thoroughly analyzed; report to Summers with any findings, immediately."

As they walked away, Tom spoke urgently to Holly.

"Summers, this is your investigation. You're officially the chief investigator on this case from this point forward. You have authorization to use any of our resources, including manpower, to assist you in any way. We're scouring this whole area for a dark-coloured or black half-ton pickup; so far, there's nothing."

Holly nodded. "Okay, keep me posted. I'm going back over to the hospital. Nona Teal called; she wants to talk."

"They already know we're treating it as is suspicious accident," he said. "It might be best to tell them about the damage to the car. Don't tell them about the possibility of a recording. And Summers, how much does the press know about this?"

"They know that there was a woman killed. No details were to be released pending notification of next of kin. Only the hospital staff know about the child."

"Good—keep it that way, and keep a tight rein on the evidence."

* * *

Nurse Brody came in with a juice bottle and food for Megan.

"Sorry to interrupt you folks, but our little angel needs some sustenance," she said. She handed the tray to Nona. She took it, hesitated, and then passed it to Joe. "You feed her, Joe."

The eating game between Megan, Lacuna, and Joe began. At one point, Megan gave the spoon to Nona. The game of three became a game of four.

Brody smiled and thought, *That wee angel is wise beyond her three years.*

"Well folks, now it's my turn," said Nurse Brody, after Megan had taken some refreshment. "I need to bathe her and change her bed."

Megan gave Nona and Joe an anxious look.

"It's okay, sweetheart. We're not leaving."

Andrew entered the room.

"Where did you go?" asked Nona.

"I made the identification. We'll be able to make arrangements to take her home, and you'll be able to see her soon."

Nona thanked him. She noticed Joe was hesitating and moving towards the door.

"Joe—please don't go. Please join us. I've so many questions I wish to ask you. You must be exhausted."

"I'm fine, Nona. I'd be glad to help you in any way I can."

They moved into a small private waiting room.

"I can't begin to thank you, Joe," Nona began. "You've done so much for us. I have to ask: was Mary still alive when you got to her?" Her voice began to crack.

"When I got to the car, Mary was gone. All I heard was Megan crying and calling for her mommy."

"She was talking, then?"

"Yes, she spoke, but only for a minute or two, and then she stopped."

Dr. Williams came in. "All the test results are in," he said. "The psychologist suggests her inability to speak is a direct result of the accident. He believes it is temporary."

"When can we take her home?" Andrew asked.

"I don't see any reason why you can't take her home later today."

"Thank you. When can I see Mary, and when can we bring her home?" Nona asked anxiously.

"You may see Mary now, if you like. Andrew made arrangements with your local funeral home."

Before Nona left, she spoke to Joe. "Please, give us your phone number and address; we wish to keep in touch with you." She gave Joe a card. "Here's ours. Joe, feel free to visit Megan any time you wish."

Joe smiled and gave her a big hug. "I will Nona…I will. I'd like to say goodbye to her. Why don't I stay with Megan while you sort out the paperwork?"

"Joe, that's a wonderful idea. We also have to speak with Constable Summers before we leave."

Nona walked to the morgue, with Andrew at her side and Dr. Williams ahead of them, leading the way. *I must see her—I have to be sure—but the pain and the shock will be great,* she thought.

Once they arrived and signed in, the medical examiner approached them and led them inside. "Dr. Teal? Please come this way. Take all the time you need. Let us know when you are ready."

Nona nodded, and the sheet was removed to Mary's shoulders. She gasped, and her knees started to buckle. Andrew was behind her and held her. Nona wanted to reach out and touch her. She placed her hand on the glass separating them. Quiet tears began to stream down her face. Feeling faint, she slowly turned away. She still had the interview with the police before they could collect Megan and head home.

* * *

Holly's mind was racing as she began to set up in the small private waiting room. It was a very comfortable room. There was a small tan-coloured sofa, a matching chair and a coffee table. She set up her computer and recorder on the coffee table.

A few minutes later, Nona and Andrew arrived.

"How is Megan coming along?" Holly asked.

"Surprisingly well. We'll take her with us this afternoon."

"That's good news," said Holly. "I'm sure you're all anxious to get home, so I'll try to make this as brief and as easy on you as possible. Are you ready to discuss the details of the investigation?" Holly asked.

Andrew and Nona nodded.

"We are suspicious about the accident," Holly began. "We're now treating it as a homicide."

"*What?*" Both Andrew and Nona exclaimed at once.

"Your daughter's car was deliberately pushed off the road, and it appears that it was planned. Her car was pushed through a weakened guardrail. Do you know why Mary was on that particular road?"

Nona nodded her head. "County Road 16?"

"Yes."

"My daughter found that it relaxed her driving to and from her place of work."

Holly paused for a moment, thinking, then asked, "Was there anyone you know of who would want to harm her?"

Nona thought slowly, shaking her head. "I don't think so. Everyone liked her very much."

"Does she have any close friends, a boyfriend or..."

"She has many friends, and as far as I know, she was not dating anyone at that time."

"I think that's all for now. You folks have a safe trip home and we'll keep in touch."

* * *

"What the hell happened, O'Brian? Teal was not supposed to be killed—it was to be a warning!"

"Yes sir, I know. Teal should not have died. As it turns out, the coroner's report states that her neck was fractured."

"You know what this means, don't you?"

"Yes, sir. A full-scale investigation will be carried out by the RCMP."

"It'll be a very thorough investigation, too. What are you doing to cover this up?"

O'Brian checked his notes.

"The truck involved was efficiently dismantled and disposed of. It was burned and the remaining fragments were buried in a thirty-foot deep gravel pit. It'll never be found."

"And the driver?"

"Terminated and cremated," said O'Brian, hoping this would satisfy his boss.

"I want you to continue to keep close tabs on Gwen Ross. Let me know if you become suspicious of anything she does, or if you feel she's getting too close," Sandforth said.

Without another word, he hung up.

* * *

Early Monday morning, Holly grabbed a Tim Horton's coffee and breakfast biscuit. She wanted to get the RCMP office in Halifax before the place got busy; she needed a head start on the day to formulate a plan. At eight-thirty-five am, she called the Forensics lab.

"Jerry, anything new on the Teal car?"

"We've gone through her briefcase; the contents are to do with her work," he said. "We found her micro-recorder. It was jammed between the driver's seat and the centre console. I think you had better come down and hear this for yourself."

As difficult as it was, listening to Mary's heart-wrenching recording definitely confirmed the lab's other findings: her death was not an accident. This recording was a very important piece of evidence.

Another technician came in. "We've analyzed Dr. Teal's phone messages," she said. "Most of them are pretty generic, but listen to message number eight." The technician cued up the recording and pressed *play*. The message was brief and to the point:

"Dr. Teal," said a male voice, "take this as a warning. Stop searching, and no further harm will come to you or your family."

"It was received by Teal's machine twenty-five minutes after the 911 call came in," said Jerry. "We've traced it to a public phone in Boston. I've asked the Boston police to check any cameras covering it."

"This must be connected to the accident," said Holly. "Mary's death was not a planned murder. It was a scare tactic on someone's behalf. Whoever was behind this phone call is guilty of murder."

Later in the day, when Holly arrived at Teal's lab, she was introduced to Dr. Betsy Goble; she had been a close colleague of Mary's and had worked at the lab for twenty-six years. She was a tall, slim, gracious woman with deep brown eyes and reddish-brown hair that revealed subtle silver streaks. Her smile was contagious.

"Please call me Betsy. Everyone does," she said as she shook Holly's hand.

"Okay, Betsy; you may call me Holly."

"How is Megan doing? I understand you saw her at the hospital."

"She's doing quite well. She is going to live with her grandmother, Dr. Nona Teal."

"That is very good news. Can you tell me what happened?"

"Unfortunately, at this time, I can't give you any details," Holly said. She was being cautious.

"Yes, I know; however, the fact that you're here tells me you're investigating it. Therefore it was not an ordinary accident."

"Very astute, Betsy; there are indeed aspects of this accident which need clarification."

"Poor Megan; she's lost both her father and her mother."

"You knew her father?" Holly asked.

"Yes. They met in graduate school and lived together for four years. They split up, but Megan was not born yet. He was older than she. When he graduated, he got a job offer in Boston that was too good to pass up. Mary still had just over a year to go before she would get her doctorate. They tried to stay as a couple, but it did not work out. They remained friends."

"What was his name, and where did he work?"

"Dr. Matthew Stone," Betsy said. "He worked for Bio Tech Labs."

Holly wrote the information down in her pocket notebook and then asked, "Betsy, you said that Megan lost her father; how did he die?"

"Excellent question; the official report stated that he was accidentally infected with a deadly virus with which he was working." She paused for a moment and continued. "That's strange, don't you think, Holly? Both Megan's biological parents died accidentally within two weeks of one another."

Holly nodded. "It could be a coincidence," she said—but Holly didn't believe in coincidences. "It's definitely worth noting. Can you tell me, in layman's terms, about the research Mary was working on?"

"She was working on phytoplankton. Do you know anything about phytoplankton?"

"A little bit," Holly answered.

"Phytoplankton is critical to the life of virtually every animal in our oceans, which cover more than seventy percent of Earth's surface. It is the first step in every marine food web."

"Even the whales?"

"Yes. Baleen, or filter-feeding whales, such as blue whales, right whales, and so on, which coincidentally are the largest marine animals; they eat very small crustaceans which in turn feed on phytoplankton. Marine phytoplankton has become an extremely important area of study for many reasons. The whole future survival of these tiny microscopic plants is in jeopardy." Betsy gave a deep sigh, and continued. "What most people don't know is that if the phytoplankton production is affected in a negative way—that is, if their numbers become reduced any more than they already are—it will negatively affect humans in a large way. Marine fisheries around the world would all but disappear; our oxygen supply would be drastically reduced—all because of the tremendous amount of pollution, especially carbon dioxide, which we humans have and are currently producing through the consumption of fossil fuels."

"But we're not going to lose *all* of them, are we?"

"Our oceans are rapidly approaching what we call *the tipping point*. Phytoplankton is already decreasing at a rapid rate. The tipping point is when this reduction reaches a point beyond which it cannot recover and keeps on decreasing."

"So, does that mean they all die?"

"You've got it, Holly. When there's no more phytoplankton, there'll be no more animals in our oceans."

"No, *no!* I don't want to hear this!" Holly said. She was surprised with how alarmed she felt. "I didn't realize how important it was."

"But Holly, you must. Every human on this planet must know what's happening to our marine environment. With no source of food, virtually every animal in the oceans will become extinct."

"And we'll lose more than fifty percent of our oxygen production on Earth," Holly added.

Betsy nodded. "One of the first to go will be the whales. There is an old expression: *As the whales go, so do we.* Earth will survive—but not as we know it."

"That is a dreadful scenario. Is there no hope?"

"There's always hope. There are signs, especially in our young people; they give us hope. Many are very upset with what previous generations have done and are doing to our planet. It has happened mainly through greed and disrespect of our environment, which started with the Industrial Revolution. However, the environmental movement is gathering support, and the term 'green' is now respected. There is hope—but we must act quickly. Education is the key."

They took a break and poured themselves a cup of coffee. Holly was deep in thought, processing what she had just learned. Then she shook her head.

"Wow...this is a lot to take in," she said.

"Yes, I know; I'm sorry I got so far off-track."

"No, I think everyone in the world should hear and know what I've just heard. Betsy, what exactly was Mary's area of research?"

"She was looking into what causes abnormal plankton blooms, such as 'red tides' which are caused when certain dinoflagellates in the phytoplankton get out of balance. Their production increases many times over normal level. Some say these are normal occurrences; however, over the last few decades, they have occurred more frequently. The concern is that they may, in part, be caused by pollution."

"I've read about this online and in newspapers. They produce some sort of poison, correct?"

"Certain dinoflagellates produce some of the most potent naturally-produced poisons."

"Do they cause the shellfish poisoning?" Holly asked, continuing to make some notes.

"Yes. Clams, being filter feeders, siphon out and eat tiny organisms, including these dinoflagellates. They are immune to the poison. When conditions are right, these single-celled plants reproduce rapidly and can have densities that exceed tens of millions of cells per litre. The shellfish concentrates these poisons, and if humans eat them, it can cause paralysis and even death by shutting down the nervous system. The toxin that they produce is called saxitoxin."

"I always thought it was the puffer fish that produced the most deadly poison."

"It and several species of dinoflagellates, and some blue-green algae produce a similar toxin. Dr. Tony Shields, a biochemist, and Mary have been working together on some aspects of these toxins. They're trying to develop antidotes for them and have published a few papers on their research."

"Were there any problems about co-authorship?" Holly asked.

"Heavens no; they got along very well. They worked out a system for co-authorship: they would alternate senior authorship on successive papers," Betsy explained.

"Is that unusual?"

"Yes, sometimes there can be hard feelings over such arrangements. Senior authorship is generally considered to be very important."

"Betsy, can you think of anyone who would have a grudge against or be jealous of Mary—or even someone who would want to harm her in any way?"

"No, I can't. Mary was very well-liked and easy to get along with."

"Fair enough," said Holly. "Still, I think I would like to have a brief chat with Dr. Shields."

Betsy nodded, and with a quick phone call, she arranged a meeting, and gave Holly directions to the biochemistry lab.

Back at her office, Holly reviewed her notes from the day. Dr. Shields, in his meeting with Holly, had confirmed what she had already learned from Betsy. Additionally, the fact that both of Megan's parents had died suddenly in suspicious circumstances made her think that Matthew was also murdered. All of these elements influenced the other, and were integral to her investigation.

Maybe Nona Teal can help clarify all this. I'll know more tomorrow, Holly thought.

She gave Tom her findings to date and told him about the arrangements to go to Grand Manan. She needed to get his permission to contact the Boston Police Department's coroner to request a copy of Stone's death certificate.

* * *

Holly was met at the St. John airport by a fellow officer. She picked up an RCMP vehicle and drove to Blacks Harbour and caught the one-thirty pm ferry to the island. She took her coffee and climbed up to the top deck to whale watch. It was a cool, calm, sunny day. Once they cleared the islands just outside of the harbour known as "The Wolves," a cool breeze came up over the icy waters of the Bay of Fundy. They spotted some high straight blows, indicating that finback whales were in the area. In just over an hour, they swung around the beautiful Swallowtail Lighthouse and into the wharf at North Head.

She had no problem finding Nona's place. It was a beautiful, century-old building that reminded one of a gingerbread house; it was painted white with blue trim and was crowned with a widow's walk with a blue railing. A ten-foot-wide wraparound deck was closed in at the west end to form a sun room; the rest of the deck was open. Holly drove up the driveway into the parking area. As she got out of the car, Megan was running down the steps, waving Lacuna and jumping up and down.

"What a beautiful place you have, Nona," said Holly as they were sitting on the deck. "Your view is breathtaking. You look right out over the Bay of Fundy."

"It was built by my great-grandfather, a sea captain, in the late 1800s; much of the wood came from old shipwrecks. We love it. There's always something to watch here."

"I didn't realize there were so many islands," Holly said.

"Grand Manan is an archipelago of many islands. Currently, only this island and White Head Island are inhabited. The island straight ahead of us is Long Island, the one beyond with the small lighthouse is High Duck Island, and over there is Nantucket Island. The one you can barely see is White Head Island." Nona had brought out a tray with both tea and coffee, fresh homemade bread, and her homemade blackberry jelly. Holly spread some butter and jelly on a still-warm piece of bread and took a bite.

"Nona, this is absolutely delicious. Thank you." There was a brief pause as they both ate, and then Holly asked, "Nona, what can you tell me about Dr. Matthew Stone?"

Nona was a bit surprised at the question. "How did you know?"

"I was at your daughter's lab yesterday. Betsy Goble told me that he had died in a lab accident."

"An accident?"

Something about the way Nona had said this revealed more than her words alone.

"Nona, do you think it wasn't an accident?" she asked.

Nona told Holly about Mary getting encoded letters from Matthew.

"Excuse me, Nona—did you say *codes?*"

"Yes. I never saw the letters or the message she finally deciphered."

"Do you still have them—or do you know where they might be?"

"The two letters were destroyed by Mary. As far as the message goes, I'm not absolutely sure what she did with it." Nona stopped a moment to think. "Mary said something about a Gwen Ross, an investigative reporter who lives in Boston. Gwen was a friend of Matt's."

"Do you know how I could get in touch with this Gwen Ross?" Holly asked.

"Her phone number is probably with Mary's papers, which I believe you have," said Nona.

After a time, Nona asked, "Is there anything further you can tell me regarding your investigation?"

"We've not found the pickup or the driver," said Holly. Then she made a quick decision to share more information. "We did find out that the accident was only meant to be a warning."

Nona's eyes welled up with tears. "Do you think Matt and Mary's deaths are related somehow?"

"I'm definitely looking into it," answered Holly.

To change the subject, Holly asked, "Did you and Mary work in the same area of research?"

"Not exactly; our research was related. Mary worked on phytoplankton; I work on zooplankton. We often joked about it. If it wasn't for Mary's phytoplankton, there wouldn't be any zooplankton."

Holly nodded. "Yes, Betsy explained the importance of the phytoplankton. I must admit I was quite ignorant of it before meeting her. I found it fascinating."

They spent some time discussing the implications of recent ecological developments; Nona was quite knowledgeable, and Holly was completely absorbed with what Nona shared.

After some time had passed, Nona glanced at her watch. "Well, you've missed the five-thirty pm ferry," she said. They watched it leave.

"Oh dear...I guess I have."

"You can catch the seven-thirty pm ferry. Would you like to come out on my research boat and we'll get some plankton for you to look at?" Nona asked.

"I would love to!"

"Great! We'll see if Andrew and Megan want to come with us."

They went out past Long Island and High Duck Island. Andrew slowed the boat to a crawl while Nona put the fine-meshed plankton net over the side.

"Why so slow?" Holly asked. She was watching Megan as she sat up in the chair behind the wheel.

"She thinks she is driving the boat," Nona said, chuckling. "The net has such a fine mesh; if we went any faster, it would produce a pressure wave in front of it and push everything away instead of catching it."

She gently pulled the net in as she spoke. Finally, the plankton net broke through the surface and was carefully brought aboard. Nona washed it down with seawater; she opened the canister and showed the contents to Holly.

"It looks like green soup," Holly commented.

"There are millions of single-celled plants in here. We'll pour them into this white tray and transfer some of it into a small dish; then we'll place them under the stereomicroscope so you can really see what they look like."

As she was focusing on the 'green soup' she said, "Very good—we have several species and a few crab larvae and copepods, tiny crustaceans, or zooplankton."

"That would be your field of study."

"Actually, my interest is in some of the larger zooplankton. You are about to enter a whole new world, Holly."

Nona showed Holly how to focus the microscope. "You can move the dish around a bit, if you like."

Holly peered through the lens. "Holy mackerel—I don't believe this! They are beautiful and so green! They're all different sizes and shapes. Look at the intricate designs on some of them; they look like miniature pillboxes. Is that a type of casing?"

"A good description, Holly; do you see all the different designs on these 'pillboxes'?"

"Wow—this is cool. Some look like tiny green helmets with long spikes on them."

"Those are the dinoflagellates. These are the organisms Mary worked on." said Nona.

Holly finally lifted her head up from the microscope. "I can't believe these tiny cells are the basis for the food web of all the animals in the ocean," she said in amazement. "If these ceased to exist...well...I can't bring myself to think of what this world would look like without fish, dolphins, and whales."

"That is why we're concerned about the amount of pollution being dumped into our oceans."

In the meantime, Andrew had washed and put away the phytoplankton net and had lowered the zooplankton net, which was larger and with a coarser mesh. He had put the boat in neutral and lowered the net to the depth of a couple of hundred meters; he was slowly pulling it up as Megan and Holly emerged from the lab portion of the boat.

"I thought Holly might like to see what the next link in the food chain looks like," he said.

"That is very thoughtful of you Andrew; thank you," said Holly.

He brought in the net and emptied the contents in a large rectangular white pan. Once again, Holly was amazed.

"Look at all that activity, and so many different-looking animals. So this is what the fish eat!"

"Smaller fish, like herring, and the very young of some of our larger fish, along with baleen whales, like the blue whale and the right whale," said Nona.

"How much would an adult blue whale eat in a day?" Holly asked.

"Several tons—and I hate to cut this short, but if you wish to catch the seven-thirty pm ferry, we'd better get moving."

As Nona was tidying up, she explained that many of the zooplankton Holly saw were larval forms of animals such as starfish, crabs, and even lobsters.

"In the marine environment, many of the animals that live on the ocean floor produce these larvae, which rise close to the ocean's surface to feed; also, the surface currents disperse a species." She kept a few of the larger crustaceans out and carefully poured the rest back into the ocean.

"They look like small shrimp," Holly remarked; she looked at the translucent, inch-long animals. They had spots of red here and there, and very black eyes.

"Those are fully-grown crustaceans, commonly called krill."

"And this is what the whales feed on, right?"

"Yes; you must come back sometime and we'll take you out to see the whales—right, Megan?"

Megan nodded her head and waved Lacuna; she danced around Holly and Nona.

On the way back in, they chatted more about the ocean and made arrangements to keep in touch. They were back just in time for Holly to catch the ferry. She had an hour and a half of quiet time, during which she wrote about her experiences. She realized how happy she had been on Nona's boat. *I can see why someone could spend their life on the ocean, loving it and being a part of it,* she thought.

Holly was in her office early the next morning. She unpacked and sorted her notes and put them in her computer. She added one comment:

> Look into the Stone case thoroughly and call Gwen Ross.

In parenthesis she added:

> (I do not believe in coincidencesww.)

The rest of the material was all to do with the phytoplankton and zooplankton, which she put in her own computer.

Her morning's mail brought a copy of the formal police report from Boston. It did not tell her anything that she didn't already know. Stamped across the bottom of the report were the words CASE CLOSED.

Maybe—but not for me, thought Holly.

She decided the only person she could turn to in this case was Gwen Ross. She called her, left an explanatory message, and asked her to call back.

Later that morning, she arrived at the Forensics lab, just as the technicians were finishing up the final sweep of the car.

"Hi, Holly—this is good timing," said Jerry.

"So I see," she replied. "Is there anything new?"

"Not unless we get some more information from her laptop. It was slightly damaged in the crash, but the technicians think they can recover most of it."

"Let me know when you do. In the meantime, I'd like all the data you currently have."

"Sure," he said. He handed her a large envelope. "These are the contents of Mary Teal's briefcase. I hope it's of some help to you."

Later, Holly received a call from Gwen. They quickly became familiar with one another, and realized that each of them could offer the other one valuable assistance.

Holly told Gwen about her conversation with Nona. Gwen explained her relationship with Matt Stone.

"Gwen, do you think Matt's death was an accident?"

"No. Was Mary's death an accident?"

"No—we have proof that Mary's car was intentionally pushed off the road. It was supposed to be a warning to scare her away from something."

"Do you believe there is a connection between the two?" Gwen asked.

"I'm beginning to think there might be, and that is why I am calling you," she said as she opened her notebook on the computer. "Nona Teal told me Mary had been deciphering a couple of letters Matt Stone had sent her. However, she didn't know what the message was. Mary never told her. Do you know anything about this, Gwen?"

"Yes, but I can't discuss this over the phone."

"Gwen, would it be asking too much for you to fly up here? Alternatively, I could come down there. Which would be best for you?"

"How about we meet somewhere in between?"

"That would be perfect."

"I have a cousin who lives near Fredericton," said Gwen. "He's been asking me to come for a visit. I'll do that."

"That would be great. We can meet somewhere in Fredericton. I think Nona should also be there."

"I agree. Holly, you should know that the American authorities are not investigating Matt's death any further. The fact that his death may now be linked to Mary's—along with any material relating to either case coming from outside of Canada—should be kept up there with you for now."

"I agree," Holly said. "See what you can work out at your end."

Within three hours, Gwen called her back, and the meeting was set for the following week in the Fredericton area.

Holly began to go through the papers in Mary Teal's briefcase. Most were work-related; she put them aside to give to Betsy Goble. She looked through Mary's more private notes and photocopied the phone bill, and placed Mary's credit cards and her wallet in a separate envelope. She left Mary's journal to last. She flipped back and forth through the previous months and discovered that Mary and Matt spoke on the phone once or twice a month. Matt sent Mary child support checks regularly. She scrutinized the pages from the time of Matthew's death to the end of her journal. A stamp collection in a Boston bank was the only new information. Mary hadn't put anything in her diary about decoding a message. On the third last page was a note to herself to put Matthew's will in her safety deposit box.

I wonder, she thought.

* * *

Holly was looking forward to meeting Gwen and seeing Nona again. Arriving in Fredericton, she took a cab to the meeting place and was surprised to see Gwen was already there. Greetings were exchanged; they ordered coffee and sat at a table out of hearing range from others.

Holly opened the conversation. "You have a very impressive resumé, Gwen."

"You checked on me," Gwen said, smiling. "And I must say likewise—for someone in their early thirties, Holly, you have been very successful."

They both laughed.

"Have you met Nona Teal yet?" asked Holly.

"No. I'm looking forward to meeting her."

Holly took some notes out of her briefcase along with a pen and a blank pad of paper.

"Did you know that Mary had possession of Matthew's safety deposit box in Boston, which contains a large stamp collection? Do you think the missing part of the decoded message may be there?"

Gwen thought for a moment.

"I doubt it. Mary never mentioned it."

"As it turns out, Mary has a safety deposit box here in Fredericton," said Holly.

"Really!"

"Don't get too excited; today is just a fishing expedition. I asked Nona if, in her presence, we could take a look at it." Looking up, Holly said, "There she is now."

A very distinguished middle-aged woman came through the door. Her naturally gray and black streaked hair cascaded over her shoulders. She was wearing a red pantsuit with a white blouse, and carried a small, stylish black shoulder bag. Holly stood up, and Nona found her immediately.

Holly welcomed her with a smile, and said, "Nona, I would like you to meet Gwen Ross."

"Gwen, it's so good to meet you. Mary told me a lot about you—all of it good," she said, smiling. "Please call me Nona. I would like that."

As Gwen and Nona were getting acquainted, Holly noticed that an especially attentive young man come in and sat two tables away from them.

"Gwen, it might be a good idea if we left here and went for that drive I promised you. We can talk in the car."

Nona agreed. Gwen immediately got the message that they had been followed.

"Let's get some coffee and sandwiches to go. There are some beautiful and quiet spots by the St. John River," Nona suggested.

Later, the three women were sitting on a bench, drinking coffee, and looking over the St. John River. Gwen asked Nona how Megan was doing.

"It was a miracle that she came away physically unscathed—but she still doesn't speak. The doctors think it's temporary."

Gwen nodded, and looked around. "This park, the river, and the whole city are all so beautiful," she said. She was checking to see if anyone was nearby, but it seemed to be safe for the time being. "All clear, Holly."

Holly turned to Nona. "Nona, I have all of Mary's personal belongings from her car," she said. "I will be giving you all of it later. I wanted to let you know that I had to read her personal journal. I'm so sorry, but I had no choice. In the last two pages, she wrote of putting something in her safety deposit box that might be important to this case."

Nona looked puzzled. "What could it be?" she asked.

Gwen, without giving specifics, filled Holly in about what Mary had already given to her.

"Mary told me if she found anything when she decoded the letters, she'd give it to you," said Nona.

"She did—however, Mary held something back. She was about to give me something," said Gwen.

"I know she trusted you, Gwen," said Nona. Turning to Holly, she added, "I've the key; why don't we head to the bank now?"

Together, they made their way to the bank. As they approached the building, Gwen suggested they drop Nona off; they'd wait outside and observe in case she was followed. Their instincts were correct: within seconds, the young man who was in the restaurant appeared outside the bank. Holly got out of the car and, acting like she was in a hurry, accidentally bumped into him, almost knocking him off his feet.

"Watch where you're going, lady!" The man barked at her.

"I'm so sorry. Are you hurt?"

"No!" he said, trying to push her out of the way. Holly showed him her police badge. He immediately became apologetic and took off, walking away from the bank.

Nona returned to the car a few minutes later with the contents of Mary's safety deposit box. She handed them to Holly. "There is not much here," she said. Nona's voice was trembling with emotion. She picked up the ring and watch she'd given Mary upon receiving her PhD. There were copies of Megan's birth certificate, Matthew's will, and Mary's will. Memories of Mary were flooding her mind; Gwen and Holly sat silent in respect. Then Holly gave the small stack of papers back to Nona. "I think you should be the one to go through these."

Nona's hands were shaking. "This may be something," she said. She was looking at a small envelope; on it was written, *If anything should happen to me, this may be important.*

Nona gasped as she thought, *Mary knew she might be in danger!* She paused, then said, "I'm sorry, I can't." She passed the note to Holly.

Holly accepted the envelope and read the message. *Please be sure Gwen Ross gets this. Her phone number is on the back.* She turned it over to Gwen.

Gwen took the piece of paper from Holly. It said, *Matthew's additional research regarding Renfrew, etc. is hidden in Uncle Bill's Place at Matthew's cabin.* There was a map with the note.

"Where is Uncle Bill's Place?" she asked.

"Uncle Bill was Matt's great-grandfather who built Matthew's cabin," Nona said excitedly. "Uncle Bill's Place is a hiding place Matt used as a child. It is not in the cabin; but on the property somewhere. That map you are holding probably shows you where."

It took them just over a half an hour to carefully come up with a plan, bearing in mind that they were under surveillance. Gwen would phone the caretaker of the cabin and ask him to call Nona to say that he saw signs of a possible break-in. Nona should come to check it. Andrew and Megan would go with her and they would spend a long weekend there. They could go on some hikes. While playing hide and seek, Andrew, helping Megan, would hide in Uncle Bill's Place. When Nona would find them, Andrew would come out carrying Megan, wrapped in a blanket.

Gwen took a photograph of the map with a disposable camera; Holly would need the original as evidence. They agreed to work on a drop site at a later date.

* * *

"Pat O'Brian is here to see you, sir."

"Send him in." Sandforth hastily removed some papers he was working on. "You've another update for me?"

"Constable Holly Summers has been rather busy with her investigation. She's been to the lab where Mary Teal worked and interviewed a couple of researchers. I do not believe she got anything affecting us. A Dr. Goble apparently mentioned Stone's death. The next day, Summers paid a visit to Nona Teal's place on Grand Manan. We have no idea of what that conversation entailed. She must have learned about the relationship between Mary Teal and Gwen Ross."

"Oh, shit!" exclaimed Sandforth.

O'Brian took a deep breath and continued. "Yesterday, there was a three-way meeting between Ross, Summers, and Nona Teal in Fredericton, New Brunswick. Unfortunately, they spotted our tail. He was either not very good—or Ross and Summers are very good. I suspect it is the latter."

Sandforth nodded his head, indicating to O'Brian that he wished for him to continue.

"They left the restaurant, drove around for a while, and ended up at a bank," O'Brian said. He then explained what happened there in terms of the brief confrontation between Summers and Sandforth's man.

Sandforth was furious. He banged his desk with his fist. "So we've got *nothing!*"

* * *

Ten days later Nona, Andrew, and Megan drove straight through to Walker Lake. They arrived late morning on a beautiful, sunny, warm summer's day. As they turned down the lane to the cabin, Nona commented on the beauty of the very old spruce trees. Andrew got Megan out of the car and they walked on the deck and around to the front of the cabin. It was extremely peaceful and serene. There seemed to be only a few people around. Megan noticed the dock and, carrying Lacuna under her arm, went running out to the end of it. Nona went with her to prevent her from jumping in the water, and sat with Megan as Andrew unpacked the car.

They entered the cabin and were very thankful that Seth had opened it and aired it out. Nona was amazed at the simplicity of the interior. She fell in love with it immediately.

"These windows across the front are a fantastic idea," she said. She went to the kitchen to unpack the groceries and make lunch. Taking their grilled cheese sandwiches out on the front deck to eat, they sat quietly and watched some of the ducks swimming around the lake. Andrew was looking at the map from Mary's safety deposit box, comparing it to the topographical map hanging above the antique dining table. Someone had outlined, in red, the boundaries of the property. It consisted of five lots. The property was about 1500 feet by 500 feet. He had found three possible places where Uncle Bill's Place might be. He took photographs with a small camera of both maps.

"I think I'll take a walk around the property to see if I can get an idea of where Matt hid his research. I may be gone for a couple of hours."

"Andrew, please be very careful; make very sure no one is following you. I think Megan and I will stay around the cabin for now."

Andrew packed himself a snack and a bottle of diet Pepsi. He found a narrow, relatively unused path running parallel to the lake. He followed it for about 400 feet and then began to look for a side path leading off in the direction of a large hill about 200 feet high. He knew the path would not be well-marked. After several minutes, he noticed what might be a path of sorts. He stepped over a couple of large, dead, fallen trees and began to weave his way through the woods. The floor of the bush was rocky. He had brought several small pieces of white string to mark his path. Shortly, he knew he was climbing up the hill. He stopped and, referring to a compass, made a couple of notes on his map. If the map was correct, he was getting very near the spot.

Andrew stopped and looked around; examining the immediate area, he saw nothing of interest. He walked on higher up the hill. He found a few caves, but none were big enough. He paused for a drink of Pepsi, checked the map again, and thought, *What if Matt reversed this part of the map?* He retraced his steps back to the other side of the hill. After another hour of searching several areas, he was getting frustrated.

Andrew had walked about forty-five feet when his eye caught something. There was an outcropping of rock off to his left. Around its base were several rocks of varying sizes. He climbed over some very rough terrain to get to it. There was a cave entrance; it looked too narrow. His intuition kicked in;

he went over to have a closer look. As he did so, he stopped to listen. All was very quiet. He came closer and moved some stones and old, dead branches.

Before him was a cave opening about four-and-a-half-feet high and two-and-a-half-feet wide. He turned on his flashlight and looked at it. There was a solid wall of stone beyond the entrance. His gut told him to look further. He began to enter this cave; immediately to his right was another opening about three feet wide. He crawled on his hands and knees. Soon there was another sixty-degree turn to his left. After crawling for about ten feet, it opened into a small cavern roughly ten feet by twelve feet, with irregular five-foot-high walls.

This has to be it, Andrew thought.

However, he didn't see anything that looked like a container of any kind.

Andrew stood quietly, and with his flashlight he began to scan the entire surface of the interior of this cave. There were several ledges and various crevices. Most of them were too small to hide anything. After several minutes, he sat down. He was beginning to think he should head back to the cabin, but he decided to take one last look. Scanning the walls he noticed, close to the floor and across from him, was a triangular crevice about twelve inches high with a base of three inches which was blocked by a similarly-shaped stone.

Andrew crawled across the floor and carefully removed the stone. His heart began to beat faster. He put his hand in; he could only reach about six inches. He took a stick and began to probe; within seconds he struck something. It sounded like metal. He carefully maneuvered it with the stick until he could grab the object with his hand. His effort was rewarded: he pulled out a small tin box.

Andrew was excited; had he found the missing papers? He very carefully opened the box and found ten or twelve sheets of paper with someone's handwriting on them. He started to read them; the top page was dated recently. Looking at the last page, he saw that it was signed by Matthew Stone. Andrew could not believe he'd found it. Removing the papers, he carefully placed everything back inside the cave the way he found it. He did the same for the entrance. He listened. It was quiet. He walked back the same way he came and removed all the string.

When he got back to the cabin, Nona was reading inside and Megan was playing on the deck.

"I was about to send out a search party for you. Did you have a nice hike?"

"I did, thank you; let's sit out on the deck while we talk."

Nona picked up a couple of beers and they went out and sat with Megan.

"I thought I would go out to scout the area to see what it would be like for a hide and seek game with Megan. Nona, I found something." Andrew reached into his pocket and pulled out the sheets of paper.

"Is that Matthew's research?"

"Yes."

"Do you think it was safe?" Nona asked.

"Yes; I certainly wasn't followed. The area where I found this is extremely rugged, and there is no way we could have used it as a hide and seek place for Megan. I left it exactly the way I found it."

He continued to describe what he had seen.

"What do you think we should do with it now?"

"Nothing at the moment." Nona was quiet. "Why don't we just hang around here for the rest of today and tomorrow? I'll call Gwen tonight. We have to go into Boston to see the lawyer about the transfer of this property and pick up Megan's stamp collection. We could ask Gwen, and see if she would like to come out for dinner, or we could meet her somewhere."

"You'll know more when you talk to Gwen."

"Yes. And we know we'll be followed as soon as we leave here. We'll have to be extremely careful when we pass these papers to Gwen," Nona said, putting them in her purse.

"Why don't we photograph each page?"

"That's a very good idea, Andrew. I'll take photos with my disposable camera and slip it to Gwen."

After a delicious barbecued steak dinner, they took Megan for a ride around the lake in the motorboat with a small, quiet electric engine. Megan loved it. She sat on Andrew's knee and helped steer the boat, or stayed beside Nona and watched everything around her.

They'd brought fishing gear from the cabin. Andrew baited Megan's line and his own, and showed Megan how to cast. Nona was busy taking videos and photos. Megan caught her first sunfish and was very excited. After touching it, Megan motioned to Andrew to throw it back. She caught and released two more before they called it quits.

While Nona was getting Megan ready for bed, Andrew made a small bonfire. In her Winnie-the-Pooh pyjamas, along with Lacuna and her blanket, Megan and Nona joined Andrew. They sang some of Megan's favourite songs, and Megan hummed along. She fell asleep. Andrew picked her up and put her to bed.

Once Megan was asleep, Nona called Gwen, and reached her right away.

"Nona, how was your trip?"

"It was great; we arrived this morning. Megan caught her first fish today and was thrilled."

"I bet she was. Did you have any problems finding the cabin?"

"No. Your directions were perfect. Andrew went for a very long hike today; he had a wonderful time exploring the property here. It is such a beautiful spot. It's very quiet and serene."

"Are you coming into Boston while you're here? If so, let's try to get together."

"We want to see you while we're here, if possible. We need to come in the day after tomorrow and run some errands."

"That would be great; how about six pm? Denny's would be a good place for Megan to eat," said Gwen.

"That sounds perfect. Andrew and I have to stop at Uncle Bill's Place on our way in."

"I'm really looking forward to it."

They were up early the next morning and they all went for a morning swim. After breakfast, Megan and Andrew went fishing. Nona stayed home and read her book. They spent the rest of the day swimming, hiking, and fishing.

The next day, they were on their way to Boston. Andrew had marked the various places they were to visit in Boston on his city map. Megan was tucked into her car seat with Lacuna and her blanket.

The stop at the lawyers was brief, but they were a bit longer at the bank. Andrew couldn't believe the size of the stamp collection. On the way to Denny's, they stopped at Staples and picked up two large metal fireproof boxes. They divided the stamp collection between them and hid them in the car. Then they met Gwen in the parking lot.

"How is everybody?" Gwen was mainly looking at Megan. Megan was humming as she waved Lacuna at her.

"That means she is happy and she likes you."

"Why thank you, Megan. I like you too."

Gwen gave a small gift bag to Megan. Megan opened the bag and found a box of crayons and two colouring books; one was about sea life.

She turned to Gwen and signed, *thank you.*

"You're welcome, sweetheart." Megan blew her a kiss, and Gwen returned it.

Andrew was helping Megan to colour, so that Gwen and Nona could talk.

"How is Megan settling in? Is there any further word on her ability to speak?" Gwen asked quietly.

"She is doing very well. As you can see, I'm teaching her sign language, which she is picking up quickly. I'm planning to homeschool her for a while. The children on the island are really accepting her as one of them. We'll see how she is doing when she is six or seven, and decide whether or not to put her into the regular school system."

"How are *you* doing?"

"I'm okay. Of course, I have my moments, but Megan keeps me busy. I'm slowly getting back into my research. It will take time."

"Speaking of your research, can I get a copy of the speech you gave in Scotland? You combined some of your research and brilliantly connected it with the need for some very quick and decisive means to stop polluting the oceans. I'm very interested in this field."

"Thank you, Gwen, for your interest. I'll definitely send you a copy."

Everyone was very hungry and there was not much said over dinner. Megan had been very good, and as a reward, she received a dish of her favourite ice cream, butterscotch ripple.

Nona looked at Gwen and whispered, "We have it!" Slightly louder, she said, "We're going to keep it for Megan. Here is a set of keys; we want you to enjoy it."

Nona passed her the keys and a disposable camera with them.

"Thank you, Nona. I'll use it and take good care of it."

Andrew was back. "I've taken care of the bill," he said.

"Thank you very much, Andrew," said Gwen.

At the car they said their goodbyes to Gwen. Megan blew her a couple of kisses and waved Lacuna at her. Gwen gave Nona a hug and whispered, "I'll read this carefully and let you know what I find." Out loud she said. "I'll be in touch. Safe trip home."

Five days later, Megan, Nona, and Andrew were back on the island. There was a message from Gwen; Nona phoned her.

"Nona, Matthew found several more cases," said Gwen. I've asked my fellow investigative reporters in those various places to look into this more deeply. We don't seem to have enough evidence to proceed at the moment. I'm sending a copy of my findings to Holly. When you're talking to Holly, please let her know that I've received word from a colleague in Nevada. There have been some strange things going on at the Center for Earth's Sustainable Resources near Area 51. It may be connected to the Boston Lab. I'll let her know if anything comes of it"

"Thank you very much, Gwen. Hopefully we will find something more in the future."

"I'm sure we will. In the meantime, keep safe, keep well and I'll keep in touch."

* * *

The Center for Earth's Sustainable Resources (US) was located in a huge 100,000 square foot, sterile, cold, multi-storied building, just outside the boundaries of Area 51, the Nevada Test Site. This and other regions in the Southwest US were associated with UFO sightings and crashed spacecraft. It was an extremely Top Secret area.

The US facility was constructed of tempered one-way glass and steel with five floors above ground and four below ground. The five above-ground stories and the first subterranean floor were devoted to legitimate research.

As one entered through the large double-glass doors with polished brass hardware, there was a two-storied foyer with limited seating space. The walls and floor were cold, white marble, and one felt most unwelcome. There was too much security, too many checkpoints, and armed guards. Behind the information desk hung a metal board with the scientists' names and lab numbers. None of the names of the scientists working on the lowest three subterranean floors appeared on this board. There was a separate, highly-secured entrance for those levels. All research and activities occurring here were funded by the Black Budget and were top secret. A separate, secret Board of Directors of what was simply called The Company would meet here at least once a year. Each of the directors had a private suite. In addition, there was a small private dining room and kitchen.

The Company not only ran these three floors, but also oversaw branches all over the world in countries such as Russia, France, Britain, Australia, and China. This 'mother company' was formed by certain extremely wealthy humans who slowly amalgamated their massive fortunes over several decades with the sole purpose of taking control of the world via its economies, governments, and militaries.

Since 1945, they'd been amassing power and money, holding many government contracts. They had people—puppets—in powerful government positions in virtually every major country of the world. All the major players were after only one thing: money and the power it gave them. They had absolutely no empathy or concern for their fellow human beings or for the planet. Everyone in their way was simply destroyed or eliminated. They had raped the Earth and continued to do so.

Some of the early leaders were actively involved in the Roswell cover-up. They knew about the meeting with the aliens when they came to help. Their help was refused. They took advantage of this first refusal and co-opted some aliens to help them. There was a certain group from Nibiru called the Anunnaki, who were more than happy to join these humans. Instead of using the technically-advanced knowledge of the

Anunnaki to help humans and the planet, The Company kept it for themselves.

The Company was run by two co-chairs. This was necessitated by the presence of a small, strong group of aliens controlled by the Anunnaki. Their leader was named Anin. The other chair was a very powerful man, George Dean, from the USA. The rest of the board consisted of representatives from the US, Russia, China, Australia, and Europe, making seven directors in all. Each one had worked extremely hard and given their lives and a good part of their fortunes to The Company. Over the years it had grown immensely at the cost of the rest of the world's citizens.

Every September, they had their regular annual meeting. Each member flew in on their own private jets. As they landed, they were whisked away in secrecy to the very bottom level of the CESR building. Each board member had their own selfish interests and would protect them at all costs. As a result, the meetings could last for days. The co-chairs, Dean and Anin, were expecting a long rough meeting this year. There would be a fair bit of politicking involved.

The meeting started quite amicably with the statement of aims and objectives. It was stressed that the list was not in order of importance.

- Peace is not profitable; keep the military strong and create wars if necessary.
- The secret governments within the regular governments must be kept strong.
- We must maintain control over the world's communication and transportation systems.
- The price of oil and gas must remain artificially high.
- We must continue to keep the general public in the dark as to what we are really doing by continuing to create diversions.

"Remember—if the rest of the world finds out what we are really up to, we are done in more ways than you can count. We're aware of an informal networking between several investigative reporters from various countries. They've not found anything yet and we'll keep it that way," said Dean.

"How do you intend to do this?" Igor from Russia asked.

"We're monitoring the group closely and will take action when and where we feel it's necessary—if the board continues to allow the co-chairs this power," Dean answered.

All agreed.

The treasurer's report, given by Maria Downs of Australia, was disappointing. No one was surprised, because the world's economies were in a recession. These economies were recovering slowly. They had kept the price of oil artificially high by creating unrest in oil-producing areas and hotspots across the Middle East.

At the end of the report, Maria asked, "What can we do to raise more funds?"

"That's not our only problem," Igor interjected. "This New Age movement is gathering steam. There is a belief out there that Earth will soon undergo a catastrophic event. Technology is bringing people of all walks of life and from different countries into this movement. It is becoming extremely difficult to control as there appears to be no clear leader."

"We'll place that concern under new business and discuss it later," Dean said trying to keep the meeting in order.

Jean Peters from the USA spoke up. "I would like us to look at the status of our current means of distracting the public while we're about to do some more tests. I would also like some more details of just what these tests are going to involve."

"We're planning a few things over the next several months. We will need everyone that is here to give us all the help you can, along with any suggestions you may have," Dean said. "It's going to take a few days to work through some plans that Anin and I have talked about. You will each receive a brief for tomorrow's meeting. I suggest we adjourn."

As the meeting was breaking up, George turned to Anin. "Do you really have a firm plan and do you currently have people working on it?"

"Yes I do; you'll receive details tomorrow morning."

"Depending on those details, Anin, there may not be a discussion. We may just do it. In fact we've done some already."

"Yes, I know. The rest of the board doesn't need to know everything we're doing."

For the next couple of days, the board argued vehemently over several of the ideas being put forth; each scenario tended to affect one or two particular areas of the world more so than the rest. Many would damage—or otherwise drastically affect—the flow of monies coming to one or more board members.

The list of plans which Anin and George drew up included the following two major points:

> *The world economy: Do nothing at the moment and let the world economy play out for a while longer.*

"This would give us more time to complete some of the projects." Igor commented and added. "What period of time are you thinking of?"

"What would you suggest?"

George passed a note to Anin which said, *How much more time do you need until the end point?*

Igor's response was quick and sharp. He was annoyed and suspicious, as he saw these notes going back and forth.

"It is not for me to suggest. It is what Anin and his people need, is it not?"

Anin and George had discussed this privately, but knowing Anin's part of the project was running into problems, George wanted to know what Anin felt he could release to the board at this time. The answer would have to be vague. George was anxious to read the response to his note. It read, *We'll need several more years before the plan for the endpoint is one-hundred percent foolproof. It could be earlier if everyone agrees to take that chance.*

George looked up from his note and levelled his gaze directly at Igor.

"We all know that we've encountered a few delays, which, for a plan of this magnitude, is not unexpected. Depending on the risk level that is acceptable to this board, the endpoint could be within the next two decades."

Igor calmed down. "Perhaps you are right," he said. He didn't want to get on the wrong side of either of the chairs. "Let's discuss these other ideas—they may determine what happens to this one."

"Excellent idea," George said. He glanced at the others. "We'll move on to the second item:

> *Release lethal bacteria in predetermined areas where we feel we can make the greatest impact on raising the general world population's fear level.*

This particular item brought a swift reaction from the entire board with such questions as:

"Are you sure the bacteria being released can be contained if necessary?"

"Are the antidotes proven to have a high success rate, if needed, for our own people?"

"Where and when do you plan to release these bacteria?"

"How lethal are these bacteria?"

"How are you going to go about doing this?"

The questions were coming all at once, and George and Anin knew they would have to keep tight control over the answers.

Anin was the first to respond.

"In our various labs, we've developed some very lethal bacteria. It is much more difficult to develop an antiserum to counteract it—especially for the more potent strains. If a human is infected with one of these, they're dead within four to six hours. We're also on the brink of testing four others along with making their antiserums."

"Where, how, and how much of this strain of bacteria are you planning to test?" Maria asked.

"That depends on how much of a threat there is—or what level of fear we wish to create as a distraction," said Dean.

Anin took over. "We can infect people in many different ways. The best way to kill a large number would be to drop the bacteria from the air using unmanned drones. This would be extremely effective. We can infect a few by carefully-selected areas where the disease would spread rapidly. It's fear we're trying to create as a distraction to focus people's attention from what we're doing. Remember how few people worldwide had SARS and died? In the rest of the world, the fear level rose."

"Oh, God!" Jean interrupted. "Did we create that?"

"No, we didn't. Another example is the AIDS epidemic. We had nothing to do with it."

"If we decide to do it in the near future, at what level, and where would you release it?" Chang asked in his usual quiet manner.

"We'll discuss it after a coffee break. Be back in about twenty minutes," said Dean.

Maria and Jean drew close to speak in hushed tones amongst themselves. "Do we have to start this whole plan of putting a distraction of this order in place sometime soon? Or are they looking for an excuse to put the bacteria out there on trial basis?" Maria asked.

"Hopefully we'll get the answer after coffee," Jean answered; she quietly added, "What do you think this meeting is *really* about? There doesn't seem to be anything new so far."

But before Maria could answer, they were interrupted.

"Ladies and gentlemen, it is time to return to our discussions. We'll do so for another two hours and then break for a two-hour lunch," Dean announced.

They took their respective places and put on their earphones to hear the translations as others often spoke in their native tongues.

"Maria, I believe you have the floor."

"Thank you, George. Do we feel this current threat level is sufficient to warrant such a reaction? Or are you doing these tests for possible future use?"

"With the New Age movement and the public clamouring for many of the covert operations to become public, I would say we are at a level four out of ten. This is a level that we don't consider to be critical, but it is one which we need to keep a very close eye on."

Anin then spoke. "As for the second part of your question: we're very close to doing some more controlled field tests which we all agreed on in our last meeting."

"I would just like some assurance that you can perform them safely—that is, keep it from spreading," said Maria.

"I assure you it'll be safe. There'll be a limited number of deaths in a few localized areas."

Dean had overheard the conversation between Maria and Jean during the break. He was annoyed then, and was even more so now.

"Maria, are you doubting our plans?" he asked.

Maria was uncomfortable with Dean's tone. "I wanted to make the point that we shouldn't overdo it at this time."

Dean displayed an expression on his face that caused Maria to feel that she may have overstepped the boundaries.

Igor added, "Thank you, Maria; you saved me from asking the same question." Looking at Dean, he asked, "Can we do a small test in a controlled location, evaluate the results, and go from there?"

"Agreed—now let's look at the next point for discussion: the use of earthquakes to cause distractions and increase fear levels. We've looked at this before. We're about to test some of our newest aircrafts; I feel we need to throw confusion into the spacecraft and UFO scenario."

Wolfgang spoke up.

"Thank you, George. We've the antigravity propulsion technology, thanks to Anin. We also have an excellent craft which we have been using quite successfully, which many have seen in flight and thought they were seeing UFOs. Two more of our spacecraft will soon be ready for initial test flights. We may need to distract the people living close to the area in Nevada where we test them. If the test is successful, we will be one step closer to our Final Plan."

"What form will this distraction take?" Chang asked. "I gather the distraction will be local?"

"That is correct. It'll be in two parts, as we need to put everyone's minds on Earth and not on the sky when we take off and land. The distraction will be in the form of two small 3.5 to 4.5 magnitude earthquakes; one as it takes off, and one when it lands. They'll be just strong enough to rattle things around for about five minutes. There'll also be a small forest fire producing lots of smoke."

Anin spoke up again. "These earthquakes are also a test to see what the lower capabilities of our equipment can do.

"So this is the real reason for this meeting," Maria whispered to Jean.

"If this works, we'll be one more step towards total planetary control, if we ever need it," Dean said confidently.

A long discussion ensued and carried over to the next day, resulting in the following decision:

> We, the board of CESR (The Company), have agreed to the following:
>
> No immediate action will be taken regarding the New Age movement; however, surveillance will be kept on it. A limited test of the bacteria will be discreetly done under tight controls early next year. The places will be kept top secret. The earthquakes will go ahead as planned.

"This meeting is now adjourned," said Dean. Then he thought, *Anin and I are in total control of The Company—and soon we will be in control of the world.*

After the rest left, George looked at Anin and said, "Okay, you go ahead and do whatever you need to do. Don't worry about anything. Have I made myself clear?"

"Perfectly."

The next day, the headlines in the Australian newspapers read, MARIA DOWNS KILLED IN PLANE CRASH. It happened over the Pacific; the plane had mysteriously disappeared. The last transmission from the pilot indicated something was wrong with the onboard computer; shortly thereafter they heard what sounded like an explosion, then nothing. All the wonderful things Maria had done for her country, and particularly her home city of Melbourne, were listed. She was well-known for her charitable work and leadership in many group organizations to which she belonged. They gave details of the highlights of her career. Her multibillion dollar company would be run by her older brother, David. A thorough search of the area was underway, but the authorities said there would probably be no survivors.

George Dean turned to Anin who was across the room and said, "Well done; that certainly was quick and efficient."

"I cannot take credit. We had nothing to do with it."

"What? Then who did?"

"I wish I knew. We must do some discreet investigations. We'll have a good look at her brother, David. We must also sanitize any record of Maria being connected with us."

PART TWO
1994 – 2005

Six-year-old Megan was still unable to speak; Nona was homeschooling her, and she was communicating through drawings and sign language. Her closest friends were Sadie and Sam, the children of Roger Wilson, captain of Nona's research vessel "Serendipity." Megan always went with Nona to collect samples for her research out on the Bay of Fundy. Joe White was like a grandfather to her and was a regular visitor on the island.

Megan loved to play on the island's sandy beaches; her favourite was Seal Cove, which was a long, slightly-curved beach that was bordered at one end by an aging old wharf propped up by huge chunks of basaltic rock with a tidal river beside it. At low tide, it was a stream; however, at high tide, it became a river, deep enough to allow fishing boats to enter and tie up at the various net sheds lining both sides of it. The far end was hemmed in by rocks and cliffs, and the upper edge of the beach slowly blended into high grasses and various wildflowers. Families brought their children here to swim and play, as well as to indulge in a favourite pastime: collecting sea glass. The broken pieces of glass were ground over the years by the sand through tidal movements and waves, patiently sculpting them into various shapes and sizes of all colours. These treasures would eventually wash up on the various beaches, and many of these pieces became beautiful pieces of jewelry.

On one very hot summer day, Nona and Megan arrived at Seal Cove with a picnic basket, beach towels, and pails. They selected a site beside a large sandstone rock that projected out into the sand. It was one of those magical days: the tide, reaching its lowest point, was turning to flood the beach. Long finger-like wisps of fog were forming near the water's edge. The breeze was playing with the wisps, causing them to dance up the beach to dissipate on the warm land, or to recede back to the sea.

Megan and Nona were strolling along the edge of the incoming tide, looking for treasures. Megan had found several white and a few green pieces of sea glass. Looking up through the wisps of fog, she noticed someone coming towards her. It was an elderly lady, stooped with age, and walking with a long stick she had found somewhere on her journeys. She had a slight limp, and periodically she'd stop and pick something up and slowly examine it; she'd either toss it back into the ocean, or would carefully place it in the threadbare cloth bag she carried. Megan was fascinated by her. She wore a long skirt that reached her ankles, and the brightest green shoes Megan had ever seen, complete with orange socks. Around her stooped shoulders hung a well-worn, multi-coloured granny square shawl. Her long, stringy gray hair, damp with fog, hung to her shoulders. An old navy tam rested on her head at a cocky angle. Megan tugged at Nona's shorts, nodding in the direction of the old woman. Before Nona could respond, a group of five teenagers passed them, and they overheard them talking.

"There's that crazy old hag," one said.

"She's not really crazy—is she, John?"

"My grandpa says she's weird and talks to herself."

Nona and Megan waited quietly until the teenagers were out of earshot. Then Nona turned to her granddaughter and said, "That's Celeste, Megan. Those teenagers are cruel. She's different, but she's not crazy."

Megan ran over to show Celeste her treasures. Celeste stopped and smiled at her.

"My, my—you've been very busy, haven't you?" she said amicably.

"Hello, Celeste. This is Megan," said Nona. "I'm Nona, Megan's grandmother." She paused and added, "Megan has trouble talking."

"Ah, yes—the car accident," Celeste responded.

Nona nodded. They chatted comfortably while Megan went ahead to explore. Before long, she found something, and turned to run back to Celeste to share her discovery. In Megan's hand was a piece of well-worn, sky-blue fluted glass, about one by two inches. Megan tugged at Celeste's shawl and handed her the piece of glass. Celeste carefully took it.

"It's so beautiful, Megan," she said, handing it back to Megan—but Megan shook her head. She gently closed her tiny, young hand over Celeste's gnarled fingers, and motioned with her other hand, pointing first at herself, then raising her open palm towards Celeste.

"Celeste, she is signalling that it belongs to you," Nona said, smiling. Celeste opened her hand and began to rub the glass slowly with her fingers. Tears welled up; in her mind, she saw a picture from long ago: a small round table with a hand-crocheted doily on which were two objects—a small, beautiful, sky-blue fluted vase containing a single white rose. Behind it and slightly off to the left was the photograph of a handsome young Army officer.

Celeste's hand trembled and she almost dropped it. Megan, understanding, took the slipping piece of glass, and carefully pressed it into Celeste's shaking hands. She looked up at the elderly woman and smiled.

"Thank you, Megan. You know...don't you?"

Megan nodded.

"I shall never forget this day and what you have given me," Celeste said.

Megan smiled again and tilted her head to one side. Celeste nodded, shrugged her old shoulders, and winked.

Megan winked back.

"Megan, that was a beautiful thing you just did. I think you made a new friend today!" said Nona.

Through a series of drawings of whales, Megan revealed to Nona that she was seeing whales in her dreams. In these drawings, one humpback appeared consistently. When Megan saw whales out on the bay, she would hum and dance. When the whales dove or moved away, Megan stopped humming. One day, Megan was sketching a humpback, and Nona realized that Megan was humming the same tune she hummed whenever she saw humpbacks in the bay. Nona wondered if this was a coincidence, so she began to record Megan humming to the whales when they were out on the bay and at home when Megan was drawing them. These melodies were virtually identical to the one she heard Joe and Megan humming at the hospital.

Several weeks later, they were on Serendipity, collecting samples, when they came close to a pod of humpbacks. Megan started humming. Within minutes, five or six humpbacks started swimming towards the boat. Megan leaned over the side of the boat and hummed louder as if she knew these gentle giants were responding to her voice.

Instantly, Megan caught sight of a magnificent young humpback swimming about one hundred feet below the surface. She watched it give a couple of strong powerful strokes of its tail as it headed to the surface; it breached about two hundred feet away from them, right where Megan was looking. Nona watched with glee as this whale continued to breach, slapping its tail and flipper. As this spectacle played out, Megan continued to hum and dance. After several minutes, the whales dove to feed.

Nona took video of the wondrous event, knowing that no one would believe her without evidence. Moments such as these confirmed to Megan that her dreams were in fact true.

Later, Megan showed through her drawings how she saw her special whale when it was underwater; it was, in fact, the very same whale that Megan was seeing in her visions. Upon studying the videos, Nona realized that the dance moves Megan was doing mimicked the exact movements of this special humpback, even when it was a couple of hundred feet below the surface!

How could that be? Nona wondered—then she remembered when Mary was her age, she too had a similar ability to see visions, but she grew out of it as she got older. Nona compared the tail pattern and discovered this whale's name was Lacuna! The next question was, how was Lacuna communicating with Megan?

As time went on, Nona was very interested in the growing friendship between Megan and Celeste. Nona had heard the odd story about the Montgomery family and Celeste. She was known for some very far-fetched stories she'd told about meeting aliens and being on a spacecraft. No one believed her; some folks ridiculed her behind her back. Nona, remembering the initial interaction between Celeste and Megan, wondered if there was some truth to Celeste being fey. Both her parents came from Stornoway in the Outer Hebrides of Scotland. They settled on Wood Island in the Grand Manan archipelago. It was a hard life. The family lived on fishing, grew their own vegetables in the summer, and made their own bread and preserves.

Celeste was the youngest of eleven children. Two died at childbirth, leaving five boys and four girls. Two of the boys died in World War II; one was a pilot in the RCAF and was shot down over Germany. The younger one went down with the Athabasca in the English Channel. Celeste's father died in a nor'easter while fishing on Georges Banks. Celeste was four years old at the time. Now she was the only one left of her family.

She lived in Seal Cove, and her neighbours kept an eye on her and made sure she was okay. Some said she knew the exact time when someone passed. Others claimed she cured injured animals that people brought to her. There was no vet on Grand Manan; Celeste would treat injured pets out of pure compassion. She wouldn't take any money—people would give her food instead.

Frequently, Megan, Sadie, Nona, and Celeste would be at Seal Cove at the same time. Megan would run over to her and walk the beach with Celeste. Nona loved to watch them as they picked up sea glass; together they would stop and look out at the ocean, and sometimes Megan would dance for Celeste.

About two months after their initial meeting, Megan and Nona met Celeste walking the beach; as they were leaving the beach, a young, frazzled-looking mother and a dark-haired little boy from the neighbourhood approached Celeste. The child's face was streaked with tears, and he had a blanketed bundle in his arms.

"Our puppy has been hurt," said the young mother. "We thought we could find you down here at the beach, so we came looking for you. Can you please help?"

Celeste dropped the two fairly large pieces of driftwood that she'd collected for her garden, and gently took the blanket from the little boy. She carefully opened the blanket, revealing a little brown and white pup with what appeared to be a badly dislocated or broken hind leg. Celeste and Megan looked at one another and nodded.

"I'll come back for the driftwood later," said Celeste.

"Nonsense!" Nona said as she picked up the driftwood. "Megan, you take the bag of sea glass while Celeste carries the puppy. Come, Celeste, we'll drive you home." The young mother gushed with gratitude, and indicated that she and her son would follow the group in their own car.

Nona knew where Celeste lived, as did most everyone in the area, since Celeste was such a distinctive character. She lived in a wee house that was painted white with yellow trim. The group arrived together and parked, and as they entered through the small, enclosed porch, Nona noticed that someone had delivered a full grocery bag.

"Oh dear—one of my angels has been here!" exclaimed Celeste.

Nona picked up the grocery bag for her, as Celeste's arms were occupied with the injured puppy.

The kitchen was bright, clean, and neat. Nona put the bag on the counter and started to put the groceries away for her new friend.

"In that linen closet are some fresh towels," Celeste said, nodding towards a door just off the kitchen. Megan went and retrieved a fluffy pink towel and diligently laid it on the kitchen table; Celeste carefully placed the puppy on it. The little boy drew closer with his mother behind him, and they watched Celeste work with quiet, hopeful eyes.

"Now, Megan, in the back shed, there is a black box with some glass jars. Would you please be a darling and get it for me?"

Megan nodded and scampered away.

"Celeste, I put the milk and meat in the fridge for you. What would you like me to do with the rest of these groceries?" asked Nona.

"Thank you, Nona. Just leave them—I'll put them away later. How about you make us a pot of tea while Megan and I look after this wee creature?" said Celeste as Megan returned with the box of medicines.

"Megan, you keep your hands on the puppy while I get some more things I need," Celeste instructed.

Megan hesitated, but when they looked into one another's eyes, she seemed to know immediately what to do. She laid her hands on the puppy and began to hum.

For a brief moment, Nona was taken aback. *She's humming the same piece she hums when Lacuna is around—the same melody that Joe hummed to Megan after Mary's car accident,* she thought. She was even more amazed when Celeste returned with her arms full of supplies; she was humming the same thing.

Nona, the young mother, and the little boy quietly drank their tea and watched as Celeste and Megan put a makeshift cast on the puppy's back leg. Nona was astonished to note that, during the entire process, Celeste never spoke; however, they kept humming, and periodically they would glance at one another. Megan was efficiently assisting Celeste, but Celeste was not outwardly giving instructions; she somehow knew exactly what she was supposed to do. Watching this, it dawned on Nona that Celeste was directing Megan through telepathy.

The whole process had taken just over a half an hour. The puppy, having been administered to, was sound asleep on a fresh towel that had been nestled inside of a sturdy cardboard box in which the young mother and little boy could safely transport home. They tucked the blanket they had originally brought around him, and thanked Celeste and Megan profusely before departing to take their puppy home.

After they left, Celeste cast a warm smile at Megan.

"Thank you, Megan. You're a natural," she said.

Megan smiled in return and signed, "You're welcome."

Nona made a fresh pot of tea and sat with Celeste.

"You're simply wonderful with children and animals," she said. "You and Megan work very well together. Can you tell me about the piece of music you and Megan were humming? I've heard it before, but you seem to know more of it."

"Does the wee one hum it often?" Celeste asked, smiling.

"Only at certain times—especially when she sees humpback whales."

"That would be the one she calls Lacuna?"

Nona was shocked.

"It's okay, Nona; Megan told me all about it."

"So, you two *do* communicate through telepathy!"

"Oh yes," answered Celeste, as if it were an everyday occurrence. "Now, about the humming: you know, Nona, Megan is a very special old soul. The piece I hum has been handed down through both my parent's families for centuries. It is an ancient piece. Unfortunately, I don't know its origin. Some of the old folk from the Hebrides say it was given to their ancestors by an angel from heaven. I find that whenever I feel down or lonely, I hum it and it makes me feel better. It also helps me to concentrate. When you visit next, I'll teach it to you."

Nona was moved by this information, and had an impulse to ask, "Will Megan ever speak again?"

"I don't know when or under what circumstances, Nona, but yes, she will talk again."

Tears welled up in Nona's eyes. "Thank you, thank you, thank you," she softly said. She took Celeste's hands in her own and smiled.

After they'd visited a bit longer and had finished their pot of tea, Nona looked at the time. "Come, Megan—Andrew will wonder where we are," she said.

"It was a pleasure having you here today," Celeste said. "You're most welcome here anytime."

As they drove home, Nona reflected on the fascinating events of the day. She was thrilled to know Megan would get her speech back; she trusted and believed Celeste, and both Nona and Megan looked forward to visiting Celeste often.

As time went by, Nona and Megan—and sometimes Sadie—went to visit with Celeste either at her home or on the beach. Sam, who had previously been part of an almost inseparable trio, began to fade into the background when he started going to public school.

Celeste followed through on her promise to Nona to teach her the unusual and ancient piece of humming. She found it helped her a great deal when she was trying to concentrate, or when she was not feeling well.

Megan was about six years old when she woke up one morning at five o'clock, screaming, "Help me, help me!"

Nona, jolted out of her sleep, could not believe her ears; Megan hadn't spoken one word since the accident. Startled, Nona ran to Megan and comforted her.

"It's okay...Megan, it's okay," she said quietly. She wrapped her arms around her.

Nona wondered if Megan was reliving the car accident. However, in previous nightmares, Megan only screamed—she had never spoken a word. This, however, was very different.

Between sobs, Megan looked at Nona with a frantic expression, and cried, "Gram, they need help! Gram, we've *got* to help them!"

"Who? Who do we need to help, Megan?"

Stumbling over her words, Megan explained that she'd had a vision of a baby humpback badly entangled in fishing gear. It was desperately trying to stay at the surface to breathe. Lacuna and two other adults were trying to hold this young humpback at or near the surface, but they were beginning to tire and were desperately calling for help.

Despite her shock and joy at the realization that Megan was actually talking, Nona calmed Megan down. Andrew couldn't believe his ears when he heard Megan speaking. He helped Megan to get dressed while Nona called Roger.

"But where exactly is this entangled whale?" Andrew asked when Nona came back into the room.

"I don't know exactly, but let's head out into the Bay of Fundy and take it from there," she said, throwing on her jacket.

Roger quickly arrived, and the four of them immediately started out into the Bay of Fundy.

"How are we going to find them?" Andrew asked.

"I'm not sure, but my gut tells me that Megan will show us," Nona answered.

Megan was beside herself.

"Megan, love, you must calm down and help by showing us where the injured whale is," said Andrew.

Megan wiped the tears from her face with both hands, and took a deep, shuddering breath to gather herself. She looked at the chart and pointed to a spot about two miles off White Head Island.

As soon as Nona realized that Megan had identified a specific location, she got in touch the authorities and contacted the US spotter plane.

"There are three whales and one very young one in distress," she said, giving them the coordinates while heading in that direction.

A few moments later the pilot of the plane responded. "In the distance we can see two more humpbacks arriving and are taking over, allowing the tired adults to have a rest. There is one adult humpback on either side of the baby, holding it up by its flippers."

Within minutes, Megan was sitting up on the bow with Nona; she began to jump up and down, singing loudly, "Lacuna, Gram—it's Lacuna!"

When Lacuna was about three hundred feet from the boat, she turned around and began to swim away. Roger followed her. The spotter plane confirmed they were on the right course and that a couple of rescue teams were on their way. They could see whale blows ahead.

"There they are!" Andrew shouted.

Roger slowed the boat down and let it drift close to the entangled baby. They didn't want to scare the whales in any way. Andrew had disappeared and came back wearing his wetsuit, with flippers and a snorkel in his hand.

The baby was so small and helpless. It was badly injured and entangled in a mass of ropes. Three of the ropes had cut in to its flesh. The young whale was exhausted and was surrounded by three other whales, plus Lacuna. Nona could not believe her eyes. The adults were taking turns—one was on either side under the baby's flippers, holding it up so it could breathe.

Lacuna moved in to relieve one of them. Megan got a message from Lacuna:

You must hurry.

They couldn't wait for the rescue teams; they were still almost an hour away. Andrew, now in his wetsuit, slipped quietly into the water. He dove down and came up about two minutes later, reporting that there were three or four long pieces of three-quarter-inch rope with several heavy metal lobster traps attached to them, hanging from the whale. He got out his knife.

"Andrew, please be careful," Nona said as Andrew slipped underneath the injured whale.

"Lacuna will take care of him," Megan said.

Soon Andrew came up again, and had Roger tie one end of a piece of rope to the boat. Taking the other end, Andrew disappeared below the surface and tied his end to the rope hanging from the whale; then he took his knife and cut the entangled rope above his knot.

Roger hauled in the rope with the traps on it, and gave another piece of rope to Andrew, who repeated the same process. Almost two-thirds of the rope and lobster traps were now cut free of the whale. Then, Andrew took two big floats and tied one to each end piece of a thirty-foot rope. He placed the rope underneath the midsection of the whale so the floats were on either side of the animal; these would help to keep it at the surface. With both lines with the traps on the deck, Roger counted over thirty traps.

No wonder that baby could not keep herself at the surface, he thought.

When the second rope was cut, the baby humpback tried to swim away. Lacuna, with the help of another whale, prevented her from doing so, and calmed her down. Andrew swam up beside it and looked into its huge eye. A very strange feeling engulfed him; something passed between them. Andrew later said that he felt strongly that the whale was pleading with him to set her free.

Andrew came up alongside the boat to talk to Nona and Roger. "I don't know whether I can do much more. The ropes have cut so deeply, I'm afraid if I pull on them she'll react violently with pain."

Just then, Megan said, "The baby doesn't have time. She'll die shortly if you cannot get more of those ropes off."

Andrew looked at Nona. "I know what Megan says is true," he said.

By this time, Roger had put on his wetsuit as well, and slipped into the water with Andrew.

"It appears that a rope has wrapped itself around her left flipper several times," said Andrew.

"With the two of us working together, we could free her from those ropes faster. The spotter says the rescue teams are still twenty minutes away. Andrew, you and I will have to do our best," said Roger.

"I agree. We'll have to be very careful when removing those ropes; they're really cutting into her flesh."

When they got closer, they could see that there were six coils of rope, two of which had dug two inches deep into the flipper. They decided to cut the loose ropes and attempt to free the flipper as best they could. It took them about ten minutes. The last part was the hardest as it was embedded in the flesh. They were afraid that, if they pulled the rope, the flipper would move in reaction to the pain. They were amazed that the whale hardly moved at all when they pulled the rope out. Both Andrew and Roger surfaced and tried to catch their breath. The right flipper was not as badly entangled, and they were able to cut it loose within minutes. They had left the tail and flukes until last; they were badly entangled and still had one rope around it with many traps on it. Andrew did not want to cut this rope; the baby would flap her tail, which would be extremely dangerous for himself and Roger.

Roger contacted the spotter plane. The nearest rescue team would be there in five minutes, so the two men decided to stay in the water with the baby until they arrived. They would leave the tail and flukes to the professionals.

When the rescue team arrived, Andrew filled them in on what they'd done so far.

"You fellows have done a fantastic job. We'll take over from here," they said.

Roger very slowly and quietly moved Serendipity out of their way. They watched the professionals finish the job. It had taken them several tries to release the rope around its tail. About twenty minutes later, a great cheer went up as they were successful, and the baby began to slowly swim; then she seemed to realize she was free. She dove and surfaced beside Serendipity; she raised her head above the water and looked at the four of them. As she slipped quietly back into the water, her mother came up beside her and gently moved her away. Just then, they heard a splash: one of the other whales breached. Lacuna joined in; it was quite a celebration. It was as if the rest of the pod were thanking everybody who had helped.

Andrew and Roger changed out of their wetsuits and gratefully wrapped their frigid hands around hot mugs of coffee. They were exhausted and cold, but they felt really good about what they had accomplished.

Nona took the wheel and turned for home. Now they had two reasons to really celebrate: Megan was finally talking, and there was a baby humpback out there who now had a chance to live.

* * *

"Nona, it's Roger—Megan has fallen off her horse. She's knocked herself out. She's in an ambulance on the way to the hospital as I speak."

"I'm on my way," Nona said. She turned to Andrew who was standing beside her.

"Megan has been hurt; we must go to the hospital immediately," she said.

Once they arrived, Sadie and Roger met them. Sadie was crying, and ran over and gave Nona a hug.

"The doctor is in examining Megan right now," Roger said.

"What happened?"

"We were on the gravel road which runs into the old gravel pit over by Ingalls Head. Something spooked Megan's horse; it reared, throwing Megan off. I was scared. I jumped off my horse and ran over to her; she wasn't moving. A woman driving a pickup came along. She quickly found a pulse and called 911. She found a blanket and put it over Megan. She said we had to keep her warm and not move her. The Mountie arrived first and he was asking us questions when the ambulance and paramedics arrived. They quickly examined her, placed her on a backboard, and brought her here to the hospital."

Sadie began to cry again. Roger put his arm around her.

"Thank you, Sadie. You did everything right." Nona paused to let Sadie catch her breath. "Did Megan have her riding helmet on? Do you know the woman who helped you?" she asked.

"Yes, she did have her helmet on. The paramedic said it was a good thing—otherwise it could've been a lot more serious. As for the lady who helped us: I think it was one of the people from away. I forgot to ask her name, but I've seen her around. She's been coming here for many years in the summers."

"How long has the doctor been with her?" Andrew asked.

"About fifteen to twenty minutes," Roger said.

As if on cue, a nurse arrived. "The doctor is with Megan and is giving her a thorough examination," she informed them.

"Is it Dr. Richards?" Nona asked.

"No, Dr. Richards is away right now. We have a locum here for a couple of weeks. His name is Dr. Hellman. We're very lucky to have him on duty right now; his specialty is head trauma. I'm sure he will be out to see you very shortly."

Within minutes, Dr. Hellman came out to see them. He was tall, with a head of thick salt-and-pepper hair and deep brown eyes. He explained his diagnosis, speaking with a Newfoundland accent.

"Megan has had a concussion," he said. "She's still unconscious, but her vitals are good. I understand that she is twelve years old?"

"Yes—when may we see her?" Nona asked.

"In a few minutes; they're just moving her from emergency to a room. I want to keep a close eye on her."

"Do you have any idea how long it will be before she comes to?" Andrew asked.

"With this sort of head trauma, it's very difficult to tell. We'll know more in about twenty-four hours."

As soon as they were able, Nona and Andrew went to Megan's room. The nurse was just finishing getting her settled. They could see a bump on her head. Tears ran down Nona's cheeks.

"Andrew, I'm going to stay with her in case she wakes up."

Andrew kissed Megan on the forehead and whispered, "I love you, Megan."

Nona took Megan's hand in hers and started to hum the tune Celeste taught her a few years back. Somehow it made her feel better, and she could've sworn Megan could hear her.

Megan was in a trance-like state, and was suspended within a timeless state of mind. She had no concept of time. It was very quiet and dark, and Megan thought she was waking up—but she couldn't understand where she was. She found herself in a large, towering cave surrounded by magnificent quartz crystals that were casting the most beautiful light she'd ever seen; there was a blend of greens, blues, and many shades of purple and indigo. She felt completely at home, and a feeling of déjà vu overwhelmed her. She heard a voice filled with music speaking to her.

"Welcome home," said the voice.

Megan looked around.

"Over here," the voice called.

She saw a very tall woman, dressed in white, with golden hair draped over her shoulders in such a way that it radiated the colours of the quartz crystals. She was sitting on a ledge about six feet up and was smiling. Her eyes reflected the colour of indigo.

"Where am I?" Megan whispered in awe. "This place is so beautiful! I know I've been here before." Megan hesitated a moment. "I think it was more than once. Have I died? Am I in heaven?"

"No. You are in a trance, and are stuck between Earth and other dimensions."

"Why am I here?"

"You're here to remember and to begin healing. You are fluctuating between a very deep, sleep-like state which you are now in, and a deeper state of being unconscious."

"Is that what you meant when you said I was in between?"

"Yes. Right now you are in a deep sleep-like state, and your brain waves are very slow."

Megan sighed. "I know I was in Atlantis when it disappeared into the ocean. I died in this very cave." She shivered, remembering it. "I don't want to be here any longer."

"Oh, but you must stay a bit longer, for we are here to help you heal."

The tall blonde woman spread out her arms, and several other tall, blonde males and females came into the cave. A very young girl came to sit at her feet.

"Wait!" Megan said, pointing at the young girl. "That's *me*! But how can it be?"

"Yes...this is you, a long, long time ago."

"I remember! I was here. I was learning to be a Keeper of the Crystals."

"Yes, you were, Megan. We harnessed the power of the crystals to give free energy to the advanced technologies."

Megan nodded, and she was very excited. "We had so many wonderful abilities; we could move objects with our minds, communicate by telepathy, and even perform astral travel. How and why did we lose all those wonderful abilities?"

"Megan, you have not lost those abilities; they are within you. You have just lost the means to activate them. However, you have already awakened your telepathic ability. Look at how you communicate with whales! Your mother, Mary, could telecommunicate when she was young. You'll soon have the full ability, and will be able to engage in astral travel and more—but first, you must deal with your own karma."

"My karma? How? Why?" Megan asked.

She was slipping back into a deep sleep again, and her vision slowly faded away. Then she found herself in a rather dark place. She could hear what she thought was humming.

Megan then experienced her second trip beyond her usual reality. She was swimming in a dolphin body; a couple of dolphins were swimming with her. She realized she'd been with dolphins in a past life and was relaxed and thoroughly enjoying it. They were undulating through the water like porpoises. She loved being several feet underwater; with a flip of her tail, coming up to the surface was especially fun. With a distinct pop, a quick blow, and rapidly inhaling some air, she would dive again. Soon they were out in fairly deep water. Below her, off to her left, she saw a huge black shape with big long white flippers slowly rising to the surface. It was a humpback whale, but it was not Lacuna. She watched it surface.

He's huge! she thought.

At that moment, she received a message from one of her escorts.

Look to your left.

She did so, and saw that three other humpbacks were resurfacing. Megan was mesmerized; these were absolutely gigantic animals. She was blown away by how graceful, agile, and fast they were.

Just then, Megan heard what sounded like a rifle shot. It was extremely loud. A young calf had slapped the water and was swimming to its mother.

He is hungry, she thought as she watched the mother hang upside down. The baby sucked up the large, steady stream of rich milk.

Suddenly, Megan felt that she could not breathe anymore. She quickly surfaced and gulped another breath of air and down she went. As she was gliding under the surface, the baby whale had stopped feeding, and the adults became more alert. The dolphin on her left gave her a message.

Look down, and be ready to move when we do.

Just below them, Megan spotted a very large, compact school of small herring. All three adults were making sounds like grunts and barks. The last of the three adults dove gracefully as soon as he saw the herring. Slipping on to his back, he gave a very strong kick of his tail and swam downwards. To avoid the sucking pull of the water resulting from his very rapid dive, Megan quickly swam to where her traveling mates were. Keeping an eye on the whales, she saw that they leveled off and spaced themselves fairly evenly around the school of herring and began to blow a rising curtain of bubbles. The herring reacted to this by forming a tighter and tighter circular column as the fish swam to the surface trying to escape. The whales corralled the column of herring which got smaller and denser and became a large, densely-packed mass. They couldn't escape, because they would not cross the bubble curtain. They were trapped, literally boiling at the surface. The three whales swam below them, turned, and with their gigantic mouths wide open, surfaced. Each whale took thousands of fish and, slowly closing their mouths, forced the seawater out through their baleen, trapping the fish inside.

Now that's cooperative feeding! Megan thought.

The whales were now resting at the surface. She began to listen to her surroundings. She knew that whales and dolphins make sounds she could hear, but some of the sounds were above and below her normal hearing range. She became aware that the whales and dolphins were not only communicating between their own species, but also with other species. The dolphins were starting to play, and their sharp clicks were overriding other quieter sounds. As she rose to the surface, she was aware of five or six porpoises making distinct pops, like someone removing the cork from a champagne bottle.

She slipped back into a deep sleep again, thinking, *Oh, I was really enjoying that. I was so happy, peaceful, and joyful; I was home.*

Megan was being monitored constantly as to her responses to light and touch. They also did periodic brain scans, along with monitoring all the regular vital signs and blood tests. There was a slight hemorrhage on her brain, but not enough to be the reason for how far Megan had slipped into unconsciousness. They couldn't get a consistent reading of her brain waves.

"Megan appears to be alternating between a fairly deep sleep state and an even deeper sleep," Dr. Hellman explained to Nona, Andrew, and Joe, who had just arrived. "She is in a trance-like state. Hopefully, within the next twelve to twenty-four hours, we will see her condition improve."

Megan felt she'd been asleep for a long time when she realized she was about to have another vision. She heard a clicking sound. She was in the ocean again swimming with her two dolphin friends. She thought, *I wonder where to this time? I really don't care; I just love doing this.*

The dolphins swam faster. Megan followed them. Her guides began to have fun performing an underwater ballet with twists, turns, and spirals in all directions. They did circles around one another and around Megan. At this point, she joined in. She, along with the others, began to dive deeper; spinning, they came soaring to the surface, broke free and leapt into the air. After performing a perfectly-synchronized arc, they returned to their watery home. They repeated this several times.

After covering several miles, Megan heard some strange noises ahead of them. It was a mixture of low short moans, pops, brays and whistles. Just then, a huge black shape moved past her to the surface.

Oh my God! We're swimming amongst a pod of six or seven right whales! she realized.

Megan swam to the surface for a gulp of air. She was trying to watch them all, but she couldn't, because they were actively feeding; they were diving deep beyond where she could see, but she could hear them. About ten minutes later, a couple of them came to the surface and blew. Megan swam alongside and around them as they took a few moments to rest before going down again to feed. She came up beside one and looked into its huge, round, black eye, and saw her reflection as a dolphin.

Instantly, she was totally engulfed in a combination of emotions such as joy, elation, and a deep, indescribable sensation she knew she would never forget. She and the whale were reconnecting. She knew, at that moment, that she was joined with a whale whose ancestors originated on Earth millions and millions of years before humans did. Their brains were very highly-evolved, perhaps even more so than humans. For a moment, Megan knew their minds had become one. This right whale was desperately trying to tell her something. A picture was developing in her mind, but before it came clear, the whale lifted his head and blew, inhaled and ever so gently hung and dove with the rest of the pod, each leaving behind it a perfect circle of calm water—their "footprints."

Megan knew in her heart of hearts what this gentle giant was trying to tell her. It was something that would change her life completely. Before she could develop the image in her mind, she slipped again into darkness.

It had been almost two days since they had brought Megan into the hospital. They were beginning to get more positive results from her brainwave patterns.

"So you're saying that the situation seems to be improving slowly," Nona asked.

"Yes. We are hoping to see the waves rise again, but this time a bit faster and for a bit longer. Can you think of anything or someone Megan knows who might help her to bring her back to us? She should have come out of this by now."

Nona immediately remembered what Joe had done for Megan several years ago after Mary's death. He had been with Megan most of the night and was resting at their place on the island. She called him and asked him to come and to do some more humming to Megan. She thought of Celeste and called her as well. She was hoping the two of them humming together would bring Megan back. Joe came in right away.

Megan had slipped into another one of her trancelike states. She was getting kind of used to this waking up and having a peculiar dream, so when it happened again, she fully expected to be in the ocean swimming with dolphins again. This time she was not. She was on spaceship of some kind. She was sitting in the chair, and opposite her was a stranger.

"Where am I?" Megan asked as she studied the tall individual sitting opposite her. He had no hair, a large head, and big turquoise eyes.

Through a translation device came a rather unusual voice.

"It's okay Megan," he said. "We are friendly, and are here to help you and your fellow humans on Earth. We mean you no harm. Do you believe we exist?"

"Yes," answered Megan. "There are countless galaxies and billions of planets and stars out there. By sheer odds, there have to be many other planets similar to Earth, as well as others that are very different to us. Some are far more advanced than we are. I believe you are from one of these."

"We wanted you to know that you are going to be okay," said the stranger, "and soon you'll be fully conscious again. You'll also remember a good deal of what you have seen and heard while you're in this current trance."

"I fell off my horse and hit my head, and I have had some pretty strange dreams."

"Megan, those were not dreams—they were visions. It's all right; this is part of why you are on Earth at this time. We needed to talk with you. We need your help. Your planet is going to be in very serious trouble soon."

"How? When is this going to happen?"

"Humans have been and still are using up at a very rapid rate much of the Earth's natural resources which are unsustainable and non-renewable. For example: there is only a finite amount of your fossil fuels such as oil, gas and coal. When they are gone, that is it—there is no more. Most of the world's fisheries are either gone or at the point where they cannot recover. The forests are disappearing at an alarming rate. One of your main sources of oxygen is being decimated; your oceans are extremely polluted. If your oceans die, so does your planet."

"You mean we are doomed?"

"Only if humans don't change their ways. Megan, there is always hope. We see glimmers of it more and more every day. People are becoming more sensitive to what is happening around them, and this number is steadily increasing—and you are beginning to demand answers. Humans cannot and must not continue to abuse Earth. They must be taught to respect every person, every plant, every animal, absolutely everything on your planet. Everyone and everything on earth are all interconnected. You are not separate entities. You are all *one*."

"If we hurt one another, or other animals and plants and beings, we are hurting ourselves?"

"Yes. Not just when you hurt one another, but also when you hurt, kill, or damage any part of this planet which is not renewable—whether it's through carelessness, ignorance, or greed. The end result is the same."

"This world is so big, and we've such a huge population; where do we start? Where do *I* start?"

"Earth's humankind needs to be educated as to how and why your planet got to this stage. Many of you already know why, and are truly beginning to turn things around. Many are turning to more sustainable forms of energy, such as wind and solar power; more people are learning to live closer to the land and respect their surroundings and their environment. There are many signs of hope; these are but a few indications."

"What about our climate change?"

"Climate change normally occurs in cycles. The cycle you are currently in is a warming trend which will eventually change and become a cooling one. These are normal cycles, and your world is full of cycles. It is the added population and tremendous extra load that humans have put on the system that is causing the problem, especially with the amount of carbon dioxide being produced. All these actions are causing the cycles to occur much faster than normal. There's been too much carbon dioxide entering your atmosphere in too short a period of time. This started with the Industrial Revolution and the burning of the carbon-based fuels."

"Is it the carbon dioxide through a greenhouse effect that's causing global warming?"

"That is one thing it is doing. There is something far more important happening, however: the oceans are the main absorbers of carbon dioxide; the plants and cycles that normally help keep the carbon dioxide balance are overloaded, and your oceans are becoming more and more acetic. This is happening too fast for the marine organisms to change and adapt to these new conditions."

Megan thought for a moment. "What will happen if the marine plants and animals cannot keep up with these changes through evolution?" she asked.

"Your oceans are slowly dying. A few organisms will survive. Your world will be a very different place; many species of plants and animals—and even humans—will be extinct. Humanity will probably not survive."

Megan sat in silence for several minutes. "You said you needed my help. What can I do?"

"Well, there are several things. Education is a major key. Megan, read up on the history of Earth, especially that of the last 15,000 to 20,000 years. This may give you a better understanding of how Earthlings got themselves to this point. Please share what you learn."

"Atlantis was real, wasn't it?"

"Yes, very much so; you were there." He paused a moment, touched a couple of buttons on the machine in front of him, then looked up at Megan. "We know you are still very young, but do you know where you're headed in your studies?"

Megan smiled; she couldn't help it. "I do—even more so now. I'm going to carry on our family tradition. The females go into the field of Marine Ecology. Gram is researching zooplankton, and my mother was researching phytoplankton before she died. I would like to follow that tradition and study the marine viruses and bacteria. I think this would be good area to work in, especially, after what you have just told me."

"Excellent, we'll help you any way we can. If you need us, let Lacuna know; she'll get in touch with us."

"You know Lacuna?"

"Indeed we do, Megan; she is a very special whale, and you are very special human. The ability that you have to communicate with one another will increase over time."

"Thank you," Megan said. She was slipping back into her deep sleep.

"Wait, Megan—there is one more thing. You've been given some very special abilities—what you call paranormal; these will develop as you need them, and we'll help you along the way."

"How?"

"You will see, my friend, you will see. Trust us, and trust yourself. Trust your visions and your intuition; you'll be fine."

Megan heard a very familiar sound behind her. She turned and saw Lacuna waiting for her. She stepped into the water and became a dolphin again, and swam beside Lacuna. Gently and slowly, she swam to the surface. Lacuna was making the beautiful humming sound Megan loved. As they surfaced, Megan found herself humming. She opened her eyes, stopped humming, and simply smiled and went back to sleep. There were hugs and smiles all around.

Within a few minutes, Megan was wide awake. She was amazed to see everyone around her. There was Nona, Andrew, Joe, and Celeste. Megan was looking at Joe and Celeste.

"I heard you humming our song. I knew it was you, and that it was time I came home," she said. Everyone nodded and laughed.

Megan turned to Nona. "Oh Gram, you won't believe where I've been and what I've seen! I must write it down before I forget!"

As Nona was getting some paper and a pen, Joe said to Megan, "You'll never forget."

Celeste added with a smile, "Megan, you had an extremely interesting experience."

Realizing Megan needed some time, Joe and Andrew went for coffee, while Celeste and Nona stayed with her. After about twenty minutes, Megan put the pen down and looked over at Nona and Celeste. "I'm sorry, I just had to write about what happened to me." She was very excited. Celeste was smiling, for she knew exactly what Megan had been through.

"Was I gone very long? Was I unconscious?"

"You were in a semi-coma for about three days, dear; how are you feeling?" Nona asked.

"I have a slight headache, that's all." She hesitated a moment. "Gram, I really need to talk to you and Celeste about my dreams—or were they visions?"

"They were visions." Celeste said.

"Like the ones you sometimes have?" Megan asked.

"Yes."

Nona looked at Megan. "The doctor thinks you should rest."

"Gram, I've slept for three days!" she said. They all laughed. "I couldn't talk when I first woke up. I was overwhelmed by what I'd experienced. Celeste, Joe, and Lacuna guided me home."

Megan almost told Nona she'd come back as a dolphin, but she felt Nona may not understand. She knew that Celeste did.

"Gram, just before I woke up, I was on a spaceship, talking with an alien." She stopped to see what Nona's reaction would be. Nona had looked at Celeste, who nodded and winked to let her know it was okay.

"Gram, I was on a spaceship. That is why I couldn't talk about it right away; I felt everyone would think I was crazy or something." Megan was excited. "I had several visions." Megan decided she'd tell them about the ones about the whales, but not the one about Atlantis.

"I was swimming with dolphins and whales twice; once with humpbacks and once with right whales. It was so beautiful and so peaceful. I loved it."

As Megan shared, she relived the experience, and just as she was finishing, her doctor came in.

"Well, Megan, you definitely presented us with a puzzle. You were in some form of a coma, yet you weren't fitting into the Glasgow Scale for comas. I want you to be careful for the next few days. Don't be worried if your memory is slow to come back in some areas. I'm leaving a report for your doctor. If you experience any of these symptoms on this sheet, report to him immediately or go to the nearest emergency centre." He handed the papers to Nona. "I guess you're free to go, young lady. Take care of yourself."

"Thank you very much for all you have done. I'll be very careful," she said.

When the doctor left Megan said to Nona, "It was so nice of Joe to come. The tune Joe was humming was the same one he hummed to me many years ago. It is very special to me."

Megan recovered, and as time went on, she continued to have visions of swimming with the whales and dolphins. She always felt so good when she awoke.

One evening, she was sitting in the living room watching a TV program about ancient mysteries, and she found it fascinating; it reminded her of the vision she'd had of talking to an alien, and she recalled his suggestion of looking into some of Earth's ancient history. She decided to do some research on it and was amazed at the number of books and publications regarding extraterrestrials, UFOs, and spacecraft. She began reading a book on the history of extraterrestrials and one about Atlantis.

She was spellbound, and was particularly interested in the warning that we are currently in a similar situation that Atlantis found itself in during its final years of existence. She read about how aliens from Nibiru, also called Planet X, or the Red Planet, first visited the planet about 400,000 years earlier, and how they had returned every 3600 years since then. About 100,000 B.C.E., the Anunnaki from Nibiru had intervened with the evolution of the human species. In 32,400 B.C.E., many celestial happenings occurred. Earth was flipped on its axis, which initiated our most recent Ice Age. The formation of the glaciers and ice caps forced humans to move. The Atlantians, at this time, were in a highly-evolved state of consciousness. The third cycle began with the melting of the ice caps, resulting in the great flood. A large number of Sirians arrived on Earth and brought their ancestral Sirian Soul Music, which was the harmonic vibration which kept Earth in balance and the portals open. When Megan read about this, she wondered if this music was still being produced by the dolphins and whales.

She read about how, between 12,000 and 10,000 B.C.E., a large comet split into three pieces crashed into the Atlantic Ocean. Atlantis disappeared below the ocean's surface. The Nakkal Brotherhood, knowing such a disaster was coming, left Atlantis. Some went to the Himalayas in Tibet where they built a very large white pyramid. Others went to the Yucatán Peninsula which became part of Mexico.

The endemic race living on Atlantis was gentle and intuitive, whereas, the Anunnaki were cold and calculating. They interbred, and the Anunnaki way of life became dominant, logical, calculating, and devoid of much emotion. They intervened and formed an opposition to the indigenous race. When Atlantis sank the Anunnaki left Earth, but returned and intervened twice; once in Sumer in 7200 B.C.E., and then again in 3600 B.C.E. in Egypt. In the latter, the Anunnaki directly interfered with the Pleiadians and the Sirians.

When Megan finished reading and making notes, she really didn't know what to believe. She would, however, keep an open mind, and would read more.

There were days when she relaxed, sometimes helping on Serendipity with Nona's research. She would more often than not just sit and relive those beautiful visions with the dolphins and whales. She saw Lacuna twice over a two-week period.

Nona noticed a slightly different behaviour; Lacuna seemed to spend more time just logging near the boat, while Megan would sit cross-legged near the stern. Sometimes she would sing or talk to no one in particular. Lacuna performed some flipper slaps, inhaled deeply, and raising her tail out of the water, she disappeared below the surface.

"Lacuna seemed different today. Is she okay?" Nona asked Megan.

"Yes, Gram. She wanted to be quiet and not get me too excited," Megan answered.

Megan had begun to read about aliens and UFOs. Her initial readings showed her that aliens had obviously visited Earth over a long period of time. Two main thoughts kept running through her mind: *Were aliens here before there were dinosaurs? If Atlantis really existed, could the beings who lived there have anything to do with our origins?*

She read about the more recent sightings of UFOs in North America. Most of the sightings began just around the end of World War II.

I've always thought the dropping of the two atomic bombs on Japan—with the resulting mushroom clouds carrying radiations out into space—started it all, she thought.

She read about Adamski, who met with an alien in the Southwest USA. They carried on a telepathic conversation which was witnessed by other humans. In 1964, a US soldier was given a document to read about an investigation about a real incident, and concluded that Earth had been visited by beings from at least four alien civilizations for thousands of years.

Eventually, Megan learned that there was a US aerospace command in charge of all space operations. It was a multinational force; but was centred in the United States where billions of tax dollars went into a Black Budget—a budget used for covert, top-secret projects. She remembered the Roswell incident, where two UFOs crashed in 1947 in southwestern USA. The day after, the US military began a cover-up of such evidence, calling the crashed space vehicle a weather balloon. They sanitized the whole area, and witnesses were threatened not to talk. In spite of the tremendous pressure by the American people and from around the world, the cover-up has continued to the present day.

Megan wondered why. She believed that it may have been because the US military knew they had no defence against aliens, if they ever attacked. Or maybe it was because one of the four aliens survived; perhaps some deals were made. One theory said that if no one knew what was going on, then the aliens would be protected from being harassed by the press, and the military, in total secrecy, could do whatever they wished; they could even make secret deals with the aliens. It would, at the very least, give them time to reverse engineer material from the crash site.

She stopped reading for a moment and thought, *There have been trillions of dollars spent in areas such as Area 51, and so many people are involved. What have they found, and why isn't the general public being informed?*

With those questions in mind, Megan fell asleep and had a vision. She was very confused at the first. She was sure she would be swimming with the dolphins. This time, that was not meant to be.

She was in a lab somewhere, watching two men in white lab coats working with petri dishes. She thought she recognized one of them, but she was not sure. They were very carefully transferring these dishes from one microscope to another. The man she thought she'd seen before was intent on looking through a microscope. The other man walked over and they were talking. She couldn't hear what was being said. The man who was standing pulled out a loaded syringe and jabbed the man sitting at the microscope. The petri dish fell and broke as he fell off the stool and lay unconscious on the floor. The conscious man picked up the broken pieces of the petri dish. He took a piece of broken glass, dipped it in the medium of the fallen dish and carefully cut the hand of the unconscious man. Megan clearly saw their faces.

"Oh my God!" she was screaming. "Stop, you're killing my father!"

Nona heard her yelling and came running.

"This must have been a very bad dream," said Nona. "Would you like to talk about it?"

Megan was wide awake and shaking. "Gram—please tell me again: exactly how did my father die?"

Nona sat bolt upright. They hadn't talked about it in any detail for years.

"I'll be very honest with you, Megan. We don't know exactly how Matthew died. We were told he was working on a lethal virus and that he'd cut himself on a broken petri dish while working alone in his lab."

"No, Gram," Megan said in a raised voice. "He was not alone and he didn't cut himself. Gram, he was murdered. I saw it all in my vision." Megan started to cry. "It was horrible, Gram."

"We all knew at the time that it was not an accident, but the company he worked for covered it up so well that there was no evidence."

"Why was he killed?"

Nona took a very deep breath and told her what happened. Megan thought for a few minutes, and then said, "Does that mean my mother's death was not an accident, either?"

"It was meant to be a warning; however, she died. The RCMP are still looking into it, even though it is a cold case; as far as we're concerned, she was murdered."

Nona went on to explain what had transpired during the months immediately following Mary's accident. Then she told Megan about how she had met Gwen. "I think you and I should go to Matthew's cabin for a holiday and you can talk with her about it."

Nona called Gwen, and filled her in on Megan's accident. She didn't mention anything about Megan having visions.

Megan was starting to ask more questions regarding both her parents' deaths. The more she asked, the more she was upset; there was a sense of urgency that needed to be satisfied. She wanted to meet Gwen and talk to her as soon as possible, so plans were made. Nona and Megan would fly to Boston; Gwen would meet them, and they would drive out to the cabin for a few days.

They arrived in Boston and were met by Gwen. After grocery shopping, they drove to the cabin, unpacked, and got settled. They each picked up a cold drink, and sat out on the deck. It was very quiet and peaceful.

"No wonder Matthew loved this place so," Nona commented as she pointed out a pair of Mergansers floating by. "Megan, your great, great grandfather knew what he was doing when he bought this property."

"Megan...you had a rather traumatic experience recently. How are you feeling? You look wonderful." Gwen said.

"It wasn't too bad; I didn't break any bones," she answered with a smile.

"But weren't you in a coma of some sort?"

"For about three days.

"Nona, I understand that you've been traveling and giving talks, and so forth. How's that going?"

"I'm very busy and frequently have to say no to requests for public speaking—otherwise, I would never be home. I do find that giving the talks is very stimulating and satisfying, though; it keeps my mind busy and sharp. It's now the other driving force in my life—the first one, of course, is Megan. She keeps me on my toes," Nona said, laughing.

"Megan, how is school coming along? What aspects do you find most interesting?"

"The sciences, especially biology; living on an island surrounded by the ocean has given me a special affinity for it. After my fall, I did some reading. I talked to Gram about it on the plane. I'm going to study marine biology at University."

"Wow, that's great, Megan! What a fascinating field to be in!" Gwen commented, smiling.

"If I do well in undergraduate school, I want to do graduate studies and carry on the work and tradition of my mother and Gram."

"I wish you the very best. Somehow, I've a feeling you'll be very successful."

"Thank you, Gwen."

Later that evening, Nona broached the subject of Matthew's death with Gwen.

"Gwen, has there been any further development in Matthew's case?"

Gwen immediately knew what Nona was referring to. The Boston police still insisted it was an accident. The RCMP was holding Mary's murder as a cold case. Gwen and Nona had made a promise after finding the additional research which Matt had hidden that Gwen would continue on with her investigation, along with other investigative reporters. Initial results had been quite promising; several more suspicious deaths had come to light. So far, there was no concrete evidence that Matthew's employers were directly connected.

"We still get a few more incidents reported now and then, and we are still investigating. We're also keeping a low profile on this. At the same time, we're looking into some real problems with the drug companies. I doubt these are connected to the lab Matthew worked for."

"Gwen, there is something I think you should know," said Nona. "Megan had a very disturbing nightmare several nights ago. It involved the day Matt was murdered."

Nona and Megan told Gwen about it. Megan was shaking and almost in tears when they finished.

"It was so very real. It was as if I was actually there," said Megan.

"Megan, in a way I think you were there," Nona added.

Gwen looked puzzled. "Could we please back this train up? I think I'm missing something."

Nona responded, as Megan was still upset.

"Gwen, ever since and during Megan's so-called coma, she has been having visions which are not only very clear, but when they are happening, Megan feels they are extremely real."

"Gram—I don't think Gwen believes I have visions," she said. Megan began to cry softly.

Gwen looked at Megan and placed her hand on her arm.

"Megan, look at me. I do believe you. I have a friend who has them. You are not alone and you've been given a very precious gift."

Megan stopped crying. "Really?" she asked.

"Really," said Gwen with a reassuring smile.

Everyone relaxed, and Megan calmed down.

"Now Megan, can you describe the lab—and more importantly, the man who was in the lab with your father?" Gwen asked gently.

"When I woke up, I sketched the man's face, and also a general outline of the lab," Megan said. She dug out the papers and handed them to Gwen.

Gwen looked at the five drawings in her hand and said, "Megan, these are excellent."

"Do you think they might help?" Megan asked hopefully.

"Well, I'm certainly going to try to match it to someone who worked in that lab at that time."

"Oh, Gram—do you think they will find my father's killer?"

"We're going to do everything we possibly can, Megan. I must warn you: it will be a long shot. If we move ahead with this, it may lead us to who it was that ordered your mother's car to be run off that road." She looked very seriously at Megan and added, "Knowing who did it and proving it are two different things."

Nona turned to Gwen. "Are you going to share this with Holly?"

"Not right away; if we can tentatively identify this man, we'll decide what to do then."

They were all awakened early the next morning by the haunting, echoing calls of the loons. The bright, warm sun reflected off the lake, forming the illusion of millions of crystals and diamonds. Megan was up early, made coffee, and was on her second cup when Gwen came out yawning.

"Bless your heart," she said as she poured a cup of coffee and sat in the old rocker. "What a beautiful and peaceful place this is!"

"I love it here," Megan responded. "Somehow I feel close to my father when I'm at the cabin." She put her book down and looked at Gwen. "You're an investigative reporter, right?"

Gwen nodded as she took a sip of coffee.

"Gram said you belong to a worldwide group of investigative reporters who are trying to ferret out the truth about all the monies that governments around the world are unable or unwilling to account for," she stated.

Gwen nodded her head.

"Do you think it all started with Roswell?" Megan asked.

"I think what happened there was the catalyst which started what we refer to as Global Watergate—a broad term which covers anything and everything the military and/or governments are doing and have done which they do not want their citizens to know about."

"That's scary. Why can't your president do anything about it?"

"There is a group here in the US doing everything they can, including taking legal action to force the government to come clean. They are slowly making headway. As far as our president is concerned: when one of our former presidents was asked this very question, he answered something like, 'There is a government within the government and I do not control it.' There is a shadow government of some kind."

"If the president doesn't control it, who does?" Megan asked.

"That is a main thrust of our investigative probes. We are attempting to find credible sources to give us clues. The really sad part of this whole thing, Megan, is that the USA brags about our freedom and democracy—and yet if we have a secret government, one could ask: are we still a credible and true democracy?"

"Isn't that a bit too harsh?" Nona said.

"I don't think so. There is just too much secrecy around where trillions of our tax dollars have gone with very little to show for it."

"Who do you think is controlling these secret governments or whatever they are? Is it only the USA that's involved?" Nona asked while making herself some toast.

"There is evidence that other militaries and governments are involved. What really worries me is the possibility that some of the wealthiest people and private corporations outside the government and the military are also involved."

"Gwen, do you think the lab where my father worked was part of this covert business?"

"The more I investigate it, the more I think they're involved in some way."

"How can we—can *I*—as a private citizen help?" Megan asked.

"By continually pressuring our governments to come clean and disclose everything they know. Force these covert groups to come out into the open. We need to know the truth; we have the right to know the truth."

After breakfast, each of them took some time to themselves. Gwen was on her computer. There were a few new pieces to add to the gigantic puzzle they were trying to solve, but nothing earth shaking. She added Megan's drawings and information to her computer. Nona stretched out on the chaise lounge reading her book. Megan sat at the table, making notes and summaries of their earlier conversations. At one point she turned to Gwen and said, "Do you believe in UFOs and extraterrestrials?"

"Yes I do. Do you?"

Megan smiled, thinking of her recent visit on an alien spaceship.

"Yes, I do. There is just far too much evidence in support of their existence. I'm totally fascinated by it all."

"The US government says that there are no such things as UFOs," Gwen said.

"Yes, but most other governments, including Russia, are much more open about it." Megan thought for a moment. "Have you ever heard Paul Hellyer's speech which he gave at the Exopolitics conference in Washington DC?"

"No, I haven't. Who is he?"

"He was our Canadian Minister of Defence under a former government. He gave a fascinating speech. You really should listen to it."

Gwen brought it up on her computer and listened to it twice before commenting.

"He really packed a lot in less than ten minutes."

"Didn't he just!" Nona said as she joined the conversation. "He certainly believes in aliens!"

"Yes, what he said carries a lot of truth—especially the acknowledgment that many decades ago we on Earth were approached by aliens who warned us that Earth was in serious trouble. They offered us their help; it was refused. Hellyer said something to the effect that our government—or was it the military?—were so paranoid that they would rather use the aliens' technology to fight them off rather than welcome them as partners in development."

Nona then added, "Didn't he also say some renegade aliens may have joined some humans to develop dangerous weapons?"

"Yes," Gwen answered.

"I have to wonder: are these covert operations not only going on here, but elsewhere in the world, too? If so, who's really in charge? How did it get so far out of hand?"

Gwen got up and got herself, Megan, and Nona another cup of coffee.

"This is what I think may have happened and how it may have evolved," said Gwen. "As you know, most UFO sightings occurred just after World War II when the world was desperately trying to recover. Then, in 1947, there was a crash of the two spacecraft near Roswell. It is almost a certainty that one of the aliens survived. I think the military, especially the Air Force, was truly paranoid, and therefore quickly started the cover-up, knowing they were totally defenceless against any form an alien attack. Then the US government got involved, and the whole thing snowballed from there. No one wanted to take the responsibility of admitting they had lied to the American public and to the world. From this, a new bureaucracy was born and has grown tramatically ever since."

She paused to have some coffee.

"How did it become worldwide?" Megan asked; she was taking notes.

"The military started to farm out some aspects of their covert research, such as the 'miracle metal' to private companies, who in turn received a top-secret status and were able to hire our top scientists to work for them. Once it metastasized into the private sector, certain wealthy humans began to pour money into these various covert projects. I honestly believe the whole business is being controlled not by legitimate concerns, but by aspects of the world's wealthiest elite and certain personnel in the world's militaries and governments. Currently we don't have any proof of this, but we're digging to find the truth. We'll find it."

"If what Gwen says is true—along with the fact that aliens exist and have visited Earth—is it possible that there is alien involvement, not only in the covert stuff, but also at the top levels of power?"

"Very good thinking, Megan; it is entirely possible, and it is more than likely the case."

"I wonder if there are good aliens and bad aliens."

"How much reading have you done in this area?" Gwen asked Megan.

"I've just started."

"May I suggest you read about some of our ancient history? I'm referring to the time around 10,000 to 12,000 B.C.E."

"I've read about Atlantis."

"May I suggest you reread what we used to call myths? I'm referring to very early Egypt and also the country of Sumer," Gwen said. She paused, wrote something down on some paper, and handed it to Megan; listed were some suggested titles.

"Thank you, Gwen; I really appreciate this."

After a few more days of rest and relaxation at Matthew's cabin, Gwen drove Nona and Megan back to the airport.

Back in Grand Manan, with only three weeks before school, Megan spent time on Serendipity with her friend Sadie, helping with Nona's research. Lacuna came alongside the boat for a visit the odd time. Megan also did some of the reading Gwen suggested.

Ever since Megan and Nona had returned from Matthew's cabin, Megan's parents were very much on her mind. One day after doing some research, Megan had walked over to the piano and picked up one of Nona's favourite photographs. Mary and Nona had been standing on the deck of Serendipity, laughing together. It was an early fall evening with a glorious sunset; shades of purple streaks were competing with vivid yellows, oranges, and reds. There was a mirror image, only slightly blurred, rippling below on the surface of the sea.

"Gram, why do you love the ocean so much? Did Mom love it too?"

Nona glanced over to see what Megan was doing. When she saw her granddaughter gazing at that special photograph, she was overcome with a wave of emotion. She cleared her throat, walked over, and sat beside Magen. Looking at the photograph, Nona had to fight back the tears. "Oh, yes, darling; Mary truly loved the ocean." She took a deep breath and smiled. "You know, Megan, your mother loved the ocean even more than I do!"

Megan was amazed. "But you're crazy about it!"

"I only got close to it when I was studying at University and worked in this area during the summers. When I graduated, I came here to Grand Manan to do my research. Mary lived here and went to school until she went away to university. As a very young child, she came out on the boat with us virtually every time we went, just like you do. Mary was always happy when she was on the water. Your mother grew up with, beside, and on the ocean, just as you're doing."

"Do you think I will love it as much as my mom did?"

"Oh, sweetheart, you already do. You've a very special friend out there. Lacuna and you have a unique relationship. No one else must ever know that you and Lacuna are able to communicate. Megan, I think you are going to have a very long and productive love affair with the ocean."

"As much as yours and Mom's?"

"I believe even more so, because you not only respect and love it, you are a part of it—a very important part."

"Thanks, Gram."

As Megan ran off to be with Sadie, Nona turned and walked into the kitchen. Tears welled up in her eyes and streamed down her cheeks. Tears of missing Mary were mixed with tears of sheer joy for Megan. She knew in her soul that Megan was meant to be as close to the ocean, the whales, and dolphins as one could without being one of them. *Then again,* she said to herself, *I think sometimes that she is one of them.*

Nona reflected on the many wonderful times she and Mary had enjoyed together, and how close Mary had been to the ocean; she also recalled how much Mary had loved her father. Mary had faithfully kept her father's letters; Nona reminded herself to sort them out so she could show them to Megan.

I wonder if those poems that Mary used to write about Grand Manan are also in that box, she thought.

She got up and rummaged around in storage, and found the box containing Mary's poetry. She found her favourite poem and began to read. Mary had been homesick the day she had written it; she had always said it was her favourite one about Grand Manan.

I've waited and waited, months and months for your return

To come to me, to cast off all of your woes to be healed;

For my peace and serenity, I know you so often yearn

So you will give yourself to me and thyself will be revealed.

On my ancient pillared rock you will come and stand;

Let its steadfastness and ageless wisdom rise in you.

Watch, feel the rhythm of my tides, which move eternally;

Know that they are Gaia's heartbeat to strengthen you.

Sail the waters of Fundy Bay, and their intrinsic power feel;

Ride her great waves and currents, and her secrets learn.

Watch marine life around you and sense their great zeal,

The great majestic whales hold all knowledge, you do yearn.

See the glorious sunrise o'er the cliffs of North Head so bold,

And know that life goes on even when all seems out of sight.

As the sun sets o'er The Whistle turning red, orange and gold,

Know that darkness is merely the temporary absence of light.

Let the millions times millions dancing diamonds on the sea

Tell you the great blessings and treasures to share and show.

Just as the zillion flickering lights of the age-old stars you see,

Each glowing brightly to give you all the joys in life to grow.

Let my storms and steady rains wash away all your fear;

Let my soft and gentle breezes cleanse your soul to purity;

Let my winds in all directions blow through your mind to clear;

Let my clear night skies with starlight lead your way to eternity.

Come to me, and you will learn the true you and your purpose in life.

I am surrounded by deep waters; you are surrounded by love so deep.

I am your special Island free of troubles, sorrows, fear and strife.

When you are here with me, you will never be alone, awake or asleep.

So let me hold you and cradle you in my arms and give you peace.

Let me rock and sway you gently as the breezes and trees sing.

Let me take all pain and worry as my ebb tides will take with ease.

Let my love engulf you, flow through you, and your truth will ring.

Nona was in tears as she finished reading it. She decided then and there to have it written in calligraphy and framed for Megan.

That evening, Megan picked up the list Gwen had given her. She bought a few of books for her e-reader and started to read. She was about to discover something which would alter her perspective on how she viewed the world around her. It had begun with her vision of being a young girl in Atlantis. She went back much further. Megan found intertwined translations of the Sumerian 6000-year-old tablets with those of the Babylonians, the Hebrew version of the Bible, and other ancient texts. She made the following notes:

- There were advanced civilizations on earth long before the Nefilim (Anunnaki).
- The Nefilim were conscious beings from the planet Nibiru, which travels a 3600-year elliptical orbit.
- 500,000 years ago, Nibiru's atmosphere began to break down. They needed to put particles of gold in their higher atmosphere to reflect light and heat back to the surface.
- They discovered gold on Earth and placed several hundred of their race in an area which is now known as Africa to mine it. Every 3600 years, they came close to Earth and uploaded the gold. This started about 400,000 years ago.
- 300,000 and 200,000 years ago, the workers rebelled and refused to mine gold. Their superiors, who were from Nibiru, took the sperm from a young male Nefilim and mixed it with primate DNA and produced a race of slaves. Note: Current science has discovered these gold mines and have proven that the first humans lived between 150,000 to 200,000 years ago. Our maternal mitochondrial DNA has remained constant since then. At about the same time, aliens arrived from another planet—Sirius—and merged with the Nefilim. At this point, our race was sterile and in servitude. The forbidden tree of knowledge brought two aspects, each with a duality: good and evil, and the ability to procreate.
- The Anunnaki built the great pyramids as astronomical devices to be used by their progeny to find their way back to Earth and to the gold.

So we were slaves of the Anunnaki. I wonder if we still are? thought Megan.

That night as Megan was going to sleep, she began a conversation with Ortho, the alien.

"You have some questions for me, Megan?"

"Yes; which planet you are from?"

"We're from the planet Sirius."

"I should have known. Don't the dolphins and whales have a connection with you?"

"Yes, they came here millions of years ago."

"Is it true—they carry all the ancient wisdom?"

"Yes, Megan. You might say this is their planet with more than seventy percent of Earth's surface covered in seawater. They are more highly-evolved than humans and are beautifully adapted to their environment. In your 'coma' you became a dolphin and swam with other dolphins and whales."

"I cherished every moment. I couldn't get over the sounds I heard. It was almost like listening to a symphony—it was so beautiful."

"Sound, vibrations, or frequencies are extremely important on Earth and throughout the entire universe."

"Why is that?" Megan asked. She was excited.

"Well, it is quite involved, and yet it is very simple. Everything in the universe has its own vibrational frequency and is unique to each human, each animal, and each plant. Even rocks have their own unique frequencies."

"Wait—are you telling me that rocks vibrate?"

"Yes, they do. You see, vibrations occur as wavelengths and the number of wavelengths per second determines their frequency. Short wavelengths produce higher frequencies, such as gamma rays and x-rays to long radio frequencies and even much longer.

"Nature has its own set of frequencies. Every star and planet, even Earth has its own frequency, called the Schuman Resonance. There are sounds within your hearing range and many sounds or frequencies above and below it. Just because you cannot hear it does not mean that it does not exist."

"So, vibrations or frequencies hold everything together, even at the atomic level?" she asked.

"Yes. You should read what your fellow humans are doing at the atomic level in the field of quantum physics. Skip the mathematical part of it and just read about their findings. I know you will find it very interesting."

"Why are sound and frequencies so important?"

"It keeps everything and every organism in the universe in balance. The whales and dolphins are here to keep the oceans of Earth in balance."

"If that is the case, then the hundreds of thousands of whales and dolphins humans have killed must make it much harder for our current cetaceans to do this."

"Along with the noise pollution caused by ships' engines and sonar, add chemical pollution from humans. The whales and dolphins are currently at the point of disappearing—unless they get help immediately. If they disappear, your oceans will be so far out of balance they won't recover."

Megan was shocked. "Oh no! We cannot let that happen! Ortho, I've been doing a lot of reading about aliens. Are there good ones and bad ones?"

"Yes."

"Are you one of the good ones?"

Ortho chuckled. "Yes, Megan. We prefer to be called 'Light Ones.' The ones you call bad, we refer to as 'Dark Ones.' Darkness is merely the absence of light and the more light there is, the less dark there is. There are many stars and planets in the universe that are inhabited by various forms of beings."

"What is the difference between the Light Ones and the Dark Ones?"

"The Dark Ones are interventionists; they've interfered and still do so with the human race. We can't help humans unless we are asked."

"Is it true the Anunnaki came to Earth to steal our resources?" asked Megan.

Ortho nodded, "Since then, we and other Light Ones were in Egypt trying to help humans to become more spiritual when the Anunnaki intervened. It is extremely important for humans to learn how to live in unison and to respect everything and everyone on the planet; you're not to be isolated individuals competing with one another and abusing Earth's resources."

"How did the Anunnaki get such control over our planet?"

"They are a very advanced technological society compared to Earth. They do things you on Earth have yet to dream about. In very ancient times, when they were exploring the universe, they came upon this absolutely beautiful blue and green planet and claimed it for their own. Ever since then, they've interfered with the human race. They broke one of the universal laws; no planet and its civilization may intervene in another planet or their civilization without their permission. Did you also read about the Federation of Light which was formed by non-interventionists?"

"Yes. I read about civilizations from Sirius, Andromeda, Pleiadea, and Arcturus which are all part of it. You are here trying to help us." Megan took a moment to think. "You are helping me. Are there others like you and me?" she asked anxiously.

"There are, Megan. You will get to know them in the future when it becomes necessary."

Megan could not hold on to this vision any longer.

Megan was approaching sixteen; she was not only having these visions; she was also beginning to have some very ugly nightmares which seemed to be connected with her father's death. She was imprisoned by nonhumans with very distorted bodies, or by hairless apes with large heads and huge yellowish orange eyes which looked into her soul. She would shiver and turn away, feeling nauseated. In another nightmare, she found herself in a dark forest being chased by an animal which ran and jumped long distances. It had big, bright, orange eyes. From time to time, it would send out a type of light beam, which stung like a hornet's sting. He'd almost catch her; it was enjoying the chase.

When she woke up from these nightmares, she would be shaking, and would be in a cold sweat. After several weeks of having these nightmares every night, she found her personality was changing. Her boyfriend Nick noticed and asked her what was bothering her.

"Nothing; I'm fine," she said.

"You've become quieter and withdrawn, and you're no longer the happy-go-lucky girl I knew," he said.

"Sadie and Sam have said the same thing," she said. She started to cry. "I don't want to be like this." Then she told him about the nightmares.

"Have you told your grandmother about them? I'm sure she's noticed this change in you, too," he said.

As he kissed her; he thought to himself, *Even her kisses have changed.*

"Gram, I need to talk to you."

"I'll make some tea; we'll go and sit on the deck."

She told Nona about the horrific nightmares. "Why am I having them? What does it mean?"

"You say they started shortly after we came back from Boston?"

"Yes, and they are getting worse; they are making me feel very anxious and angry."

"After the weekend with Gwen, how did you feel?"

"I was excited about learning more about the Secret Governments."

"Yes—but how did you feel after telling her about seeing your father being killed?"

"I guess I buried it."

"How do you feel about it now?"

Megan thought for a few minutes. "I'm angry, Gram. I'm really furious that my father could have been killed and that his killers got away with it. They also killed my mother, and still nothing was done to bring them to justice." Megan began to cry uncontrollably. "Gram, I'm so mad, it just hurts *so* much!"

"You're having a very normal reaction, Megan; let your tears flow. It's the best thing for you. You are in the anger stage of mourning. It's been a long time coming."

Eventually, Megan calmed down.

"How about I get us a couple of muffins and some tea?" Nona suggested. Andrew was already sitting in the kitchen, eating a muffin.

"Is Megan okay?" he asked.

"I think her parents' deaths, and how they died, are finally beginning to hit her hard. With our help, she's going to have to work this through herself. It's going to be a very difficult thing for her." She kissed his cheek and took the tray with tea, muffins, and blueberry jam, and returned to the deck and Megan.

Megan had gone very quiet while Nona had gone to the kitchen. Nona tried to get her to talk some more, but it was obvious that the conversation, for the moment, was over.

Nona tried several times over the next few days to get Megan to open up. She had no luck. Megan was very withdrawn. Nona and Andrew were getting very worried.

Nick also was unsuccessful in getting her to talk. The following week, he broke up with Megan. She took it very hard, and began to withdraw even more. She lost interest in everything she'd been doing, and got mixed up with a slightly older group of teenagers. Despite Sadie and Sam's warnings, Megan started going out with a boy named Tim.

He was a bit older than Megan and was part of a wild gang. He worked on the lobster boats from November through June; during the summer and fall he did odd jobs around the island. On most evenings, he hung out with the rest of his buddies who loved to party. The RCMP was called often due to noise and fights. Drugs were passed around freely and Megan began to smoke pot. She started to drink heavily and often did not come home at night.

Nona and Andrew were sick with worry. They tried talking to Megan, but to no avail. Nona had called Joe; he too was unsuccessful. They all knew exactly what caused Megan to rebel. She was hurt badly and was running away. She was not only angry—she was in denial.

Megan had been running with this gang for a few months when Nona's phone rang at around two am. There had been a motorcycle accident. Tim had been killed; Megan was in hospital. She was seriously injured, but would be okay. She had a broken leg, a couple of broken ribs, and a bruised spleen.

Nona and Andrew rushed over to the hospital and waited for what seemed like hours before they could see her. When they did, Nona took one look at her and said, "Megan, I love you so. You are going to be okay."

Megan began to weep. "Gram, I'm so sorry. I've been such a fool. I feel so stupid."

"Whatever happens, Megan, we are with you and we love you."

"But Gram…I'm pregnant," Megan said. She began to cry.

Just then the nurse came in to give Megan some pain medication. Dr. Williams talked to Nona in the hall.

"I'm so sorry, Nona; Megan lost the baby."

Nona's knees began to buckle. Andrew caught her and helped her sit on a chair.

The doctor continued to explain what happened.

"It was a result of the accident; she miscarried. It was a boy, but he wasn't developing properly. She would never have been able to carry him to term."

"Have you told Megan yet?" asked Andrew.

"No."

"I'll tell her," said Nona.

"Just so you know: her blood tests were negative for drugs or alcohol. We plan to keep her for a few days."

Nona gathered herself. "I'm going in and see Megan. Andrew, would you please phone Sadie, Celeste, and Joe, and let them know what has happened?"

Andrew kissed her. "I'll be back shortly."

When Nona returned to the room, she found that Megan was sleeping. Not long after, she woke in pain. Nona rang for the nurse, who gave Megan a sedative.

"I'm so sorry, Gram. I was so mad and so hurt. I know now I should have turned to you and Andrew, but for some reason, I couldn't. I ran away. I've made a real fool of myself."

"You know I understand, and you can talk to me anytime," Nona said as she wiped Megan's tears away.

"Gram...I'm pregnant."

"Megan...I hate to tell you this, but the baby was damaged in the accident; you miscarried on the way to the hospital."

"You mean I lost the baby?"

"Yes, Megan, you did, but through no fault of your own."

"I was going to talk to you about getting an abortion."

"What? Why?" Nona was surprised by Megan's remark.

"It wasn't Tim's." Megan began to cry. "I was raped by a couple of his so-called buddies."

"Oh Megan, I'm so, so sorry. Did Tim know?"

"I told him last night. He went very quiet and went over to his buddy's place and beat the crap out of them. He came back and we went for a bike ride. We'd gone a few clicks when he started to drive erratically. He took a spell of some sort. The next thing I knew I was in the ambulance."

"Do you wish to press charges?"

"I've given it a great deal of thought. I don't think so. I was drugged at the time, and you know the reputation that gang has. There's no evidence. Tim's friends knew about it, and they have their own method of dealing out justice. I need to talk to someone about it, though—not just about the rape, but the whole experience I've had. This whole wild phase was the result of me being so hurt and mad about what happened to my parents. I was angry at the world. I know I need help."

Nona took Megan's good hand. "Knowing that you need support and asking for help is perhaps the hardest thing to do. It is the first step in the healing process."

Megan's mind flashed back to the Crystal Cave in Atlantis. "Yes, I'm going to begin my healing," she said.

They were both in tears, and hugged one another.

Sadie called Sam at university and told him about what had happened to Megan. Sam was three years older than Megan and was in his second year of geology. He and Megan were best friends. Sadie knew he would want to know about the accident. The only part she left out was that Megan had been pregnant and had lost the baby. She would never tell him.

"I'm coming home on the weekend; tell her I'll be in to see her," he said.

By the time Sam got to see Megan, she was feeling better. As soon as Megan saw Sam, she began to cry.

"Oh Sam—I've been a fool. Will you ever forgive me?"

"Of course I forgive you. What do you think friends are for?"

"Sam, I've missed you so."

"I've missed you, too," he answered. They talked a bit more until Megan began to get tired. "Meg, you get some rest; I'll be back later," he said.

As he left her room, he vowed he would help her any way he could.

Megan came home after three days. She had several very willing helpers, including Papa Joe, Sadie, and of course Nona and Andrew. Joe had taken a couple of weeks off for holidays and was staying with them. Megan was going to need his help.

Whenever Sam came back to the island for a visit, Megan was always first on his list. They would sit, walk, and talk, and just be together. Sometimes Sadie would join them. It was like old times. The Megan they knew was back. She'd learned the hard way that life can be very unpleasant; life wasn't always fair. It could be extremely painful.

One weekend, Nona packed a picnic lunch, and Sam and Megan borrowed Sam's father's car to go White Head Island. It was late August and a beautiful clear day. He drove out to the lighthouse over the very narrow road covered with rather large smooth stones. Megan sat quietly.

"Look, Sam—someone is out there gathering seaweed at low tide," she pointed out.

They parked the SUV near the lighthouse and walked the all-terrain track along the edge of the ocean. It always took Megan's breath away when she came around the last bend and saw that first heady glimpse of the huge, beautiful, sandy beach. It was extra big as it was low tide.

She stopped and took a few deep breaths and exclaimed, "Oh Sam! I do love it so!"

They went to their favourite spot about two-thirds along the beach. They dropped their things and walked the rest of the beach in silence. Returning to their spot, they opened the picnic basket and began to enjoy the feast Nona had prepared them. There were chicken and beef sandwiches made on home-made all-grain bread, slivers of celery and carrots and home-made veggie dip. Nona had also included a bottle of Megan's favourite white wine. To top it all off they found homemade blueberry muffins.

"Are you going to the party at Cathy's tonight?" Sam asked.

"What I'd really like to do is have a quiet evening with Gram and Andrew. You're welcome to join us if you like," Megan said hopefully.

"I would like that, Megan; thank you. I'll be there."

Megan had slipped badly in her school work and was sure she wasn't going to get the grades needed to go to Dalhousie University in Halifax the following year. Sadie had told her in no uncertain terms that they were both going together or not at all. Her biology, math, and chemistry teachers made course outlines for her to follow and gave her some shortcuts. Under the circumstances, they would even let her try some make-up tests for the ones she'd missed. Her other teachers followed suit as they all believed she could do it; they were there to help her any way they could.

When Joe heard this, he was surprised at the amount of help and generosity that the people of the island were giving to Megan.

Nona grinned from ear to ear: "This is Grand Manan, you know!"

They both laughed. "It sure is, and I love it," said Joe.

Megan went every Tuesday afternoon to a psychologist in St. John. Megan liked her immediately. She was told it could take weeks or months to make progress, but somehow Megan knew it would not take that long.

Megan's life fell into a pattern of therapy sessions. While doing this, she never forgot the conversation she had with Papa Joe as they sat together on a piece of driftwood on Stanley's Beach. They had been walking up and down the beach talking about many things, and then sat on her favourite log.

"Are you still having those nightmares?" Papa Joe asked.

"No, Papa Joe, and I'm so glad they're gone."

"What about your visions?"

"While I was with the gang, I never had visions. Since I've come home, I've had a few short ones, but I can't remember them."

"As you heal, your mind and soul will come back even stronger than before. When they do, you must pay very close attention to your intuition and visions."

"I will, Papa Joe."

"Remember, the more you heal, the clearer things will be. Also, if you need help, please just ask."

As they got up to walk home, he added, "Megan, you are still carrying a lot of anger and hatred for those who killed your parents. You'll have to learn to forgive them. You do not have to forgive the acts, but you must forgive the persons. Face all your fears head-on, because your karma is holding you back. When you rid yourself of your anger and your fear, you'll be amazed how much more free your mind will become. You'll have clearer visions, and they'll come with more frequency. You may even be able to do astral travel." With that, he smiled and winked at her.

"Joe, you're my guardian angel, aren't you?" she asked.

Joe just smiled and leaned down and kissed the top of her head.

As they were walking home, Megan asked Joe, "You mentioned karma when we were talking; what does it mean?"

"It's Hindu in origin. It is the sum of a person's actions during a lifetime. Karma can be good; it can also be bad. In your case, Megan, you have to deal with what happened during your wild time and you must learn to forgive—not only others, but also yourself."

It was about two weeks after her talk with Joe that she had her first clear vision. It was short but encouraging. She was back in the Crystal Cave.

"Welcome my child—or should I say, young lady? You have been through quite an ordeal. How are you feeling?"

"Every day I feel a bit stronger. You knew this was going to happen. Why didn't you warn me?" Megan asked.

"This was something you had to experience first-hand. You needed this so you could grow and become more understanding of what some of your fellow humans are going through. It will help you to empathize and to help them in turn. You're going to be a much stronger woman for it."

"I think I understand," Megan answered. "Forgiving is very hard work, but I'm working on it. It's hard, because I've such a hatred for them."

"It *is* very difficult, Megan, but you must. Please keep working on it. It will come, and all of a sudden, you will know. It will feel as if a huge weight has been lifted from you."

The rest of the group, which had been there before, entered the cave. Together, they were singing and humming the most beautiful sound Megan had ever heard. It went right to the core of her being. She recognized a small part of it; it was what Joe and Lacuna were humming as she surfaced from her coma.

"That is part of what we call the Wam sound that we brought from Sirius a long, long time ago. It is an integral part of the frequencies which hold this galaxy together. Someday, Megan, when you're ready, you'll discover it again; you already know it. We'll all sing together..."

And then, suddenly, Megan awoke to the alarm clock.

Megan frequently went out on Serendipity to help Nona and visit Lacuna. She always felt it was a privilege to be out on the ocean. She had a special experience just before she went off to university. They had stopped to have some lunch. It was a gorgeous August day: the weather was very calm, with hardly a breeze, and the visibility was excellent. She noticed some very high, straight blows to the east. They were finback whales. They waited to see if they'd come closer. There were an abnormal number of the bigger gray seals around; they were behaving differently as they formed a large loose circle around the boat. Not only were their heads out of the water, but their shoulders were as well. They looked like sentries on watch. Megan saw a few finbacks coming closer. They dove and disappeared for a few minutes when Nona shouted, "More are coming from the west!"

Before they knew it, they were watching a loose pod of over a dozen finbacks swimming around them. The seals held their positions; several more finbacks arrived. Surrounding Serendipity, they put on a spectacular show. As the show was getting underway, a large group of white-sided dolphins joined in. The finbacks would dive and come up fairly close to the boat; as they did so, the white-sided dolphins were riding their pressure waves; some came clear out of the water. This went on for several minutes.

Nona thought they were just having a social time. Megan, however, upon hearing their guttural, deep, throaty sounds, realized that this was more than just play. At least twenty-three finbacks and dozens of white-sided dolphins were involved. Megan knew they were communicating with one another and with other whales in the area. She spotted a pod of five or six humpback whales. Lacuna was one of them. They stayed outside of the circle. Soon the activity of the finbacks and the white-sided dolphins began to die down and they began to disperse. Megan had this very strange feeling that they were trying to give her a message, but she couldn't understand it. The humpbacks were still around and moved over to the boat. Lacuna swam over and came alongside. Nona knew Megan and Lacuna were communicating in their own special way. They stayed there for about twenty minutes, and then began their trip home.

Nona was puzzled. "That was really something!" she exclaimed. "I've seen smaller groups do a similar sort of thing, but nothing like that! What do you think it was all about?"

"I knew the finbacks were trying to tell me something," Megan answered. "Lacuna heard them and explained the finbacks were asking me to please help them sometime in the future. I promised I would do everything in my power to do anything to help the whales and dolphins."

As time went on, Megan continued to have her visions. Most were comprised of swimming with the dolphins. Sometimes she woke up laughing at some of the maneuvers they were doing. One of her favourites was when dolphins would come straight out of the water, walking on the surface for a few seconds. When she tried to do this, she would come out of the water, fall straight back down, do side flops, back flops, belly flops, and everything in between; eventually, she succeeded. She came up a bit slower, and as soon as she broke the surface, she started wiggling her tail—and for a second, she was walking on water. She felt fantastic.

"I love life!" Megan said as she woke up.

Sam was frequently on the island during the summer. He spent as much time as he could with Megan. They often went to White Head Island, either by themselves or with friends. It was getting near the end of the summer. Megan and Sam were sitting on the beach relaxing when Sam asked, "Megan, what are your plans for the future?"

"You know how much I love the ocean—and you know about some of the visions I've had. I'll be studying marine biology at Dalhousie University in Nova Scotia. I've pledged myself to follow the same path as my Gram and my mom, and study marine microplankton. It is something I must do. I cannot stand by and watch our oceans slowly die." Tears began to well up in Megan's eyes at the thought of what the oceans—and the entire planet—was up against.

"Meg, I understand. If this is what you want to do, go for it!"

"Thanks for your support, Sam. It means a lot to me."

They started to gather up their things; Megan turned to Sam. "I know you're studying geology and going into your final year. Are you going to graduate school."

"If my marks remain good, I want to do a Master's degree and maybe even a PhD."

"Sam, that's absolutely wonderful. I wish you all the best."

They packed up the remains of their lunch. Both realized that summer was over; they wouldn't see each other except at Christmas and study break. They were very quiet and in their own worlds for the entire walk back to the car. Putting their things in the car, Megan said, "Let's sit on those rocks for a bit; I really don't want to go back yet."

As they sat looking out over the Bay of Fundy, her throat began to tighten. She began to have trouble breathing.

"I won't say goodbye; I can't. It hurts too much," she said.

Sam couldn't help it—he hated seeing her cry, so he carefully put his arm around her.

"Then don't say goodbye. Just say 'so long.'"

"I know. One phase of my life is ending and another is beginning. I'm sad and excited all at the same time. Sam...please, hold me for a moment or two. I'm going to miss you terribly."

"I know, Meg...I know. I'll miss you too."

As he sat there holding her, he felt something deep inside. He realized he was falling in love with her. It took every bit of fortitude to slowly release her.

"Are you okay now? We had better get moving, or we'll miss the last ferry."

"Okay," Megan sighed.

Sam helped her up, and wanted so very much to hold her close to him and kiss her and tell her how he felt. During the drive home, they were both very quiet; when Sam dropped Megan off, he was invited in by Andrew, but he politely declined and left. As he drove away, he called out, "I'll be at the nine-thirty ferry tomorrow morning to see you off!"

He had very mixed feelings as he drove home.

Should I tell her or not? Not now, he decided. They both had enough on their plates. If it was to be, it would work out in the future.

Megan woke early; she had another vision. She was with Ortho on his spaceship.

"I wanted to wish you well, Megan. You are about to embark upon a new leg of your predestined path. Whenever you need our help, you have but to ask."

"How will I know I'm on my predestined path?" she responded.

"You'll simply know. How did you know going to Dalhousie University was the correct choice?"

"I just knew. It *felt* right. I'm very comfortable with my decision. I know I'll be doing postgraduate studies on oceans."

"Very good; you know the feeling. As long as you have that feeling, you are on the correct path."

She smiled as she woke up. She had a heightened feeling of self-confidence. All was well.

Megan was up early and so was Papa Joe. They took their coffee and toast out to the deck. After they ate, Papa Joe lit his pipe.

"I love the smell of pipe smoke; there is something very soothing about it. Do you have any special advice for me?" she asked.

"Megan, you are now a young woman and are heading into a new phase of your life," said Papa Joe. "Know that you are safe and loved by many. You have a phenomenal support group; never hesitate to use it. You must try to live in the present. Take the best memories from the past and the lessons you've learned along the way, and let the rest go. You must live in the now."

"You do, don't you, Papa Joe?"

"Yes, honey, I do. Once I learned to do it, I've been at peace with myself."

"You once told me, Papa Joe, that it was not easy to forgive someone who has hurt you deeply. One must learn to forgive."

"Megan, I was once so angry and full of hatred that it almost killed me. I was an alcoholic—a bad one."

Megan was surprised at hearing this and asked, "How did you overcome it?"

"One never really does. I had a couple of really good friends who never gave up on me. Through their example and caring, I made it."

"Were you ever married, Papa Joe?" Megan paused: "I'm sorry...perhaps I should not have asked."

"No, Megan, it's okay. Yes, I was. She left me while I was serving in the US Navy. That's when I started to drink heavily. I've not heard from her since. I never remarried."

Papa Joe began to hum. Megan recognized the melody and she quietly joined in. Joe looked at her and smiled.

"Papa Joe, where did you learn that song?"

"My grandfather taught it to me many years ago. His father taught it to him. It came down through generation after generation. Where it actually originated, I don't really know, but when I hum it, something happens inside, and it makes me feel very peaceful and content."

"Me too, Papa Joe—and I think I know where it came from."

"Where?' he asked, smiling.

"In a vision of being in a crystal cave in Atlantis long ago, I heard the most beautiful, etheric music being sung. It was mostly hummed; what you hum is a small part of it. I was told one day I would remember it and that we would all sing it together. It has something to do with what she called the Wam which they brought to Earth from the planet Sirius."

"You know, my grandfather told of a legend that says, 'When the world is one and at peace, this entire song will be sung by millions of beings.'"

"Joe, you know Lacuna knows the bit we know and much more. I wonder…"

Nona came out on the deck. "I guess we'd better get ready to go. Andrew has put Megan's things in the car."

Megan kissed Joe as she stood up; she could tell that he was contemplating her words.

He smiled again, saying, "Could be, could be…"

There was a crowd at the wharf in North Head to see her off. Most of her friends from school were there. Many of them would also be leaving in a couple of days to go to college or university. Sam, Sadie, and their father Roger, along with Papa Joe, crowded around her, wishing her luck and all the best. Andrew and Nona stood close by, smiling; they were very proud.

Nona smiled and whispered, "I know that Mary is thrilled." Tears began to slowly run down her cheeks.

"So long," said Megan to each one as she hugged them.

Sadie was crying. "I'll really miss you, Megan." Next to her was Sam. She looked Sam in the eye, and said very softly as she hugged him, "It's okay, Sam. I know, I know. It'll all be okay; you know I have to do this."

He smiled. He couldn't believe his ears. He hugged her and whispered, "I'll see you down the road. Be careful."

Next, she hugged Papa Joe.

"I know you are my very special angel," she said.

Thanking everyone and waving, she joined Andrew and Nona as they ran for the ferry.

The first several weeks were very busy for Megan as she was getting settled. The first time she got home was for the Christmas and New Year holidays. She was very excited to visit with everyone, especially Sam, who was also home. They spent a lot of time together chatting about this and that. Sam had been accepted at Queen's University in Ontario to study for his Master's degree. Megan was pleased.

"Sam, that's great news! I'm so pleased for you. It probably means we'll not see one another as frequently. I will miss that; however, both of us have to do what we have to do. We can phone one another and e-mail one another often."

"I know, Megan. I'll miss you too. You're correct; we each must follow our individual paths for another few years. We're both going to be so busy with our studies that time will fly by."

"Sam, I know you love me—and I think you know I love you, too" she said honestly.

They hugged one another, both of them knowing in their hearts that they would be spending their future together.

The night before they returned to their respective universities, Sam took her out for dinner. The two of them spent a very quiet evening together discussing what their futures might look like. When they parted, they vowed to each to go steady, even though they would be miles apart.

Sam drove Megan home. They hugged and kissed, holding one another.

That night, Megan had a very special vision with Ortho. Seated in a semicircle were at least two dozen others ranging in age from six years old to their early twenties.

"Hello, Megan. Please come and sit beside me. We thought you might like to meet some of your fellow humans who have similar abilities to yours."

After introductions were made, Ortho told her, "There are hundreds of you with special abilities, and more are arriving each day."

"Why are we here today?" a little boy with red hair asked.

"To start with, you're going to get to know one another, and you will come to realize that each one of you is here for a reason. Many of you will be working together to help heal Earth. Each of you has your own unique part to play, and some of you will unite into teams. If the humans currently living on Earth do not change their ways, Earth may not survive. It is going to need all the help it can get. We see positive movements; however, it will not happen fast enough," Ortho said.

"Well, can't you help us?" asked the little redheaded boy.

"We are allowed to help, but we are not permitted to interfere. That is why we are in contact with thousands of other young people and children at this time. We'll continue to call on each of you, and you'll call on us. Remember, none of you are working on your own. Each of you will grow stronger, and in some cases, you will develop different special abilities. Before you can awaken these, you must rid yourselves of all negative thoughts and feelings and learn to face your fears and conquer them. Once you do this, nothing will stop you from fulfilling your purpose here on Earth." Ortho looked around. "Go now, and know you are not alone."

Ortho spoke directly to Megan, telling her, "Megan, you've chosen to study marine bacteria and viruses, which is exactly what you are called to do. Because of their extreme importance as a linchpin in the whole marine system, it is critical that the study of them be brought to the forefront so they can be protected."

"Are you saying that something is going to happen that will cause this 'linchpin' to fail and cause a catastrophic collapse in the oceans?" Megan asked.

"That is a distinct possibility. That is why you are going to be needed in a key position on Earth when and if it happens."

Megan was astounded. Waking up, she thought, *I will do my best.*

She thought she heard a voice from the distance saying, "We will help you."

Even though Megan was away at university, she was keeping her appointments as required with her psychologist. After one of these appointments, she went home to the island to visit. Megan was looking at some of the books lying around.

"Gram, you're reading about spirituality. Is this a new area of interest for you?"

"Not really; it is a bit of a story, actually."

"Please tell me about it. Is it about religion?"

"First of all, you can be spiritual and not be affiliated with any religion; or, you can be if you wish. Spirituality is a belief rejecting the idea that the only way of furthering one's spiritual growth is through some form of organized religion. Spirituality is a way of allowing one to discover the essence of who we are, why we're are here, or even whether there is life after death. I feel very spiritual when I'm experiencing the sheer beauty and complexity of the ocean, when I see a gorgeous sunset, when I hear a moving piece music, or see a newborn baby."

"You mean, when you experience something with your heart," Megan added. "What I feel when I love you, Andrew, and Lacuna, or when I'm seeing visions can be called a spiritual experience."

"Only if you're truly moved by it. It is a way of seeing and feeling things you can't explain."

"Does one have to believe in God in order to be spiritual?" Megan asked.

"If you mean the way some religions portray God—no, not necessarily, though many who are spiritual do belong to organized religions. Many who are spiritual believe that there is some form of a higher force."

"You were brought up and trained as a scientist and taught if one can't prove something exists, it doesn't. How did you become interested in spirituality?"

"I think as a child, I was very spiritual. I went to school, and attended Sunday school. Somehow I got brainwashed. Instead of thinking for myself, I accepted what I was taught; I didn't question it. I remember that I eventually questioned what was being done and taught in the name of religion. I drifted away from going to church. I'm not saying everyone should do this. Everyone has the freedom of choice. You must at all times be true to yourself."

Nona served tea and biscuits as she continued sharing.

"I did start to really question some of the science and the way it was being taught at university," she added. "Take the theory of organic evolution, which by definition means that living organisms change over time. This is true. We simply have to look at the fossil records to see it. I questioned that the Darwinian Theory was taught as a fact. If one questioned it, you were given a vacant look or told to shut up. People forget it's a theory."

"But Gram, wasn't Darwin right?"

"To a large degree, I think he was. It was the interpretation—'Survival of the Fittest'—which has caused a problem...the idea that evolution occurs only by competition. I believe that many are changing that expression to 'Survival of the Best Adapted.' This allows more ideas to be considered."

"I understand; but tell me more about your exploration of spirituality, please."

"When I really started to take it very seriously was after your grandfather died. I was devastated. I had a very dear friend who spent hours talking to me. She read parts of books on spirituality. For a long time I listened, but I didn't absorb it. Then one day, out on Serendipity, we came across a courtship pod of right whales which came close to the boat. One female was surrounded by several males. The female rolled over, and in mid-roll, she stopped and we were eye to eye. Her eye was huge and ancient. It was an infinitely calm gaze and somewhat distant. There was neither warmth, nor friendliness, nor coldness, nor indifference; it was remote and calm, filled with the wisdom of the ages. Her soul was on a higher plane. When I met the eye of this whale, I understood how far we are from God and how close whales are to the Creator. They want and have tried, over and over, to share their knowledge with us. I wondered, *Have they truly given up on us, or do they still want to make contact?* It was because of that very brief encounter that I began to really heal and read everything I could about spirituality—and I still do. I know from watching you and Lacuna that they have not given up!"

Megan was enthralled by what Nona had just told her. "Gram, may I borrow some of these books?" Nona picked out two or three; she was happy to share her spiritual journey with Megan.

All evening, Megan read. That night, she found herself back in the Crystal Cave in Atlantis.

"Well, you're home for another visit," The lady in white said. She was sitting beside Megan. "You must realize you are well on the road to healing—physically, mentally and spiritually."

"Why do humans have to go through so much anxiety and pain?" Megan asked.

"It is all part of finding the real you. It can be very painful at times. As you grow and get to know yourself—your *true* self— you will find it is a beautiful experience."

"How do I do that?"

"You are already doing it, Megan. You still haven't come to grips with your parents' deaths. There is still a lot of anger, and the inability to forgive is still inside you. I know you're working on it through various avenues. Follow their advice; only work with those which work for you."

"I still feel that I need some extra guidance regarding this. Can you help me?"

"Yes; write on a piece of paper the act and how it makes you feel deep inside."

"I've tried. I get very angry and I put it away."

"Keep doing it, Megan. The more you do it, the more you'll be able to face that anger. Over time, your anger will lessen. I know it is extremely difficult; but, you must do this."

She was determined to follow this advice.

At breakfast she asked, "Gram, did you go through a time when you were in conflict between science and spirituality?"

"I did, initially. Sometimes I felt like there was a war going on in my mind. Slowly, I came to realize science is okay in its place. There is so much going on out there that can't be proven by science. Just because it can't be proven does not mean it does not exist. Our western way of thinking has done a lot of damage in the long run."

"In what way?"

"I feel there are two major factors. First: science, technology and medicine have become so advanced and powerful that they seem to take over our lives; they are almost like gods to us. Second, we are so inundated with the need to win, at any cost. Competition and greed are very ingrained in many humans. They've become brainwashed. We've real problems thinking about and practicing spirituality. With the arrival of the New Age, the trend seems to be changing. Caring and respecting one another and the environment in which we live is becoming more and more important. We are not separate from one another, nor from the environment in which we live."

"I've just been reading about that!" Megan said excitedly. "We are not separate from one another, but are interconnected with each other and the world we live in. We must respect one another, respect our planet, and stop abusing her before it is too late. We got into a discussion at university this week about quantum physics. I'm not talking about the mathematical part; we were talking about some of the findings at the subatomic level." Megan went on to explain further.

"A quantum is a discrete quantity of light, and our entire world occurs as extremely rapid short bursts of light which are very fast and close together. When you see a bird flying, it is made up of a series of individual events happening so fast that we can't see the individual events; instead, we view it like a video or movie. These bursts of light are *quanta*. Quantum physics allows for such theories, which explain such things as parallel universes, and time travel. It allows for several scenarios or possibilities to exist in a parallel fashion at the same time. Experiments in Britain and the USA showed that a quantum particle's behaviour could be altered by people being in a room where the experiment was being conducted. When the number of observers increased, their influence on the particles also increased. Because quanta occur in bursts, there are spaces between them.

"There is a concept of parallel universes, where several possibilities could exist simultaneously, like a series of parallel highways. The spaces between the quanta are called 'choice points' which are points in time when one can jump or cross a bridge between possibilities. You can change the outcome of something by altering your beliefs."

"So there might be a lot of truth in the old saying 'mind over matter.'" Nona said as she chuckled. "Megan, did you know that there are two satellites in orbit that measure the strength of Earths' magnetic fields? Twice in recent years, they've picked up a marked spike; one was when Princess Diana was killed, and the second one was 9/11 when the twin towers in New York came down. It's called 'collective consciousness.' When a very large number of humans are experiencing the same emotions, an electrical field of some sort forms beyond our physical bodies and connects up with other similar electrical fields.

"There is a quote of Albert Einstein's that is very appropriate here. It went something like this: 'We require a new manner of thinking, if mankind is to survive.' I find this quotation to be very thought-provoking," Nona said, clearing the table. Megan joined her.

Now I know why Ortho wanted me to read this material, she realized.

* * *

During the first decade of the millennium, a group of very wealthy young people whose families had made their money by investing in such areas as oil, gas, and various other unsustainable Earth's resources began to realize that these resources would soon be running out. They started to put their money into banks, preferred shares, and so forth. Some of their children who were aged between twenty and forty lived their lives the same way their parents did—using and abusing the planet's resources with no consideration for others. They didn't care for the environment. Their attitude was, "If it's there, I'll take it, even if I don't need it." It was an attitude of entitlement.

Within this wealthy class was a small but growing number who were starting families; they had the foresight to realize that Earth was in bad shape. It was overcrowded with humans and there was an out-of-control birth rate. Earth couldn't feed them; disease and starvation was rampant in densely-populated areas. Natural resources were running out; drinkable fresh water was becoming less and less available; pollution on the earth, as well as in the air and the ocean was out of control.

A few of this generation were sitting around a pool at a very expensive resort in the tropics. A sixteen-year-old girl came up to her father and asked, "Dad, why are we here?"

He gave her a flip answer. A young lad came over to support her.

"Sir, I think your daughter wants to know why we are living it up without a care in the world while our planet is dying; why are we doing nothing about it?"

The father had no answer.

This got the attention of several other young people who came over. They joined in the discussion. It culminated with a core of young people vowing they were going to learn more about the situation and investigate what they could do to help the planet. Their initial motto was RESPECT EARTH—DON'T ABUSE HER.

Word spread rapidly throughout the world via the Internet. Within months, they had several thousand people of all ages and walks of life, from schoolchildren to senior citizens—all with a common desire: to find a solution to Earth's problems so their children and grandchildren could have a decent, healthy, safe place to live.

The next step was to build a type of think-tank—a lab complex—and to hire top people from all over the world to come and work there. Together they hoped these people would work as a team. There would be no interference with their work by the owners. There would be absolutely no pressure to compete for research funds. All would be paid equally and there would be no pressure to publish. The idea was to encourage free thinking with the future of Earth being of paramount importance. They chose Canada to build this complex for several reasons: Canada still had many of the natural resources, and their economy was relatively strong. It bordered on four of the five Great Lakes, and of great importance and concern was that it also bordered on three of Earth's oceans: the Atlantic, the Arctic, and the Pacific. The lab complex was built near Halifax, because of the strength and the reputation of Bedford Institute nearby, as well as the relative closeness to MIT in Massachusetts and several other federal labs in the Maritimes and New England.

This complex was started in 2005 and was due to be finished in about 2010. At that time, they would search the world for personnel to work there. It would start with several areas of study and research: economy, communications, medicine, nutrition and food production, epidemiology, oceanography, chemistry, physics, and biology. In biology, the emphasis was to be put on the marine environment.

PART THREE
2010 – 2020

When Megan was in the process of finishing her post-doctorate at Yale, she was asked to come for an interview at what was called The Centre for the Future. Megan was ecstatic about the possibility of working there. They were very impressed with her work, especially in the area of marine microplankton and her ability in the bioengineering of DNA. Megan was thrilled; the position carried a lot of prestige and she would be closer to home, which meant that she would see Sam more often.

After she left for Glasgow University, they had seen each other during holidays, but only for brief periods of time. When he heard she got the job in Halifax, he was ecstatic. He was going to take a week's holiday so he could be with her.

Megan came home to a true Grand Manan welcome. Everyone was there; even Sam had made a special trip home from Australia to be there. They had a huge dinner and a party followed. Megan was overwhelmed and made sure she talked to everyone. At the end of the evening, she and Sam went for a quiet walk on the beach. Sam was so thrilled for her; she would be working in the Maritimes. He was currently working in Melbourne for the Canadian government on earthquakes, and had about three years left in his contract. The two of them had already discussed the obstacles they faced in trying to keep their relationship strong over such a long distance. Tonight they were discussing it again.

"Sam, I'm tired, and we're going in circles. If it's a nice day tomorrow, could we go over to White Head? I promise we'll discuss this more."

Sam put his arm around her and kissed her. "Why don't we camp over there?" he said.

Megan looked at him and gave him a sweet smile. "I would like that."

Driving home that night, Sam promised himself that, out of his love and respect for Megan, he would let her take the lead.

When Megan came into the house, Nona was still up.

"Well, you look like the cat that swallowed the canary," Nona said as she was putting away dishes.

"I hope you don't mind, and I hope you'll understand...Sam and I are planning on going camping on White Head for a day or two," Megan said, blushing.

"Well, it's about time!" Nona said. She laughed and gave Megan a big hug.

"Has it really been that obvious?"

"Since the day you said goodbye to Sam—when you were leaving to go to Scotland—I could tell he was crazy about you and that you loved him, too. Let your heart lead you, Megan, and go with the flow. Now go and try to get a good night's sleep. I'll pack a picnic basket for you to take with you."

Sam arrived the next morning, wearing a bright smile as he came bouncing up the steps.

"Hi Gram," he said to Nona. He'd called her that since he was a little boy.

"Good morning, dear," Nona answered warmly.

Sam picked up Megan's bag and the basket. "Wow, this basket is heavy!" he commented. "Thanks, Gram."

"My pleasure," Nona said. Megan joined them at the front door.

"You two have a wonderful time," Nona said.

The pair smiled and waved, and made their way to the car.

Soon they were quietly driving to Ingalls Head. They watched the ferry come around the head of the wharf; it slowly glided into the loading ramp.

Sam turned to Megan. She looked at him.

"I know, it's going to be okay. We're going to have a wonderful time, aren't we?" she said.

"Yes, we are," he said as he raised her hand to his lips. Something like an electrical shock wave went right through Megan. It was something she'd never experienced with any other man she had been with—and there had been a few.

Once they arrived at the beach, they noticed that there were three families at the nearest end—but the rest the beach was empty. Breathing a sigh of relief, they walked to their favourite spot near the far end. Sam pitched the tent on a grassy area among some evergreens. Megan opened the basket, and Sam sat on the blanket. Megan was laughing as she pulled out a bottle of white wine.

"Sam, this is exactly the same wine we had the day before I left for Scotland. Oh, my Lord, there's another one." They both laughed.

"That's our Gram!" Sam said, and he poured them each a glass.

"Here's to us," they said in unison.

They laid a small fire and lit it. As the fire crackled in the twilight, the sun was at the precise point where everything in its path turns to gold.

"This is my favourite time of day," Megan said. She began to hum, and rested her head on his shoulder.

"Mine too," Sam said. He paused as he listened to Megan humming. "Meg, what is that beautiful piece you're humming? I love it."

"It's something Papa Joe taught me years ago. There are no words to go with it. It's a very haunting and beautiful melody. I love it." The two of them sat there while she taught him the tune, and as they hummed together, they watched the sun slowly disappear as it surrendered to the night. The colours were unbelievably beautiful, starting with layers of gold mixed in with reddish and purple highlights. The wisps of white clouds danced across the sky and glowed in brilliant reds and oranges.

Megan was quietly and deeply moved, and her eyes welled up.

"I can't believe I'm finally home—but you're still going to have to go back to Australia. Sam, it's so far away," she said. She turned her face towards him, and he gently wiped her tears away with his thumbs. Cradling her head in both of his hands, he lowered his face to hers and, ever so softly, he licked away the last traces of her tears.

His whole being was trembling and he could feel the blood surging in his body. He wanted her, but at the same time, he loved her so much, and he did not want to hurt her. He pulled away slightly so he could see her, and he looked deep into her eyes.

She stopped crying and whispered, "I love you, Sam. I love you so much. I always have." She was overcome by a feeling of unprecedented peace; in fact, she felt as though she had just moved into another dimension. Time seemed to stop, and the only thing that mattered was that they were together and in love.

Sam stood up, bringing her with him; he softly caressed her face as they explored each other. He held her tight as he could feel her knees begin to buckle. Their lips met; they were hungry for one another, and their passion and desire grew as they kissed. At one point Sam stopped so he could see her face.

"Maybe we should go to the tent," he said.

Megan looked at him and softly said, "No." She kissed him and whispered, "Here, Sam...on the beach."

They held one another, still kissing. He slid his hands up under her sweater, and caressed her nipples and breasts. With a sense of urgency, he removed her sweater, and held her close to him. Moving his hands lower, he quickly removed her bathing suit as she removed his. They sank to their knees, still caressing each other with their hands and tongues as he gently lowered her to the blanket.

His eyes surveyed her completely; he had never seen such a beautiful body.

"Oh Meg, I love you," he whispered.

This time when they kissed, he slid his hand over her abdomen, paused for a second, and slowly slid it between her legs.

She let out a low groan and whispered, "Please, Sam—*now!*" She never had felt such passion or desire. For the first time in her life, she felt truly alive.

"Now we're going to move into the tent, my love, and we can carry on where it's warm," Sam said, sweeping her up in his arms.

The next morning, they awoke to beautiful sunny day.

As they lay together, Sam whispered to her, "This is not the way I planned it."

She turned to look at him, wondering what he meant.

"Meg, I love you," he said. "Will you marry me?"

Megan's eyes filled with tears. "But, Sam...you're going on a contract to Australia for three years, and I can't quit my job. I promised to stay there for at least seven years." She began to cry. "I really want to say yes, Sam, but…"

"We'll be engaged, and I'll come home as often as I possibly can," he interjected.

"And I can come to Australia, too. Oh Sam, I don't want to be away from you that long!"

"Meg, we'll work something out. I promise you we will."

"Oh, Sam—then yes, I *will* marry you!" she said.

"There's only one problem," he added. "I was so excited when I packed to get ready to come here that I left the ring at home."

They both laughed.

"Well, let's go and get it, and tell our folks. We can come back here later today," Megan suggested.

"The ever-practical Megan; okay, we can leave our stuff here—no one will touch it. It's Grand Manan, after all."

When they told both families the news, they were ecstatic. They were not surprised, however, as each had a feeling that this had been coming for some time.

After spending time with their families, they returned to the campsite. Sam got down on his knees and asked her to marry him, the way he had envisioned it. They spent another night filled with love and passion.

Sam was leaving for Australia the next day.

The next day, when it was time for Sam to depart, he went to Megan's where they could say their goodbyes in private. They were both in tears, and held each other tight, dreading the moment when they would have to let one another go.

Reluctantly, Sam left. A few minutes later, Megan drove down to the end of Fishermen's Wharf. As the ferry was pulling away, Sam was on the stern deck, and they waved with both arms to one another.

Megan got back in her car and returned home in tears; Nona was there to comfort her.

"I have a surprise for you; I suspect it will help soothe what ails you," Nona said with a smile.

Megan saw a basket with food and a thermos. She stopped crying as the realization of what Nona meant dawned on her.

"We're going out to sea!" Megan exclaimed.

Nona smiled and nodded.

Megan had been waiting for this moment for several months. It was not that she hadn't visited Lacuna since she left for Scotland; in fact, she'd flown home a couple of times, but she'd only seen her once when Lacuna was on her summer feeding ground in the Bay of Fundy.

With a burst of renewed enthusiasm, Megan put on some warm clothes, and out they went.

Once they were out to sea, Lacuna came out to greet the boat—with her new baby tagging along behind her.

"Oh Lacuna, he's gorgeous! I'll call him Shadow," Megan said; she was beside herself with excitement.

Shadow was swimming around and around boat. He would dive and come up on one side or the other. When he did this, he would roll onto his side and raise his long, thin white flipper, waving it around. After several minutes, he began to calm down.

"Oh Lacuna—I love him! He really loves to show off," Megan said, laughing.

Then Lacuna, Shadow, and Megan went quiet for a while. Soon, the baby whale was hungry, so they left.

It's so nice to be home. Now I'm fairly close by; I'll be over here as much as I possibly can, Megan thought.

During dinner, Andrew asked, "When do you start your new job? You must be getting excited!"

"Yes, I'm *very* excited; I start in a couple weeks," answered Megan. "I'll have to go to Halifax this coming week and find a place to live and see more of the facility where I'll be."

"The whole architectural concept of that facility is friendly and welcoming," Nona said. She'd toured the facility during its grand opening. "Education of the public—from all walks of life—is one of their main purposes, and the organic approach to the design encourages this."

"Who will you be working for?" asked Andrew.

"I'll be working on my own, but at the same time, I'll be on a team of researchers which will be collaborating with other teams. I'm thrilled! It's a very different approach to research—and a very welcome one."

Early the next morning, the news on television announced that there had been an 8.2 magnitude earthquake in the Pacific, just off the South American coast.

"That is two this month. I swear they've been increasing in frequency, especially when you look at it from a global point of view. For the past few decades, it seems this old earth is just ripping herself apart!" Andrew said.

"Also, the strength of the storms—especially the winds along the east coast—have been more frequent and stronger," Nona added. "And along with the increase in earthquakes and storms, new diseases are arising and spreading quickly in heavily-overpopulated areas. They're literally wiping out thousands of people at an alarming rate, and there is no known cure for them. These diseases seem to run their course, disappear, and then pop up again in an area far away from where they started. It's driving the medical people wild. They can't treat it—and it is instant death if you get it. They can't seem to find the source."

Andrew turned Megan. "What do you know about the situation with the marine environment? I know it's not good—but how bad is it?"

"It's bad, Andrew; we've already lost about twenty percent of the phytoplankton due to the increased acidification, and we're beginning to see the trickle-down effect in the very noticeable decrease in fish populations worldwide."

"What will you be working on?" Andrew asked as he began to clear the table.

"We've lost a large fraction of our marine bacteria and viruses, and they are vital to virtually every marine ecosystem there is. There are two major species of microscopic cyanobacteria with as many as 100,000 to 200,000 bacteria in a drop of seawater. These cells break down the large and small pieces of dying or dead plants and animals, thus releasing nutrients back into the system for photosynthesis to occur. The viruses are even smaller. They don't have cell membranes; they exist as naked DNA. They need to infect other organisms in order to survive. Try imagining millions of viruses in a drop of seawater. Their densities are higher closer to shore, where most of the nutrients are located."

"What do these viruses do?" Andrew asked.

"Viruses, in order to survive, must infect other living cells. They use the host cell's DNA to replicate; this kills the host cell. In the marine environment, it is the viruses that control the number of bacteria. In other words, they keep the ocean's food webs in balance. You could say that the viruses and bacteria constitute the linchpin of marine ecosystems."

"Are we humans and our pollution responsible for all this?" Andrew asked.

"We're currently in a natural cycle; Earth warms up before it cools to what some call a mini ice age. It won't happen in our lifetime. It's a very natural cycle; however, we certainly have greatly contributed to the disastrous state that our planet is in—not only to the oceans, but to the land and also our atmosphere. We're slowly killing our planet and ourselves along with it."

Another news bulletin came over the TV.

"Thousands have died, and thousands more are dying, due to a huge outbreak of yet another bacterial disease in India," said the news anchor.

"Oh my God—this is the third one, and probably the worst one in two years! What's causing these diseases?" Nona asked.

Megan was at a loss for words. They all looked at the TV report with grim expressions, but none of them had answers.

* * *

Gwen and her fellow investigative reporters around the world had been busy over the previous several years, gathering evidence on the top-secret labs worldwide. These were Black Ops at their blackest; they were particularly watching the CESR in Nevada. Initially, the same people gathered there annually. More recently, one or two would come for a day or so, and others at different times. They had a mole in the security force on the second subterranean floor. He'd been able to get some photos with a tiny pen camera. The results were not great, but with computer enhancement and comparing flight plans, along with other data, the investigative reporters were able to put names to four of the five:

1. Wolfgang Schmitt from Germany, an extremely wealthy industrialist
2. Chin Chang from China, a wealthy, secretive businessman
3. Jean Peters, an American woman, hailing from a wealthy family who had made their fortune from oil
4. Richard Worthington from South Africa (who had replaced Maria Downs).

Gwen and her colleagues were developing quite the file on these people. Of special interest to them was what businesses they were in and if there was any connection between them; any unusual movements, activities, and meetings were highlighted.

A few questionable links between them had been discovered, but there was nothing solid enough to act upon. The investigative team had also turned their scrutiny towards any suspicious mass deaths from unknown causes. They were carrying on what Matt had started many years ago, and it was here that they were beginning to make some progress.

Out of seventy-one incidents over the previous ten years, ten had been caused by naturally-occurring bacteria or accidental poisonings. That left sixty-one suspicious occurrences resulting anywhere from seventeen to 304 deaths per incident. In these cases, one hundred percent of those infected died within twelve to thirty-six hours. About six years earlier, there had been a jump in the total numbers that died. Two occurred in large, heavily-populated areas: the first resulted in over 3000 deaths in China, and then four months later, 6350 died elsewhere in Asia. From then on, the numbers grew exponentially until they reached 200,650—in this case, this number was on a small, heavily-populated island in Indonesia. It had, in fact, wiped out the entire population of the island. Then, the team received the news revealing that there may be over a million who have already died in the most recent epidemic in India.

Gwen phoned her counterpart in India. "Do they have any idea of the cause yet?"

"Not really; I was talking with a doctor, and he said that the symptoms in this outbreak appear to be different. He didn't offer me any details. He promised to get back to me later."

"Phone me right away when you have anything—anything at all," said Gwen.

This whole business is getting more and more suspicious. It's almost like there is a third or fourth party involved, she thought.

* * *

George Dean was furious.

"Anin, are you and your people responsible for this disaster in India? And if you are, why was I not informed beforehand?"

"Take it easy, George—we're not responsible; we've people looking into it. We think that it is a mutation of a naturally-occurring bacteria."

"You assured me at start that there would be no interference from your friends in space."

"If it's not natural and we didn't do it, then we'll find out who did and put them out of business," Anin said. He was adamant.

I wonder if I can really trust him any longer—but, then what choice do I have? thought George.

* * *

Gwen continued her research into Matthew Stone's death. She had a lot of work to do on the current project on drug companies. As a result, she didn't get to Megan's sketches for a several weeks.

I hope they are accurate enough to give us a match of some kind, she thought.

She reread the original file of Matthew's. Next she brought up the file on the lab where Matt had worked. She already had a list of over 200 employees. The names of the scientists who worked on the lowest floors were not there. She called Jamie, a computer-savvy friend who was also a cryptographer, and told him what she was trying to do.

"If the list is well-hidden, it may take quite a while to find. I'll do my best," said Jamie.

Gwen thought for a moment. "Narrow your search by looking at the five years before and after the year Stone was killed.

"I'll see what I can do for you."

Two days later, Jamie had managed to get the full laboratory directory. "It took some doing," he said. "It should be showing up in your email now, Gwen."

Gwen opened the attachment, and scanned down the file until she found the name of Dr. Matthew Stone. Along with his name, there were several others. By crossing off all the female names, she was left with six male names.

The man I'm looking for has to be one of the three who worked closest with Matt, because he trusted whoever did this to him, she thought. She noted that he had two lab assistants. *If I'm really lucky, one of these two will match Megan's sketches. All I have to do is find a photo of each of these guys.*

Being an investigative reporter, Gwen had cultivated many contacts. One of these contacts happened to work for the government licensing office in Boston. She had done him a huge favour a few years back. She called and asked him to look up two specific names.

"If you find current licenses, please scan a copy of their photos to me," she said. Her contact had hesitated, but he owed her.

A promise is a promise, he thought.

Within an hour, the email attachment came through with only one photograph—and it didn't match Megan's sketch.

Damn it—I knew this was a long shot, she thought.

She called her contact again. "The photo you sent is not the man I'm looking for," she said. Can you keep looking?"

"There's nothing in the current files. I'm going back through earlier years. I've just found one from about fifteen years ago. I'm sending it to you now."

Another email came through. She compared this one to Megan's sketch.

Well, I'll be damned...we have a match. Now I have to find you, Mark Adams.

She immediately got on the phone and called a private investigative firm she'd used a few times; she hired them to find this Adams person for her. All she could do in the meantime was wait.

A month later, she called for an update.

"Gwen, it's been very difficult; two months after Stone's death, Adams disappeared. We are currently working on the premise that he changed his name and is hiding. We found his sister in Houston; she has not heard from him. We'll keep looking—however, it doesn't look promising."

After several months, Gwen heard back from the private investigator.

"Gwen, we found Mark Adams. He lives in Houston, Texas, under an alias. He's in hospital with terminal cancer and is not expected to live."

"How much time does he have?"

"A few days, a couple weeks at most. We tried to see him—however he is at the stage where it is family only. His sister is currently looking after him. We talked to the nurses; he is lucid and has requested to see the minister."

"A deathbed confession won't be much use, because of the confidentiality of the situation," said Gwen.

"That is true. Hopefully he will talk to his sister, Martha, and tell her what he did. We will let you know immediately if anything transpires."

It was an extremely hot day in Houston and Martha had been rushing around getting her errands done. She was out of breath and perspiring heavily when she arrived at the hospital. She took the elevator to the third floor. As she was about to enter Mark's room, she could hear voices.

A nurse stopped her. "Your brother is talking with his minister. I'll get you a coffee and you can wait in the quiet room."

Martha sat all alone in the small room. She turned off the TV and gazed into space. She was thinking of the small farm where they had grown up together. There was just the two of them; she was three years older than Mark. They were not really close until he moved to Houston three months earlier and had sworn her to secrecy. He had never married. Martha, however, was happily married with three children.

She'd noticed that her brother had changed. He used to be a very happy-go-lucky man; now he was much quieter, and at times, introspective. She put it down to his work as a lab technician in an extremely busy hospital. She felt that something had happened to him while he worked in Boston. Maybe it was a love affair which had ended badly. And why had he changed his name? Martha had made up her mind: she was going to have a serious talk with him, as he only had days to live.

"Martha, you may see him now," said the nurse. As they walked into his room, he turned away.

She quietly approached his bedside and softly said, "Mark, it's me Martha."

He turned and looked at her. He had been crying; his eyes were bloodshot, and were swollen with large black circles below them. He took her hand, and in a very weak voice said, "Martha, I have done something horrible." He was trembling; he took a couple of deep breaths and asked her if she'd brought the pad and pen he'd asked for.

"Yes, I did, and a digital recording device, too—in case you wanted to record something for the children."

"We'll record what I'm about to say. I also want you to write it down." He paused and began to speak. "I'm going to tell you something I did a long time ago. Several years ago, I killed a man."

Martha was shocked. "Mark! What happened?"

"I was working in the Boston lab. I never told you, but I was a technician in one of the covert units working on viruses which I found out later were part of a biological weapons program."

Martha was astonished. "Isn't that illegal?"

"Yes...and virtually every major world power is covertly working on some form of it. There was a scientist—a Dr. Matthew Stone—who must have stumbled onto something the lab was doing. He was about to talk, and they wanted him silenced." He stopped and gathered strength to continue. "I was ordered to infect him with a virus, but not the one we were working on. They told me it would make him very ill. Pat O'Brian, the head of security, ordered it."

"Why did you do it?" Martha asked.

Tears began to flow. "If I didn't do it, they would have killed you, Martha. I had no choice. They held that threat over me, and they had my name changed and moved me around the country. I'm dying and had to tell someone. I confessed to the minister." He squeezed her hand. "Can you ever forgive me? Martha, I never meant to kill him."

"I know, Mark. It was really an accident. You were used; of course I forgive you."

The two of them sat quietly for a few minutes.

"What do you want me to do with the note and recording?" Martha asked.

"Don't give it to the police. In my wallet, you'll find an email address. Martha—you must email the information to this individual before you leave the hospital," Mark insisted.

"I will, Mark. I'll do it right now at their courtesy computer. You rest. I'll do this and be right back. I love you, Mark."

"I love you too, Martha."

She kissed him on the forehead, squeezed his hand, and left. Her head was spinning. She couldn't believe what she'd heard.

She placed the digital recording device in a secure place in her bag and, hugging the bag close to her body, decided to think about what to do with it later. With the note in her hand, she rushed to the first floor and, as calmly as she could, spoke to the hospital concierge about using the courtesy computer. Once she was online, she sent an email to a Gwen Ross in Boston. Then she immediately had the original hard copy of the note shredded.

As soon as her email was sent, she logged out and cleared the history tab on the computer. Feeling an increasing sense of urgency, she ran to the elevator to go back to the third floor. When she entered Mark's room, there were two nurses at his side.

"He's asking for you," one of them said quietly. As she approached his bed, she could see that he was having trouble breathing. Tears welled up in her eyes as she took his hand. She leaned over and whispered, "It's done."

Mark looked up and smiled. "Thank you Martha...I love you," he answered.

His already-weakened grip on her hand weakened more, and a moment later, he was gone.

* * *

Gwen was in the kitchen making a cup of soup and a sandwich when she heard the soft beep of an alert on her computer, indicating that an email had come in. She went over to the laptop and checked, and was completely thunderstruck at what she saw.

"Oh my God!" she exclaimed. She carefully read the message three times, and then called her investigator's number.

"Is Mark Adams still alive?" she asked.

"I just got a call from my agent. Mark passed away a few minutes ago. He had two visitors today: a minister and his sister. She stayed for a while and took some notes, left for a few minutes, and came back just in time to say goodbye to him."

"Do you know if the sister was ever followed?"

"No, she wasn't, Gwen."

The next morning, Gwen made three phone calls. The first was to a Detective Boyle in the Boston police force; he was someone she trusted. She would meet him at ten forty-five am. Afterwards, she called Holly and sent her a copy of the email. Then she called Nona.

"Nona, remember those sketches Megan gave to me?"

"Yes, I do. Don't tell me..."

"Yes." Gwen filled her in. "I've a meeting with a detective I trust this morning. I'm positive Matt's case will be reopened. I'll keep a very close eye on it. I'm going to search for this person called O'Brian. We still might find a connection to Mary's murder."

"Megan is going to be so pleased."

After finishing her call to Nona, Gwen called Jamie to find Pat O'Brian. An hour later, he called and confirmed. "A Patrick O'Brian is still working as head of security at the lab in Boston," he said.

Gwen's meeting with detective Boyle went as she expected. He promised to look into it, but couldn't promise anything; it was a closed case. A written confession from a dying man meant he could not be questioned. Gwen took this in stride; she knew Boyle well and had worked with him a few times. At first he would be cautious, but he would be extremely thorough.

Gwen had phoned Nona on Friday; since Megan was coming home for the weekend, Nona decided to wait and give Megan the news when she arrived. Megan arrived on the eleven am ferry, and they were sitting on the deck having lunch when Nona told her that Gwen had called.

"Now, I don't want you to get overly excited," Nona started, "but you should know that she found the man in your sketches."

"Where? What does this mean?" Despite Nona's warning, Megan was immediately excited.

"The man in question has died."

"Oh," Megan said, suddenly deflated.

"He signed a deathbed confession, naming the person who gave him the order. Apparently he was told that whatever he gave Matt would actually not kill him," Nona said quietly.

"So where does Gwen go from here?"

She's tracking down the person named in the confession. It is only his surname, so it may take her awhile. We'll have to be patient and see what unfolds."

Gwen's phone rang.

"Gwen, I went back to the system I used to find Mark Adams," said Jamie. "His full name is Patrick Grant O'Brian; his current age is sixty. He worked in the same lab complex at the same time both Matt and Mark were there. He's head of security."

"After you send me this material, I suggest you sanitize your computer of any trace of Mark Adams and O'Brian. Thanks a million Jamie; once again, you've done a fantastic job."

As she ended the call, she thought, *Now we're getting somewhere.*

Right away, she called Detective Boyle.

"Arthur; I think we should meet."

"The usual place in a half hour," he responded.

Gwen got in her car and drove a circuitous route. She arrived just in time to see Boyle walking into the Café Green. She joined him and ordered a Western and a coffee, and as she sat down, she placed an envelope on the table in front of her.

"What have we here, Gwen?" Boyle asked.

"You may have this information," she said, tapping the white envelope. Boyle reached for it, but she put her hand on it to stop him. "But not just yet, Arthur."

He would have to be patient; he knew her well, and he trusted her. "You're being very cautious. It must be important," Boyle said as he winked at her.

"It might be very important. I have information on the man named in the confession."

"How did you settle on the name Mark Adams in the first place?"

"I was given it by a reliable source who I can't reveal." Gwen took a couple of sips of coffee and continued. "When this breaks, Mark's sister, Martha, may be in danger. She'll need protection."

"Let's see what you have, and then we'll decide how to handle it."

Gwen explained why she thought Matt was killed and that Dr. Mary Teal, Matthew's former girlfriend, was also killed in Canada a very short time thereafter.

"It sounds like something illegal was going on at the lab facility here in Boston. Have you any proof I can act on?"

"Nothing strong enough, but we're working on it. That's all I can say about the lab for now."

"What's in that envelope?"

"Open it and see. As usual, it didn't come from me. I'm concerned this individual may already have bolted. If he is still here, we'll have to work fast."

"Okay Gwen, this sounds very interesting."

"What I'm going to tell you now will make it even more so. When I made my initial inquiries right after Matthew's death, I was given the runaround. I was not allowed to talk to O'Brian, nor could I get an interview with the head of the lab at that time, Dr. Marshall Sandforth."

"And now we know it *wasn't* an accident," Arthur added.

"Exactly; I don't think O'Brian did this himself. I think the order came from Sandforth."

Arthur took out his pen and made a few notes. "Well, if he is still here, I'll bring him in for questioning."

"May I suggest you immediately place him under protective custody? Sandforth is still here in Boston."

"I'll get a search warrant for O'Brian's home and office."

He pulled out his cell and quickly made a call.

"Great, that's good news," he said to the person on the other end of the line.

Boyle ended the call and looked at Gwen.

"They're tracking down O'Brian right now. Gwen, this could be big."

"Arthur, it could be *huge*. It may, in fact, be the tip of the iceberg. So...we'll stick to our usual arrangement?"

"Yes—what I know, you'll know. What you know, I'll know."

* * *

Within four hours, Boyle had what he needed. He waited until O'Brian left work; he was afraid that approaching O'Brian at the lab would set off a chain reaction. A surveillance team was following O'Brian. He'd stopped at a grocery store, and as he got out of his car, he was taken in for questioning. His phone and the contents of his car were confiscated.

O'Brian was absolutely furious.

"I don't even know the man you're talking about!"

"It may be a national security issue," said Boyle.

"*What?*" O'Brian yelled. "*What* are you talking about?"

"You'll find out soon enough."

Boyle knew that mentioning national security was a bit iffy. He also knew that he had until the next morning before there would be interference from another agency.

They took him to an outlying small police station, as he knew reporters were always sniffing around the main stations in Boston.

"Where are you taking me?" O'Brian demanded.

"Somewhere safe and quiet," Boyle said as he pulled up to a small brick building. They walked in, and went directly to a quiet room at the back.

O'Brian was still insisting that he'd done nothing wrong. He was trying to keep his mind clear, but fear was creeping in.

"As per regulations I'm recording this interview," said Boyle.

"I'm innocent. I'll say no more until I get a lawyer."

"Okay, then I'll do the talking. First of all, I have a written confession that has been signed by one Mark Adams stating you ordered him to silence a Dr. Matthew Stone. He states he worked at the same lab you work at here in Boston. He was a technician for Stone, and you threatened to kill his sister, Martha, if he didn't cooperate."

"That's a lie."

"You told him the syringe you gave him contained a virus which would make Stone very ill. Stone died, didn't he? You knew it would kill him, didn't you?"

"No, I did nothing of the kind."

"You were ordered to do it, weren't you?"

"No."

"You did it on your own?"

"No. Please, I need a drink of water."

"In a moment—so, you're saying that you were not involved?"

"No, I wasn't. I did not kill Matt."

"How did you know everyone in his lab called him *Matt*?"

"You just told me."

"No, I didn't. I never said his name was Matt."

"You did so—when you arrested me."

Boyle decided to change his tactics. He got O'Brian a jug of water.

"You were ordered to kill him," said Boyle.

"No, I wasn't."

"Then you really are going to take sole responsibility for this murder?"

"No, I am not. I want my lawyer."

Boyle's pager went off and, picking up the phone, he said, "Yes, yes, okay."

He turned to O'Brian. "We can protect you, you know."

"From what?"

"Don't you mean from whom?"

"What are you talking about?"

"Your boss, Sandforth."

"Sandforth!" O'Brian exclaimed.

"Yes. Marshall Sandforth ordered you to kill Matthew Stone, and you're going to take the fall for it. Pat, when we're finished with you here, we will turn you over to the Canadian authorities."

"What for?"

"For the murder of Dr. Mary Teal."

"What? You've got nothing."

"No? We'll let you sit here and stew a bit. Think it over, Pat. We'll help you."

"Help me? How can you possibly help me?"

"If you confess, we'll put you in a safe house and in witness protection. We really want the guy who gave the orders." Boyle rose to leave and turned. "O'Brian, what do you think your boss is going to do when he finds out Mark confessed and that you are in police custody—especially if we don't find it necessary to keep you? What would you do if you were in his shoes?"

Boyle left the room and phoned the forensics computer unit.

"There was a $200,000 cash deposit in O'Brian's account two weeks after Stone was killed. We're looking into who deposited it. It also looks like he has an encoded file. We are attempting to decode it now; it may take a while," they reported.

Boyle returned to the room and noticed that O'Brian was looking very uncomfortable; he was starting to sweat.

"So, Pat—how did you spend the $200,000?"

"What $200,000?"

"The money you received for killing two people."

O'Brian sighed in defeat. "You'll keep me in protective custody, won't you?"

"Only if you tell us the truth."

"He'll find a way to get to me and kill me, whether I confess or not."

"Maybe he'll let you live."

"Not this guy; he's a paranoid maniac."

"Are you ready to tell us who gave you the orders to kill two people, and why?"

"I have no idea why, but Sandforth was terrified of whatever Stone had found."

"Will you testify in court to this?"

"If I live long enough." He was tired and shaken. "May I call my lawyer now?"

"By all means," Boyle said as he handed him the phone.

***

Sandforth had just got word that the police had a signed confession from Adams regarding the murder of Stone. He picked up the phone to call O'Brian, there was no answer at his home. He tried O'Brian's cellphone. Again there was no answer.

"Where the hell are you?" he said in a very angry voice.

He sent a security detail to find him.

"Sir, his car is not here, and he has not picked up his evening paper. His neighbours said the cops were here around five-thirty pm, and that they took some stuff from Pat's place."

"Damn!" he cursed.

He started to dial his police contact and stopped. It was after hours. He phoned his home, but no luck; he was out with the boys and left his cellphone at home. As a last resort, he called the main police station; O'Brian was not there. Sandforth was really getting worried.

Where can he be? Something does not feel right.

He'd call the pilot of his private jet and get out of the country for a few days until he could find out what was going on. Putting a few things in his pockets, he packed lightly, and locked his work files and computer in a private vault on the lowest floor. He went directly to the airport.

* * *

Boyle had O'Brian's signed confession and was about to leave the room when O'Brian said, "I hope the old bastard gets what he deserves. You know, Boyle, I really hate him. I was getting suspicious of what was happening, especially on the lower floors. When I told Sandforth I was quitting, he said my wife and three children would come to serious harm if I left. I had to stay. He ruined my life, and I'll never forgive him. This is the reason I'm helping you."

Boyle turned to him. "Does he have a private jet?" he asked.

"Oh God, yes. He's probably on it as I speak, escaping the country."

"Give me the details, and if he hasn't already left, I'll get airport security to detain him."

"Be careful, Boyle; he has them under his thumb, too. I wish you luck in catching that bastard."

"I've arranged to have you moved to a safe house. Homeland Security may wish to speak with you. We've also started the paperwork to get you into the witness protection program. O'Brian, you've done the right thing."

* * *

Sandforth tipped the cabbie and entered the airport. He relaxed a little bit when he saw one of his people on duty. *This should be easy*, he thought.

A security guard had just put his cellphone back in his pocket. As the line got shorter and shorter, Sandforth was sweating. He wondered if he should make an excuse and step out of line and wait until he'd calmed down, but decided it would only draw attention to himself. He convinced himself he would be okay. He removed his $600 shoes and placed them in a tray with his wallet, his laptop, change, and keys. He went through the scanner feeling confident. He was putting on his shoes when an older security guard approached him.

"Dr. Sandforth? Please follow me."

Sandforth knew he had no choice. Upon entering a small room, he was aware of three other people there.

"Excuse me, could someone tell me what is going on? I have a plane to catch."

"Dr. Sandforth, I'm Detective Boyle, and we would like you to come with us."

"Why should I?" Sandforth was indignant.

"We have some questions about the death of a Dr. Matthew Stone who used to work for you."

* * *

Boyle had contacted Gwen and filled her in on the arrests of O'Brian and Sandforth.

"Did O'Brian have anything to say about the lower three floors of the lab?" Gwen asked.

"No, he has no knowledge of the research, other than they were funded through government/military contracts and that they were working on some form of viral or bacterial bio-engineering. None of their work was ever published or will be published."

"What was his overall impression of those lowest floors?"

"He told me that he felt that something very wrong was going on there. His rationale was based on the secretive procedures one had to go through to get in there, not to mention that two people were killed because they discovered something so dangerous to Sandforth that he had no choice."

"I think he's correct," Gwen agreed.

"O'Brian confirmed that Sandforth gave the order to kill Stone. He found out before we picked him up that we had taken O'Brian into custody. We suspected he would attempt to flee the country. We stopped him at the airport. I'm currently in the process of moving Sandforth to a safer place to question him. I'll let you know where we take him."

* * *

"We have a slight problem." George Dean said to Anin. "I've been informed that our lab in Boston has been compromised."

"In what way?" Anin snapped. He was very busy; he had no time for trouble from the lower levels of jurisdiction. He had enough problems of his own.

"Both the head of security and the head of the lab are currently in police custody—and maybe federal custody—on murder charges. I need your consent to close down the Boston facility.

"Is there any direct connection between you and that particular lab?" Asked Anin.

"No, thankfully." George updated Anin on the so-called accidents that caused the deaths of Matthew Stone and Mary, and the details of the cover-up of the two murders.

"Were these murders done on Sandforth's orders, or by someone higher up?"

"It was Sandforth alone; he is extremely paranoid," George commented.

"What was behind these arrests—do you know?"

"The man who killed Stone made a deathbed confession."

"What was the research which caused all this?"

"At that time, it was vital to the genetic bioengineering of certain bacteria. One of the bacteria they developed was the precursor of the one we're about to test in Russia."

"Well, this puts an end to that test, doesn't it?" Anin said. He was very annoyed.

"Not necessarily; after the Stone incident, that research was moved—along with the scientists involved—to our lab in Melbourne, Australia."

"Fine. Now make sure that Sandforth doesn't talk."

* * *

"Where are you taking me?" Sandforth demanded.

"Somewhere safe. We think your life is in danger."

"From whom?" Sandforth asked, but he knew exactly who would be after him. The realization cut like a knife in his chest. "Please hurry; I've a plane to catch," he said.

"Sorry, but right now I think the safest place for you is with us. We are your best bet to stay alive." Boyle turned to one of his fellow officers who was handing him a phone.

"Someone from Homeland Security says it is paramount he speaks to you about Sandforth," the officer said.

"What did you tell him?" Boyle asked.

"I told him that I didn't know where you were."

Boyle nodded and turned back to Sandforth, who was agitated and perspiring.

"There was no phone call from Homeland Security, Boyle—you just made it look like there was," Sandforth accused.

"Well, Sandforth, whether it was or wasn't, it doesn't really matter. If you like, we'll wait here and let them come. If Homeland Security takes you, you'll have no rights. If it wasn't Homeland Security, your bosses have found out and want you eliminated. Your only choice is to come with us."

"No matter what I do, or where I go, my life is over," Sandforth said in a forlorn voice.

Boyle's phone rang again. He listened for a moment, then said, "We're on our way—we'll meet you there."

They rushed out of the room and headed out the back way. Driving in an unmarked car, Boyle said, "Duck down as we pass that black SUV ahead. I believe it is Homeland Security."

"Why are you doing this for me? You could've just left me there. Won't you get into trouble for doing this?"

"Maybe—as to why, well, there's someone who has been wanting to talk to you for years."

"Who might that be?" Sandforth asked.

"Gwen Ross."

* * *

Boyle was right. It wasn't National Security that called. His boss was trying to silence Sandforth. The Boston lab was under surveillance; some people and equipment were being moved.

Gwen was certain Sandforth's lab was still involved in highly-classified research. The only way she was going to get any further was to get someone like Sandforth to talk.

Boyle liked Gwen and how she operated. She had given him O'Brian and Sandforth. He owed it to her, himself, and the general public to get to the bottom of all this. Since he had talked to Gwen, he was convinced that Sandforth was up to no good. He was terrified of the possible outcome if he didn't help stop it.

"I think I've got a way to do this. Gwen, come to this address as soon as you can. Make sure you're not being followed; come alone, and don't park close to the building."

Gwen picked up her laptop and followed Boyle's directions.

If we handle this properly, we might get our foot in the door, she thought as she was driving.

When she entered the tiny house, she took her first look at Sandforth.

My, he looks ill, she noted.

He was very pale, was slightly slumped over, and was pacing the floor.

"Good evening, Boyle," she said.

She looked at Sandforth. "And I understand that you are Dr. Sandforth."

"Please, Ms. Ross, call me Marshall."

The three of them sat down at a round table with a recording device. It was Boyle who spoke first.

"We don't have much time before someone catches up with us; if you wish to talk, you'd better start now."

"I really don't know where to start. No matter how hard you try to protect me, no one can. I am done. I'm as good as dead. They will find me sooner or later and kill me."

"Who are they?" Gwen asked. She knew she was looking at a condemned man.

"I wish I knew. My orders come from various locations, and I never know who I'm really talking to."

"Is it the same person each time?" asked Boyle.

"I think so."

It was Gwen's turn to ask a question. "Do you know anything about the people you work for? Do you know where their headquarters are?"

"We are not the only lab facility. There are several others worldwide. When I joined The Company fifteen years ago, I was told we were the only one."

"You found out differently." Gwen said. "How did you find out?"

"I was called into a meeting one day and was told we'd received a very large grant to study viruses and bacteria; we were to work on bioengineering their DNA."

"You are talking about genetic engineering, which is illegal." Boyle commented.

"There are certain labs licensed to do it, and are very carefully monitored. These top-secret labs are doing it illegally. We were assured all was okay; most of the funding comes to us through the military. We were very fortunate to get such great funding. It allowed us to have the best of everything."

"Did you hire the staff yourself?"

"I hired the scientists working on the non-secret projects. Those working in the 'For Your Eyes Only' labs were hired through the parent company."

Gwen sat up straighter in her chair and asked, "Can you tell us the name of your head company?"

Sandforth was becoming very agitated again; he was slow in answering.

"I guess I'm dead whether I tell you are not," he said.

There was a pregnant silence.

Sandforth sighed and said, "It is the CESR—the Center for Earth's Sustainable Resources—which have their headquarters near Area 51 in Nevada."

Gwen could not believe her ears; *This might just be the crack in the case we've been looking for*, she thought.

"Do you know the names of any of the directors of the CESR?" she asked.

"I have my suspicions. I overheard a conversation which led me to conclude that one of them was called Dean. I don't know if it's the first or last name. I heard a dependable rumour that there was an alien on the board as well." Sandforth paused to catch his breath. "The whole lower part of the underground section of that lab, especially the lowest level, is untouchable," he added.

"Do you know why these bioengineered viruses and bacteria were made?" Boyle asked.

"When Stone was killed, we were developing a type of bacteria that had a very short lifespan; it was extremely deadly. After a certain length of time, it would self-destruct, leaving no trace."

"Was it being tested on small, isolated groups around the world?" Gwen asked.

"Yes, it was."

Gwen had to catch her breath. "Was the fact that Dr. Stone found out about this the reason you had him killed?"

"Yes," Sandforth admitted. He was exhausted.

"Was Dr. Mary Teal aware of it?" Gwen asked. Her voice was getting edgy.

"We had strong evidence that she was, and we knew she had contacted you. We didn't know how much she knew. The plan was just to scare her off. It went very wrong."

Boyle was checking his notes. "Are you currently working on this bacterium?"

"No. It was moved, along with the two scientists who were working on it to another lab after Stone was killed. After that, our funding was cut by fifty percent."

"What is your lab complex currently working on?" Gwen asked.

"We're working on some anti-serums for that organism and others."

"How far are you along?" Gwen was getting excited.

"We've an antiserum for the first one we bioengineered."

"What were these organisms going to be used for?" Boyle asked. He couldn't help but be upset.

"I was told that it was a biological weapon of some kind. These labs are funded by Black Budgets and therefore they are top-secret."

Boyle's burn phone rang. "Yes. Tell them I'll meet with them shortly. Do they have proper ID? Give me a half an hour; that will be a good place to meet."

"Who was that?" Sandforth had turned gray. "I'm afraid. Are you taking me with you?"

"No, they're coming here."

"Who?" Sandforth began to pace around the room."

"It's okay. I arranged for a trusted associate of mine in the FBI to take you into custody. You will be much safer with them, than either Homeland Security or us. The RCMP in Canada are going to want talk to you also; the FBI is their best link." Boyle winked at Gwen.

"So, what is going to happen to me with the FBI?"

"Sandforth, because you have been cooperative, I would suggest you call a lawyer and follow his advice. The FBI can make deals we cannot."

There was a knock at the door. Boyle turned to Gwen and said, "You had better leave now. Go out the back way."

Sandforth had asked for a piece of paper and was writing something on it. As he rose to say goodbye to Gwen, he slipped her a folded piece of paper with something in it.

"I'm very sorry for what I did; I felt I had no choice. Maybe this will help," he told her.

Gwen didn't have time to say anything; she moved swiftly and quietly to her car. She got in and waited for the big black SUV and Boyle's car to leave. She touched the piece of paper; four small SD cards fell out. On the paper some passwords were written.

As she drove, she tried to figure out what would be the best way to use the memory cards and codes Sandforth had given her. She stopped at her bank and withdrew a great deal of cash. She bought a new laptop and several burn phones.

I'm so glad that I thought to put my own computer and all my notes in my car when I left home, she thought.

She started to drive again, and a little voice in her mind said, *Why don't you just keep driving north and go visit Holly in Halifax?*

It seemed like a good idea to her.

She stopped at a Starbuck's for takeout and bought some food and coffee. While she was sitting in the parking area eating, she took out the new computer, set it up, and started to copy the files. While they were loading up, she called Holly.

"It's so great to hear from you, Gwen. What's up?"

"We got O'Brian and Sandforth to confess; they are now in FBI custody."

"That was quick."

"The Boston police picked up Sandforth as he was trying to leave the country. The detective in charge is a very good and trusted friend of mine. I have a copy of the initial interrogation."

"That is fantastic. Can't wait to hear how you guys did it!" Holly exclaimed. She was excited.

"I'm sending you some information regarding both O'Brian and Sandforth. It must be kept off the record for now."

"No problem."

"Holly, I have another favour to ask of you. I must get away from Boston asap."

"Come up here, if you can."

"When I left the city, I found myself heading north."

"Are you in serious trouble?"

"Not with the police. A lot depends on when and what Sandforth tells the FBI. I have a feeling he's not going to talk. I'm sure my house and office are going to be watched by Sandforth's people. Can you arrange a place for me to stay?"

"You can stay with me."

"Thanks, Holly. I'll drive straight through."

"Where are you crossing?"

"At the Calais/St. Stephen border; I should be at the border early tomorrow."

"Let me know when you're about two hours away from crossing and I'll have an RCMP officer meet you. In the meantime, if you need anything, call me on my cell. Drive carefully."

"Thanks, Holly. I'll see you soon."

Holly immediately called Nona and gave her the news.

"Holly, that is fantastic. Do you have any of the details?"

"Not really; Gwen is on her way up here to stay with me for a while. I wanted you to know that O'Brian and Sandforth are in jail and are likely going to be charged with murder."

Gwen drove for a couple of hours; eventually she pulled into a gas station to fuel up and to get something to eat. She sat in the car eating, turned on her new computer, and began to transfer the data on the SD cards. He had given her files upon files of information. She decided she would drive and let the computer do its thing. She drove out of the gas station and headed north.

***

"Anin, I told you—Sandforth has just disappeared. Did you have anything to do with it?"

"No, George—calm down and tell me what you know."

"He was going to fly out of the country, but his plane never took off. He made it to the airport, but security took him off somewhere."

"Why didn't you intervene?"

"We tried the Homeland Security route, but it failed. He was initially with a Detective Boyle, but I just got confirmation that Sandforth is now with the FBI."

"Well, you know what you have to do."

Dean felt a shiver go through him. *Yes, I've no choice,* he realized.

It was now almost midnight. He could not take a chance on whether Sandforth had talked or not. It really didn't matter. He called a drill. All the viruses and bacteria were moved to a safe area. All personnel was evacuated. Then he hit the red button. Sirens blared through Boston. Fire departments would respond, but it would be too late. Absolutely everything in the lowest floor would be destroyed beyond recognition. Firefighters would not get in.

He phoned Anin and simply stated, "Done."

***

Gwen called Nona; she felt she needed to talk to her. She put her phone on speaker and dialed.

"Hi Nona, it's Gwen. I'm so glad I got you."

"Holly called and gave us the message. Are you all right?"

"Yes. I'm driving north and I'm going to stay with Holly for a while. I'll give you all the details later. Tell Megan this all happened because of her vision and her sketches. I know it has taken years, but we got them. I'll definitely come and see you."

"Gwen, thank you so much for all that you have done. Be safe."

"Andrew, where are you?" Nona called out.

He came running. "I don't know all the details yet, but I've received news that O'Brian and Sandforth are in jail. The FBI have them. I must call Megan." Tears were beginning to flow, and Nona was having trouble speaking.

"I'll dial her number and you can talk to her," said Andrew.

Megan had no sooner finished talking to Nona about the latest updates when Holly called.

"I was just talking to Gram. I can't believe it!" said Megan.

"Believe it, Megan. It's true. The FBI contacted me and confirmed. Have you any plans for tomorrow?"

"I'm going to be home to be with Gram for a few days."

"When are you planning to leave? I'm meeting Gwen in St. John tomorrow and it would be great if you could be there, too."

"That would be awesome."

Holly told Megan about Gwen's plan. "We would have to leave very early in the morning," she added.

"You figure out the timing and I'll be ready. Tomorrow is Friday; why don't the three of us pop over to the island for the weekend together? I know Gram will definitely go for it," said Megan.

"That's a superb idea. We'll take my car," Holly said.

Gwen was exhausted when she got to the border. It was about eight am. The cars were moving slowly. Finally, just when she thought she would fall asleep at the wheel, she was at the immigration and custom booth in St. Stephen.

"May I please have your passport?" asked the agent.

Gwen handed it over.

"How long do you plan to stay in Canada?" he asked.

"I'm not sure."

"That's okay. Because of the cameras, I'm going to look as if I'm asking a series of questions. I would like you to play along, Ms. Ross."

Gwen was slightly surprised, but she nodded and said, "I'll do my best."

"I'm going to have a rather stern look on my face and shake my head. Then I'll ask you to pull over to the customs building."

Following instructions, she went over to the customs building. There was a handsome, sandy-haired RCMP officer there to greet her. "Ms. Ross, I presume; Constable Holly Summers sent me. I'm Constable McKenzie—but please call me Ryan."

"Will do," answered Gwen.

"We're going to leave your car here. Then we're going to search your car and confiscate everything. You may keep what you want to take, and we'll store the rest for you."

Gwen was wide awake now. "So we're going to make it look like a drug bust?"

"Yes, we're going to make it look like we're arresting you. Then in about ten minutes, we'll be on our way to St. John where we will meet with Constable Summers."

By the time they'd driven through St. Stephen, Gwen was nodding off.

"I'm so sorry, Ryan," she said. "I'm just so exhausted."

"Don't be sorry, Gwen; You rest and I'll drive. Holly knows we're on our way."

About an hour later, the three women were sitting in a Tim Horton's in St. John having a coffee and some lunch. They were at a table in a back corner where they felt safe.

"I can't begin to thank you enough for believing in me and following up on those sketches," said Megan.

"It's us who should be thanking you, Megan," said Gwen. "How is Nona doing?"

"She has mixed emotions. She's relieved, but she's also a bit shaken up. This has brought my mother's death to the forefront of her mind once again."

"It's probably a good thing for Nona, and for you, too; hopefully it'll bring closure for both of you."

Holly nodded in agreement. "Can you tell us some more about what happened?" she asked.

For the next half hour, Gwen filled them in on how she had tracked down Mark, and how she was given his written confession. "His sister is in the witness protection program with her husband and children. She is a very brave woman," she said. She explained how the confession led to the arrest of O'Brian which in turn led to the arrest of Sandforth.

"How did you and the police get each of them to confess so quickly?" Megan asked.

"O'Brian had been threatened and was trapped by Sandforth and ended up hating him. He knew his only chance to stay alive was to cooperate and tell the truth. Sandforth recognized that the same held true for him as well. The evidence against them both is strong, and I'm positive they will both be found guilty of murder. Holly, I'm not sure what will happen regarding Mary's murder, but there'll definitely be some form of cooperation between the RCMP and the FBI. We'll just have to wait and see how the two trials turn out in the US first."

"Does this help your investigation into what is really going on in some of these labs?" Megan asked as she drank the last of her coffee.

"They were testing a very virulent strain of bacteria when Matt was there and he suspected what was going on, but he couldn't prove it. According to Sandforth, he was just getting too close to the truth and he eliminated him. The bacterial strains were moved out of Boston. They lost fifty percent of their funding, and Sandforth was very bitter and angry about it. I think this helped him to turn on his superiors."

Gwen's phone rang. "Sorry, girls, I have to take this. I'll be right back." She got up and stood a discreet distance away as she took her call.

"Is Gwen in any danger because of all this?" Megan asked in a very soft voice.

"She might be—not from the law, but from whoever is running those labs."

"Well, ladies, here's some incredible news: the lower level of the lab complex in Boston was totally destroyed by fire overnight," Gwen said as she returned to the table.

Holly was very concerned. "Where does that leave your investigation?"

"I'm not really sure," Gwen said. "The murder charges will stick, though—of that I'm certain. I'm not sure how this will impact our investigation into their research, however."

Holly looked at her watch. "Maybe we should get underway."

Megan smiled. "Gwen, we've a surprise for you: the three of us are going to spend the weekend on Grand Manan."

For a moment, Gwen was stunned. "That's absolutely wonderful!" she said. "But...I've nothing to wear. I left very quickly; I'm wearing all the clothes I have."

"Hmm...I guess we'll just have to go shopping here before we leave St. John," said Megan.

For an hour they had great fun picking out clothes for Gwen, and after their purchases, they headed to Grand Manan. While they were waiting for the ferry, Gwen phoned Boyle for an update.

"I'm in a bit of trouble with my captain, but he'll get over it. He can't do much to me, as the FBI congratulated him on having such a cooperative detective on his police force," he told her. They both chuckled at this.

"Are they talking?"

"To a degree, O'Brian is, but Sandforth isn't. Both were denied bail and have lawyers. Sandforth hired one of the best in Boston. It won't do him any good."

"Can you tell me anything more about the fire at the lab?"

"The fire chief told me the walls of the underground floors contained explosive incendiary devices. They were set off by a remote device. Everything was destroyed. Fortunately, no one was hurt; the labs were evacuated earlier in the day."

"Do they have any suspects in mind?"

"No, but it was probably the head of the company that owns and controls it. Gwen, I think you'd better stay up there for a bit, just to be safe. I'll keep in touch."

Once they'd arrived on the island, Megan, Holly, and Gwen were given a wonderful welcome by Nona and Andrew. Andrew fixed them all a celebratory drink and they sat out on the deck. Then he quietly disappeared; he was barbecuing steaks for dinner. Nona was anxious to hear more details. Holly and Megan went inside to help Andrew, giving Nona and Gwen some quiet time together.

They all had a wonderful time over dinner. In the evening, they had a bonfire; it was early summer and there was a cool breeze coming in off the Bay of Fundy. They were having so much fun that Gwen forgot the stress of the previous few days. Eventually she broke away from the gathering as she was getting very tired. Before Gwen went to bed, she checked her new computer to quickly review what had been downloaded. She was amazed at the amount of material. It was going to take a long time to decode and sort the files. She packed it all in her new briefcase and crawled into bed.

After a breakfast of bacon and eggs, ham, sausages, homemade toasted bread, and homemade blackberry jelly, they sat on the deck enjoying a calm and sunny morning.

Over coffee, Nona asked, "How would everyone like to go out on Serendipity? It's such a beautiful day."

"Lacuna is back! I knew it!" Megan exclaimed.

"Is Serendipity a boat or something?" Gwen asked.

Everyone was chuckling as Nona explained. "Serendipity is our research vessel. If you look, she's the white boat with a red haul, at the far end."

"Who is Lacuna?"

Nona quickly answered, "Come with us and you'll see." Nona winked at Megan. "Grab some warm clothes from the cupboard there, and let's be off."

Megan had telepathically sent a message to Lacuna. This would be the first time she would see her this summer.

About an hour later, Megan shouted, "Whale blows, twelve o'clock!"

"What are blows?" Gwen asked.

"Whales," Holly answered, laughing. "Are they single or double?"

"Doubles, and lots of them. There's a large pod of humpbacks headed our way," said Nona.

"I've never seen whales in the wild," Gwen said. She was thrilled.

"Well, you are in for a wonderful experience," Nona said. The distance between the boat and the whales was closing quickly.

"They're swimming right towards us!" Holly exclaimed.

A few moments later, Andrew slowed the engine and slipped it into neutral, explaining to Gwen what he was doing.

"We're not allowed to approach a whale within 300 feet; however, if they come to us, that's okay."

With that, there was a double breach by the two leading whales. Megan was on the bow jumping up and down. There was a thundering splash as the whales hit the water simultaneously.

The noise was deafening, and the resulting spray missed the boat by a few feet.

Gwen was holding on to the railing. She couldn't believe her eyes. She was speechless. Before she could catch her breath, another whale in the pod did a partial breach, which was followed by two more simultaneous breaches. The two whales that breached first came up alongside the boat.

"Gwen, I would like you to meet Lacuna; Lacuna, this is my friend Gwen," said Megan. Lacuna rolled over and on her side, and slowly lifted her very long white flipper; then, very slowly, she hit the water with a rather quiet slap.

Gwen was laughing with tears rolling down her cheeks. She raised her arm and waved and lowered it slowly.

Just beyond Lacuna there were two smaller whales. Megan whistled, and one came over to the boat and did exactly what Lacuna did.

"This little guy is Shadow, Lacuna's son," she said.

The pod, led by Lacuna and Shadow, decided to put on a show for Megan and her friends. It was quite a sight. There was a lot of tail slapping, flipper slapping, breaching, and tail bobbing. Megan was dancing about the boat. Before the show was over, Nona, Gwen, and Holly were also dancing and singing.

Slowly all went quiet and calm. The pod moved on, but Lacuna and Shadow stayed at the surface beside the boat. Megan was straddling the gunwales, quietly humming. The others sat on the opposite side with Andrew, watching the scene before them.

"What a beautiful and incredible experience!" said Gwen. "Thank you, Nona. I've never seen anything like this in my life. It's just what I needed."

"You're very welcome. You are more than welcome here anytime," said Nona.

Gwen leaned over to Holly. She nodded towards Megan and whispered, "It's like they're communicating."

Nona overheard, and quietly answered, "They are; they have been doing so since Megan was three years old."

Gwen remembered the weekend with Nona and Megan at Matthew's cabin when Megan told her about her vision.

"I should have known," she said, awestruck.

On Sunday, Gwen, Holly, and Megan returned to Halifax. Gwen began a thorough search of Sandforth's files. She went back to the time around Matthew's murder. She put the legitimate files aside and looked for material on the covert studies. She studied the specs and blueprints and took the computer down to the rec room to get Holly's opinion on what she had found.

Holly studied the descriptions, diagrams and blueprints. "I've never seen anything as advanced as this. They really were hiding something. Have you found anything suspicious around the time Stone was killed?" she asked.

"Not really— a couple of days before Matt died, Sandforth had met with O'Brian in his office and had requested that O'Brian take care of a problem. I'm sure he had more detailed files somewhere. I wonder if they were destroyed in the fire."

"You could be right, but he must've given you something."

"I'm sure he did. All I have to do is find it." Gwen's phone rang, and she politely excused herself. When she came back, she said, "That was Boyle. Sandforth committed suicide."

"What? How could he? He was in jail—wasn't he under a suicide watch?" Holly asked.

"They really don't know. They think his lawyer may have smuggled something to him."

"What about O'Brian?"

"The FBI was shaken by Sandforth's death, and has virtually made him disappear. With the two confessions, it's virtually a closed case." Gwen commented. "I'll phone Nona later and let her know." She paused for a moment or two. "That makes these files the only link we have to uncover what happened in that lab. I'm hoping to find some details which will get our foot in the door of these Black Budget facilities."

"I sure hope so. Do you have much more material to go through?" asked Holly.

"I've only just begun."

After four days, Gwen came across an obscure reference buried in a series of other files. It was a notation written beside the description of a bacterium which was being bioengineered. It was virulent, could rapidly spread by touch, and could cause death within hours. Gwen tried again to find the origin of the note and to whom it had been sent. There was no direct evidence of the source other than the notation appearing to have been in Sandforth's handwriting. The name on it had been blacked out. There was a notation: *Lab Z – 5, 413*. She found a file which described the layout of the entire building. Looking at the description of the various floors, she learned that the above-ground floors were designated in the normal fashion of one, two, three, etc., but those below ground were marked *Z –1, Z –2, Z –3,* and *Z –4. Z – 4* would be the lowest floor, and 413 would be the lab. Gwen was about to give up when she spotted a notation of a lab: *Z –4, 412*. Attached to it was a memo which read,

> *Ted, please note: Dean will be here in two weeks.*
>
> *—M. S.*

Wait a minute! Gwen thought, *Sandforth said something about a man called Dean. It couldn't be a coincidence. Dean has to have been one of the directors of CESR in Nevada.*

She phoned John Gray, an investigative reporter in that area.

"Is there someone whose first or last name is Dean who works at the CESR?" she asked.

"There is a Dr. George Dean who is currently the head of the lab, and has been for many years," answered Gray.

"What do you know about him?"

"Not very much; he keeps to himself. He has some rather interesting visitors periodically."

"Okay John, thanks."

She had her lunch and went back to the Sandforth files. Later in the afternoon, she found a file of personal notes. Before she could get into it, Holly had come home.

"How did things go today?"

"Very interesting, Holly," she said. Over a bottle of beer, she shared an update on what she had found so far.

"I found a Dr. George Dean who is head of the lab near Area 51 in Nevada; there is definitely a connection between that lab and the one in Boston."

"Do you suppose it was he who gave the order to have the lowest level of the Boston lab destroyed?"

"I think that's more than likely, Holly." Gwen took a couple of sips of beer. "After supper, I'll go back and look at some more of his files and see what I can find."

By nine pm, Gwen was tired and bored; most of what she read was a repeat of what she had already seen, so she took a short break. As she sat down, she saw a page which was dated about two months after the murders. She found a note which was written by Sandforth:

> This morning, I was notified by The Company that, due to the 'bungling' of the deaths of Stone and Teal, our research into the biological weapon Stone had found out about would be terminated. As of midnight tonight, the three scientists

currently working on it in Boston, along with all their research and equipment, will be removed to other countries. My research funding will be cut by fifty percent. To say that I'm furious would be an understatement. In spite of their standing orders, I'm going to record the names of the three scientists for my future protection. Their names are:

Dr. Joseph Lampson

Dr. Margo Ellsworth

Dr. Donald Uxbridge

It is worth noting that Uxbridge is going to Russia, whereas Ellsworth and Lampson are going to Melbourne Australia.

—Marshall Sandforth III.

After reading this, Gwen immediately called Holly to come and have a look. Once Holly had viewed the information, her comment was very straightforward: "I'll have those names traced tomorrow. Is this what you're looking for?"

"Hopefully, this will begin to get us somewhere. There are still many files to look at."

Holly phoned the next morning. "We've been able to confirm that Lampson and Ellsworth are still currently working in Melbourne. We think Uxbridge is somewhere in Moscow."

"Holly, this is fantastic. Thank you so much!"

Gwen tried to catch her breath and said, "Thank you, Sandforth—I found it."

She immediately phoned her contact, Syd Logan, in Australia.

"Syd, I've found something. Do you have a list of all the lab employees in Melbourne?"

"I do indeed."

"Is there a Dr. Joseph Lampson, and a Dr. Margo Ellsworth on that list?"

There was a pause as Syd leafed through his notes.

"Yes, there is. Both are microbiologists."

"Can you find out when they started there? Anything you can find out about them will be incredibly helpful, Syd—dig as deep as you can."

* * *

Sam was in an art gallery in Melbourne looking at a group of paintings when the curator spoke to him.

"You're interested in these particular paintings," the curator observed.

"Yes, I find his style rather intriguing, especially his seascapes."

"David is highly-respected painter in Australia. Would you like to meet him? He's bringing in a couple of his paintings, and I believe one of them is a seascape."

"Why, yes—I would very much like to meet him. Thank you!"

Shortly thereafter, the curator approached him once again, and was accompanied by another individual.

"This is the painter I was telling about—David Downs," said the curator.

"I'm Sam Rogers—pleased to meet you," said Sam. They shook hands. "I'm very interested in your seascapes."

"The ocean is my favourite subject. Would you like to see the one I just brought in?"

"Yes, I would."

David turned a painting around, and Sam gasped.

"My God, David—this is incredible. Where did you paint this one?"

"On the east coast of Canada; it is a group of islands called the Grand Manan archipelago."

"I was born and raised there!" Sam said.

"What a coincidence! It's from a photograph I took when I was on holiday about five years ago."

"How long were you on the island, David?"

"I was there for two days. I flew into St. John's, Newfoundland, and rented a sailboat called *Prediction*. I sailed down to the Bay of Fundy, and then back to St. John's."

"You know, for years I've tried to paint, but I'm not very good at it," said Sam.

"What do you do for living?" asked David.

"I'm a geologist. The Canadian government contracted me to come here to work on earthquake activity in this area. I paint as a hobby."

"Why don't you come over to my studio sometime, and I'll give you some painting tips?"

"That's very generous of you, David. I'm certainly struggling with my technique. If it's okay with you, I would really like to buy this one of Grand Manan. My fiancée is from the island—we're getting married next spring or summer—and I know she would love this painting."

About three weeks later, Sam called David. When he looked at David's card, he wondered why an artist would be living in such an upscale part of town. When they spoke, they made plans for the following weekend, and arranged to have Sam bring his current artistic projects over to David's place early in the morning, when the light of the day was at its best.

After they finished their phone conversation, Sam looked at the address again and decided to run a search on David online; as he'd hoped, there were multiple results which offered a great deal of information.

Now I know why he lives there, Sam thought. He realized why the name "Downs" sounded so familiar: David's sister, Maria, died in a plane crash several years earlier, and David had taken over the family's company. However, he was president in name only. The family was counted among the twenty wealthiest in the world; it owned several companies, including a pharmaceutical lab on the outskirts of Melbourne. He noticed the list of its products and noted one area: the genetic engineering of viruses and bacteria.

I must call Megan and see if she knows this company, he thought.

He phoned her immediately and told her about David Downs, and that he was going to get help with his painting.

"Do you know anything about a drug company called Downs Pharmaceuticals? They specialize in viruses and bacteria, as well as bioengineering antiserums."

"It does sound familiar, but I can't place it," said Megan. "What are they working on, specifically?"

"I'll see if I can find out anything more," said Sam.

The next day, Megan phoned Gwen and asked her if any of the Downs Companies were on her watch list.

"Yes, there is one in Australia near Melbourne. Why are you asking?"

Megan told her what Sam had said.

"Megan, it is probably nothing, but tell Sam to be careful. We are watching that company very closely. We think it might be related to the Boston laboratory."

"I'm going down there for conference in about two weeks," said Megan. "I'll check into it myself. And Gwen...is everything okay?"

"Yes, but it's a good idea to stay alert," Gwen answered. "I wonder...would you mind if I traveled with you?"

"That would be great! You're up to something, aren't you?"

"You could say that. There are a couple of people I wish to talk to personally. I also think it might be a good idea for me to get away for a bit, and I've never been to that part of Australia. I'll probably only be there a few days."

"Don't be silly. It's a long way to go. You should stay longer and explore!" said Megan.

As Gwen hung up, she wondered if she should tell Megan the truth about the connection between the Boston and Melbourne labs.

The wrought iron gates with the coat of arms of the Downs Estate were anchored by two large cylindrical granite pillars. At five minutes after nine am, Sam pressed the intercom button, giving his name when prompted; he was let in immediately. He drove up the long winding lane lined with endemic shrubs. He could see the main house perched on a hill with a greenhouse off to one side near a large white horse barn. As he drew nearer the house, he noted a mixture of formal and informal gardens. The three-storey house was constructed with hand-cut stone and was partially covered with ivy. He parked his car and walked up the flagstone path to climb five matching steps to a stone porch. Two large bay windows flanked either side of the huge hand-carved wooden doors. On either side was an elongated, leaded stained glass window of intriguing geometric shapes.

David met Sam at the door, and invited him in to a large foyer which had two spiral staircases, one going up on each side. The house was tastefully decorated in a natural colour scheme, and many of David's paintings adorned the walls. After a tour of the house, David then led Sam to his studio, which was a charming old repurposed greenhouse. Attached to it at the far end was a covered walkway leading to the original gardener's house, which David had converted into an office and apartment. Sam was enthralled with the eclectic nature of the interior; there were canvases of all shapes and sizes. Some were blank, others were finished, and there were still others that were at many stages in between. Sam was deeply impressed and loved what he saw.

The tutorial session began with working on a seascape; Sam was having a difficult time with the waves and whitecaps.

"Here, let me show you a little trick," said David. "Think about what actually forms the wave. It is water tumbling over itself; so take your brush with a dab of white paint and place it on top of the wave and give it a little spin in the direction the wave is moving." David stood back and watched carefully while Sam attempted this. "There you go; that's much better."

They continued working for a while, and Sam was having great fun practicing his whitecaps. For a few minutes he watched David paint. Then David asked, "When is Megan arriving?"

"She'll be here in a couple of weeks," answered Sam.

"May I ask you a rather unusual question?" David asked.

"Certainly," answered Sam.

"Is your wife's name Megan Teal—granddaughter of a Nona Teal?"

"Why, yes...it is," answered Sam, suddenly feeling uncertain.

David smiled. "My wife, Shelley, is actually an admirer of some of the work that Nona Teal has done. This is a wonderful coincidence—if you believe in coincidences, that is. I had wondered if we had people in common when you mentioned Grand Manan at our first meeting. This confirmed my gut feeling that we did!"

Sam nodded, but he was still a bit surprised at the connection. He smiled back at David and said, "Small world!"

"Yes," David said. It really is." He seemed sincere, but Sam was on alert.

"I'm going to go out on a limb here," David said, "and ask another question that may seem odd: Does Megan have a friend named Gwen Ross?"

"Yes she does, as a matter of fact," Sam carefully answered.

How did he make the connection between Megan and Gwen? he wondered. He didn't have a chance to ask.

"I've tried to call Ross; her answering machine is full," said David.

"As an investigative reporter, I understand that Gwen is pretty busy; we never know where she is one day to the next," said Sam.

"Does Megan know of her whereabouts?"

"She might."

"May I ask you a favour? Would you please call Megan and have her give a message to Ross?"

"I'll ask her to, but I can't guarantee anything," answered Sam.

"All I ask is for you to try, please. I know that this seems out of left field, but it truly is important."

That night, Sam called Megan and explained the rather unusual turn of events. Sam gave her David's unlisted number who in turn gave it to Gwen.

"This is truly unbelievable—and more than a coincidence," Gwen said when she got the message from Megan.

She immediately called David.

After ten minutes of conversation, Gwen told him, "I'm coming to Melbourne with Megan in about two weeks, and would like very much to have an interview with you. How do you feel about that?"

"I'd be happy to meet with you," David said.

As soon as her conversation with David was finished, Gwen phoned Megan.

"I don't really understand why or how this connection happened—this very same individual turned me down several times years ago when I tried to get an interview with him!"

"Do you think he knows of a link between his lab and the Boston one?" Megan asked.

"We'll find out in the near future. By the way, I got on the same flight as you."

Sam was waiting at the gate. Megan was first to come through immigration and customs, and he spotted her right away.

"Meg, I've missed you so much," he said as he hugged and kissed her.

"Me too," she said.

Sam was still holding Megan in his arms when Gwen came through. The three of them walked to the baggage claim and retrieved their luggage before heading to the airport parking lot.

"Gwen, I hear you're going to have an interview with David."

"Yes, Sam—and I'm thrilled about it! I've tried for ages to get one with him."

"He certainly seems very anxious to talk to you. When and where is it?"

"Tomorrow morning, his place."

"You'll love it; his place is incredible."

"How about we all grab dinner?" Megan suggested.

"Thanks, Megan, but I think you two love birds need some time together, and I'm going to be very busy getting my notes together for tomorrow's interview. Thanks so much for including me, though. Do you mind dropping me off at my hotel? It's not far from the airport—I'm just staying at the Holiday Inn."

After a brief ride, they arrived at Gwen's hotel. After she pulled her suitcase from the trunk, she turned and smiled at Sam and Megan. "Have a good night, you two!" she said.

"See you tomorrow," Megan called out.

Sam and Megan got caught up on each other's news over dinner. Sam told Megan about David Downs and his wife, Shelley. He described their magnificent home and spectacular art studio.

"They're so down-to-earth, though," he said. "You would never know, other than the estate, that they are worth billions of dollars."

"I'm really looking forward to meeting them," Megan said sincerely.

"As it turns out, Shelley admires the work Nona has been doing with the Universal Harmony Movement that she first initiated at the Glasgow Conference back when you were just a few years old. She really believes in it, and is very active here in Australia in spreading the word."

"It sounds like Shelley and Gram would get along well together," Megan said, yawning. She was exhausted from the flight.

"You're tired," said Sam. "I'll settle the bill, and we'll be on our way."

Finally, they were settled in Sam's apartment; Megan had been very much looking forward to spending the night with Sam. She showered and crawled into bed. Sam showered afterwards; as he approached the bed full of anticipation, he had to smile: Megan was sound asleep. He shook his head, climbed in bed beside her, and carefully snuggled in. She stirred a bit, partially opening her eyes. "Sorry," she murmured, then immediately fell back to sleep.

"Not to worry—we have a fortnight together," Sam whispered.

The next morning, Megan was awake early. She began to caress Sam, who was instantly awake; thus began an hour of sex and passion that left them both exhausted. They fell asleep again in each other's arms. When Megan awoke again, she slipped out of the bed, showered, and made breakfast. Sam awoke shortly after and joined Megan.

"Sam, shouldn't you be getting ready for work?"

"'I'm taking the next several days off just to be with you," he said.

The phone rang. "Yes, David, they arrived safe and sound. Thanks for checking. Oh, yes? One moment—I'll ask her."

Sam put his hand over the receiver. "Shelley and David would like us to join them for dinner tonight," he told Megan.

"That would be great," she said.

Later that day, when Gwen arrived at the Downs' estate, she was welcomed by David himself, and not by one of his staff as she'd expected. She was immediately impressed by him; he appeared to be in his late forties or early fifties, but it was hard to tell as he was clearly quite physically fit. He was quite confident while being approachable and engaging.

I'll have to be careful in my questions and alert to his answers, she thought.

Likewise, David felt that Gwen was unlike most reporters he had dealt with, and he realized he'd have to be careful with his answers.

As he gave her a tour of the house, Gwen was enthralled with the large hexagon-shaped room; two walls lined with bookshelves faced one another. Two other walls had large rectangular windows draped in a fine fabric. There was a fire crackling in a huge stone fireplace; the mantle and sides were hand-carved and inlaid with Mother of Pearl. An original Rembrandt painting hung over the fireplace in the wall opposite the entrance. A beautiful antique crystal chandelier hung from a medallion in the centre of the ceiling.

"This truly is wonderful, and so beautifully decorated," she said.

"Thank you. My grandfather had this added. We spend most of our evenings here."

They sat in cozy deep red leather chairs. In front of them was the most fascinating round coffee table Gwen had ever seen. A two-inch top consisted of wood heavily marked with a curved grain, which sat on a cypress tree trunk.

A slightly graying woman brought in a tray of goodies and coffee.

David opened the conversation. "Ms. Ross, I apologize for ignoring your previous requests for interviews."

"I understand you don't to talk with reporters," she said, smiling.

"That is true."

"Why me, and why now?" Gwen asked.

David noted these two questions were asked with a genuine interest. He responded in like fashion. "Ms. Ross—may I call you Gwen?"

Gwen nodded.

"When my sister went missing, I wasn't talking with anyone other than my wife."

"I understand," Gwen said. *I'll be quiet for a minute or two and let him talk,* she thought.

"When I first heard of Maria's death, I was devastated. She saved my life. She stood by me; because of her, I kicked my alcohol and drug habit. Through her encouragement and guidance, I got back into painting, which has become the central element of my life."

"Did you have investigators look into the plane crash?" Gwen asked.

"I did, but they found nothing new."

"Do you have any idea of what happened and why?"

"I did wonder if she had been murdered."

"And now?"

"It's...a mystery," David said quietly.

"Do you have a firm of specialized investigators still working on it for you?"

David was stunned by this question. *Is she fishing?* he wondered. He felt momentarily that he was being cornered, and he didn't like it one bit.

"What makes you ask such a question?" he asked.

Gwen smiled. "You did inherit the entire Down's fortune and all the company's investments, did you not? I would be very surprised if you didn't have some sort of surveillance over these companies, considering you personally have nothing to do with their day-to-day running."

"I never wanted to be in the business sector. Gwen, may I request that this whole interview be off the record?"

"Yes—we can speak off the record," Gwen said. She could see that it had to be this way if he was going to talk at all.

"I have a private security and a private investigative service," David continued.

Gwen nodded. "You are very wise in doing so, David. I know you will not reveal the names of these organizations, nor will I ask you to. Please be assured that I respect your privacy."

David began to relax a bit. David had made up his mind and sat back in his chair. "I've had my investigators do a full background check on you," he admitted.

"I would not expect anything less," said Gwen.

"You certainly have had a very successful career."

Gwen smiled. "I have been blessed with being in the right place at the right time."

"Tell me, Gwen: what made you become one of the original members of the International Investigative Reporters Organization—the IIRO?"

Gwen looked at him and saw a twinkle in his eye. "Well, you must have a pretty good idea, if you've had me fully investigated," she said.

"I know this group is working on uncovering the existence of Covert Governments. What are you ultimately looking for?"

"My bottom line is to seek out the truth, and right now it appears to be a never-ending quest."

"You've made a recent breakthrough about a Boston laboratory."

"Yes, I gather you know of the arrests which occurred there recently."

"Yes I do. I also know about Sandforth's death."

Gwen nodded. *So...this is the reason behind his willingness to do this interview,* she thought. *I must be very careful here, because I'm still not sure which side he is really on.*

"Yes, his death was unfortunate. He'll never be tried for the deaths he ordered," she answered.

"You mean the murders of Megan's parents?"

"Yes—and probably there are others we'll never know of."

"Gwen, I need your help with something. I feel I can trust you."

"You can."

"I've been rather suspicious of one of the labs we own located just outside of Melbourne. I'm suspicious of what is going on in a special underground complex there. My investigative company can't find out much about it, nor can they get confirmation on where the funding is coming from."

"It sounds to me that you have one of the international covert Black Labs."

"That is what I've suspected for a long time," David commented.

"I'm not surprised you can't get anywhere. These labs have security well beyond anything you can imagine," Gwen said. "Why do you think I might be able to help?"

"It's a gut feeling I've had ever since you cracked the Boston case."

"I had help, David; a Detective Boyle was also involved."

"And now you're on the run, right?" he joked.

Gwen laughed. "It's not the first time in my career I've had to slip out of the USA."

There was a tapping on the door, and Shelley came in. "Lunch is ready," she said.

Introductions were made, and they moved to a small cozy dining room.

In the course of conversation, Shelley said, "Gwen, I believe you know Dr. Nona Teal—am I correct?"

"I do, Shelley," Gwen said.

"I've been following her work on initiating the Partners for Universal Harmony for some time," she responded. After discussing the finer points of the movement, Shelley asked, "Do you think Dr. Teal would come to Australia and speak to our groups here?"

"I'm sure she would. Why don't you give her a call and see? I know that she can be rather difficult to reach as she's quite busy, but I'll be happy to put you in touch with her. Since we're thirteen hours ahead here in Melbourne, it's a rather awkward time to phone her, but perhaps we can make sure that you two connect over the phone this evening."

"Thank you, Gwen. That's a wonderful suggestion, and I appreciate your help in reaching her."

Once lunch was over, Gwen and David returned to his study. When they were sitting down again, Gwen spoke more directly about the topic that was weighing on everyone's mind.

"So David, you're suspicious of what is going on in your Melbourne lab?"

"I certainly am, and after your conversation about the Universal Harmony with my wife, I believe you can see one of the reasons why. Is there anything you can do to help us discover what is happening here?"

"Unfortunately, I can't reveal my source—and I must ask that you keep whatever information I give you to yourself. It is imperative this information doesn't get back to me." Gwen had made up her mind over lunch; if she was going to get anywhere at all with the Australian situation, she would have to start trusting someone, and right now that someone was David Downs.

"Then I guess we'd better start trusting one another," David said as he reached out to shake her hand.

Immediately, Gwen wrote three names on a piece of paper and handed it to David. After the names, she simply wrote the word *here?*

David looked at the piece of paper. Something on that list triggered a memory, so he pulled out his laptop and did a brief search. It took him a couple of minutes to find what he was looking for: the list of employees at the Melbourne complex. After reviewing the list, he took a pencil and circled two names on Gwen's. "Well, what do you know?" he said as he returned the sheet of paper to Gwen. "We have a match."

Gwen saw that the names of Ellsworth and Lampson were circled. "We sure do!" she said, smiling. "Can you confirm when they started here?"

After additional research, David confirmed their start date. When he told Gwen this date, she said, "Matthew Stone and Mary Teal were both killed within a few weeks prior to that date."

David gave a low whistle and checked another file. "When I look at the documentation for our receiving department for that time period, I see that we had a very large and unusual shipment of new equipment which arrived around that time," he said. "This stands out in particular as the shipper and contents are unidentified. Our standard process for all of our incoming shipments is to have the name and address of our suppliers recorded as well as a detailed description of what we've received. That's not the case at all for this shipment."

"Did your funding also increase at that time?"

David scrolled through more files on his laptop until he found the relevant accounting spreadsheet. "Yes—by sixty percent. What does all this mean, Gwen?"

"It means, David, that I'm about to tell you something that will shock you to your core. Can we please have some coffee? This is going to take some serious explaining."

Over the next hour, Gwen methodically described the entire story, linking information from the week before Matthew's and Mary's death all the way to the present.

David was shocked and dismayed. "You're telling me that I own one of these covert labs which are genetically engineering deadly microbes which are being used to terrorize and instill fear into the human race? I don't believe it!"

"I'm afraid it's true—and we now have some evidence to help prove it."

"How are we going to proceed?"

"That will take a great deal of careful planning," replied Gwen.

David sat staring at the fireplace. Finally, having made up his mind, he turned to Gwen.

"I think I know someone who can help us," he said. He stood up and said, "I'll be right back."

Gwen could hear voices. She was going over things in her mind when the middle-aged woman who served them coffee earlier entered David's study, with David right behind her.

"Gwen, I would like you to meet Angela."

Gwen was very puzzled, but she rose to shake hands with the newcomer. "Angela, this is Gwen, the investigative reporter I told you about," he said.

Gwen was getting edgy. "I thought our talk was to be purely confidential. Please explain."

David couldn't help it; he gave a quiet little chuckle. "Please, Gwen, I think you'd better sit down. "I must apologize—I didn't introduce Angela properly. Her name is Maria. This is my sister."

He waited to see Gwen's reaction.

"But..." Gwen started. She was shocked and surprised into silence.

Maria came over to Gwen and sat beside her and spoke quietly.

"It's true, Gwen. I'm Maria Downs, and yes, I'm alive. Before I explain, I must insist that you not call me Maria; Angela is my name now, and only the three of us in this room know the truth. I can help you, but you must also help to keep me safe by referring to me as Angela Monterey, a cousin of David's. Okay?"

"Okay," Gwen said. She was still stunned and confused.

"David just told me about the breakthrough you made regarding the covert labs," Angela continued. "I'd like to hear more. Why don't I tell you part of my story first, and then we can go from there?"

"That sounds like a good plan," said Gwen.

"I think this discussion calls for something to drink," said David. "I'll leave the two of you to talk; I'll be back in just a few moments." He left the room and closed the door quietly behind him.

There was a moment of silence; each was absorbed in a myriad of thoughts. After a minute, Gwen took the lead and said, "Before you begin, may I ask how long it has been that David has known that you were alive?"

"I came to visit him just a few years back. I just had to see him. At first, he was very suspicious of me. I think he thought I was a reporter or an investigator of some sort. I told him I was a distant cousin on our father's side of the family, and mentioned a couple of things about our father that only he and I knew. He let me stay the weekend."

"Did he figure out or even have the slightest suspicion as to your real identity?"

"No—I had a series of plastic surgeries, and had worked hard to change my personality and speech patterns. Still, I was amazed that he didn't clue in right away."

"When did he discover who you really were?"

"By my third visit, we were getting along quite well, and he suggested I stay longer. One evening while Shelley was out, David and I went for a walk; he started to tell me how much he missed Maria and how close they had been. My heart was breaking—I couldn't stand it." Angela paused while she dabbed her eyes with a tissue, then she continued. "As we strolled along, I stopped him. He turned to me and asked if I was okay. I took his hand like I used to and asked, 'What if Maria were alive?' He was stunned, and then he looked right into my eyes. I was crying by that time, but I had to tell him. 'Yes, David...it's me,' I said. I thought he would faint, but instead he held me in his arms and said, 'Somehow, I always hoped, and I always prayed. In my heart, I just knew you were still out there!' From then on, I lived here in our home—not as his sister, but as his cousin."

Gwen couldn't help it; she too was crying. "But why did you wait so long?" she asked.

"I had to, Gwen. You of all people must have a good idea of who I was and what I was involved in."

Gwen was immediately sobered by the cold, harsh reality of this reminder. "Yes...yes, of course," she answered.

"I know—you must have some questions."

"I do."

At this point, David returned and had brought some wine.

"So how are you two getting along?" He smiled and gave his sister a wink.

"Gwen knows, David; I told her the truth."

"I had hoped you would. Thank you for doing so, Angela. How far long did you get?"

"I was just at the point when I told you who I really was."

"Ah, yes. I can see that both of you have shed a few tears," David said as Angela laughed.

"It truly is an incredible story, but I must admit that I'm really curious about the plane crash, and what you experienced afterward," said Gwen.

"Actually, there was no plane crash."

Gwen was intrigued. "You mean...it was faked?"

"Yes. Let me backtrack a bit. Gwen, you must know from your research that I initially had inherited the businesses from my father which included a directorship on the board of the CESR in the USA. I was totally shocked at their agenda. I'll tell you more about that later, but suffice it to say that I didn't agree with what was going on; I couldn't understand why my father was so involved. I found out that the Melbourne lab was handling something that was considered top secret, and when I tried to find out what it was, I was told in no uncertain terms that it was none of my business—furthermore, I was warned that if I didn't stop asking questions, something terrible would happen to David. I felt I had to go along with it; I had no choice." She paused to have a drink. "Then I realized our lab was not the only one involved, and I learned of the many other things that the covert governments were up to. I couldn't stomach it. I knew they thought I was the weak link on the board, and I wanted out."

"You couldn't just walk out?" Gwen asked.

"Actually, I could have, but they would have killed me and David. I knew I would be able to expose them someday, but only if I stayed alive. It took me over a year to develop my plan."

"It must've been very difficult for you," Gwen stated.

"It was. I had to make them uncomfortable to the point that my participation was no longer desirable to them."

"You were playing a very dangerous game," David interjected.

"Yes, it was. I knew the last board meeting I attended was to be the critical one. I had to criticize some aspect of their plans, and I did so. But now I'm getting ahead of myself. Several months before that meeting, I began to formulate my plan and put together the various components."

"How did you manage to fake the plane crash?" Gwen asked.

"I found a small, struggling computer technology company that was extremely good at creating scenes for videos, movies, and the like. Their only problem was lack of funds which they needed to buy the best equipment possible. I contacted them through a third party and made a deal with them: if they produced a short video for me, I would buy them the necessary equipment. What they did was so realistic that I couldn't believe it."

"But how did you make the plane disappear?"

"I paid my pilot a great deal of money, and he ditched it in the Pacific somewhere. Apparently, no one was significantly suspicious."

"But Angela, as I remember it, they did find some debris," Gwen said.

"Yes—that was intentionally jettisoned the day before the plane was ditched."

"Incredible!" Gwen said, then asked, "How did you arrange all the plastic surgeries?"

"I flew to South Africa as a heavily made-up elderly woman with a fake passport. I stayed there for a few years, had a series of six plastic surgeries, acquired a South African passport in the name of Angela Monterey, and came to Australia."

"How did you manage to pay for all this?" Gwen asked. She was spellbound.

"Many months prior to my disappearance, I began transferring money to a Swiss bank account."

"Wow! It all worked out so well for you. I really admire what you've done—it could not have been easy. At any point, you may have been found out. What an incredible story!" said Gwen.

"It's not over yet," Angela added.

"That's right," David said. "Because of you, Gwen, we might be able to break things wide open."

* * *

Megan and Sam had enjoyed an absolutely wonderful day. They drove to the beach and had a long walk; having packed a picnic basket, they ate their lunch while relaxing and watching the swimmers and the children playing in the sand.

"Tell me, Sam, what is David Downs like?"

"He is a great guy—a multibillionaire, but to meet him, you'd never know it. He's down-to-earth and is very good to his employees. His wife Shelley is a lovely woman; she's very independent and clever. Her involvement here with Universal Harmony is outstanding."

Megan nodded. "So, I talked to Gram about Sandforth," she said.

"That would have been a significant conversation," Sam said. "How did Gram take the news of Sandforth's death?"

"She wasn't totally surprised, but she was upset, at first, that she wouldn't see him go to prison. By the end of the conversation, however, she said that he obviously lived in hell when he was here on Earth, so in her own way, she chose to forgive him. Her philosophy is that if one is unable to forgive, they are not free to move forward."

After another couple of hours at the beach, they packed up their belongings and headed back to Sam's place. When they arrived, he found a message on his phone from David:

"The interview with Gwen went very well; she's still here and will be staying for dinner. How about you two come over at around seven-thirty this evening and join us? Shelley and I would love to meet Megan."

"That's great news!" said Megan. "Gwen said that she felt she'd be very successful if she even got as much as an hour with him."

That evening, Megan and Sam arrived at the gates of David's country estate. Once they were out of the car, they were greeted warmly by Shelley, David and Gwen.

"It's so nice to finally meet you, Megan," said Shelley. Megan handed her the bottle of wine that Sam had picked out for her, having known her favourite, and Shelley smiled in thanks. "Sam has said such wonderful things about you."

"Welcome to Australia," David added welcoming them into his home.

After a lovely meal of roast beef, gravy, a medley of root veggies, accompanied by a local award winning red wine, home-made apple pie and local cheddar cheese was served, followed by freshly-ground coffee. After dinner and dessert, they moved to the library and sipped some fine Australian liqueurs. During dinner, the conversation had been lively and light, but now, the tone of the conversations became more serious.

"Megan, I'm fascinated by the type of open research you're engaged in; tell me, is the complex where you work really living up to the original statement of purpose? And does it function well?" asked Shelley.

"I must admit, for the first while it was difficult, because everyone there found it a challenge to become accustomed to the new innovations. It's taken a few years to build, but we work well together. There is a strong move towards team research, not only within each discipline, but between disciplines, which has resulted in some very interesting findings."

"What is your field of research?" David asked.

"Marine viruses and bacteria, plus I do some bioengineering."

"Do you think these viruses and bacteria we've been seeing in various countries which seem to be causing large numbers of humans to die are natural or bioengineered?" David asked.

"If they're not being caused by natural mutations, then it must be some form of genetic engineering," Sam commented.

"That is our fear. If this is so, we could have a very serious global situation on our hands. There are some people who believe the AIDS virus was created by someone to try to reduce the world's population. This is only a theory, but what if it's true?" Megan said.

"If these viruses and bacteria are being bioengineered, who is doing it—and why?" Shelley asked, shaking her head.

"Again, there's a theory going around that they are being produced by what some people call Secret or Shadow Governments which are potentially aligned with various militaries around the world. It could even be one or more groups of extremely wealthy people. It may, in fact, be a combination of any or all of them." Megan said. "Gwen, you have some pretty interesting ideas of what might be happening. Would you like to explain them?"

"Certainly—but before I start, I want to be clear: none of these ideas originated with me; they have been published and discussed for quite a while. I'll give you an overview of the three main points:

"First: Certain countries, such as the US and Russia, are actively trying to cultivate arms in outer space, and there may be nuclear weapons involved.

"Second, whoever constitutes what some call the Power Elite, for lack of a better term, have led the way in the abuse of Earth's resources for their own greed and profit. It is a well-known fact that the Earth is on the brink of a disaster, which may well bring about the end of the human race. It is believed by some that certain aliens have quietly contacted humanity's powerful leaders, offering assistance to heal the Earth. These leaders refused. These are the same human leaders who are thought to be in control of such things as the Black Budgets; they are also suspected to be the financial contributors of many covert laboratories and research centres that are involved in top secret activities. The Power Elite know Earth is doomed, but they don't care. They have made deals with certain aliens. If these humans cooperate with them, these same aliens will rescue them and move them to another safe planet. Later, when Earth recovers from the disaster; the aliens will bring them back. These humans will then be in absolute control of Earth.

"Third, we are using up Earth's resources, which some aliens desperately need for their own planets and civilizations; these aliens need to wipe out a huge percentage of humans before these resources are used up. At the same time, they still need a certain number of humans to survive in order to do the mining and processing of these resources."

David frowned. "That all sounds rather negative. Are there any hopeful signs that this Power Elite can be weakened or defeated?"

"Yes, I believe there are," Megan said, smiling at Shelley. "Your wife and my Gram are very good examples of the awakening of the human spirit. There are thousands of people with similar ideas developing very strong interconnecting grassroots movements around the world. An increasing number of people are asking questions, demanding accountability and disclosure from their legal governments about where all their millions of unaccounted tax money have been spent—especially as there is very little to show for it. What have the Black Budgets been used for, and what are the governments keeping from us? Why has there been so much secrecy?"

"In the United States, more money is being put toward the Black Budgets than to our educational system," Gwen added. "It is a pretty sorry state of affairs when the education of our young people and their welfare is a lower priority than these Black Ops. However, there are many US citizens who are actively bringing this knowledge to the general public, raising awareness about what is really going on. I believe this sort of thing is happening in many other countries as well, but to a lesser extent than in the USA.

"It's as if our governments think that the general public either cannot or will not think for themselves. We have been subjected to so many cover-ups by the powers that be that many people either no longer listen or care. They are so overwhelmed that they won't try. Having said that, there are signs that this sense of apathy is beginning to change. Ultimately, this is why we developed the International Investigative Reporters Organization—because we believe that the Power Elite is a global threat."

"Wow! I've heard rumours to that effect," said David. "I wonder if all the so-called secret governments are under the control of some form of centralization, such as the one you're calling the Power Elite."

"I lean in that direction," Gwen said. "That's what our group of reporters is seeking to uncover. We're trying to find out the truth."

Megan nodded in agreement. "We need people to truly wake up to the fact that life on Earth is rapidly moving towards extinction—mainly due to the human factor. At the same time, we must realize this trend can be stopped, altered, and maybe even reversed."

"How on earth—pardon the pun—can that be accomplished?" David asked.

Shelley leaned forward. "There are very positive signs that humans are much more aware of what's been happening, and are trying to work on healing one another and the planet," she said. "However, I feel it has to be a global effort. No one country or continent can do this. We have to put aside our differences and work together in a cooperative manner towards this common goal."

"Well said, Shelley," said Megan. "I think the grassroots group which you and Gram are so involved in, along with many similar ones, are excellent platforms."

"Yes—and cohesion between the many different groups is one of the main things we're trying to achieve together," Shelley added. "I would love to speak with Nona, if possible, and invite her for a speaking engagement here. Gwen and I discussed this possibility earlier today. Do you think it's a good time to reach her right now?"

"Certainly," said Megan. "It's morning where she is; I can call her and make introductions over the phone."

Shelley offered the phone to Megan, who then called Nona.

"Good morning, Gram," she said, "I'm having a delightful time in Australia with Sam and Gwen. We've made new friends, and one of them is a great admirer of yours. We're over at their home as they had us over for dinner, along with Gwen. May I put you on the phone with our hostess? Her name is Shelley."

"Of course, dear," said Nona. "I'm glad to hear that you're having such a good time. Pass the phone over to Shelley, and after we're done talking, I'll say goodbye to you."

Megan handed the phone to Shelley with a smile. Shelley took the phone and began speaking.

"Dr. Nona Teal—I'm so pleased to have the chance to speak with you. Your granddaughter Megan is a lovely young woman, and I feel that you and I have some common interests. I wonder if you'd be interested in coming to Melbourne to speak about Partners for Universal Harmony."

"It just so happens I'll be going to New Zealand late this month," said Nona. "I have the two weeks before and about three weeks after my New Zealand trip before I'm required to be back here in Canada. Have Megan give you my email address and phone number, and send me the details. I'd love to come to Australia as well, so see what you can work out on your end, and we'll go from there."

After Shelley and Nona exchanged a few more pleasantries and finished speaking, Shelley returned the phone to Megan, who said her goodbyes to her Gram before hanging up. Shelley was very excited to have spoken with Nona, and was looking forward to facilitating a speaking engagement for her.

Shortly thereafter, they noticed that it was beginning to get late; the evening was winding down, so the conversation eased back to lighter topics. An hour later, Gwen, Megan, and Sam took their leave, and offered many thanks to David and Shelley for such a wonderful evening.

The next morning, Gwen received a phone call; it was Angela.

"I was wondering if we could spend some time together today to have a good, uninterrupted talk," she said. "I think we have much of value to share with one another."

"I'd like that very much," said Gwen.

"Perfect. How would you like to come to the estate for lunch today at one pm? We'll take it from there and see how the afternoon unfolds."

After an excellent lunch, they took their coffee and dessert—an exquisite strawberry shortcake—to the rose garden. It was a quiet and private place to talk, and provided a tranquil setting in which to visit.

"This was one of my mother's favourite spots; she would sit here by the hour and read," said Angela.

"It's so beautiful," sighed Gwen, "and very peaceful."

Angela sipped her coffee and settled into a luxurious teak lounge chair.

"Gwen," she asked, "Can you share with me what you know about Sandforth? Were you able to find out much from him?"

Gwen was both open and circumspect as she described the death of Matthew Stone and Mary Teal, and the many years of subsequent investigation. She also told her about the actual arrest and outlined briefly what had followed.

"Did Sandforth give you any information other than his confession?" asked Angela.

Gwen hesitated. *If I'm going to get her to help, then I'll have to trust her; after all, she's trusted me with the details of her identity,* she thought. She decided to open up a bit more.

"Yes, he gave me some passwords and access to his computer files," she said. "I think he was trying to atone for what he had done. In fact, that is how I found out about the move of the two scientists from Boston to Melbourne."

"Did you bring the passwords with you?"

"Yes...but I must admit that I'm hesitant to share them."

"I understand, Gwen. How about you and I look at them together? I recall from my days on the board that there was a type of universal code used to transmit sensitive information which might be of some help to you. I could probably help decode any material which was sent during my time on the board."

Gwen paused for a few moments to think it over, and then decided.

"Okay, let's do that," she said.

"How about we each gather our data and our thoughts and meet again tomorrow?" Angela offered. "I can take you to our beach house; that way, we'll get in some swimming and relaxation while we go over the material together, and we can stay there overnight."

Gwen felt that a foundation of mutual trust had been established, and thought that this sounded like a fine idea. If they put their heads together, the results had good potential. She decided to take Angela up on her offer.

"You tell me the time, and I'll be ready!" she said.

Angela picked up Gwen the next morning, and off they went.

"It is a beautiful day; where exactly are we headed?"

"Out to Torquay. It's very quiet there; we can relax, walk on the beach, or swim."

The drive was scenic, and Gwen happily took in the surroundings as Angela drove. An hour later, they were sitting on the deck watching the waves pound and tumble ashore. After some refreshments and a walk on the beach, they came back to the beach house, ready to begin their research.

"I've my laptop and a USB drive with some of my old files," said Angela. "They just might be of some help." Once their computers were up and running, they were ready to go. "Where do you think we should start?" Angela asked.

"Try bringing up anything you have for two to three weeks before Matthew Stone was murdered and for the same time period afterwards."

"This is interesting," Angela said. "It seems that there was a lot of testing of about three different bacterial strains, then it suddenly stopped."

Gwen glanced at Angela's data. "That confirms what we already know."

"Yes, but look here, Gwen—they were far more extensive and widespread than we thought."

Gwen leaned over and looked at the screen where Angela was pointing.

"Wait a minute...are those coordinates correct?"

"They should be...why?"

"What are our coordinates here?" Gwen asked.

Angela turned on her GPS and entered the longitude and latitude from the file. They were not looking at land; they were looking at water. They double-checked. "I think we better check all of these locations." Angela stated. Of the forty-nine locations, forty were on land; the remaining nine were in the open ocean.

"I don't understand." Angela said.

"Neither do I!" exclaimed Gwen:

"Were they testing one or more of these viruses or bacteria on marine life, or were they dumping some there?"

"Let's take this one step further," Gwen suggested as she was searching some of her old notes.

"What are you looking for?"

"Angela, at the time just after Matt's death, we found some research he'd done. I believe we are now looking at the same findings."

They cross-checked their data; sure enough, almost all of what Matt had found corresponded with many of the forty-nine locations that Angela found.

Angela was calculating the amount of time and effort it would take to check all these out. "We should contact David and ask him to check out all of the coordinates we have; he'll be able to get the results far faster than we could. I'll phone him and make us some coffee. It's time we took a break."

They were relaxing and having a drink when the phone call came from Stuart Cameron, one of David's research assistants.

"The land locations you gave us for those dates show that in each case, there were mysterious deaths reported, numbering anywhere between fifteen to forty-five people. No cause was found."

"What about the marine locations?" Gwen asked.

"Now this is where it gets interesting. We've got answers back for five of them so far, and so far there is a trend: these locations are within one hundred to 400 miles of land. Corpses of both whales and dolphins were found washed up on shores in those general areas; cause of death is unknown. The marine biologists who examined some of them suspect they died from either a viral or bacterial infection."

Angela thanked Stuart and asked him to keep on trying for the other locations.

"Why would they be testing these viruses or bacteria on marine life?" Angela asked Gwen.

"I'm not sure, but Megan may have a clue," Gwen replied. "While you were on the phone, I was checking for any additional similar incidences after Matthew died. I found nothing until about three years afterwards. It appears that the testing of these microbes began again and they may have culminated in the horrendous death toll recently in India."

"Were they ever able to get a sample from that outbreak?" Angela asked.

"No, that bacteria had an extremely short lifespan, and was virtually untraceable."

"Let me contact Megan and see if she knows about these marine incidents."

* * *

That evening, after speaking with Gwen on the phone about researching incidences of potential microbe testing on marine life, Megan wished to talk to Lacuna in order to gain a deeper understanding. She lay down in bed and gently relaxed into a meditative state. As she opened her mind, she found herself talking to Ortho.

"We're bringing you both through a portal in this region," he said. "We can only hold you both for a short time, so please be brief."

Megan was immediately excited. "I've a couple questions," she began. "Lacuna, can you give me information on the mysterious deaths of whales and dolphins?"

Lacuna communicated some very disturbing information in video-like pictures. What she saw made Megan cry. There was a family of dolphins swimming near the surface when a small canister exploded in their midst. A whitish cloud formed around them, and in minutes they were dead.

Megan was weeping. "Oh Lacuna! Who would do this?"

Another vision was of a small aircraft flying close to the ocean. It dropped a small canister directly into a pod of five humpbacks. Three whales dove immediately, but two didn't get away in time.

Megan closed her eyes as Lacuna sent one last message to her.

Help us, please, Megan...please, help us.

"I will, I promise!" she responded.

She turned her mind directly back to Ortho.

"Can you help? What's going on?"

"That was the result of an earlier experiment of genetic engineering."

"Why are the dolphins and whales being killed?"

"They are being warned not to help the humans in any way; if they do, they will pay a huge price"

"Were those whales part of her family?"

"No, Megan, they weren't her immediate family. It happened thousands of miles away; the whales and dolphins can communicate with one another over great distances. Why do you think all the oceans are interconnected?" He paused a moment and answered his own question. "The cetaceans are responsible for keeping the oceans in balance, not just the oceans, but the whole planet."

"Is it true they carry all the ancient wisdom?" Megan asked.

"Yes, it is. The dark forces know if cetaceans and humans could ever work together, there would be no chance for them here on Earth."

"They'll do anything to keep us apart."

"Yes—and they almost succeeded in getting the humans to hunt whales to virtual extinction."

"Are they still dropping those canisters?" she asked.

"Not recently, but they could start again at any time if they feel a need to. Our time is up, now, Megan. Go in peace."

"Meg...Meg..."

Sam was calling her softly. She woke up and found herself in his arms.

"Oh, Sam!"

"Meg, you've been crying."

Megan told him what she'd seen. "Sam, I have to help them. I simply must."

"You will, my darling; you'll find a way, and I'll help you any way I can. Now rest and try to get some sleep tonight."

The next morning, Megan called Gwen on her cellphone.

"I can't tell you how I know this," she said, "but I've confirmed that there was indeed experimental testing on marine life, which resulted in the deaths of many dolphins and whales. They were killed by the Power Elite by dropping canisters of bacteria directly on their pods."

"Is it ongoing?" Gwen asked.

"No, it's not, but it could start up again anytime."

"Thanks for the confirmation, Megan," said Gwen. "I'll keep working on my end here and will let you know what we come up with. I'll check in with you later."

"I think we've come as far as we can along this line of research, for now," said Angela as she handed Gwen a coffee. "Let's try something else. Do you have that set of numbers from Sandforths' files handy?"

"I do," said Gwen. "Let's look at this one first and see if we can make anything of it." She pulled up a file and highlighted the numbers *71211822249227*. "It appears to be all one long number. What could it possibly be? Could it be a secret account?"

"I think I know what it might be. Print out the alphabet and place a number above it, and then put a series of numbers below it—only this time count backwards. Perhaps numbers correspond with letters—for example, the seventh letter of the alphabet is *g*, the first letter of the alphabet is *a*, the second letter of the alphabet is *b*, and so on."

After trying that method, Gwen and Angela agreed that it wasn't getting them anywhere. With that theory, the highlighted numbers only spelled *gabaahbbbdibbg*, which didn't make sense. They went back and separated the numbers into various combinations; they still got nowhere.

"This is frustrating. Maybe we should try the reverse; A=26 and so on."

"I don't think we're going to get anywhere with this. This was top secret information encrypted by a professional. We need an expert to crack the codes—someone we can trust."

"I agree. Our best bet is to hire a cryptographer," Gwen said. "I know of someone with those qualifications—a young man who has worked for me back home on other research projects."

"Would he come here?" Angela asked.

"He might, if we give him enough of an incentive."

"You mean money?"

"Yes, if we pay him well, I'm sure he'll be willing to come to Melbourne. He's pretty mobile."

"Money is no problem. I'll cover the cost."

"Perfect—I'll phone him now."

When Gwen contacted Jamie, she explained that she was working on a sensitive story and needed his expertise to help break a code. "I should tell you now—you'll be decrypting some sensitive material and it may be dangerous."

"Has this anything to do with the Boston lab?" Jamie inquired.

"Indirectly, yes it does. We'd like to bring you here as soon as possible. We'll pay for your flight and at least twice your fee, as well as your meals, accommodations, and any additional expenses."

"With an offer like that, how can I refuse? Just tell me where I need to be and when."

"Well, you're coming to Australia, and we need you here now. How soon can you be ready?"

"It won't take me long—about three hours."

"I see here online that there's a flight leaving Boston in six and half hours," she said. Angela was scrolling through the airline's website on her laptop, looking at reservations, with Gwen was glancing over her shoulder as she spoke. "Does that work for you?

"I can manage that," said Jamie.

Gwen nodded at Angela, who pulled out her credit card to pay for the flight. Within moments, the ticket was purchased.

"Done!" said Gwen. "You're flying business class; I'm sending your ticket by e-mail right now. I'll pick you up at the airport tomorrow when you arrive."

The next day, they were at the airport just in time to meet him.

"Hey Jamie—over here!" Gwen called.

"Gwen, it's so good to see you!"

"This is my friend, Angela Monterey," said Gwen by way of introduction.

"You must be exhausted," Angela said.

"Not really; I slept most of the time. It's the first time I've travelled business class. It was great."

"Well, let's get you to the hotel," Angela said. They made their way to the parking lot, located Angela's car, and put Jamie's things in the trunk.

Once at the hotel, Jamie went up to his room to freshen up, and then he joined Gwen and Angela at the bar. Each ordered a beer, and Angela and Gwen explained what they'd found so far regarding Sandforth's files.

"We'll show you the actual files tomorrow. There are a lot of them and most of them are in some form of code," said Angela.

"You've had a long flight, and the jet lag may hit you hard. How about you get a good night's rest, and we can pick this up tomorrow?"

"That sounds good to me," said Jamie. "I must admit, I'm a bit weary after all."

"No problem, Jamie; let's meet in the lobby at ten am tomorrow, and we'll go from there."

* * *

After a handful of days snorkeling at the Great Barrier Reef, Megan and Sam returned to Sam's apartment. The light was blinking on his answering machine.

"Meg, there's a message here from one of your team workers—a Sandy Johnson—asking you to call your lab," he said. He handed her the cordless phone.

"Sandy, I just got your message now," said Megan, returning the call. "I was offline for a few days, so I haven't had time to check email or cell messages. What's happening?"

"Megan, regarding your request about the whale and dolphin deaths: you were right—there were several incidences. We sent you an e-mail with the details."

"Great—I'll check the email as soon as we're done talking. Can you tell me if there were there any autopsies done?"

"Yes there were, and it appears that the cause of death was a bacterial infection of some sort. However, in every case, they didn't find any evidence of the actual bacterial cells. Is there anything else we can do on our end?"

"Yes—put out a worldwide alert to keep a watch for any further occurrences. Thank you Sandy, I really appreciate it."

After hanging up the phone, Megan forwarded Gwen copies of the emails that Sandy had sent her. According to Sandy's findings, there were more incidences than Gwen had told her about, including a couple that were close to Australia.

Megan had a couple of days left before returning home. Sam had gone back to work, so Megan and Gwen had lunch and went to the beach for the afternoon. Gwen wanted to talk to Megan a bit more about the whales as well as the email that Megan had forwarded.

"You've been very busy the last several days, Gwen," said Megan. "Even though I've been away for about a week, I still get the sense you're getting somewhere with the Melbourne lab."

"You really can read minds, can't you?"

"Only if one is open to it," said Megan, smiling.

"I see," said Gwen, becoming a bit more serious. "Well, I do feel you should know more about what is happening."

"Only if you wish to tell me."

"Megan, we may be getting somewhere. It's a very slow process and I have to be to be very careful." She told Megan the highlights of the decoding process, but gave no specific details.

"Did you take a look at the email I forwarded you about the coordinates for the cetaceans killed?" asked Megan.

"Yes, I did, and I found it fascinating. I'd love to hear more of your thoughts."

"The first thing that jumped out at me is that some of the incidences were very close to Australia. I wonder if there is any connection with the lab here?"

Gwen frowned. "I wish I had a concrete answer for you. To be honest, I'm baffled as well. Why are they killing dolphins and whales? It doesn't make any sense."

Megan nodded, and then explained what Ortho had told her about how whales hold all of Earth's wisdom, along with the possible interconnection between whales, dolphins, and humans. "The killing of whales could be a warning to them not to help us," she said.

"And to think that humans almost hunted them to extinction..." said Gwen, shaking her head sadly.

They both went quiet for a while, contemplating the enormity of this revelation.

After a few moments, Gwen asked, "Do you think that whales, dolphins, and humans will work together someday?"

"Yes...yes, I do; there are myths and legends from all over the world showing it has happened many times. And just look at my connection to Lacuna."

"Tell me more, please."

"Well, seeing that we're in Australia; let's begin here. There are several coastal tribes here who have very close connections with dolphins and whales. The Mirning on the south coast have a legend about a great white whale, Jiderra, which came from Sirius along with seven sisters from Pleaides. The seven sisters drove Jiderra onto the rocks where he turned into stone, thus providing a connection between humans and whales. In 1996, a large white whale was seen in that area. There are other legends right across Polynesia, and throughout the Pacific region—Hawaii, China, Japan. In India, there were dolphin beings, half-human and half-fish; they were called Vishnu; and in Sumer they were known as Oannes. They were also very prominent in Egypt and Greece; hence, the boy on a dolphin statue."

"Wasn't there something about a tribe in Africa and dolphins?" Gwen asked.

"There is: the Dogon tribe have cave paintings of a half-human, half-dolphin that are thousands of years old. There are drawings of the Sirius Star and its orbit, which were only confirmed by astronomers recently. They also proved that the pattern of their orbits was exactly as the Dogons had drawn it in ancient times. The amazing thing about this orbit is that it bears a striking resemblance to our DNA helix. They called these dolphin beings *Nommos*. In all cases, these dolphin/humans brought civilization and advanced technology to many of these regions."

"So, we did at one time work closely with cetaceans," Gwen acknowledged.

"Yes—and I honestly believe we will again. We have to if we're going to save this planet that we call home."

"What happened? How did we get so separated?" Gwen asked.

"Probably because humans, having the freedom of choice, chose a path of greed and destruction rather than one of peace, love, and forgiveness."

"Megan, that seems to be true—especially when you consider what the Power Elite are doing; we as a world civilization can't let them get away with it. There are two to three thousand of the greediest, richest, most powerful families trying to control the rest of the six billion individuals on the planet. Many are beginning to wake up to what is really going on and are trying to do something about it."

"I know—just look at how fast the Universal Harmony Movement and other groups like them are growing and how many ordinary citizens are pushing their governments to come clean about Black Budgets, UFOs, and aliens," Megan said.

"It's too bad you won't be here to hear Nona's speeches."

"Will you?" asked Megan.

"Yes. I'm making arrangements to stay for a while longer."

"That's great Gwen; I know she'll be glad to have you here."

"I'll be glad to see her at her speaking engagement for sure—and I'm staying as long as it takes to get some concrete information regarding the Melbourne lab."

* * *

Jamie had been working on the Sandforth files for several days when he called Gwen.

"I've loaded all the data. I've run it through several decoding programs and I think I've found something of interest. I think you should come over to my hotel room and have a look."

"Thanks Jamie. I'll be right over."

When Gwen arrived, Jamie had his laptop running and had rigged up three auxiliary monitors to display extra data.

"Lord, Jamie, I don't know how you do it. One screen is enough to drive me nuts sometimes—you've got four here in total!"

Jamie gave a confident smile; he knew he was good at what he did. "There's plenty to look at," he said

"What have you found?"

"First, let me say that it's no wonder you were having problems, Gwen. Sandforth was using a very complex filing system, with several different complicated codes. The man was paranoid." Jamie pointed to the first screen. "This file contains a series of numbers," he said. "It's a research proposal for genetically engineering a bacterium capable of breaking down oil spills."

"This is interesting, and a legitimate use of research," Gwen commented.

"True, but look at the second screen."

Gwen studied it for a moment. "It's the same date, but the content is different."

"Watch this," Jamie said as he pulled up files on monitors three and four. "Again, it's the same date. Let me explain something before we look at the content: each of these files with the same date was encoded with a different code, yet I believe they're all dealing with the same subject."

"Yes, that makes sense," Gwen agreed as she read each of the screens one through four. She was making notes as she went. "How very clever."

"The first two appear to be legitimate proposals regarding an oil-eating bacterium, but the last two are for a different bacterium." He brought up page two of the proposal. Gwen saw it immediately. They were looking at the equipment required and the cost of each piece. "They're virtually identical, but why go to all that trouble?" Jamie asked.

Gwen gave Jamie some background so he would understand what might be going on in the Boston and Melbourne labs. "What you've just found could be the tip of the iceberg. If we continue, we may both be in danger from the Power Elite or Secret Governments. This is why I've given you the background information—so you can understand more comprehensively what you're getting involved in. I'm dedicated to exposing them; are you still in?"

"I'm already in," said Jamie.

Gwen nodded, and pointed back to the first two screens. "Okay, then: I believe the first two proposals are cover-ups. If anyone looks at them, they will think all is okay. Screens three and four are the actual proposals which went through the Black Budgets."

"So this is what I'm looking for?"

"Yes—and any possible connections with other scientists and labs worldwide."

"I'd better get moving, then; there are a lot of these files to decode. Before you go, I found something else. I'm not sure it means anything; see what you think."

Jamie brought up another set of deciphered files about the bioengineering of a bacterium, called E. coli MMB 39. There was a series of coordinates listed under trials. Gwen was startled when she saw a particular one.

"Jamie, can you please bring up a map or chart? I want to see where these latitudes and longitudes are located." As he did so, she exclaimed, "I knew one of these looked familiar! Enter and run the locations of where the dead dolphins and whales were found," Gwen added as she handed him a sheet of paper.

"Most of these are on coastlines," he said.

"Jamie, can you get data on the ocean currents for these regions?"

"Yes, but it would be faster if you contacted the Australian Oceanographic Division, especially if you wish something more detailed than just the general currents."

"You're right, Jamie. We'll need tide tables to begin with." With pen and paper, they listed what they wanted in the way of tidal currents, regular currents, and weather conditions for each day of the previous three weeks leading up to the date that the corpses were found.

"With this information, we will hopefully be able to determine, by backtracking, the general area in which these animals were infected," Jamie said, "but we'll probably have to wait a day or two for answers."

"Fair enough. I've got to head out now, but before I go, I wanted to ask: did you find any reference to an Ellsworth or Lampson?"

"I did, but there was nothing new."

Gwen left feeling excited; she immediately called Angela to fill her in. She wanted to call Megan, but decided to wait and see if the oceanographic data would yield anything.

* * *

Margo Ellsworth was deciding whether she should sign a five-year extension. While doing this, she had a flashback: she was in her Boston office many years ago. Larry Lampson, her colleague, was there. "I don't believe it. I will not move. They can't make me do this—can they?"

"Margo, I don't think we've any choice. Let's look at our contracts and see if The Company can move us without our consent." Larry was very upset. A bacteriologist, he had been with The Company four years longer than Margo.

They read their contracts. "Here it is, on page six, third paragraph down," Larry said.

"Dammit!" Margo said.

"Talk about your fine print," Larry added. There, in fine print, were two specific sentences:

> The Company reserves the right to move an employee currently assigned to a covert lab to any location or laboratory of The Company's choice. No reason shall be given, and all expenses related to such a move shall be paid for by The Company.'

"I never dreamed it would happen," said Margo.

They each had signed their respective twenty-five-year contracts and had initialed each page showing they'd agreed.

"You're right Larry—we have no choice, but it doesn't mean I have to like it."

Larry got up and left her office. She crumpled up the contract and tossed it into the waste paper basket.

"That won't help you," said a voice.

It was her boss, Sandforth, standing in her doorway.

"Margo, this was not my decision. It came from my boss in Nevada. This whole section is being moved to Australia. You have one month to pack and get ready. Until such time as you find a place, you'll be staying at a hotel, and we'll supply you with a company vehicle."

He turned and left, closing her office door.

Margo just sat there and stared at the door. She suspected it had something to do with Stone's death.

Was his death an accident? she wondered.

Silence was required. Each scientist would work on their own or with another, and in her case it was Larry. Whatever they were working on would be kept a secret between them. When a particular piece of research was completed, a new project would be given to them. The Company's research was compartmentalized. The rationale behind this was that if their research got out, a competing company would steal it.

Being innocent and just out of post-graduate studies, Margo jumped at the chance of working in an area of research that explored the Earth's sustainable resources—in her mind, that was positive, and the pay was very good, too. However, she had begun to question their work ever since Stone's death. She was getting a bad feeling about it. *Trust your intuition when in doubt* was a phrase her mother had often used. As she pondered these things, her telephone rang and brought her back to the present.

Having worked for The Company for several years, she was very bitter. She'd heard that O'Brian and Sandforth had been arrested and charged with murder. This reinforced her suspicion that The Company was involved in illegal activities. But she was trapped; she wanted to get out, but was afraid to. If she was allowed to, she would be watched constantly— or even worse, they would do something to her memory so she would have Alzheimer-like symptoms.

Margo had seen it happen to Larry four years ago. He had wanted out. One day he was fine, and the next he passed out in the lab and had been taken away. Margo found out he was in a long-term care facility. He had a stroke. Whether the stroke was natural or not, she'd been with The Company long enough to know better than to take a chance. She held onto the belief she could do more to bring The Company down by staying alert and in their employ. Then she signed a five-year extension to her contract.

Over many years, she gathered important information which she had encoded into her poetry and short stories. No one suspected her; many of her poems were considered silly. Whenever she was asked why she wrote them, she would simply say, "Just playing with words; I need to do this and crosswords to keep my mind sharp." She was often the brunt of jokes. She honestly believed one day the joke would be on them.

She had played the game so well that security had lessened over the years to the point where she was infrequently followed. She'd become boring, according to security.

Margo attended some conferences to help keep her current in the world in bioengineering. At a recent conference, she'd met and had a brief talk with a Dr. Megan Teal. The name Teal rang a bell; Megan was Mary Teal's daughter. Margo wondered if she could leak information to Megan. No, that would put Megan's life in danger. There had to be another way...another connection, somehow.

She saw an ad for a series of talks to be given by a Dr. Nona Teal, whom she quickly found out was Megan's grandmother. She couldn't believe her eyes.

I don't believe in coincidences. This was meant to be. I have to meet her, she thought. *This may be my one chance. I'll go and play it by ear.*

* * *

Shelley had just met Nona at the airport. "Nona, we're thrilled to have you here in Australia, not only to speak about Universal Harmony, but also that you have agreed to stay with us."

"It's been a long time since I've been to Australia; I'm looking forward to my visit here."

After dinner, Shelley and Nona sat in the library and discussed how they were going to proceed. Her first speech would be in Melbourne the next day. She would speak in the following communities: Brisbane, Sydney, and Adelaide during the next ten days.

Shelley hired one of the large halls in Melbourne and was very pleased to see it was virtually full. She estimated a crowd of at least 180. They started on time. Shelley began her introduction.

"Nona is a marine ecologist, and a well-known speaker. In a presentation she gave in Glasgow many years ago, she combined her two main interests in a very clever way: she intertwined her knowledge of the oceans with the Universal Harmony Movement. Since then, she has been travelling the world giving speeches. Today I've asked her to speak on Universal Harmony. Please welcome her to our country."

Loud applause ensued.

"Thank you, Shelley, for that wonderful introduction. This is the second time I've been to Australia, but the first time to this area. I'm looking forward to talking to you and also visiting other parts of the country.

"I'm here to share with you a message—a message not of my own, but one shared by thousands who believe we can make a difference. Shelley tells me many of you are newcomers to this Harmony Movement and has asked me to explain it and why I feel it is so important.

"When I say *oneness*, I'm not referring to each of us as a solitary being, or even that humans are the one dominant species. I'm referring to something much, much greater. In Western Thought we generally believe that we are all separate from one another. As a species we've the God-given right to use and abuse any living organism, plant, or animal—any of Earth's resources such as minerals; oil and gas. We tend to use and abuse these at will. Yes, we were given dominion over Earth. We are to protect it, not abuse it. Somehow, we have lost respect, not only for each other, but also our environment. Earth is in very serious trouble. Many of us realize that what we were taught to be right, we now see as wrong. Not all of it, but much of it.

"You may ask, how does the idea of harmony work? Where did it come from? Why do we need it now? What does it really mean? As I've said, oneness means we are not separate. We are not separate from one another. We are not separate from the plants and animals, nor are we separate from the soil, rocks, lakes, and oceans. Each and every one of us is an integral part of this planet.

"Let's compare Earth to the human body. Our bodies are made up of billions of cells which are all interconnected and work together in a functioning body. Each plant, animal, mineral, drop of water is like cells in our body. It takes all organisms to make a properly functioning Earth. I believe each and every one of us all over the world knows deep down inside that this is the real truth. This truth has been around forever. Many of us in our society seem to have lost it. Others still live by it; the various indigenous peoples around the world, like the aboriginals here in Australia, are examples. Also, many of what we refer to as Eastern philosophies still practice it.

"I believe the universal harmony idea is built on three foundations which are interconnected. I will attempt to show you why:

"The first foundation says that humans are a social species. Imagine if you were forced to live on your own with no one to talk to, share ideas, laughter, and joy with; imagine if there was no one to love or to love you in return. I shiver when I think about it. It would be an extremely boring life."

There was laughter throughout the audience.

"In fact, most animals are social to some degree or another. We need other humans to exist to be alive and to procreate. Yes, we are interconnected. We will talk more about this in a few minutes.

"The second foundation establishes that every living organism, be it plant, animal, or microbes, carries its own unique DNA; genes. The exception is identical twins. If all the genes of a given species were put together, we would have what is called a gene pool for that species. Each individual of that species is an expression of its gene pool. The key to remember here is that each individual is unique because of their unique DNA.

"The third foundation is probably not as well-known as the first two. I first read about it many years ago; it rang true to me as I know it has to others. It is based on understanding of frequencies—that is, the number of vibrations or wavelengths occurring in one second. I'm not going into a complicated physics lecture; however, I must explain why frequencies are so critical. We are all familiar with wavelengths and frequencies such as radio and TV signals, x-rays and, of course, sound. These are all part of an electromagnetic spectrum. How dreary would our world be without sound? There would be no music, birdsong, or talking—although that last one might come in handy sometimes."

The audience laughed again.

"We all know there are many sounds and frequencies we cannot hear; a dog whistle, for example, and also most of the whale songs which are below what we can detect. Yes, frequencies are part of the study of physics. They are also an intricate part of everything. Absolutely everything and every organism vibrates; it has its own unique frequency. Even the chairs you are sitting on vibrate and have a frequency. Every atom vibrates with its own frequency. Remember the periodic table which decorated part of a wall in your chemistry lab?"

A rather loud groan went through the crowd.

"I can tell by your reaction that you do. Each atom is unique with its own electrons, protons, etc. whizzing around the nucleus in their own orbits."

Most of the people in the audience were nodding in agreement.

"Atoms form molecules and molecules form compounds such as sugars and proteins. In turn, these compounds combine with others to form tissues, tissues form organs, organs form systems, and systems interconnect to form your body. The point I'm making is that everything is made up of various combinations of molecules and compounds. Therefore, everything vibrates and has a unique frequency. Even stars and galaxies have unique frequencies. Earth has its own frequency, called the Shumann Resonance, which is very low."

Nona took a sip of water and continued.

"Let's go one step further; this is where it gets really exciting. We are going to discover resonance and harmony. This sounds like music, doesn't it? We all know music is made up of notes and chords. Each octave is made up of eight whole notes and five sharps and flats, giving us thirteen notes in all."

Nona had turned on her computer to a simulated grand piano. She struck middle C which produced a pure sound.

"This note C has its own very specific frequency as does F, G and so on." She played the scale slowly. "Okay, now if you play certain notes together, you get a chord." She played three different chords. "These produce a rather pleasant sound." Then she played a chord, but put a note in which didn't belong.

The audience groaned.

"That one didn't resonate, did it?"

A loud 'no' came from the audience.

Then she played a simple melody with all the notes in tune, followed by the same melody with two notes off key.

The audience groaned and laughed again.

Nona then played another more complex piece with four notes off key. They all groaned and plugged their ears. Quickly she played the same piece with all the notes in tune.

Everyone smiled and clapped.

Shelley came to the front as the emcee, and spoke to the audience. "On those pleasant notes, we'll take a twenty-minute break, after which Dr. Teal will put it all together for us—I hope in a harmonious fashion."

The audience clapped and were chatting with one another as they made their way to the room where tea and coffee awaited them.

Margo Ellsworth was really looking forward to the speech; she was not disappointed. During the break, she enjoyed talking to others. Angela approached her. She'd recognized the name Ellsworth from Margo's name tag.

"Dr. Ellsworth, I'm Angela Monterey, co-chair of the session. I don't think I've seen you here before."

"No, this is my first time. I wanted to hear Nona Teal speak. I'm interested in the harmony idea and have been for some time."

"We would love to have you as a member."

"I would like to find out more about it first."

"Certainly; I'll arrange to have an information package made up for you."

"I would like that," Margo said. She was nervous.

"How long have you lived in Australia? I notice a slight American accent."

"About twenty-five years; my work brought me here."

"Where do you work? Are you an M.D.?"

Margo relaxed a little bit. "No, I'm in research."

"Oh, how interesting; we must talk about it sometime. Excuse me, dear, I'm being waved at. Enjoy the rest of Nona's speech. Don't forget to pick up your package as you leave tonight."

"Thanks," Margo said. She breathed a sigh of relief and wandered back to her chair. Her mind was no longer on the conference; she was trying to figure out what to do.

Should I leave now? she wondered. *I'll wait and see what happens. This may be my only chance to contact someone.*

Angela went over to talk with Gwen.

"I just met Dr. Margo Ellsworth. It isn't a coincidence. She told me she moved here from the states about twenty-five years ago."

"How interesting; I'll see if I can speak with her after the talk and before the workshop begins. Don't worry, I'll be very careful and nonchalant."

Gwen returned to the lecture hall and made sure she sat two rows back and slightly to the left of Ellsworth.

"Welcome back, everyone."

Nona continued her speech.

"Just to recap: absolutely everything and every being has a unique frequency. Mine is different from Shelley's, as hers is different from anyone else's. Each of us has a unique genetic or DNA profile. Although we have the same tissues and organs, and are made up of similar cells, the DNA in each of those cells in a given person is different from anyone else.

"If all the cells in a given tissue or organ are in resonance or in balance with one another, that tissue or organ is said to be healthy. However, if these cells, for whatever reason, are not in resonance or out of balance, a disease of some sort may result.

"Now let's look at family dynamics. For example, there is a mother, father and three children. The mother and father are constantly arguing, or one is constantly putting the other one down. They are not only hurting each other, but they're also hurting the children and themselves. This family is unhappy and dysfunctional. Why? Because they're out of balance, and are not in harmony or resonance—whereas the family that gets along well is forgiving and practices unconditional love, and is happy, healthy, and harmonious. This shows us that a happy, healthy person, family, neighbourhood, etc. are positive, because there is respect and love for one another. Unhappy people, families, and organizations, etc. are negative to varying degrees, because there is a lack of love and respect for one another.

"This negativity can be taken further and can occur in communities, cities, states, provinces, even between countries. Negativity acts as a separating, competing factor. Positive environments, on the other hand, can produce uniting and cooperating attitudes; negative versus positives, dark versus light, plus all shades of gray in between. This is all based on whether frequencies are in balance or not, and to what degree.

"Let's look at an even larger picture; an ecosystem perhaps. A forest, a desert, coral reef, or an ocean; each of these depends on the component parts working in harmony—that is, keeping themselves in balance. If all of Earth's ecosystems are in balance, then our planet is in harmony and very healthy. However, if one or more of Earth's ecosystems are out of balance, then the Earth is not in harmony and is unhealthy. The more out of balance it becomes, the more Earth becomes dysfunctional.

"Earth has been very resilient for millions of years, adapting to changes, even major ones. She's evolved and adapted and thus survived. Yes, species have evolved and changed over time and adapted. Some become extinct while others survive. Thousands of species have become extinct in just the last hundred years or so, mainly due to the activities of humans.

"What is different in the last hundred or so years? It is the presence of humans, as we are the newcomers? The latest scientific information says that <u>Homo sapiens</u> arrived on Earth about 200,000 to 400,000 years ago, which is extremely recent on the evolutionary clock. For thousands of years, our species lived in harmony with Earth; this balance held for centuries and centuries. When did we get out of balance? Why are we out of balance? Most authorities believe it began with the Industrial Revolution. Initially it wasn't a problem, as Earth's population was a lot smaller than it is now. As our population grew, so did the consumption of our planet's unsustainable resources. Our technology and knowledge in virtually every field has grown faster in the last sixty or so years than the previous several thousand years put together. The world today is extremely different than it was just sixty to seventy years ago.

"We all know there are serious problems facing us here on Earth today, and most of them have been caused by humans: overpopulation, starvation and diseases, unsustainable resources that are running out, and climate change, just to name a few. Earth is resilient, but not that resilient. Earth is very close to the tipping point—the point at which there is no return. Earth needs help. Earth needs us. We need Earth. We can help her. We've already started. It is through grassroots movements, and peaceful movements like the Harmony Movement. There are many groups with thousands of people worldwide taking similar approaches to ours.

"It all starts with each and every one of us realizing we're not separate individuals; we're *one*. All humans are part of one another and all that is around us. We must learn to respect and love one another and everything surrounding us. We must stop abusing ourselves, each other, our land, our forest, our oceans, our world, our planet, our Earth. It is the only home we've got. We must make sure it survives so our children, grandchildren, and generations to follow have a decent place to live and love. After all, we are all *one*."

The audience rose clapping, shouting, "Hear, Hear!"

As they settled back in their chairs, Shelley thanked Nona profusely and added, "Before we open the floor for questions: Nona has agreed to run a workshop after we have had a bite to eat."

Shelley then opened the floor for questions. We would like to hold the question-and-answer session to between twenty and thirty minutes, as we would like to follow up with a brief workshop. The floor is now open to questions."

The attendees were orderly and respectful in their questions, and asked the following questions:

"Dr. Teal, are you saying that absolutely everything vibrates?"

"Yes, everything has a frequency, because everything vibrates. Each animal, including us, has a unique frequency. Rocks, minerals, water, stars, planets, and galaxies all have their own frequencies."

"Anything which disrupts that frequency causes that object or organism to be out of balance, out of harmony?"

"Correct; the degree of disruption determines how much disharmony results."

"Are you saying if each of us love and respect one another and our environments that Earth will begin to heal?"

"Very good question; it's a good start, and is an excellent foundation to build on. Humans must learn to respect one another, no matter what country, origin, race, religion, or social paradigm we embrace. We must acknowledge and respect each other's beliefs and do this honestly and openly. Even though forgiving past hurts, injustices, misunderstandings; crimes, wars etc. may be difficult to do, we must do it. If we don't forgive, and begin to trust and respect one another, things will continue the way they are. If mistrust could become trust, if hatred could become love, if disrespect became respect, think of what could happen, especially if it spreads worldwide. Competition would become cooperation. There would be no more war, only peace. Crime would slowly disappear. The richer countries would reach out to the poor countries to help, and diseases would decrease and perhaps even disappear. We would stop abusing Earth by polluting and overusing her unsustainable resources.

"I know many of you think this is utopian and impossible. I believe it is possible. I also know it'll take time. We have to start somewhere, and I feel the Harmony Movement plus similar grassroots groups which are growing and spreading will be the answer."

"Where do we start? Where do I start?"

"You start with yourself and your family and friends, then strangers, neighbourhoods and so on; it's catching, because our very nature is to be social. Think of times when someone has reached out and helped you. It made you feel better. Now think of the times when you have unconditionally helped someone. Maybe you made a pie or casserole for a neighbour who lost a loved one, or took the time to listen to someone, or took the arm of an unsteady senior to cross the street. I see many of you are smiling. It made you feel good inside. We do care for one another. Even smiling at a stranger or offering a cheery hello can mean a great deal to someone. You see, we're not solitary individuals; we are all interconnected. When you leave here today, try to be more compassionate and helpful to your fellow humans. It'll make you feel good. It will make others feel good and they may even pass it on. We are humans. We have the freedom of choice. We can be negative or we can be positive. Positive is far more fun and it feels good." At this, there was a loud applause.

"How can I get past the feeling that the world's problems are just too overwhelming and one person can do nothing to help?"

"When you feel like that; please think of the Universal Harmony Movement. You are not alone. You are not separate. You are part of all there is. Remember, each and every part which makes up Earth is like a single cell in your body. Every cell is important and interconnected with each other. One cell cannot survive on its own. It takes all of the cells, the unit component parts, to make the whole function properly. You are not alone.

"If each of us has a positive nature and practices the rule of love and respect in all you do and say, you become a wonderful role model. Try it with your family and friends. Start with eight people; perhaps five will like how they feel when they too are positive. Then these five each inspire another five; that makes twenty-five. It spreads; we see it spreading across the globe day by day.

"Think of the catastrophes, big and small, that have occurred; 9/11, when the Twin Towers in New York came down; consider as well the massive destruction of a hurricane, or flood, or the neighbourhood home destroyed by fire. Yes, there are various government agencies and groups that come to help, but also, there are ordinary citizens who will arrive to help—and they do it unconditionally. There is almost always one or two that lead the way and others follow. As I've said, it is our nature to respond to help, because we care. We love to be helpful and it feels good, it feels positive. So, to go back to your original question: *you* be the spark; sparks can ignite fires. Ignite your family and friends and see what happens."

"Dr. Teal; I agree with the Harmony Movement and I know it works. My question is, will we, along with similar groups, ever attain the numbers required to really turn this planet around?"

"Yes; I will explain why. It is called the Maharishi Effect. This happens when a small group of individuals peacefully meditate or pray together to relieve a negative stress factor; the effects are felt beyond that small group. There are many examples of this. Peace, in part, came to Northern Ireland, because a few women gathered together from both sides of the conflict and prayed for peace; through peaceful marches and other initiatives, they took a positive lead. Several years ago, bombers were literally on their way to bomb Iraq. People from all over the world prayed together for peace, and for the first time in history, the command went out to abort. I believe in the mid-1990s, there was an asteroid on a collision path with Earth. It mysteriously changed course and missed us. Also in the 1980s, crimes and suicides were reduced in certain major city centres because of small groups praying for peace and harmony. For centuries it has been shown that as little as one percent is required to make changes; some say only one-tenth of one percent. So yes, I believe we humans can peacefully make changes and help Earth to heal."

"But how does it work?"

"It is through what is called the collective consciousness. Probably the best way to explain it is through an experiment which was done years ago which is now been referred to as the one-hundredth monkey. I see a lot of you are smiling and know the story; for those who don't, I'll summarize it for you. Off Japan, there is a group of small islands inhabited by small monkeys which were starving. Humans dropped sweet potatoes on the sand of these islands for them to eat. The monkeys didn't like eating potatoes covered with sand. After a period of time, a very young monkey on one island picked up a potato went over to a stream, washed it, and ate it. Of course it didn't take long for all the other monkeys to follow suit. The strange part about this is that although this only occurred on one specific island, all of the monkeys on these isolated islands and the mainland began washing and eating the potatoes. There was no direct contact between islands. Therefore, there must've been something—which is now called collective consciousness—that allows ideas to be passed between individuals by means that do not involve contact of any kind."

"Do you believe there are such things as secret or shadow governments which are trying to control us?"

"It is a well-known fact that certain governments are spending huge amounts of taxpayer's monies on covert or secret projects which are so secret that only a very select few are privy to their work or findings."

"Who controls these secret governments?"

"This has been written about a lot. Apparently, there are between 2000 and 3000 persons belonging to some of the world's wealthiest families who are in control of the rest of the almost 7,000,000,000 of us. They control governments, militaries, banks, production of oil, gas, etc."

"But how are they doing it?"

"Money is power; like many, I don't have proof. I suggest each of you read books in this area to get a better understanding of what really is going on."

"Is it true our oceans are in danger—and if so, what is causing it?"

"Yes; being a marine biologist, I can attest to the fact that our oceans are very close to the tipping point. Some of it is a natural cycle, such as climate change. The problem is caused by some of our human activities resulting from the burning of fossil fuels;

oil, gas coal etc., along with our other activities. These have and are causing an unnatural increase in carbon dioxide which increases the pressure on the problems of climate change; melting ice caps, and the acidification of the oceans. On top of this, we have been using the ocean as a huge garbage dump for years and continue to do so. This pollution is on our coastal continental shelves where the vast majority of our fisheries are located. Overfishing, bad and harmful fishing techniques, oil spills, and undersea mining are all contributing factors."

"Is it true the phytoplankton, those microscopic plants that live predominantly over the continental shelves; produce fifty percent of the world's oxygen?"

"That's true; a very high percentage of our phytoplankton is located in exactly the same waters which are being polluted. This is one of the main reasons why scientists are very concerned with the increase of the acidification. It's increasing much faster than some of the species of phytoplankton can adapt, and are therefore becoming extinct, which means the amount of production of oxygen is being reduced. Some say we are currently very close to the tipping point where the phytoplankton may not survive. If this is the case, then Earth will have to do with fifty percent less oxygen. Phytoplankton is the basis of virtually every food web in the ocean."

"If the marine phytoplankton dies, then our oceans would die as a result?"

"Yes."

There was a loud gasp from the audience.

"What can we do to help prevent that from happening?"

"There are many things already being done. I believe what you are asking is what as individuals can we do to help."

Shelley interrupted at this point. "That's what we're planning to do in the workshop to follow. There are sandwiches and coffee available. We would like you to pick up some paper and pencils as you leave this room to go to the lunchroom. While you're having a bite to eat, think of some ways which we as individuals can help the oceans and Earth in general. We'll start the workshop in about a half an hour in the lunchroom.

"On behalf of everyone here, I would like to thank Nona for such an inspiring and edifying talk. I think each and every one of us has learned a great deal today. She certainly has given us a great deal to think about."

Once again, Nona received a standing ovation.

As Shelley and Nona were tidying up, Shelley said, "Well, we sort of got off track there with some of those questions."

"Not really; they were all related one way or another with the fact that we need to learn to respect each other and our environment. It tells me they wish to help in any way they can, which is a very positive thing."

During the last half of Nona's talk, Gwen had noticed that Margo was a bit fidgety and at times was not really listening. She seemed distracted. As the crowd started to file out, Gwen made sure she was just behind Ellsworth and managed to bump into her. "I'm so sorry. Are you okay?"

"Yes, thank you, I'm fine," Margo answered.

"I'm Gwen Ross; may I get you a coffee or tea?"

"My name is Margo Ellsworth," Margo responded. As she turned to shake hands, she caught her breath: she saw the word reporter under Gwen's name, which was displayed on her name-tag. She was scared.

A wee voice in her head said, *This is your chance.* She instantly relaxed and smiled. "Yes, I would love a coffee and a bite to eat."

They got their coffee and plate of sandwiches. "Let's sit over here," Gwen said, heading for a quiet corner. "Margo, you look a bit shaken; are you sure you are okay?"

"I'm okay; I'm just a bit hungry."

"Well, this plate of goodies should help," Gwen said. She was doing her best to put Margo at ease.

"I see you are a reporter. What brings you to Australia?" Margo asked tentatively.

"I'm a friend of Nona's." Gwen didn't want to scare Ellsworth off.

"Her talk was very informative and moving. She is an excellent speaker," said Margo.

"May I call you Margo? Please call me Gwen. You're in research, yes?"

"I'm a microbiologist. Are you working on a story while you are here?"

Gwen made a decision to be frank. "I'm looking into what is called the Black Budgets—taxpayer's money which is used in covert programs."

"Oh." Margo paused. "Are you getting anywhere?"

"Not really," Gwen replied. "Especially in the US; the various covert secret projects are so well-guarded that it is virtually impossible to find out anything."

Margo nodded. Gwen took the pieces of paper and a couple of pens, and suggested they make some ideas for Nona's workshop.

"Good idea," said Margo.

They began to make a short list of ideas. They switched papers to compare. On the bottom right-hand corner of Margo's paper was written, *Please help me; I can help you.*

It was all Gwen could do to keep calm.

"Why don't we put our ideas in priority in case we only get one or two chances to suggest one?" Gwen suggested.

Margo had noticed that Gwen had blacked out her request; beside it, she'd written, *Yes; how?*

"I like this idea. Let us compare our priorities," said Margo.

On a third piece of paper, they put down several ideas. As they were doing so, Margo looked like she was doodling, but in fact, she had printed two words:

Purse. Bathroom.

"Okay, so we don't want this one, or this one," Gwen said as she tore off the bottom inch of the piece of paper and slipped it in her pocket.

They headed to the washrooms. Gwen noted there were three empty stalls side-by-side. She nodded to Margo, who went first; Gwen took the one next to her. She placed her purse on the floor next to Margo. Margo slid it under the partition and a minute later slid it back.

They didn't sit together when the workshop began, and Gwen noted about fifteen minutes later that Margo was leaving. Gwen was beside herself; she wanted to see what Margo had put in her purse.

After the workshop was complete, Gwen and Angela took their leave from Nona and Shelley, who were still talking to some of the people.

"Gwen, did you know Margo had a shadow with her tonight?"

"I suspected as much," answered Gwen. They were now getting into Angela's car.

Gwen was rummaging around in her purse.

"Angela, she gave me something."

She pulled out a medium-sized notebook and began to leaf through it. "This is very strange; it's a notebook full of short poems! There appears to be a letter with it."

It took them several minutes to reach the estate. Angela had phoned prior to leaving and arranged for them to have a late-night snack.

"We'll go to the library for a drink and look at what Margo gave you," she said.

Once they were settled, Gwen opened the notebook and started to read it. Margo had written instructions in bullets:

- Take this information and put it to good use.

- I'm a microbiologist at the Downs research complex – twenty-five years!

- I work in the covert section. I have helped to genetically engineer some bacteria which I know are lethal and are biological weapons.

- All aspects of research are compartmentalized. We only know what we are working on.

- I'm sure what I'm doing is illegal. I'm sorry.

- The poems — the key is on the last page.

I hope this helps.

Margo L. Ellsworth.

"I hope whatever is in these poems is enough to move forward," Angela said.

Angela told David what had happened and how Gwen had received some very important information.

"Well, what do those poems really say?" he asked.

"Hold on, David. We just got this book, and it is in some form of code."

"Not again; it seems like everything you two are currently looking at is in one code or another."

"Well, these days, if you are dealing with covert stuff of any kind, I'm sure most of it'll be in code. Jamie is currently dealing with codes within codes within codes," Gwen explained.

"We must photocopy this book and put the original in a safe place," said Angela.

The next morning, Angela and Gwen met at Jamie's hotel room. As usual, he was busy analyzing data that was simultaneously displayed on his four monitors.

"Hi Jamie—any word regarding the oceanography?"

"Yes, I just finished it. Most of it was useless. I'll let you look at it."

Have you had any further luck with the Sandforth files?"

"I'm still working on those."

"Jamie, we've something else here for you to decipher." Angela handed him the book of poetry.

Jamie flipped through it and he started to laugh. "These are just short poems!"

"283 to be exact," Gwen said, handing him a piece of paper. "I believe this is the key to deciphering them.

Jamie looked at it and smiled. "Very ingenious, I must say." He started to enter the poems into the computer just as Angela and Gwen left.

A couple of days later, Gwen heard from Jamie.

"I believe I'm finally getting somewhere."

"I'll be there shortly," Gwen said, picking up her purse and briefcase. On the way over, she picked up a couple of coffees and some sandwiches.

A short time later, she breezed in.

"Thanks, Gwen," Jamie said as she offered him the refreshments. "What you've given me appears to be bits and pieces of information that Ellsworth has picked up over the years," he said. "I'm still trying to put things together. It's like a large jigsaw puzzle. However, this is strange—can you cross-reference the bacterial code name we found in Sandforth's file?"

"Here it is," Gwen said. "There has to be a relationship between the E. coli 39 from Sandforth's file, and the E. coli 49 and E. coli 69 that we have here." Gwen thought for a few moments, then asked, "Did you come across anything which may be associated with DNA? Check on the Internet for the components of DNA and then put them into a search program to see if any words in Margo's poems correspond. I'll wait while you do that." Gwen pulled up a chair.

"The main atoms involved are hydrogen, oxygen, nitrogen, carbon and phosphorus. The genes themselves are made up of varying combinations or chains of four different protein bases: adenine, A; cytosine, C; guanine, G; and thymine, T. They apparently form pairs; for example, AT, and CG. And these in turn are attached to the sugar/phosphate compound to form a chain called a nucleotide. A and G are purines, and C and T are pyrimidines," Jamie said, reading off the computer screen.

"So let's enter the keywords: adenine, cytosine, guanine, thymine; also their abbreviations: A,C,G, and T. It may be a good idea to add these words: nucleotide, purine(s), pyrimidine(s)," Gwen suggested.

"What about also entering DNA and deoxyribonucleic acid?"

"Good idea—and why not put these DNA-related words not only into Margo's files, but also Sandforth's files?"

"It will take a while to process all of this," Jamie said.

"Call me if you come across anything interesting," Gwen said as she was going out the door. She called Sam on her cellphone.

"Sam, are you busy for lunch?"

"No. Why don't we get together at the restaurant we took Megan to in a half hour?"

Gwen had shopping to do and arrived at the restaurant a bit late.

"Sorry, Sam, I got tied up in traffic."

"No problem; I just got here myself." He gave her a hug. "How was Nona's speech?"

"Fantastic, Sam. She was great and I learned a lot. Have you heard from Megan lately?"

"Yes, I was talking to her last night," he said as they ordered their lunches.

"So, I was thinking," said Gwen, "you've a fairly good background in genetics; can you explain a few things about it to me?"

"I'll try, Gwen. Is there anything specific you want to know about genetics?"

"I'm mostly interested in the bioengineering side of it."

"I'll start with a definition. Genetic engineering is the direct technical manipulation of an organism's genetic makeup— its DNA. It was the DNA of bacteria they first worked on early in the 1970s, but it wasn't until the early 1980s that they genetically modified bacteria to produce insulin. In the mid-1990s, genetically-modified foods were developed; now we see tomatoes that have a longer shelf life, as well as insect-resistant or herbicide-resistant plants."

"Is it legal?"

"The regulations covering bioengineering differs from country to country."

Gwen shook her head. "So this means covert, top secret labs funded by Black Budgets could bioengineer viruses and bacteria without the public being aware of what they are doing."

"It's highly probable. Biological weapons and their development is illegal; many countries are doing it and probably through covert labs."

"If they made that much advancement in the '70s, '80s, and '90s, there must be some really advanced things occurring now."

"There have been in many fields. In medicine, we now have specific bioengineered serums and also antibodies for protection again certain diseases. There are many good ethical uses for bioengineering, but I agree, there are probably some very unethical and illegal things which have been created."

"It is very much a two-edged sword," Gwen commented."

"Yes it is—like so many things humanity has invented."

"Do you know if there are complex computer programs that can model what various permutations and combinations of the building blocks of DNA look like or what they can do?"

"Yes, there have been tremendous advances in that field. They'll give you an idea of what will happen.

"Let's say hypothetically that you developed a lethal bacteria or virus which they thought would kill fifty percent of the world's population of fire ants. The only way to know if it did what it was designed it to do would be to test it on an actual colony in its natural environment. Are there computer simulation programs available to explore such scenarios?"

"Yes there are, but very few exist, and even they are highly-regulated and monitored. They are virtually unavailable."

"Do you know of any?"

"Gwen, you are really on to something, aren't you?"

"I am, Sam, but unfortunately, there're many reasons why I can't talk about it."

"I understand," Sam said. "Has this anything to do with why Megan's parents were murdered?"

Gwen nodded.

Sam wrote something on a piece of paper. "Here is my private phone number if I can be of any further help."

Gwen frowned; she already had his number. She took the piece of paper; he had written *Down's lab in Melbourne.*

Later that afternoon, Gwen returned to Jamie's hotel room to see how the decoding project was going.

"This is what I've been able to get from Margo's poems so far," said Jamie. "I can't make any sense of it."

He brought up the data on monitors one and two. "The poems are in chronological order. The first one is dated over twenty years ago. These are the results of the first ten poems."

Gwen was puzzled. There were several encoded instances of the use of the G's, A's, T's, and C's. What was Margo trying to tell them?

"Jamie, let's go back to the DNA on this other computer, so that the two screens are side-by-side." "From what I gather, DNA consists of two long threadlike strands bound together." Gwen observed. "The bonds between the two strands are formed between a specific purine and a specific pyrimidine; that is, G to C; or C to G; and A to T; or T to A. So let's try running this whole thing again, putting in these four combinations: GC, CG, and AT and TA."

In very short order, they had a whole long list: TA, CG, GC, AT, CG, TA, and so on. Every so often there was a break, then a different chain would come out. Soon, several hundred different chains appeared on the screen.

"It looks as if Margo is giving us a map of a piece of DNA. You say Margo's poems appear to occur in sets, or chapters of some kind?" Gwen asked.

"It seems that way."

"This is the first set we're looking at."

"Yes, it is. I see what you're getting at, Gwen. I will run the rest and keep each set separate and in chronological order. There's over twenty years of poems here; it's going to take quite a long time to do this."

"Take as long as you need."

Gwen left and called Angela to meet her for coffee.

"Angela, I've been to see Jamie. It appears Margo has encoded in her poems some aspect of DNA."

"What! How did she manage to do that?"

"She must be an extremely intelligent woman. The poems are real mixture of rhyming a few lines to long ones; she has also written several short stories. If she had not supplied the key that goes with them, we would never have deciphered anything."

"So what did you actually get?"

"It appears to be strings with two letters; TA, CG, GC, AT and so on. Some of the strings are very long; some are short and everything in between. I've got Jamie doing the whole book of poems and short stories. Jamie says it will take a few days to enter all of it and get results."

"What do you think it all means, Gwen?"

"I'm not sure, but both bacteria and viruses are known to be easily bioengineered; in other words, their DNA can be changed and manipulated."

"We also know Ellsworth and Lampson were working on genetic engineering in our covert lab!"

"That's true. I had lunch with Sam today and he explained what can be done with DNA. It is extremely frightening stuff, and we know the Power Elite are probably doing it."

"What are we going to do with all this data that Margo gave us?" Angela asked.

"Sam says there's a highly-classified computer program that reads genetic information and can run simulations. This program can decrypt genetic code and give you a good idea of what it can do."

"That's very scary. How can we access it?"

"It's extremely difficult to come by and very expensive. Access is restricted, and it's highly monitored by government officials. However...there's a rumour, Angela, that your lab has one."

"What? I'll talk to David; maybe we can use it."

"You can try Angela, but I don't want to put Margo in danger."

"Then there has to be another way."

"There just might be, Angela. Leave it with me."

Using her burn phone, she called Megan.

"This must be very important if you're using the burn phones."

"It may or may not be, Megan." Gwen described the computer which Sam had described. "Do you know of such a decoding program?"

"Actually, we have one here. It's not the latest version, but it is pretty good."

"How tightly-scrutinized is it?"

"It really isn't, because the one we have is out of date, even though it's only three years old. We've a new one on order. Because this is an older version, the government may check it now and then. Why are you asking?"

"I'm not too sure yet until I see the results of what Jamie is currently running for me. Our initial results show us we've received some data from the Melbourne lab which appears to be series of DNA nucleotides. I've no training in genetics, so I'll need your help."

"By all means, phone me when you know what you want to do; I'll see what I can do to help."

About ten days later, Gwen heard from Jamie.

"I just finished all the analyses and we have pages and pages of nucleotides. I have grouped them together the way you wanted."

Gwen rushed over to see exactly what he'd found. "Jamie, this material is far too complex for us to try to figure out. I've a friend at home who'll be able to help us. Make a copy of all this information. We'll put one set along with your programs in a safety deposit box here in Melbourne. I'll take the second one with me. Once you have done this, wipe your hard drive and leave the dummy files of drug research intact."

She told him she was leaving him in Australia as she may need him again in the near future. She gave him some cash and would have Angela put some more in his account. She suggested he take a holiday, and take his burn phone—but he was only to use it if it was absolutely necessary to get in touch with her. She stayed with Jamie until he copied everything and wiped his hard drive. He packed up a bunch of things he would need for the next little while and left with Gwen. She took him to the beach house; he could stay there as long as he wished. Under no circumstances was he to go back to the hotel. She had called Angela who met them at the beach house with a new car for Jamie.

"Jamie, this is your car to drive around the country. We highly recommend you take an extended trip through the outback or somewhere else inconspicuous, beginning in the next couple of days," Angela told him.

"This DNA must be very important to go to all this trouble," Jamie commented. "Thank you, ladies, for the car and money you've given me. I'll do as you say."

Gwen smiled. "If I call you from Canada and tell you to get out, you must do so immediately. If you feel you are in danger or are being followed, call Angela. She will take care of you. These are all precautions; I doubt if anything will happen to you."

* * *

Gwen flew back to Canada the next day, and Megan met her at the airport.

"If it's okay with you, Megan, could we go back to your lab and have a quick look at this DNA material?" she said as soon as she arrived.

"Absolutely," Megan agreed.

"I can't tell you where this information came from. It is definitely to do with genetics we couldn't figure it out," said Gwen.

They stopped by Tim Horton's and brought coffee with them to the lab. Once they were there, Gwen produced the memory sticks. They sat at the long oak desk and began to look at the material on the computer.

After several minutes of studying the strings of nucleotides, Megan said, "It appears there are several different genetically-engineered microbes. Most seem to have been aborted—however, there are three that were not. Two are bacteria and one is a virus. The two bacteria are both derivations of the bacteria E. coli—a bacteria normally found in our large intestine that, if ingested, makes us very ill. Its DNA can mutate or change naturally, and has done so in the past; when it does, it can be lethal. These are genetic maps of bioengineered bacteria."

"So E. coli is a good choice to bioengineer into a lethal weapon?"

"Yes; the first set of nucleotides are denoted by Margo as: MMB39, MMB49 and MMB69. The MMB stands for *marine mammal bacterium*. The numbers tell us that MMB69 is the latest strain to be bioengineered. The other sets of nucleotides are also modified E. coli. She called these Hs905, Hs945 and Hs1031. Hs stands for *Homo sapiens*."

"Is the second strain specific to humans?"

"We'll have to check by putting all this information into the program before I can tell you what each one is designed for. Do you by any chance have the raw data with you?"

Gwen reached into her purse and gave Megan another external memory drive.

"I'll run this through the program to see if there is any hidden information."

Late the next day, when Gwen and Megan saw the results from the complete set of data, Megan realized they were onto something big.

"We now have a more complete picture of the bacteria in the first set," she said. "The additional data on MMB69 gives us a few more things: its life span is less than two to three hours. After three hours, it self-destructs. It's only useful as a biological weapon on relatively tight groupings of marine mammals. Once an animal is infected, it will bleed to death within three to five hours."

"Does the bacterium Hs1031 act in the same way?"

"Yes, and it appears to be specific to humans. They also die in the same way."

"So, the one that infects humans would be very effective if it's used on crowds or densely-populated areas. My God, Megan, this is very scary stuff!" Gwen exclaimed.

Megan nodded in agreement. "The question is what do we do with this information? If it got out to the public, it would cause panic!"

"It would also cause the Power Elite and their allies to increase security, and maybe even force them to go so deep underground they would never be found. We need to think very carefully about this. I imagine every major law enforcement agency has a mole or two within them. We can't go there."

Gwen agreed. "Somehow, I need to get some of this information to Angela."

"Wait for a day or two; I want to have a closer look at this data and make sure I haven't missed anything."

* * *

Sam was busy packing and organizing to return to Canada when his cellphone rang.

"This is David—I just heard you're going home. I thought you still had several months left."

"The Centre where Megan works has seconded me to go there. Something's come up where my area of expertise is required."

"When do you have to leave?"

"Early next week; I don't know whether I'll be back or not."

"It'll be wonderful for you and Megan. We'll miss you terribly."

"I'll certainly miss you, Shelley and Angela very much," said Sam.

"Can you come for dinner here on Saturday night?" David asked.

"I would love to."

Late on Saturday afternoon, Sam was in the library at the Downs Estate having a whiskey on the rocks with Shelley, Angela, and David.

"Sam, have you learned anything more?" David asked as he sat down beside Shelley.

"I really wasn't given too many details. The Canadian government is currently paying my salary, so they're in charge. They wish me to work with an American, but beyond that, I was not given any more information. I don't mind, though—I'll be headquartered at the Centre in Halifax. I'll finally be home with Megan."

"That is wonderful, Sam—I'm so pleased for you both," Shelley said, poking at the fire. "Do you think they'll be sending you back here?"

"There's a possibility, but for the foreseeable future, I'll be in Halifax."

"Will you be seeing Gwen?" Angela asked.

"I will."

"If I give you a box, will you please take it to her for me?"

"I would be more than glad to."

* * *

Megan was very upset about the material Gwen had brought from Australia. She tossed and turned for hours. Once she finally fell asleep in the wee hours of the morning, she had a visit from Ortho.

"Megan, you're worried about what to do with this new information," he said.

"Very," Megan answered.

"You have every right to be worried and upset. Unfortunately, things are going to get worse. In the near future, you'll obtain more evidence. At that point, you'll be able to move ahead. Certain new people will enter the picture to help you. Do nothing with the evidence you currently have. Store it in a very safe place until you need it."

"Can you give me a hint of what is going to happen?"

"Sorry, Megan—all I can say is that you'll recognize it when it does happen, and you'll be okay."

Megan watched as Ortho faded into the background, and she fell back into a deep sleep.

* * *

Sam was finally home, and thankfully, his plane was on time. An hour later, Megan found herself wrapped in his arms, and her whole world changed; nothing else mattered or existed—just Sam. All was well once again. She loved this feeling; it was her version of what heaven must be like.

Once they were in Megan's car, driving into the city, she said, "Sam, I can't believe your contract was cut short. You're not only home, but you'll be working through the Centre. The angels must be smiling on us!"

"Meg, this move took me totally by surprise. I cannot believe my luck. I'm to phone the head of your team—a Dr. Roland Jones—and make an appointment. He'll explain the area of research that they need my help with in more detail at that time. Apparently it has to do with earthquake simulations."

"That's very interesting—but that area of study was not part of your doctorate, was it?"

"No, that's what's so strange about it. I mean, tinkering around with earthquake simulations was a game for me, but it certainly was not part of my thesis. The only person who knew about my interest in it was my supervisor."

"Well, I guess you'll find out tomorrow."

Sam's appointment was for nine-thirty am. He went with Megan, and she introduced him to Dr. Jones just before departing to her own office.

"May I call you Sam? Please call me Roland," said Dr. Jones.

"Yes, of course, Roland," Sam answered.

"Sam, you must be wondering why we called you on such short notice. We had a call from a Dr. Alan Croft in Nevada; he needs your help with something to do with earthquakes. Do you know him?"

Sam smiled. "Yes, he was my doctoral supervisor." *Ah! That explains the connection,* thought Sam.

"He wants you to go to Nevada to work with him on a project of some sort, after having cleared it with the Canadian government. However, the government wants you to stay in Canada. We were looking for a geologist, so it seemed to be a perfect fit for you to come here to work."

"That explains a lot—thank you."

"You'll have an office and lab here. You are free to travel and work with whomever you wish. We would like very much if you would be part of our team."

Sam was very impressed with the subsequent tour and with the people he met. He liked the atmosphere and the freedom he'd been given, as well as the lack of pressure to publish. Within an hour, he was sitting in his new office. He called Alan Croft and accepted his invitation to visit him in Nevada. He would fly out in a few days.

The same day that Sam began his work in Halifax, he made sure he hand-delivered the package Angela entrusted with him. Gwen took it home and opened it. On top of the contents was a letter addressed to Gwen.

> My dearest Gwen,
>
> Having just been diagnosed with terminal cancer, I've decided that it's time to release all I know about the Earth's Sustainable Resource Center (CESR) in the USA, along with our lab here in Melbourne. This information, I'm sure, will be of great interest to you. It may also help to bring down part of the infrastructure of these damnable lab facilities around the world. Mind you, most of this information is not current. What I am giving to you now is virtually everything I know from the time I joined the board until the time of the plane crash.
>
> I was forced to join the board of the CESR; I had no choice. It was my father who held that position. The business part of the estate was given to me. If I'd refused to join the board, they would have killed David.
>
> Although much of this information is now out of date, I'm sure it'll give you a solid base upon which to build. The blueprints and schematics of

the entire building complex of the Down's lab in Melbourne are still accurate. I believe most of the network labs around the world were built around the same time and from the same general blueprints. Of note is the security system and how it functions. The lowest of two or three underground floors are where the 'Black Ops' experiments are located. This may be valuable if a raid is organized, which I would love to see happen! It's the only way to get any concrete evidence. Remember: if the CESR board even catches a whiff of a raid, they'll destroy those floors just like they did in Boston.

I know the list of board members at the CESR Area 51 are the same—all but one. There are two co-chairs: one of them is a scientist by the name of Dr. George Dean, and the other is Anin. Anin is an alien whom I believe to be particularly dangerous. He is under the control of the Anunnaki.

Please use any of this material in any way you see fit. Keep it very safe, and tell no one; if the Board ever finds out that you have, you'd be in extreme danger.

If you don't want this responsibility, I'll understand fully. If this is the case, destroy the contents of this box.

I've also enclosed the details of the staged airplane crash. There is enough information here to validate my actions if the authorities should doubt your story; I've given a sworn affidavit that everything

I've given you is the solemn truth. David has the original, and I've enclosed a copy.

I did not know you for very long, but I feel I knew you well. You are a wonderful person, and I thank you for being my friend.

Please, be *very* careful.

Love you,

Angela (Maria)

Gwen was shocked. Overcome with tears, she quietly folded the letter and replaced it in its envelope. She immediately phoned Angela, and David answered.

"Oh, David...I just opened Angela's parcel and letter. How is she? I had no idea."

"Neither did we. It's been a huge shock for everyone. She's here at home getting around-the-clock care. The doctors say she has only a few days left." David's voice was full of emotion. "She is very weak, but I know she would love to talk to you. She is heavily drugged, so her speech is not clear."

"Thank you, David—and God bless."

She waited as David brought the phone to Maria.

"G...Gwen?" said Maria. Her voice was so weak that Gwen could barely hear her.

"Yes, Maria, it's me. I had no idea you were so ill!"

"No...no one did...it...was...a secret."

"I just got the package and read your letter. I haven't fully studied the contents yet. I know they're going to be extremely helpful, and I fully intend to follow through with them. Thank you for your courage to come forward. It must not have been easy."

Maria started to cough badly.

"Don't try to talk any more, please. Know that I love you, and that I'll miss you terribly. Be assured I'll do my very best."

Maria's coughing fit continued, and David took the phone.

"Gwen, it's David again. Maria really appreciated your call."

Tears were streaming down Gwen's face. "I would really like to come down and see her, David."

David was crying too. "I don't think it's a good idea. Maria is slipping in and out of a coma."

"Oh, David! I'm *so* sorry!" she said. She paused to catch her breath. "Please tell her I'll use this material to the best of my ability. My thoughts and prayers are with you all."

"Thanks, Gwen."

Gwen put down the phone and was sobbing. She had mixed emotions of grief, along with shock. The responsibility that came with the knowledge that Maria had imparted would be enormous and would be extremely dangerous.

Taking a deep breath and wiping her tears away, she set about sorting and analyzing the material. An hour later, she had several sorted stacks of papers, photographs, notebooks, etc. on Holly's dining room table with a note on top as to what was included in each pile. She entered the following list, putting the most recent ones at the top into her laptop.

MOST RECENT

- A thin envelope labeled 'More data from Margo Ellsworth'.

- Recent information regarding the Black Ops lab located outside of Melbourne, Australia.

- The blueprints of the lower levels of the lab and the schematics of the alarm system and location of the bombs in the various walls of said lab.

- The most up-to-date surveillance reports of David's private investigator.

BEFORE PLANE CRASH

- A list of labs and the scientists around the world involved in the illegal bioengineering of bacteria and viruses.

- Some objectives of the Board at the CESR

- A list of some of the projects up to the time of the plane crash.

- Evidence that there are military outposts in space.

POST PLANE CRASH

- A detailed log of Maria's disappearance— how she went underground, and how she reappeared after several years.

- Maria's affidavit as to how she became involved with The Board, how she survived, and why she came back.

- A rather large envelope which contains various bits and pieces of other information.

By the time Gwen had finished, it was getting close to five pm; she knew Holly would be home soon. She repacked all the material into the box and hid it in her closet. She was anxious to look at this new information, but she knew she would have to wait; she still hadn't figured out what she was going to do with it.

Half an hour later, Holly came in.

"Anything exciting happen today?" she asked.

Gwen was taken aback for a couple seconds, and answered, "Exciting may be the wrong word for it: I received news today that my friend Angela in Australia has been diagnosed with terminal cancer and only has a couple of days to live."

"Oh Gwen, I'm so sorry!" Holly poured herself a drink. "May I pour you one, too?"

"Yes please."

Holly, giving Gwen her drink, asked, "How old is she?"

"In her sixties, I think. Apparently she's known for a while she that she had terminal cancer, but she kept it a secret."

Gwen's cellphone rang. It was Megan.

"How are you doing?" Megan asked. "We just heard from David. I was shocked when I heard about Angela. Gwen, I'm so sorry. I know you two were very close. If you feel like it, why don't you come over for a bit this evening? I know you and Sam would probably like to talk."

Gwen went over to Sam's place for eight o'clock that evening. Megan met her at the door and hugged her. "Oh Gwen, I am so sorry."

Sam came in from his study. He looked at Gwen, shaking his head, and came over to hug her. Gwen collapsed in his arms, and he held her while she cried. Megan prepared drinks for each of them, then they sat together without speaking.

It was Gwen who finally broke the silence. "Sam, I wish to thank you for bringing me Angela's box."

"You're very welcome, Gwen. Angela was adamant that it had to stay in my possession at all times."

"Yes—I want to talk to you both about this, but I don't know where to start."

"Take your time, Gwen. Just try to relax, and talk when you are ready," Megan suggested as she poured Gwen another rye and ginger ale.

"Before I start, Megan, I just need to ask: how much does Sam know about the work you're doing?"

"He knows we've been working on bacterial DNA."

"I only know the generalities—no specifics," Sam said.

"I did tell him that it may be connected to the reason why my parents were murdered."

"I haven't read any of it yet, so I can't discuss it. I've just finished sorting it," said Gwen. "There is some very important information in it, including more data from Margo. I'll bring it to the lab tomorrow," she said.

The next day, Gwen went to Megan's office.

"Here are the DNA sequences Angela sent me," said Gwen. "I hope they're useful." Gwen had brought a Tim Horton's coffee for each of them. Sandy took her coffee, along with the data, and went into the lab, leaving Gwen and Megan alone.

"I need to talk with you," said Gwen.

"Okay," said Megan as she drank her coffee. "What is it, Gwen? What's happened? Is it to do with what was in that box?"

"Yes. What I'm about to tell you—"

Megan's cellphone rang, interrupting them. Casting an apologetic glance at Gwen, Megan answered the call. She listened for a moment then said, "Yes, she's right here. Just a moment please...Gwen, it's David."

"Oh no!" Gwen said. She knew it would be bad news as she took the phone. "David..."

"Gwen, Maria is gone" he said, his voice breaking. "She died in my arms about twenty minutes ago. Before she passed, she told me about the box and its contents. We're well aware of what will happen to the Downs name when the news breaks, but we can live with that. What I can't live with is the knowledge of what our lab is doing. Maria trusted you, and so do I, so I wanted to call you right away to let you know."

"She was very brave, and so are you, David. I give you my word: I'll do my very best. Please let me know of the arrangements; I'm so sorry that I can't be there, but I assure you I'll do my best to destroy these Black Ops labs."

There were tears in Gwen's eyes as she handed Megan her cellphone.

"Angela is gone...she died about a half hour ago."

"Gwen, I'm so sorry. Is there anything I can do?"

"Not at the moment, but thanks, Megan. I think the best thing we can do is to carry on and work on the information we've received."

They sat quietly, sipping their coffees. Gwen wiped away her tears, took a deep breath, and squared her shoulders. "Now I'm completely free to tell you the whole story as told to me by Maria," she said.

"Gwen, I'm confused. Who is Maria?" Megan asked.

"Angela and Maria were the same person—David's sister." Gwen paused for a moment to gather her thoughts and to let Megan process the information. "Maria Downs inherited the Downs family's assets including the lab in Melbourne."

"The same lab that Margo Ellsworth worked where the DNA sequences came from?"

"Yes. Along with the assets came a seat as one of the directors of a huge lab complex called the Centre for Earth's Sustainable Resources, located near what is referred to as Area 51 in the Southwest USA. Most of this facility is dedicated to legitimate research into our natural resources. However, there is an area below ground which houses a huge lab involved in bioengineering bacteria. This is also the headquarters for the directors who are in charge of dispensing a large part of the Black Budget, along with the millions of dollars contributed by the world's wealthiest families. Maria couldn't stomach what they were doing. During the few years she was on the board, she gathered as much information as she could without drawing their suspicions. In her last meeting, she asked a question she knew would make the co-chairs nervous. On her way home to Australia, her plane crashed, and she died—or so the world was led to believe. Maria went very deep underground, changed her name, and underwent several plastic surgeries. A few years later, she reappeared back in Australia as a long-lost relative on their father's side. She visited the Downs Estate posing as Angela, a distant cousin. Even David didn't recognize her at first. About two years ago, Maria finally told him who she really was."

"How long have you known that Angela was Maria?"

"Shortly after I arrived in Australia. Maria had been looking for someone to confide in as she knew she only had a few weeks to live."

"She never told you about her cancer?"

"No Megan, she did not. I guess she didn't want people to treat her differently."

"So you really don't know as of yet what exactly is in the information she gave you?"

"Not really. I do know it's extremely damaging to the board of the CESR in the USA. I think there are many other things that are equally damaging. I think it's Maria's way of making peace with herself. I have to do something with it in a way that will do the most damage to the Secret Governments and The Company. Hopefully there'll be enough of these documents to put a stop to their illegal activities."

"Gwen, you must be extremely careful—you could be sitting on huge powder keg. This is very dangerous stuff. How are you going to handle it?"

"If there was some way of leaking this information so that it can't be traced back to you, it might get others who have related information the courage to come forward."

"True, Megan, but before I make any further decisions, I need to take a detailed look at what I've got. I'll need a secure place to work on it."

"You can work on it at the Centre," said Megan. "You've been there often enough that everyone is accustomed to your comings and goings. You use the extra desk in my office to set up your computer, and you can share my vault."

Early the next morning there was a knock on Megan's office door, and Sandy entered.

"We have the preliminary results. This is another strain of E. coli which is different from the one we already have. Megan, would you like me to go ahead with a full analysis?"

"Yes—please run a full comparison to the others."

Sandy nodded as she left.

Gwen produced a medium-sized envelope and gave it to Megan, which she opened immediately. She pulled out several sheets of paper and some photographs.

"Gwen, do you realize what this is?"

"I'm not sure, but I know it's in Margo's handwriting."

"It's a description of the development of this new bacterium from start to finish how, and why it was developed. Gwen, we may have the genotype for the bacteria responsible for the epidemic a while back in India. We'll know more when Sandy finishes the complete analysis."

"I must see if I've received any information about that epidemic," Gwen said. She checked her email and found several replies. "Most of these replies are negative, but two are of interest. One states that it was definitely a mutated strain of E. coli There was a cover-up. The other one agrees that it was a mutated strain of E. coli, and he's tracking down a lead."

"Let's hope we get some more information soon," said Megan.

* * *

Three days after Sam arrived home in Halifax, he was flying to Nevada to see Alan Croft. Sitting together in his office, Alan looked at his computer screen.

"I don't know what I'm dealing with; come here and have a look," he said.

Sam watched the screen as data and seismographs began to flow in.

"Alan, where did these come from? Am I reading these correctly?"

"They are from an area north of the Aleutian Islands in the Bering Sea—an area not known for earthquake activity."

"I see. I'm going to need to look at these more closely."

"Thanks, Sam; I'll leave you to it."

"This is very strange," Sam said, speaking into a recording device. "There is something very unusual about these patterns."

Sam immediately called Alan back in.

"Alan—are these still occurring?"

"Not at the moment. What are you thinking?"

"My gut tells me that these wave patterns are not a normal earthquake. Coming from this area, I'm questioning it. Have you notified Washington?"

"Yes. They said our Navy had done exercises in that area last week. They didn't use any explosive devices. They are sending a couple of ships back there to check the area."

"We should re-examine all earthquakes that have a magnitude of four or less on the Richter scale over the past several months. I know we usually don't look at these seriously, but I've got a gut feeling."

Over the next two days, they found several more seismographs with a similar pattern. None of them were stronger than 3.5. Some were from Indonesian waters, just north of Australia, a few were just off Guatemala on the ocean floor, two were in the Indian Ocean, and the last one was in the Gulf of Mexico. They lasted only seconds and were not near areas considered to be particularly active earthquake zones.

On the third day that Sam was there, Alan called him from his lab.

"Those earthquakes are back," he said. "They're stronger—between four and five—and are located in three different areas. All are on the ocean floor off Alaska, Japan, and Bolivia."

"Alan, I would like to run some simulations on your computers."

"Absolutely—go ahead," Alan answered.

Sam was just loading his programs into the system when Alan shouted, "Sam, come in here!"

Sam ran across the lab.

"Look at this!" Alan said. Data was streaming in from the Pacific Ocean on the big screen. They were looking at more of these strange earthquakes.

"Where are they coming from?" asked Sam.

"Off the coast of California, about 250 miles out!" exclaimed Alan. "There is a cluster of four—no, five. They are all the exact same strength. Is it my imagination, or do they form a star?"

Sam's mind was racing: "Al, I think I know what this is."

He ran back to his computer and loaded a program. Alan followed him, staring at the screen.

"Look at this. Remember when I went off on a tangent and was playing around with simulations?" said Sam.

"You had some silly idea about...oh my God!"

"Alan, these aren't ordinary earthquakes. These and the others are all man-made."

Alan's assistant had just joined them. "What? That is impossible," he said.

"I'd postulated several years ago that if one had a source of tremendous power and was able to focus it on a very specific spot and depth, one could damage the Earth's crust, fracturing it, producing an earthquake," said Sam. "I ran a simulation and showed that it could be done. At that time, there was nothing man-made that was powerful enough to cause this to happen," said Sam.

"So what's changed?" asked Alan.

Sam, shaking his head, said, "Antimatter—someone's found a way to make, store, and focus it!"

"Who? It's extremely explosive, expensive, and difficult to store."

"Good question, Alan. There are only two sources I can think of with the funds and expertise to do this. Both answers you're not going to like. You may not even believe them."

"Try me."

"You know about Black Budgets and the secrecy surrounding them?"

Alan nodded.

"In many parts of the world, there are secret governments which are made up of certain regular government and military personnel, along with some of the wealthiest elite on Earth. They're an incredibly strong force controlling most of what the rest of us in the world do."

"I suspect that there's a lot of truth in what you're saying," Alan said. "What is the second source?"

"Well, how about aliens with very advanced technologies? It all started with Roswell." Sam went on to explain the theory of governments and militaries making deals with aliens.

"I would like to think the US really had no idea what they were getting themselves into until it reached the point of no return." Alan commented.

"This is where it gets interesting," Sam answered. "Have you heard that NASA has been looking for and has found a planet or two which can sustain life as we know it?"

Alan nodded in agreement.

"Consider if there was a deal made that went something like this: Earth gets to the point when life here is no longer viable for humans. Aliens would transport humanity's leaders and the families of the Power Elite to another planet. Then, when Earth recovers, the aliens would return this group of humans to Earth. They would be in total and absolute control of the Earth. In return, they would make deals with the same aliens to use Earth's natural resources."

"Wow!" Alan exclaimed. "But why would they want to cause earthquakes?"

"There are two possibilities: one, they are illegally mining minerals from our ocean floors, or two, they wish to keep us distracted from what they are doing by keeping the level of fear high."

"Keep us distracted so we will not search for the truth?" said Alan.

"Exactly!"

Alan shook his head, then looked at Sam. "How many people do you think believe in this conspiracy theory?" he asked.

"You would be surprised at the numbers—especially now that there are more sightings of UFOs and other phenomena."

"But the US government still denies the existence of UFOs."

"There are many countries which don't agree, including Russia, Canada, and many others," Sam said.

The two men sat quietly, deep in thought. Then Alan spoke up and said, "Okay—our main problem right now is this: what can we do about these man-made earthquakes?"

Sam thought for a few minutes. "We're going to have to be extremely careful. If the people who are causing these earthquakes find out we know, they'll try to discredit us any way they can."

"Or worse," added Alan.

"We don't have conclusive evidence. Whom can we trust?" said Sam.

"For the moment, let's keep a close eye on any further occurrences of these earthquakes. In the meantime, it would be very interesting to know if there has been any other unusual activity in these areas, such as UFO sightings at the time these earthquakes occurred."

"How do we go about doing that?" Sam asked.

"Leave it with me. I have some friends who are into aliens and UFOs. I'll contact them and see what I can find out."

"Great idea; I'll go home and work on simulations and let you know the results."

* * *

"How are your trials and tests coming along in manufacturing the earthquakes and tsunamis?" Anin's superior asked.

"Very well, sir. We just created a small cluster of five of them off the coast of California. They were less than five on the Richter scale as we don't want to draw attention to them until the need arises."

"Can you make them much stronger if necessary?"

"Definitely; we could go as high as between nine and ten."

"And you're positive that no one on Earth—even Dean—is aware of how far you've progressed with the antimatter beams and bombs, and how destructive they are?"

"Positive," Anin said—then he paused for a moment.

"Is there something else?"

"Yes—Dean contacted me; the humans wish for assurance that we'll hold up our end of the bargain."

"This offends me; who do they think they are, questioning us?"

"I agree, sir, but we still need their help."

"Yes, I see. What kind of assurance are they looking for?"

"They seek confirmation stating that we'll completely fulfill our end of the contract."

"Do you think it's just Dean being paranoid, or is it a true consensus of the Board?"

"What difference does it make? Let's give them the confirmation. Whether we keep it or not is another story."

* * *

About a week later, Sandy was getting her final report ready on the new bacterial strain. Megan and Gwen were in the process of summarizing the results from Maria's information when Megan received a phone call from the Canadian Coast Guard. They reported that a plane arriving in Gander from Iceland spotted three or four whales floating on the surface of the ocean about fifty miles east of Newfoundland. They were floating belly up on the surface. A Coast Guard ship was sent to investigate. They called Dr. Megan Teal, knowing she was interested in any reports regarding dying or dead cetaceans.

Megan immediately requested a helicopter to transport her to the scene, and she awaited the arrival of the ship. When she saw the dead animals below, she requested the pilot fly as close to them as possible. The scene chilled her to the bone. There were three adult humpback whales and a very young one. There was no damage to indicate that a ship had hit them. Megan was desperate. She had just watched one of the adults die. The young one was in great distress.

When the Coast Guard vessel arrived, she immediately brought the captain up to date, emphasizing that it was necessary to get samples as soon as possible. Four crew members in hazmat suits, along with Megan, were on their way to gather these samples within minutes. There were special precautions that needed to be taken when approaching and taking samples from such large animals.

Megan quickly got her equipment ready and began to take swabs from various parts of each whale. She had special transport vials with the growth medium already in them. They used specially-made long poles with wire loops on the end and took swabs from several locations, taking samples from the young one first. It was barely alive. The crew shot it and put it out of its misery. She moved from one whale to another, collecting samples in the same manner. As they moved back towards the ship, Megan gathered the vials and placed them in special aluminum transport tubes. There were eighty-eight vials in all. While they were trying to haul the baby aboard, Megan was taping aluminum tubes together for the trip home. Suddenly, someone shouted, "Captain, look to the east!"

Before the captain could react, another yelled, "It's in the west, too—it's all around us!"

The captain gave orders to prepare for an oncoming storm, and sent a message to Megan to go below and hold on. Megan knew something very serious was about to happen. She left her hazmat suit on, and put on her heavy jacket, stuffing the samples inside it as well as inside her boots. She felt the ship start to heave, and before she knew it, they were caught in the middle of horrendous waves. The storm came out of nowhere and everywhere at the same time; there had been no warning by way of darkening skies or cooling temperatures. There was a deafening roar as it crashed down upon them, and within seconds, two of the crew were swept away; no one saw or heard their screams of terror. The waves heaved, sank, and formed steep chasms, and as the waves shattered into a million icy daggers, the numbing water crashed and tore into everything and everyone on board.

A strong arm picked Megan up and threw her into the forward hold, and she fell in a heap, barely missing a young cadet. The two of them were the only ones in the hold; both were soaking wet and shivering. They desperately grabbed the nets, trying to find an anchor to save themselves from being flung against the metal hull of the ship. Megan looked up just in time to see the watertight lid being lowered and screwed down. The only way she felt she could survive was to wrap herself as best as she possibly could in the nets. The last thing she remembered before losing consciousness was being thrown against something very hard; the pain was excruciating.

The captain managed to send several distress signals before he was flung hard against the bridge wall and knocked out; he was subsequently washed overboard. When a rescue helicopter reached the last known location, they were amazed to see the ship still afloat in relatively calm waters. They lowered a couple of men to the deck of the ship, but they found that none of the ship's crew was on deck. The rescuers performed a full search of the vessel, and as they opened the forward hatch to the hold, they heard someone moaning. With searchlights beaming, they saw two people wrapped in the nets below. The cadet was dead, but the other was alive. Carefully cutting away several layers of nets, they found Megan. They radioed the chopper, and once they had Megan secured in the stretcher, they loaded her up and headed back to St. John's. Megan did not come to until she was in hospital.

When she finally regained consciousness, she gazed up to see the tears streaming down Sam's face.

"We thought we'd lost you, Meg!" he said.

"Never—I'll never leave you!" she whispered in response.

The next day, Megan was much more lucid and able to listen and talk for short periods of time. Her memory was not quite back yet. Sam told her what had happened as best as he could without having been there on the boat with her. She began to remember the storm.

"What happened to the crew and the boat?" she asked.

"Megan, of the ten on board you're the only one who survived. The crew were washed overboard, and the man with you in the hold was found dead. The ship was badly damaged. It should have gone down, but did not."

"My angels were with me," Megan sighed.

"The storm you encountered was a localized one, about fifty miles in diameter. The climatologists told us that it was nothing they had ever seen before; it only lasted about a half an hour. It was like a very large tornado."

"The winds and the waves were moving in all directions simultaneously. It was truly beyond description, Sam. It was pure hell!" Then Megan remembered something important. "I suppose the samples we took were all lost?"

"No" said Sam. "The long metallic tubes you had inside your jacket and boots were retrieved and have been sent to your lab."

"Did any of the tissues reveal anything in the way of bacteria or viruses?"

"Your lab called about three hours ago; most of the samples are okay. They figure only four of them were damaged. The rest are being processed as per protocol."

"Sam—the lab needs to keep the samples and their findings a secret."

"That procedure is in place."

"Good," Megan said. She was getting very tired.

"I'll take care of everything sweetheart. Just rest."

It was five hours before Megan was awake again. Nona was beside her bed. Megan opened her eyes, and they both began to weep.

"Gram, it was terrifying—I thought it was the end of the world!"

"It's okay, darling. You're here in St. John's, Newfoundland. It was the Canadian Air Force Search and Rescue who found you, and you're safe."

"I know—I hurt all over."

"Considering what you've been through, you're very lucky. Your left arm is broken in two places; you have three broken ribs, your left leg is broken, and you have a very badly sprained back. The surgeons and doctors say you'll be fine, but you must rest. You're not to go back to work for four to six weeks."

"But Gram, I have to—"

"I know. Sam and I have talked. I understand the situation, and we're working something out." Nona said. "You get some sleep now. Sam will be here after supper."

Megan was almost asleep by the time Nona left.

As quickly as she fell asleep, a vision of Ortho appeared. As she heard him call her name, there was a gorgeous burst of light with shades of purple shimmering like a cascading waterfall. She opened her mind's eye; standing there beside her was Ortho and the lady from the Crystal Cave. Both were smiling at her. The lady's eyes were like amethyst; they were clear, and full of unconditional love. Ortho introduced her as Saron, his mother.

"Saron—I feel that you were on the boat and that you saved my life."

"Yes, my child. It was I and many more."

"Thank you...thank you so very much. I did perceive that I was not alone, and that there were others present aside from the cadet."

"Yes—you are beginning to really see!" Saron said, smiling.

"Can you tell me what happened? Why did the crew have to die?"

"Their purpose was to guide you to the dead whales to get those samples so you, Sam, and Gwen can work together to find the truth about what really is happening on Earth."

"I guess all of us on Earth are here to fulfill some purpose or another."

"Yes, Megan—but the difference with you and certain others is that you know what your contract or purpose here is. It is also the reason you've been allowed to open certain psychic abilities. Each of the four accidents you've had to date has awakened a special gift for you to use in your quest for the truth. This time, your ability to communicate with Lacuna will be greatly enhanced. By the way, you didn't realize it at the time, but it was Lacuna who led you to the dead whales."

"Please tell me about the storm," asked Megan.

Ortho looked at Megan and said, "Unfortunately, Megan, it was a very serious storm. It was not created naturally. Tell Sam he's on track with his interpretation of his earthquake simulations and their causes. Tell him to believe in and act on his intuition. He'll meet someone very soon, and he'll know instantly that he can trust this person. You must not tell him this, as he must follow his instincts."

"In a previous vision, you showed me many others of all ages, working hand-in-hand with you, and others like me. Is this still happening?" asked Megan.

"Oh, yes, very much so. Humans of all ages are helping. The young will lead the way. It is your generation that will lead the breakthrough to world peace and to heal Earth. Know that you are never alone," said Saron.

"Yes, indeed," said Ortho, smiling. "Megan, I hear someone calling you!"

The images of Saron and Ortho were dimming, and the sound she knew so well was becoming closer and louder. Megan laughed as she opened her eyes.

"Papa Joe, I knew it was you. You were with me on the boat, too, weren't you?"

"Yes, dear Megan, I was," he said, smiling.

When Nona came in that morning, Megan told her about parts of her vision. Her mind was still spinning in several directions when the nurse came in with a sedative.

While Megan was recovering, Sam had been phoning and sending e-mails to let their friends and coworkers know that Megan, although badly injured, was going to be okay. He also called Alan to see if he could check with his sources in climatology to see if they had found the cause of this localized and violent storm; he had an uneasy feeling about it. He had talked to experts in Canada and Iceland and no one had an answer.

Sam had picked up dinner to go, and headed to the hospital in time for visiting hours; Megan was waking up when he entered her room.

"I smell Chinese food," she said. "Thank you, darling."

"How are you feeling?"

"Sore after some of the x-rays this morning; I felt better after my sleep, though," she said. She picked up chopsticks in her good hand and began to eat.

"I called everyone. They all send you their love and get-well wishes. I called your lab as well. They've cultured each sample, keeping each one well isolated from each other. They are following your protocols exactly. No one knows you have them. Word is that you're very lucky to be alive. I still can't figure out how you rescued those samples. I guess there are powers and beings out there that we are only beginning to comprehend."

Megan looked at Sam, smiled, and thought, *If he only knew—but then again, maybe he does.*

They sat together quietly, each deep in their own thoughts. Megan asked, "Have you thought any more about what could have caused that weird storm?"

"Yes. It's all theoretical at this point, but if someone has developed a way of producing large amounts of antimatter to concentrate it into a beam and aim it at a given spot, it could do a hell of a lot of damage in a very short period of time, resulting in a well-controlled earthquake. With antimatter, it would be many magnitudes greater." Sam took a sip of his coffee: "Now, what if this antimatter was aimed at the ocean surface and, instead of holding it in one spot, it was swung in a circular fashion with a radius of about twenty miles?"

"Could that possibly create a storm like this one?" Megan asked.

"I believe it can, but I need access to my computer to run a simulation. Antimatter is extremely expensive to create. Currently, there is no way on Earth we can store nearly enough unless..." Sam's eyes widened with realization. "...unless there actually *is* a way that we haven't considered yet."

"Could antimatter bombs have been placed on the ocean floor for earthquake production? Is it possible to place such bombs on the ocean surface to produce a very powerful cyclonic storm?" asked Megan

"I'm sure it's possible; I'll run some simulations and see."

They were interrupted when the nurse came in with Megan's medication.

"Would you please close the door as you leave?" Megan smiled at Sam. "I wish to have a quiet talk with my husband."

The nurse was grinning from ear to ear as she left.

"Sam, could there be *another* explanation for sources of this antimatter?" she asked once the nurse was gone.

"What do you mean, Megan?"

"Well, in spite of the military trying to prevent alien contact, there have been a couple of well-documented encounters recently—two in 2015, and one so far this year; all of them have been peaceful and located in remote areas. What if Gwen is right? What if there are some aliens who have built alliances with secret governments? We've suspected for years that some planets have civilizations which are far more technically-advanced than ours."

"Are you saying some dark-minded aliens may have teamed up with certain illegal groups on Earth?" Sam interjected. "If that's what you're saying, I see where you're coming from. If this is true, it could explain everything—it could be even something far more dangerous than antimatter."

"Do your simulations when you get home, Sam, discuss it with Alan, and go from there," suggested Megan.

"Okay, but it does show a possible alien aspect and a connection with Earth's governments—so whom can we trust?"

"You'll have to be extremely careful. Maybe Alan knows someone who knows someone."

Her surgeon came in with her chart. "Good news, Megan: we've checked your x-rays. You are to be discharged tomorrow morning." He then turned to Sam: "Were you able to make the appropriate arrangements for transport?" he asked.

"Yes, all is arranged."

Megan was amazed yet confused when they arrived at St. John's airport. The next plane did not leave for five and a half hours.

"Sam, do we have to wait five hours?"

"Not at all—we've a surprise for you. They proceeded through security quickly and smoothly. Before she knew it, she was being wheeled out on the tarmac.

"It's okay. Andrew called Rance; he sent this private jet for you, knowing it would be far more comfortable flying this way," said Nona.

"The only reason they discharged you early is because the hospital knew you wouldn't be on a regular flight," said Sam. "If we didn't do it this way, you would still be here a few more days—and we know how important it is for you to get closer to your lab and team."

"Andrew is at your apartment overseeing the installation of the hospital bed and some equipment for physiotherapy. He's also installing Skype on your computer so you can be in direct contact with them through videoconferencing."

Megan was overwhelmed and very tired. Sam covered her with a blanket and sat with her, holding her good hand. By the time the jet left the runway, she was sound asleep.

They were greeted by Andrew at their apartment in Halifax. The plan was for Nona to stay with Holly; she would come over during the day to keep an eye on Megan and prepare meals.

Even after Megan settled into her apartment, she was exhausted from the trip. Still, within an hour of arriving home, she checked with her lab and found that all was progressing on schedule. By the next day they would be ready for the next step, and would be in contact with her. As soon as she finished checking in with them, she fell asleep; she was still profoundly exhausted.

Once Megan was asleep, Sam quietly went to his office down the hall, and found a very intriguing message from Alan. He called him back right away.

"Alan, did you find someone who'll understand what we were talking about—someone we can trust?"

"Yes, Sam, and he wants to meet with us at your earliest convenience."

"What is his background?"

"Fred Maxwell has a Master's degree in astrophysics and was an analyst with the Air Force here for many years. He worked with the team which investigated all aspects and reports of UFOs, aliens, etc. Since he retired a few years ago, he's been traveling around the United States and the world giving seminars and talks."

Sam was puzzled. "You mean...the US government allows him to do this?"

"Not only do they allow him to do this—he's being encouraged to do so. He works under a set of very close guidelines given by the powers that be. The US government realizes that well over sixty percent of our citizens believe in UFOs and extraterrestrial life—yet it is hesitant to admit that such things exist, because it would be telling the world they've been covering up and lying to their own public for years."

"So Fred is kind of an ambassador who is softening the blow they know is coming?"

"You got it, Sam. Even the US president is behind him, knowing there'll be more contact with aliens."

"Okay, Alan, you arrange a time and place with Fred and I'll be there. Megan is safely home and is surrounded by family. She also realizes these man-made earthquakes and weird storms are extremely important and that it's critical to find out what's causing them."

"While you were in St. John's, there was a similar cluster of three 4.0 quakes off of Japan. You'll find the data on your computer. Why don't I arrange the meeting with Fred to be in Halifax? I have family in Connecticut and would like to visit them at around the same time."

"Alan, that would be fantastic!"

The next morning, Sandy Johnson came over to the apartment to visit Megan and to discuss what their next step regarding the bacteria cultures should be. Nona had made coffee and some delicious-looking cookies, left them beside Megan, and went out shopping. Megan was sitting in the La-Z-Boy chair with her leg up, with her laptop open and running when Sandy came in.

"Megan, you're looking pretty good considering the trauma you experienced."

"Thanks. I'm feeling okay, but I tire quickly and I'm still in pain."

"You're bound to be," said Sandy. She poured a coffee for each of them, and briefed Megan on exactly what they had done with the samples from the moment they received them to the present.

"The samples have yielded some very interesting results," she said. "This is a strain of E. coli which I've never seen before."

An hour later, additional results came through. "These are genetically-engineered bacteria," said Megan. "Run these and compare them to the whale samples."

Sandy sent the passwords to the lab so they could access the files Megan had just given her. "Run these genotypes against the new whale bacteria and get back to us asap," she told the lab technicians.

When the results came back a few minutes later, Megan was not surprised.

"I was afraid of this," she said under her breath.

"They're almost a match. Megan, where did you get those genotypes?"

"I'll tell you, but first we must secure this data at the highest level."

After the data had been duly secured, Megan explained. "This bacterium does not occur naturally. They are bioengineered and are extremely deadly, especially to marine mammals."

"But who's doing this, and why?"

At this point, Megan gave Sandy a general overview on Black Budgets and Secret Governments.

"Okay Megan, I understand what you're saying, but where did those genotypes you have come from?"

"Sandy, I'm sorry, I cannot say—not until we get more information from these new bacteria."

After Sandy left, Megan called Gwen to come over. Gwen listened to Megan's story of the storm along with the explanation about their recent discovery of a new bioengineered bacterium.

"How close are these genotypes to the ones in the information we received in Australia?" Gwen asked.

"Very close; it's the most recent one—let's call it E. coli 79. I believe it's far more deadly and dangerous than we originally thought," answered Megan.

"Where do we go from here?"

"We should wait for more results before we proceed further."

Four days later, once Megan had the conclusive evidence she needed, she met with Gwen to review Megan's findings.

"Do you feel we now have conclusive evidence that the bacteria you found in those whales are in fact connected with the lab in Australia?" Gwen asked.

"It's a more advanced strain of the bioengineered E. coli, which they called MMB 69. It enters the body with food or with breathing. As soon as it reaches a given temperature and is near living cetacean cells, it is activated. It quickly multiplies and causes a hemolytic reaction; the animal bleeds to death in a few hours, so ultimately, it is fatal. If it doesn't infect another cetacean, it only lives one to two hours."

"Does it have some form of a resting stage, like a spore or something?"

"No, it's very easy to control. It could be used on a group of marine mammals, and it would be effective on wiping it out. A barrier-like distance would prevent it from spreading to other cetaceans."

"What about antibiotics?" asked, Gwen.

"It appears to be resistant to any of our known antibiotics."

Gwen was totally amazed at what she'd just heard. "Talk about a biological weapon! Do we have a perfect match to the genotype MMB 69 that we received from Australia.?"

"Gwen, the genotypes are close, but it's not an exact match; we can't say it was made in Australia. It could have been engineered in a similar lab anywhere in the world."

Gwen was puzzled. "From what you've described, I'm wondering if that massive epidemic in India a couple of years ago was caused by a human form of this strain of bacteria. All the reports coming out of India stated the epidemic was caused by a naturally-mutating strain. If the bacteria died off as quickly as this one, could it have been bioengineered?"

"There were no samples retrieved from any of the deceased. If there were, they were destroyed, or someone very high up in India put a gag order the results," said Megan.

"I'm going to contact my counterparts in India and get them to take a closer look."

"An excellent idea, Gwen—you do that, and we'll go from there."

"Before I go, I have one more question: what is the status of the E. coli from your whale samples? Will you be able to keep some alive in case we need them for evidence?"

"Yes, Gwen, I believe we can. It's an extremely dangerous bacterial strain, but we have the equipment and the expertise to handle it. Tomorrow I'll ask the team to start to bioengineer a counteractive serum."

* * *

Sam was at the Halifax airport greeting Alan and Col. Fred Maxwell as they exited customs.

"I've made arrangements for both of you to stay in one of our downtown hotels overlooking the harbour," said Sam. "The scenery here is beautiful; hopefully you will get a chance to experience some of it while you are here."

By the time they got settled in their room, it was noon.

"Why don't we order room service? That way, we can talk where it's quiet," suggested Fred.

"Excellent idea!" Alan said, picking up the menu.

Once their orders were made, they enjoyed some fresh, strong coffee, and Fred decided to bring the conversation to the heart of the matter.

"Sam, this is the first time we've met; I'm sure you have many questions you wish to ask me."

"Yes, Fred, I do. I understand that you worked near Area 51, which is reputed to be a very top-secret zone. You are retired you travel the globe speaking about UFOs and aliens. Why?"

Fred smiled. "Several reasons: first and foremost, I and many others working there did not agree with or condone much of what was being developed and kept secret. Of course, the development of new types of military equipment and weapons have to be done in a top secret location—however, there are aspects we feel are not legitimate, and the public, who is footing the bill, should know about this. As a result, a group of us approached the government and asked them to reconsider their denial that UFOs exist. Recent surveys show that over sixty-five percent of US citizens believe there is life on other planets and alien spacecraft. We feel it's time for our President to come clean, and to apologize for keeping the public in the dark."

"I've read a lot about what is being called Cosmogate, and that most other countries do believe in UFOs," said Sam.

Fred nodded, and continued. "I was asked by the President and given clearance to talk about certain aspects of what we know about aliens, spacecraft, and so on, in order to slowly uncover the truth—the truth that there definitely are aliens, and contact has been made in the past."

"But are you only allowed to say certain things and not others?"

"Yes."

"But the general public must be told in order to understand why certain things are happening, so we can be less afraid; with more understanding, we could be more helpful when full contact is made in a peaceful way," said Sam.

"Alan has told me what you've discovered, Sam. With that said, we must establish a strong level of trust between us in order to go any further," Fred continued. "I'm going to tell you, off the record, some things I'm not allowed to speak of in public. Are you ready for this? Can we trust one another implicitly?"

"Yes, absolutely," said Sam.

Fred nodded, and continued. "Here's the undiluted truth: we have been in contact with several different alien civilizations over the past several decades. Some of them have been friendly and wanted to help, but were turned down by the US. They were feeling very strong and confident after World War II and decided they could protect themselves without any help. We now realize that the sightings of UFOs—which have increased greatly since the end of World War II—was triggered by the dropping of the two atomic bombs on Japan. The resulting radioactive clouds which rose into the atmosphere appear to have caused great concern about the planet's safety and our impact beyond our planet. You are aware of several incidents with UFOs in the US, am I right?"

"Roswell, etc.?" asked Alan.

"Yes, that was the start. Our military moved in, and the cover-up began. Since then, we've had UFOs land, and meetings with various aliens and deals have occurred. Not all of these deals have been favourable. Early on, deals which looked positive on the surface have turned out not to be to our benefit after all. I'm sure you've heard of the Anunnaki."

Alan and Sam nodded.

"Their initial offer to help was positive in helping the US to develop new and very powerful weapons," Fred continued. "Remember, this was the time of the Cold War and nuclear bombs. As a result, the American military was becoming increasingly powerful, and some of the wealthiest, greediest families on Earth created a partnership with them."

At this point, Alan spoke up again. "Fred, what you're doing is gently alerting the world to the truth. If this is so, why hasn't this powerful 'dark' group tried to silence you in some way?"

"There are three main reasons: first, I'm not giving out any absolute proof in my speeches, so I'm not an immediate threat to them; second, I believe they feel they are all-powerful, so they assume that at this stage there is absolutely nothing that any of the seven billion people on Earth can do to stop them; third, they're far too busy getting ready for something big, which we know nothing about. They're not really paying attention to someone like me."

Sam opened his briefcase and made eye contact with Alan, who nodded back to Sam.

"My gut tells me I can trust you, Fred," said Sam, "and I want to thank you for what you've shared with us."

"Fred, Sam has found something of extreme importance," Alan said. Fred looked at Sam expectantly.

"Over the past few years there have been 4.0 earthquakes caused by unknown forces," Sam began. He paused to gauge Fred's reaction.

"I've been told this," said Fred, "but no one has discovered how they're being triggered. I'm very interested in seeing what you have found, Sam."

Sam felt encouraged to continue, and with Alan's help, he showed the locations of the epicentres, dates, strengths, and seismographs of these unnatural quakes. Fred was particularly interested in the simultaneous five quakes in the Pacific off the California coast. Then Sam split the screen and put the seismographs of two quakes of the same magnitude side-by-side.

"The one on the right is from a natural cause. The one on the left is from one of the five quakes I just showed you. Can you detect any differences?" he asked Fred, who studied them very quietly.

Fred nodded. "Yes, I can; the ones caused naturally are all different. The spikes are different heights, and the overall patterns of the spikes are distinctly different, whereas the quakes you believe to be created unnaturally have patterns in which the spikes are similar. The five off San Francisco are almost identical to each other. Sam, I do believe you have something substantial here, but it seems to me that it would be impossible to create a force strong enough to produce a magnitude 4.0 quake, wouldn't it?"

"It would be considered impossible, Fred—unless we can produce huge amounts of antimatter and have the ability to control and focus it at very specific spots. Do we have that capability on Earth, Fred?"

Fred frowned. "Sam...we may."

Sam and Alan were stunned. "What do you mean?" Alan asked.

"Well, I've heard rumours that a huge lab was carved into a mountain near Area 51—a place that's so top secret that not even the US president knows what's going on in its facilities. There are some extremely advanced technologies dealing with space travel and biological weaponry that are apparently housed there. They produce a large amount of antimatter; how much, we don't know. It's said as well that there are similar facilities in northern Siberia, Australia, and the Canadian north."

"Are there aliens working in these places?"

"I believe so, Sam."

"Then these artificial quakes and storms, like the one that almost killed my wife, could well have been caused by humans with access to such equipment—or could it be that some alien force is doing this?"

"At this stage, I believe anything is possible," Fred answered.

Alan, who had been listening intently, asked: "Regarding the artificially-induced quakes and these very destructive storms: what is the purpose of them—especially if all the superpowers have access to this technology? It's as if a very small group of humans are preparing for a war in space."

Fred got up and paced the floor, trying to come up with an answer that was safe to give. "What we've been discussing must be kept between the three of us at all costs. I can't give you an exact answer. My hands are tied; if I did tell you, I would be breaking the trust of the President of the United States and my Commander-in-Chief."

Alan coughed. "You mean to tell me you've a direct contact with President Kingsley?"

"Yes Alan...I do."

"Where do we go from here?" Sam asked.

Each sat deep in their own thoughts. Fred broke the silence, and asked, "Sam, may I have your permission to inform the

President of your finding? You are a Canadian and are not compelled to do so."

Sam turned to Alan. "I hope you'll understand, Alan, but I need to speak with Fred alone for a moment, please."

"Certainly," Alan said as he quietly left the room.

"Have you heard of Dr. Megan Teal?" Sam asked once he and Fred were alone.

"Is she not the woman who survived that incredible storm in the North Atlantic recently?"

"Yes. She is. She is my wife."

"Oh, Sam! How is she doing? I understand she was badly injured."

"She was. She is recovering and is healing at home here in Halifax."

Fred sensed that Sam wanted to talk to him about something involving Sam's wife. "What is it you want to tell me, Sam?"

"Megan knows all about my simulations. We've discussed them and their possible causes extensively. She is a microbiologist and works here at the Centre for Peace."

"I know of it. There are some very interesting studies and findings coming out of there; I follow them closely," said Fred.

"I would like you to meet her. She has some incredible information."

"Sam, I would like to, but only if she's up to it."

"I know she would really appreciate it if you could come over to our apartment. She is best in the mornings. I'll let you know about time and place after I've had a chance to speak with her."

Half an hour later, Sam left for home, feeling he'd somehow made a huge step forward in getting recognition for his ideas and findings.

"Is that you, Sam?"

As he was putting his briefcase down he bent over and kissed Megan.

"How did your day go with Sandy?" he asked, sitting down beside her.

"We're beginning to bioengineer a serum to counteract the new bacteria. How did your meeting with Alan and Fred Maxwell go?"

"Very well indeed, Megan. Maxwell is very intelligent and down-to-earth. Meg, I like him and I trust him. I followed my intuition."

"What did he think about your theories and your simulations? Was he the least bit interested?"

"He was quite interested; he listened to my explanations closely and asked a lot of questions."

"Did you discuss your hypotheses as to how these unnatural storms and quakes were being caused?"

"We did. He was extremely interested; he also told Alan and I a few things which unfortunately I cannot speak of, as he swore me to secrecy. I can tell you, however, that I'm on the right track. The problem is finding the proof."

"You will, I know it," Megan said. "I'm happy for you."

"He really wants to meet you. He knows about the Centre and he wants to talk to you about the trauma you've just been through as well as the work you are doing."

Megan looked at her calendar. "I don't meet with Sandy again for a couple of days," she said. "Do you think tomorrow morning would be too soon?"

"I'll call him and see if ten am tomorrow is okay." Megan nodded, and Sam came back with a glass of orange juice for her.

"I spoke to Fred; ten am tomorrow is perfect."

"Sam, do you think I should tell him about this new bacterium and my other findings?"

"Why don't you play it by ear, Meg? Ask him some questions and see what your gut tells you."

Megan laughed. "That advice sounds familiar!" she said.

Fred arrived on time the next morning and was welcomed at the door by Sam.

"Good morning, Fred. I hope you had a good night."

"I did, Sam. I must admit, though, that I woke up often thinking about what you had shown me." He followed Sam as they spoke, and went into the living room where Megan was sitting in her La-Z-Boy chair.

"Darling, I would like you to meet Colonel Fred Maxwell. Fred, this is my wife, Megan."

"Pleased to meet you Colonel Maxwell."

"Please, Fred will do just fine, and the pleasure is all mine."

Fred shook Megan's good hand. In his other hand, he had a magnificent bouquet of roses in a variety of colours. "For you—with best wishes for a full and speedy recovery."

"Thank you, Fred," she said. She gave them to Sam to put in a vase. "That was very kind of you. Are you enjoying Halifax?"

"Very much indeed!" Fred said. He rose from his chair when Nona came in with a tray laden with tea, coffee, and fresh blueberry muffins.

"Gram, this is—"

"Hi, Fred. How are things with you? Busy as ever, I'll bet."

Fred gave Nona a big hug. "I wondered if you two were related," he laughed. "It's so good to see you again, Nona. It's been a while. You look well—and as beautiful as usual."

Sam had returned with the roses, and he looked at Megan with the questioning expression. Megan smiled and shrugged her shoulders.

"You two obviously know one another," Sam said.

"Our paths have crossed a couple of times on our separate lecture circuits," Nona said, laughing.

"Gram, will you join us for a coffee before you go out?" Megan asked.

"I'd love to, sweetheart, but I've an appointment downtown in twenty minutes."

"I'll call you," Fred said to Nona. "Maybe you and I can go out for dinner while I'm here."

"Fred, I'd love to. Thank you," Nona said. She kissed Megan on the cheek and left.

"Well, that was a wonderful surprise!" Fred said as he sat back down. He turned to Megan. "Tell me about this adventure—or should I say misadventure—that you had recently. I'm particularly interested in your description of the storm."

Megan glanced over at Sam, who gave a little nod.

Megan told as much as she could remember about the storm. When Megan finished, he said. "It is a miracle you're here to tell your story. I'm sure Sam has told you a bit about me and our meeting yesterday."

"That he did, Fred. I wish to thank you for listening to his theories. To reassure you, Fred, Sam did tell me a bit of what happened yesterday, but he also made me aware of certain aspects discussed between you which are to remain a secret. I respect this, as does Sam."

"Your candour and reassurance are appreciated, and I thank you," said Fred. "Sam tells me you are in the research field of bioengineering bacteria and viruses at the world-renowned Centre here in Halifax. I would love to have a tour of your facility, if possible. I know you are not well enough to do so, but perhaps you could arrange one for me."

"By all means, Fred. May I ask you a question or two?"

"Certainly," he said. He glanced at Sam, who was smiling.

"Do you believe that UFOs and aliens exist?" she asked frankly.

"I've not only seen UFOs, I have been on some of them, and have met with aliens from several different civilizations."

Megan was not surprised. "What were these aliens like?"

"Most of the ones I've met are friendly, inquisitive, and extremely intelligent. They have technologies well beyond ours."

Megan was fascinated by his answer. She immediately knew she could trust him. "Thank you, Fred. Now I suppose you would like to know why I was on that ship a couple of days ago."

"I'm very interested."

Megan told him everything she saw and did the best she could. The only part that she left out was her vision with Ortho and Saron. When she finished, Fred asked if she could show him the bacteria she had found. Megan turned on Skype and requested Sandy to show the slide of the MMB 79.

"So, this is the bug that killed those whales?"

Yes," Megan replied.

"Sandy, could you please put some of our stored whale blood on a slide and add some of the MMB 79 bacteria?"

Fred could not believe his eyes. The computer program displayed on screen what was seen under the microscope, he could see that the bacteria cells were attacking all the blood cells and quickly multiplying, further attacking nearby blood cells to the point where there was nothing left but bacteria. Then the bacteria began to disintegrate.

"I would not have believed it if I hadn't seen it with my own eyes. It's like something that you would see in a science fiction movie. How can you connect it to killing the whales?"

"I took the samples of the bacteria you just saw from the open bleeding sores on these animals," Megan explained.

"How exactly is it transmitted, and how does it work?" Fred asked.

"This particular strain is specific to whales and dolphins," Megan explained.

Fred was shocked. "Are there no antibiotics or such that can destroy it?"

"No. This bacterium was bioengineered illegally."

"Thank you, Sandy—I think we've seen all we need for now," Megan said. Sandy nodded, and they both logged out of Skype.

Fred was deep in thought. He was frowning as he tried to figure out what and how much to say.

Megan spoke up first. "I'm going to tell you more, but on the understanding that what you are about to hear and what you have seen so far is only the tip of the iceberg. Also, you must hold it in strict secrecy."

"I understand and agree," Fred said.

Megan told him the facts she knew of and that she had proof that certain underground labs around the world were involved and interconnected." It was in two or more of these covert labs where deadly bioengineered bacteria and viruses were being produced. One or more strains of these microbes have already been used both on humans and marine cetaceans," she said. "There are probably more out there. This one appears to be the deadliest." Megan paused and took a large sip of coffee. "Fred, what do you think these so-called Secret Governments are up to? Why are they killing humans, causing minor earthquakes, and creating unusually violent, localized storms? Why have they developed these bacteria?"

"We are not one hundred percent sure it's them," said Fred, "however, there are two separate but related theories which may explain all of this. Earth is critically ill. If something doesn't happen soon, our planet and virtually every living being on it will die. This is our current status." He went on to explain the theories of the deals made between certain aliens and so-called Secret Governments. "The aliens get our natural resources, such as some of our rare metals and freshwater, and in return the Secret Governments get access to their advanced alien knowledge, along with a promise that the elite will be given sanctuary on another planet when Earth dies."

"So in both scenarios, the 2000 wealthy elite plus an unknown number of military and government officials live, and the rest of us seven billion humans are expendable?" Sam said angrily.

"Yes."

"If there was some way we could expose the truth about these 'dark forces' and what they've done, would that help?" asked Megan.

"Yes; they're trying to keep the rest of us not only distracted, but also in a constant state of fear. They wish us to keep from finding the truth." Fred said.

"Their security is so strong, and they are so powerful—how can anyone possibly stop them?" asked Megan. She felt frustrated.

"Between Megan's findings and mine, we've some evidence," Sam interjected, "but I don't feel it's enough. Who could we give it to that is strong enough to get it out to the general public —the citizens of Earth? We are up against some very powerful beings."

"We have to start somewhere, and fast," Megan added.

"Megan, I may have a way," Fred said. "Only a very few people know this: I've a direct line of contact with President Kingsley."

"What? Really!" exclaimed Megan.

"Yes. He's enraged by the Black Budgets. One of the main reasons he hired me was to gather comments from the people who attended my lectures and seminars. I was also to gather observations and ideas from the general public worldwide. He wants to know what the general overall as well as specific feelings people have regarding aliens and UFOs. Having said that, I would like to have permission from both of you to contact him and tell him of your findings." He hesitated, and added, "I give you my word. He'll listen. You don't need to answer tonight.

Think about this very carefully, and let me know your decisions tomorrow."

After visiting for a while longer, Fred took his leave. He thanked them profusely, and Sam walked Fred to the door. He came back and found Megan deep in thought.

"Meg, you realize if we do this, our lives will never be the same."

"I was thinking the same thing. On the other hand, if we don't take this opportunity, would we be able to live with ourselves?"

"It's what we've been trained for. With our combined expertise and experience, I believe we can do this. We can make a difference," Sam said with confidence.

"I agree," said Megan. "And there may be others out there who have bits and pieces of information which would add to the strength of our findings."

Sam nodded. "Are you going to tell Gwen and Sandy?"

"Not yet. Let's see what happens when Fred shows Kingsley our findings."

The next morning, right after breakfast, Sam called Fred and told him of their decision.

"Wonderful, Sam! I know Kingsley will be more than interested. Thank you—and thank Megan for me. I called Nona last night when I got to the hotel. She and I are having dinner tonight."

In the early afternoon, the phone rang.

"Megan, Fred here. Thank you for agreeing to allow me to move forward with your research. I contacted President Kingsley; he is extremely interested. I've a non-official appointment with him the day after tomorrow. May I come over and get some data? Not all of it, by any means—just enough to illustrate the key points of both of your findings."

"Of course. Sam is out just now, but he'll be back shortly. I'll check with him, but I know that he'll agree. Are you busy for lunch tomorrow?"

"Lunch would be great, as I booked a flight to Washington for eight-fifteen tomorrow evening."

"Perfect. If you don't hear otherwise, Fred, lunch will be at around twelve-thirty pm."

"Lovely. See you then!"

Sam arrived home shortly afterwards. "Any news?" he asked.

Megan was smiling and had a twinkle in her eye. "Fred called; he talked with Kingsley last night, and he's very interested in both of our findings."

"That's exciting!" said Sam.

"It is indeed," said Megan. "Fred's coming for lunch tomorrow, and would like to pick up a brief on our specific and general findings to take with him for his next meeting with Kingsley."

"Well, I guess we'd better get busy."

They both spent the rest of the day writing up their respective reports for Fred. Every so often, they took a break for coffee or tea, conferred with each other, and got each other's opinions on what they had accomplished to that point.

"How long do you think these should be?" Megan asked during one of their breaks. "I'm sure Kingsley doesn't have a background in the sciences, so I think we need to put it in a non-technical format."

"You're right," he said. "Let's use diagrams, photos, or other graphics to get our main points and findings across. That way, he'll not only have a picture in front of him, but also a short explanation of each one."

"Good idea, Sam. I like it. We don't want to bury him with words—after all, Kingsley is a very busy man. What do you think about keeping the material to five pages and see what happens? It's already five-thirty, and it'll take me the rest of this evening to pull it all together. I'll put the polishing touches on in the morning."

Sam agreed, and got up to put their dirty dishes in the dishwasher. Later, there was a knock on the door, and Nona answered it. Fred was there with a beautiful box of chocolates.

"These are for you and Megan to share," he said.

"Thank you, Fred. Please do come in," Nona said.

Fred went into the living room to say hello to Megan. "How are you feeling today?"

"Very good, I feel better and stronger every day. I can't wait to get out in the fresh air."

Nona came in, ready to go. "Fred's going to drop me off at Holly's after dinner," she said.

"Have a wonderful evening," said Megan. "See you tomorrow morning."

Nona had very kindly made dinner for them. All they had to do was microwave it.

"I wonder how well Gram knows Fred?" Sam said. He was tidying up after they ate.

"I had a chat with her this morning. Apparently, they've known each other for several years. They met in Washington five years ago. While attending and giving talks there, Fred was in Gram's audience when she was giving a short seminar and workshop on behalf of the Partners for Universal Harmony. They had lunch together. They are friends Sam, nothing more."

"I didn't say anything," Sam said, laughing. "I know very well that Gram is in love with Andrew." They both chuckled.

"Well, back to work for me," said Megan.

Megan was getting extremely tired at about nine pm. She could no longer concentrate. She wheeled herself into their bedroom and called Sam to help her change and get into her hospital bed.

"Oh Sam, I do so miss sleeping with you, but these damn casts and my back being painful are getting in the way. I miss you so much."

He leaned over and kissed her. "I know darling, I miss you too."

Megan smiled as she looked up at Sam playfully. "Just think of the fun we'll have catching up," she said.

Sam laughed as he went back to his study.

The next day, Nona arrived midmorning. "Hi, Gram. How did your dinner go with Fred last night?"

"I really enjoyed myself, Megan. We discussed our lecture tours and how people's attitudes are definitely changing. It's very interesting. We both agreed that many of us humans are truly searching for something. We never seem to be fully satisfied. The more we have, the more we seem to want—especially when it comes to money and material goods."

"There's that old saying: 'Much wants more.'"

"Right, Megan. What seems to drive many of us is competition and greed, but unfortunately both also tend to damage cooperation and sharing. How many of us have far more than we actually need? This seems to be especially true in the Western and European cultures—not everyone, of course; Heaven knows even in the wealthiest countries there is still a great deal of illiteracy and poverty."

"Wouldn't it be wonderful if the rich shared with those who are starving and homeless, not only in our own countries, but in others as well?" Megan added.

Nona nodded, and continued. "So many are asking 'Who am I? Why am I here? Why can't I find peace and happiness? Are we the only beings in our galaxy or in the cosmos? Why do we feel that Earth is isolated, a one-of-a-kind?' It is as if our collective minds have been waking up to a new reality."

"We have a desire—no, a *need*—to know the truth," Megan added.

"So, to that end, Fred is traveling the world, making people more aware of aliens, UFOs, and so on."

"And you, Gram, are doing roughly the same thing on a more personal level by teaching the idea that we humans are all interconnected with one another and with everything on Earth. We are *one*."

"Fred is lecturing on the cosmic level whereas I'm lecturing on a planet level. We discussed the idea that perhaps we should do an experimental series of lectures together. We would combine the two concepts not only of harmony on Earth but throughout our galaxy, and eventually beyond."

"Gram, that's a fantastic idea—I love it! You are going to do it, aren't you?"

"I'll discuss it with Andrew. I'm sure he would agree. He would come along with us and take care of all the arrangements."

"Fantastic!" said Megan. Sam entered the room, smiling.

"What's all the excitement about, you two?"

Megan quickly explained what she and Nona had been talking about.

"What a great idea!" Sam exclaimed. "I just got a call from Fred. He was very pleased with our decision. Have you told Gram yet?"

"No, Sam. Why don't you tell her?" said Megan.

"Gram, you know about the research that Megan does and what I do, right?"

"Yes, I know the general overall aspects."

"Well, Fred is very interested in both of our respective findings."

"I know. He mentioned it during dinner. Did you know he has a direct connection with Kingsley?"

Sam and Megan chuckled and together answered, "Yes!"

"Fred said he was coming over here today to have some further conversations with you, but he did not say about what." Nona got up from the table. "I guess I'd better make some lunch."

"Could you please make enough for one more? Fred is coming over to join us," Sam said as he got up. "It's probably a good idea for us to spend the next hour going over our respective summaries and make any minor changes before he arrives, just to be sure that all is in order."

"Gram tells us you might be getting together on an upcoming lecture tour," Megan said when Fred arrived. "I think it's a really good idea."

"Thanks, Megan. We thought a series of about five or six different cities throughout Canada and the United States would be a good start. If they are successful, we'll see about going global."

"I think a tour with both of you speaking is a superb idea," Sam said as he put lunch on the kitchen table for them. "Nona said to say hi, and that she's going to call you later this afternoon."

"Here are our summaries, ideas, and comments," Megan said. She was pleased to see Fred's reaction as he skimmed through them.

"These are great—and our timing is perfect! I'll be able to see Kingsley tomorrow afternoon. I'll call and let you know how it went."

They chatted a bit more during and after lunch. Fred, looking at his watch, said, "I guess I best get going. Thank you for allowing me to do this. I've a strong feeling that Kingsley will be extremely interested. Again, I want to assure you that it'll be kept in the strictest confidence."

"You're welcome—and thank *you* for bringing our research to Kingsley's attention," Sam said as he showed Fred out.

* * *

"It's so good to see you again," President Kingsley said as he greeted Fred with a warm handshake. "How was your trip?"

"Thank you, Mr. President. I believe my trip was extremely successful." He pulled a couple of folders out of his briefcase. "I brought the information in this format as I didn't know whether you would want this material on your computer or not."

"You feel these two young Canadian scientists have found something important?"

"Yes, I do. I assured them that it would be for your eyes only."

"I understand, Fred. Please show me what you have."

An hour later, Kingsley and Fred had discussed what the President now held in his hands. "Good Lord, Fred! This is very sensitive material. It is just what we've been looking for!"

"Yes—but the big question is, where do we go from here? What do we do with this information?"

"Before we go any further with this, I would like to talk with these two scientists as soon as possible. Can you arrange for them to come here to Washington in the very near future? I'd have to meet with them secretly and in a secure area."

"Yes, I understand," said Fred, "but there's a logistical problem: Megan Teal was in a horrific accident a few days ago. She was the only survivor of that wicked storm in the North Atlantic."

"I remember hearing about that. It makes this information we have even more interesting. You have obviously met with her. How is she recovering?"

"Very well, though she was quite badly injured. She has two fractures in her left arm, broken ribs, and a broken leg. She is recovering at home and is supposed to stay put for at least a couple of more weeks, if not longer."

"You don't think Megan's doctors will let her travel in the near future?"

Fred thought for a moment. "I had a feeling you would want to meet with Megan and her husband Sam in person, and I agree that this meeting is a very important one. I could, with your permission, try to set up a way to get them here somehow. How long would you think such a meeting would take?"

"I think perhaps you should set aside two to three hours."

"Okay. Check your schedule and give me a couple of different times you'll have free over the next couple weeks, and I'll see what I can do about getting Megan and Sam here."

"How do you plan to do that?"

"Megan's left arm is very badly broken. She was telling me that her surgeon is a bit worried about it setting properly, but he told Megan that she was entitled to get a second opinion. As far as I know, she hasn't yet done so. If we could get her an appointment with a top surgeon here in Washington, and we can have it coincide with one of the days you also have free."

Kingsley smiled. "I know of such a doctor, and she owes me a favour. Let me see what I can arrange from this end. Give Megan a call and see if she'll agree to come, provided she can make the trip this soon in her recovery."

"With your permission, sir, may I phone her now?"

Kingsley nodded and gestured towards the phone on his desk. Megan picked up the phone on the third ring.

"Megan, Fred here. I have news for you and Sam—is he home?"

'Yes, he is. I'll put him on the speakerphone."

While Megan was calling Sam to join her on the phone, Fred and Kingsley had also put on the speakerphone on their end.

"Megan and Sam, this is Baxter Kingsley," he said.

"Mr. President! How are you, sir?"

"Very well, thank you. More importantly, Megan, how are you feeling?"

"Thankful to be alive, and I'm doing very well."

"I want to let you both know that I'm extremely interested in your findings, and would like to discuss them further with you."

"Thank you very much," Megan and Sam answered in unison.

Fred spoke up and asked, "Megan, do you wish to get a second opinion on your left arm?"

"Yes, Fred. I would," she answered.

"If you think you're able to travel here to Washington sometime in the next week or so, I'll make the arrangements from here. You and Sam will be guests of the US government."

"Wow! The president must feel this is very important."

"I do indeed," said Kingsley.

"Darling, if you feel you can make the trip, let's go for it," said Sam.

"You can take that as a definite yes from both of us," said Megan.

"Wonderful! I'll talk to you again in the next few days when I've made concrete arrangements," said Fred before ending the call.

After hanging up, Megan and Sam looked at one another in disbelief.

"We're going to meet with the President of the United States!" Sam exclaimed. "What are we going to tell Gram?"

"We'll tell her that I'm getting a second opinion on my left arm which involves me going to a surgeon in Washington DC. My appointment will be confirmed in the next few days. I imagine we'll have to keep this a secret at least for now. We better get all our data and information ready."

That night, just before Megan went to sleep, she had a vision. It started with Lacuna sending her a message of thanks for her coming to the aid of her fellow whales.

"I know it was you, Lacuna; you were our guide. We've identified the bacteria that killed them—it was bioengineered by humans. We are working on an anti-serum for it. I assure you we'll find out who is behind this."

Yes, you will, Lacuna conveyed. She dove and disappeared into the depths below.

Ortho and Saron appeared.

"You are progressing very well with your healing," said Ortho. "We know that next week, you and Sam are going to Washington. All will be well. You are both correct in trusting Fred, and you can also trust Kingsley. He is a good man and will do the very best he can to help."

"Megan, we've a surprise for you," said Saron, smiling. She beckoned someone to her. As she did so, several dolphins swam into Megan's vision. "We thought you might like to go for a swim with your friends."

With that, Megan totally relaxed, and before she knew it, she was in the middle of dolphins swimming around; periodically, one or two would come up beside her and very gently touch her, pushing her here and there. Megan loved it. She was in heaven, and all her pains were gone. She began to swim herself and play as she had so many times before. Their clicks and squeals were music to her ears.

We love you Megan. We'll always be with you.

She heard this refrain over and over and over again and never tired of it. It became part of her. They swam and played for what seemed like hours. They created streaks of gray and white twisting, turning, soaring, diving and performed movements ballet dancers can only dream of. Megan wanted it to continue forever, but they slowly moved to the surface. The joy and sheer fun, and best of all, the unconditional love they shared was beyond anything that Megan had ever experienced before.

As Megan woke up, she thought, *Why can't we humans be like that? That's the way life should be.*

She moved to turn over. The pain in her back was gone! She lay there in a moment of disbelief. Then slowly, very slowly, she rolled over onto her other side. No pain! She wanted to stay just like that; she was worried if she moved again the stabs of searing hot pain would come back. She was still in this position when Nona came to help her wash and get dressed. Megan was afraid to move.

"Megan, are you all right? Has your back gone into spasms again?" Nona asked, worried.

"Gram, the pain in my back is gone. It doesn't hurt anymore!"

"That's wonderful!" Nona said, not quite believing it.

Very slowly, Nona helped Megan to sit up and have a sponge bath. She got dressed, and moved into her wheelchair.

Megan was smiling. "Gram, seriously, I no longer have any pain. I've no pain anywhere in my body. None—it's all gone. I can't believe it!"

Megan and Nona were laughing as they went into the kitchen. Sam joined them.

"Well, you two sound very chipper this morning—what's up?"

"Sam, I have absolutely no pain whatsoever anywhere in my body!"

"That's incredible! Let's hope and pray it stays that way," Sam said. He was thrilled.

"Oh, I believe it will," Megan said. She smiled and thought, *Thank you Saron, thank you, Ortho—and many, many thanks to my dolphin clan.*

Within three days, Megan and Sam had confirmation of their meeting with Kingsley, and Megan had an appointment with an arm and a hand specialist in Washington DC. Two days later, Fred met them at Dulles International Airport. "Megan, you look as if you've almost recovered; you look so well. It's so good to see you again." He shook hands with Sam. "I hope the arrangements I've made will be suitable."

"I'm sure they will be. You certainly arranged everything quickly, and we really appreciate it; thank you," Sam said, pushing Megan's wheelchair.

"I've never been to Washington before. I'm looking forward to being here. I still can't believe we're going to meet Kingsley in person!"

"He is most anxious to meet both of you. I've rarely seen him as excited as he was when I showed him your research."

"I certainly hope we'll meet his expectations," Sam said as he shut the back of the black SUV.

Once they were en route, Fred said, "I've made reservations for you at the Crowne Plaza City Center Hotel for two nights. Megan's appointment is at two-thirty pm tomorrow with Dr. Margaret Burton at the George Washington University Hospital. She's considered to be at the top of her field in the USA."

"I can't thank you enough for doing this, Fred," Megan said. Sam wrote down the information.

"No problem," Fred continued. This hotel is downtown and close to many of our tourist attractions. The day after tomorrow, we're going to move you to Camp David, which is in the beautiful Catoctin Mountains in Maryland. The President will meet you there. You'll find it a very comfortable and relaxed environment. The exact timing of the meeting will be decided soon."

After settling into their room at the hotel, Megan rested for an hour while Sam unpacked and read up on some of the main attractions in the Washington DC area.

"Did you find something of interest?" Megan asked when she woke from her nap.

"Yes, Meg—if we have time, we'll go to the Smithsonian Museum of Natural History, and if you're not too weary, we can go out for dinner."

"That sounds good—as long as I'm well-rested for my doctor's appointment tomorrow."

When they returned, there was a message for Sam to call Alan Croft.

"Alan, what's up?"

"We've got another series of artificially-induced quakes."

"Where?" Sam turned on his laptop.

"There are two more regions involved. One is in Indonesia, with a cluster of four 5.5 quakes, and the other cluster of three is just off Hawaii. They are stronger and occurring more frequently."

"It's as if whoever is behind these is getting ready for something big," Sam said, studying the seismographs." I'll do some work on these, Alan, and get back to you soon."

Megan checked her email, finding a message from Sandy. "We're starting to get some positive steps towards a possible anti-serum for MMB 79," she said.

"It looks like both of us have some additional information for the meeting the day after tomorrow," Sam said. He shared his new findings with Megan.

"This is really getting scary," said Megan.

"That it is. I hope that Kingsley will have some answers and advice for us."

Megan's appointment with Dr. Burton was on time, and the results were very positive. Dr. Burton, upon studying her x-rays, commented, "Megan, you are healing very well. In fact, better and faster than I ever expected. It's almost a miracle! I think that we can change your cast and give you a lighter one for your arm."

"That would be wonderful. Thank you!" Megan said, smiling.

"I'm going to see if I can get an x-ray of your leg. I'm anxious to see if it's healing at the same rate as your arm."

An hour later, while Megan was being fitted for a new arm cast, Dr. Burton popped in.

"Looks like this is going well. We're trying to also put a lighter cast on your leg, and I think we can get started with therapy on your leg."

Megan could not believe her ears. "This is fantastic! Thank you very much."

It was late afternoon when they were met again by Fred in a government SUV; they were subsequently driven to Camp David.

"What a beautiful park!" Megan said.

"We're very proud of it. It's in the middle of the blue mountain range, and most of it is open to the public. Only the area of Camp David is off limits. You'll be staying in a small cabin on the grounds, and you are free to explore the area. There are many beautiful vistas, lakes, and streams, and many of the trails are wheelchair-accessible."

"Do you know when we'll be meeting with the President?"

"Yes. We just got confirmation. He'll arrive at around ten am tomorrow and will have lunch with you both at twelve-thirty pm. He'll have a more formal discussion with you afterwards. I'll have dinner with you tonight in the main residence."

After lunch, Megan and Sam waited for Kingsley to join them in the library, which was added in 2015 to accommodate the ever-increasing number of books. Skylights in the ceiling provided natural light. The west wall consisted of alternating bulletproof windows and tiers of floor-to-ceiling electronically-controlled bookshelves. A huge bay window and window seat occupied the centre of the east wall and was flanked by bookshelves. At the far end, there was a stone fireplace with a hand-carved oak mantelpiece. Above it hung a painting, framed in pewter, of a beautiful woman—Kingsley's fiancée, a medical doctor who was killed while serving in Afghanistan. In front of the fireplace was a comfortable seating area, consisting of an oval marble coffee table with two chairs, and a matching sofa upholstered in rich chocolate leather. The wall with the entrance door was covered with state-of-the-art electronic equipment. A bird's eye maple work table, surrounded by high-back oak chairs upholstered in tan leather, formed the focal point. Scattered around were small work centres.

Sam had a chance to look at several of the titles on the bookshelves. Many were first editions of beautiful leather-bound volumes by a diverse selection of authors. He was in the midst of checking out the series of books by Charles Dickens when Fred and the president entered the room.

After introductions were made, the President said, "Megan before we start discussing your findings, please tell me about your experience with the storm. It must have been terrifying for you."

"To the best of my recollection, sir, one minute it was calm, but within seconds, fierce winds came in from every possible direction and were so strong that it was virtually impossible to stand up. The rain was coming at us horizontally. We couldn't see." Megan went on to tell him of how she was put in the hold, and how she had wrapped herself in the nets in the watertight compartment. "I must have blacked out after that, because it's all I remember."

"I understand you were the only one who survived. How did you manage to save the samples you took from the whales?" Megan looked puzzled, and glanced at Fred. "It's alright, Fred told me all about it," said Kingsley. "You were very brave and lucky to survive. How would you like to proceed?"

"Seeing as we are discussing the storm, perhaps it would be a good time for Sam to answer any questions you have regarding his antimatter theories," said Megan.

"Mr. President, as we discussed earlier, our technology is now capable of creating antimatter," said Fred, "but the challenge is in creating a means to store and control it. The question is, can our technology make and handle the quantity necessary to create this type of storm, let alone cause an earthquake of a 4.5 magnitude?"

"I've been working on that over the past several days," said Sam. "Not having the specifications of the equipment currently being used to control such a beam of antimatter, it's very difficult to come up with an answer."

"If I could get you that data, Sam, would that help?" asked Kingsley.

"It definitely would."

Kingsley nodded at Fred, who made a quick call. "We should have that data in our hands before nightfall," he said once he hung up the phone.

"Now, since we're on the topic of antimatter, what about these artificially-induced earthquakes you and Alan Croft found?" asked Kingsley. "Have you found any more since Fred told me about them?"

"Yes, sir. We've found more sets in the past couple of days which are a bit stronger."

"Sam, I've had our Navy check out the star-like burst on the seabed off San Francisco. I'm currently awaiting their findings."

"Could these quakes be caused by antimatter bombs placed strategically on or in the ocean floor." asked Megan.

"Unless it was deep water, I don't see why not," Sam answered. "I did some simulations based on that idea here they are." Sam passed his computer to the president and began to describe what the various graphs meant. "So, the quick answer is yes—a submarine could easily carry and place such bombs very accurately. An antimatter bomb would have to be encased in a very strong outer shell due to the increased pressure. The depths of the starburst was about 200 feet—well within a possible depth range to create what we've seen from the five simultaneous quakes. The big question is why. None of these artificially-induced quakes are strong enough to cause any damage or tsunamis."

Megan piped up. "Oh God—I just thought of this: what if that is not their real purpose? What if it's for undersea mining? We know it's going on under very tight control. Are these quakes part of legal or illegal mining?"

"Good point," Kingsley said. "I'll request all the information and locations of any known undersea mining being carried out in US territorial waters. If the Navy is still in the area, I'll have them check for any radioactivity in the waters around the epicentres, and will direct them to bring back some cores as well. I'll also alert the Air Force to keep surveillance over the region and will order a similar probe of our Alaskan waters. If there is illegal activity going on in these areas, it will be stopped immediately." He then turned to Megan: "I believe you have something for me?"

Megan switched on her computer. "We have a total of at least three bioengineered strains of the bacteria E. coli and one virus. There are two distinct forms: one is named E. coli MMB 79 which we matched to swabs I took recently from the humpback whales in the North Atlantic. The second one is E. coli Hs1031 which our analysis tells us is unique to humans. These bacteria are spread by contact and cause the infected animal to die within two to three hours, by hemorrhaging to death. We're currently studying the exact mechanism. If either of these strains fail to infect a new host during that time period, they will self-destruct between two and four hours"

Kingsley had been listening intently. "In other words, someone developing Hs1031 has come up with a very dangerous and lethal biological weapon."

"Yes, sir. The third strain of bacteria we have just received information on is another strain of E. coli which we'll call X for now; we are informed that it has been bioengineered. The virus is still being investigated. Our lab in Halifax is currently developing an antiserum for MMB 79, and also for Hs1031."

"Do you have any idea of when the antiserum will be ready for use?"

"Not yet."

"I see," Kingsley said, making a few notes: "You say you can't reveal your sources at this time. Why is that?"

"Actually, this material came to me through a third party. The original source is extremely reliable. Because of the confidence agreements involved, I cannot say more. I apologize, sir."

"I can respect that," said Kingsley.

Sam was sitting quietly. "Sir, these secret labs are very powerful; with very tight security it's virtually impossible to get near them," he said.

"Yes, we've had many a discussion regarding this. The general consensus is that they'll either have to be infiltrated, or we have to somehow deactivate the security systems and the triggering devices to prevent everything from being destroyed. So far we have no solution. We do have a couple of undercover men in place in two of these labs."

"Can they be contacted?"

Kingsley hesitated before answering. "Yes, Megan, they can—but I can't give you any details. They are to remain quiet until they're activated."

"I gather the dismantling of these labs will have to be from the inside out rather than outside in, if you wish to keep the evidence from being destroyed."

"Correct, Sam, but the question is, how? Thanks to you and Megan, we do know some of what they are up to; clearly, it's becoming imperative to act quickly." Kingsley glanced at his watch. "It's getting late. We'll continue this discussion in the morning." He glanced at Fred and nodded. They all stood up as the president left the room, except for Megan who remained in her wheelchair. Fred accompanied the president and closed the door behind him, leaving Sam and Megan alone once again.

They both sat in silence for a few moments.

"Well, that was an interesting and revealing session. Meg, you must be exhausted!" said Sam.

"I'm weary for sure, and my mind is going six ways to Sunday. I'd better call Gwen—I feel she may in fact hold a key or two in the information she received from Maria."

"Good idea, Meg. I'll tidy up my notes while you do so. Make sure you use your burn phone to call Gwen."

"It's a good thing we bought some new ones yesterday. I arranged with Gwen before we left that I would ring twice on my old cellphone, disconnect, and call her again on a new burn phone immediately afterwards. She'll use an alias—Anna Stone."

Megan reached Gwen quickly.

"Hi 'Anna'—things are progressing well here. I can't give you any details, unfortunately. We've discussed our proposals with someone high up in the firm. He is very excited at what we have to offer. I didn't give any details about your part of the equation—only that what you have to offer could be critical to the merger. Both Sam and I trust this person completely and I know he is anxious to talk to you."

"You mean, he would like access to the information regarding our foreign accounts?"

"Exactly. How would you like me to proceed? I know you'll want to maintain confidentiality."

"Yes. In order to proceed, I would like the following: first, protection and assurance that none of this information is to be used without my consent; second, to be involved in the discussions as to how this data will be used; third, my source will not be revealed."

"So, with all of those conditions in place, do I have your permission to speak tomorrow morning on your behalf?"

"You do."

"Very well. 'Anna,' you should know that what you have may break this whole merger wide open. Thanks again for your trust and participation."

"Does she agree to help?" Sam asked once Megan was finished her call.

"Yes, Sam—with certain guarantees."

"Kingsley knows a lot more than he is saying. He's still not sure whether to totally trust us, and I understand. Maybe if he talks to Gwen, he'll understand better and trust us more."

The following morning, the meeting continued in the library.

"I'm very pleased with what we accomplished yesterday! I expect a report from the Navy soon," President Kingsley said. "Megan, what can I do to get your source to come forward? I feel we need all the information we can get if we're going to be able to stop these labs."

"My source would like to come forward, but because of the nature and sensitivity of the material and how she attained it, she'll require certain guarantees."

"What sort of guarantees?"

"Protection, and assurance that she will be involved in any discussions as to how the material is to be used. She'll not reveal her source."

"Protection is no problem. Involvement in discussions regarding the use of her material will be negotiated between her and myself. We will respect the anonymity of her source."

"Would you like to talk to her?"

"Indeed I would."

"She is using the alias of Anna Stone, and knows she'll be talking to someone high up in the US government; however, she doesn't know that she'll be speaking to you unless you tell her."

Kingsley nodded. Megan, using the same system as the previous night, made the call.

"Anna Stone speaking."

"Hi, it's me. There is a gentleman here who wishes to talk to you. I went over your wishes, and he is willing to honour them."

Megan gave the phone over to Kingsley.

"Anna, this is President Kingsley speaking," he said as he put her on speakerphone.

There was a moment of silence as the shock hit Gwen.

"Sir, I wasn't expecting it to be you!"

"I totally understand. I've been in discussions with Megan and Sam regarding their findings. Megan hinted that you may have some further information regarding some covert labs. Is this true?"

"Yes, sir."

Kingsley went over the guarantees with Anna, and confirmed what they both agreed to. She pledged to cooperate, and was willing to release some if not all of the material she had in her possession.

"I gather this information is extremely sensitive. May I suggest you proceed to the nearest airport and get to Washington as soon as possible? I will arrange a meeting, and we can go from there. You can call Megan on this phone with your arrangements. Sam and Megan will meet your plane, along with a security detail, and will bring you to meet with me. All of your expenses will be reimbursed. Will that be satisfactory?"

"Yes...yes, sir."

"Good. You've made the right choice," said Kingsley.

Gwen was still in shock when the call ended. Then she leapt into action. She had made two copies of the contents of the box. She placed each copy in a safety deposit box in two different banks. One set of keys she kept, and the other set she gave to Holly. Gwen made plane reservations which would get her into Washington late afternoon; then she called Megan.

Kingsley, Megan, and Sam had taken a break and were having coffee when Megan got Gwen's call. "Anna will be arriving at three-thirty-five this afternoon at Dulles Airport," she said.

Kingsley entered with an aide who had a laptop under his arm. "I have the naval reports so far; they are not complete, but they soon will be."

The three of them sat down at the antique library table, and the aide quickly set up the laptop with a projector, pulling down a screen on which they would view the data.

"I believe your instincts were correct in our discussion yesterday, Megan. It appears the starburst formation of the five artificial quakes is related to illegal mining of the ocean floor. We've been especially cognizant of sea bed mining in general. The samples taken in the area show two things of interest: First, there are minable amounts of uranium, plus higher than normal concentrations of rare earth elements such as promethium, which is used in nuclear batteries. Secondly, there was no sign that atomic devices were used. Here are the photos. It appears the whole area has been damaged. What are your thoughts, Sam?"

"Whoever did this is getting ready to mine the earth's crust. May I suggest more cores be taken over a grid of the area, so we can see which minerals are there? Additionally, the data shows that no atomic devices were used, indicating that some aspect of antimatter was involved."

"Great idea, Sam. I'm putting that region under tighter surveillance. Are you absolutely certain that all five of these artificial quakes occurred simultaneously?"

"I am, sir," said Sam. Immediately, Megan interjected.

"Unless—and this may sound crazy to you, sir, but I must ask: could it be aliens?"

Kingsley looked at Megan. "I guess anything is possible; we know the Secret Governments have aliens working with them, and heaven knows what they've developed. They could easily have a craft and an antimatter source that I know nothing about."

He was interrupted by a knock on the door.

"Enter."

Another aide entered the room. "Mr. President, here are the Navy and Air Force reports regarding the Alaskan waters," he said, handing the president a USB flash drive. The aide then quietly departed.

"Thank you," he said. He inserted the USB flash drive into the laptop, which, through the projector, displayed the data onto the screen "As you can see, the Alaskan artificial quakes are a mirror image of what we found off San Francisco. It's like another illegal mining operation. There've been a number of reports from fishing vessels, of sightings of UFOs on the dates you requested. Some fishermen reported five UFOs flying in the area on the same day that the cluster of artificial quakes occurred. Sam, can you give me the exact locations and times of all the artificial quakes you have on file? I want to contact the countries where they occurred."

Sam transferred the data to a fresh USB flash drive for Kingsley, who took it and placed it in his briefcase. "I've also included my findings regarding the unusual storms which have occurred, along with the dates they happened," said Sam.

Kingsley nodded with approval as he stood up. "I think that is all for now. This has been a great start. I have other matters to attend to in the meantime, so why don't you take a break? It's just over an hour's drive to the airport from here. Security will be following you at all times. We'll meet again for dinner, and you can bring Anna with you at that time."

They met Gwen at the gate with hugs all around. Sam loaded the luggage in the trunk, and Gwen and Megan sat in the backseat so it would be easier to talk. As they pulled out of the airport parking lot, a black SUV fell in behind them, and there was a similar one a couple of cars ahead of them.

"Well, he certainly wasn't kidding when he said you would have security with you at all times, Gwen," said Megan."

"No kidding!" she answered. "So, tell me—what's the President like?"

"He's very nice. I find him down-to-earth and gracious. You'll be having dinner with him, along with Sam and I, tonight."

"This is so exciting! Where am I staying?"

"At Camp David, with us."

"We met with him yesterday afternoon and again this morning," said Sam. "He has seen all the information we have on the bacteria. We've had very in-depth talks about the artificially-induced quakes, and he was extremely interested in our findings. Gwen, he really wants to go after the covert labs. I think it's one of the things he wants to talk to you about."

"Does he know who I am?"

"No. He thinks your name is Anna Stone, but not to worry—we told him you were using an alias."

"I'm just worried that when he finds out I'm investigative reporter he'll not want to talk to me or trust me."

"I don't think it'll be a problem. He'll have you checked out within minutes by his security staff. He'll ask some very incisive question. When he finds out you were instrumental in bringing O'Brien and Sandforth to justice he'll trust you. I'm sure of it."

They arrived back at Camp David in plenty of time. Megan rested, and Gwen took a shower and got settled. Sam, on the other hand, was on his computer; he found two more suspicious quakes: a 4.5 near the Galapagos Islands, and a 5.0 just off Iceland. He made a copy of each seismograph and added some notes. Then he poured each of them a drink.

"Gwen, have you heard of any funeral arrangements for Angela—sorry, I mean, Maria?"

"They are having a private, quiet family service. She is to be cremated."

"It's too bad she missed knowing you're going to meet the President of the United States."

"She would have got a big kick out of it I'm sure. Megan, do you think the President is really going to try to force the government to come clean?"

"I know he wants to, but it's a matter of gathering enough evidence. It'll be a very tricky and dangerous thing to do. I sure hope he is serious and that he'll win out somehow."

After a while, Sam said, "Well, girls, it's time to go for dinner. Are you both ready?"

"Boy, I'm nervous and a bit scared!" Gwen said as she got up from her chair.

"Oh, Gwen, just be yourself! You'll be fine," said Megan.

When they entered the private dining room, Megan was amazed to see how cozy it was. The rectangular cherry table had all its leaves removed. There were four very comfortable looking chairs. A matching buffet with mother-of-pearl inlay with paintings of flowers above occupied the far wall. At the opposite end was an intimate seating area, consisting of a matching set of two chairs and a sofa covered in rich chocolate leather; a very welcoming fire was blazing in a marble fireplace.

Kingsley arrived just behind them; Gwen followed Megan.

"Mr. President, I would like to introduce my dear friend and colleague Ms. Gwen Ross."

"So this is 'Anna Stone.' How are you? It's a pleasure to meet you."

"Good evening, Mr. President; I'm honoured to be here."

Dinner consisted of a stuffed meatloaf and gravy from the president's grandmother's recipe accompanied by roasted baby potatoes, assorted vegetables, and a California salad. His mother's homemade apple pie along with local old cheddar cheese was a major hit. They retired to the fireplace area for coffee and liqueurs. The conversation was general and light when Kingsley turned to Gwen.

"Okay...I think I've placed you," he said. "Gwen Ross, you're a renowned investigative reporter, are you not?"

"Yes, sir. I hope that won't be a problem."

"No; in fact, it may well be an asset. Weren't you involved with the Boston lab affair?" He stopped and thought for a moment. "Yes—in the arrest of O'Brian and Sandforth. Congratulations!"

"Thank you! I had a great deal of help from Megan; they were responsible for ordering the murder of both of her parents. Detective Boyle was vital in the actual arrests of both men."

"So that is the connection between you and Megan. What've you been up to since?"

Gwen looked over at Megan. Megan nodded and said, "Go ahead, Gwen."

"Sandforth realized he was dead, no matter what, so he slipped me a piece of paper with several passwords on it and four SD cards. Fearing for my life, I fled to Canada where I stayed with an RCMP officer in Halifax. Once I was there, Megan and I worked on Sandforth's files. From there, I went to Australia for a few weeks, following a possible lead back to Canada."

"Very interesting," said Kingsley. "Why don't we move to the library and relax in a more comfortable atmosphere and talk about this more."

Once in the library, an aide brought in a tray with coffee and a selection of liqueurs; a robust fire crackled in the huge stone fireplace, creating a welcoming atmosphere. Kingsley turned to Gwen.

"So, Gwen, tell me: seeing that you're a reporter at heart, are you planning to write a story about this?"

"You are direct, Mr. President. My answer is simple: not at this point—not until I've more facts. Depending on what you wish to do with the material, will govern what I can and can't do."

"Well answered," he said. "Will you divulge your source?"

Gwen smiled. "No sir, I can't at this moment."

"Then I respect you even more. Now, I imagine you have a question or two for me?" he said, smiling.

"I do. I'll also respect that you may not be willing or able to answer."

Kingsley nodded. "Excellent; then we're on the same page," he said." What would you like to know?"

"Do you acknowledge the existence of a covert government and Black Ops within the US?" she asked in a frank manner.

"Yes."

"Thank you for your honesty, sir. I'd like to emphasize that Megan and Sam have both worked very hard to collect and analyze this important data; their diligence, in fact, almost cost Megan her life. Are you going to act on the information they've offered?"

"Yes. I'm not sure exactly how, but yes."

"Thank you, Mr. President. Now I believe you have some further questions for me."

Everyone relaxed and laughed.

"Yes, Gwen, I certainly do. Could you please tell your information without revealing your source? I've arranged for your protection for as long as necessary. The nature and substance will determine your further involvement with these discussions."

"For the moment I'll only speak in hypothetical terms with no specific details. If you feel these general situations would be of interest, then we can discuss further involvement on my part and yours."

President Kingsley smiled. "Touché, Gwen. I understand."

"Hypothetically speaking," Gwen began, "if you could get your hands on certain blueprints, details of the construction, and the security system of one of these secret labs, would that be helpful?"

"Depending on the detail, yes, that would be very helpful."

"What if they were so accurate that it would enable someone with the right expertise to disable the security system and anything connected to it, without anyone knowing?" Gwen asked. "What if you were given very detailed lists of Black Labs, along with specific names?"

"Those two pieces of information alone would be critical. Do you have any more hypothetical information?"

"Yes, Mr. President, I do." She hesitated for a moment, and then she handed him a piece of paper. On it was printed the words *Area 51*.

"What do you know about Area 51?" he asked.

"Quite frankly, the information I have places my life in great danger."

"Gwen!" Megan interjected. "You can't be serious!"

"I'm very serious, Megan."

President Kingsley was also surprised. "If you have the actual information you've presented hypothetically, especially if it relates to Area 51, then I think we need to have a serious talk."

Gwen nodded, took a deep breath, and began with a brief description of the motives behind and the means of the deaths of Mary Teal and Matthew Stone. She went on to relate the subsequent arrests, and the destruction of the lower level of the Boston lab; she also described Sandforth's files and her trip to Australia.

"And now Megan has shown you evidence of the genetic makeup of some bioengineered bacteria. Those came from an Australian source who I can't name."

"We only know that it's one of the Black Labs—but we know nothing more," Kingsley interjected. "Sorry, Gwen, please continue."

"Thank you, Mr. President. I met a gentleman named David Downs, and his wife Shelley and I became good friends with a distant relative of his named Angela. However, in actuality, Angela was Maria Downs who was supposedly killed in a plane crash many years earlier; she was reported as deceased, but she did not die in the crash. It was staged. Maria changed her identity to Angela after going into hiding and having several plastic surgeries. Up to the time of the plane crash, Maria was a board member of the Center for Earth's Sustainable Resources near Area 51. This board of directors were and are a secret group which oversees and controls some of the so-called Black Laboratories around the world."

"We've always suspected some very secretive Black Ops going on there, but we could never get any proof," said Kingsley.

"Well, we now have some proof, and a lot more information: I recently received a box which was Maria's, and it contains material which is very damning to the CESR"

"I see—but I thought you would not release the name of your source."

"That was before we agreed that this meeting would be off the record. Also, Maria has very recently died of cancer."

Kingsley was quiet for a moment, and had a pensive expression. "How much does her brother know?" he asked. "Is he also involved in the CESR and the activity in the Melbourne lab?"

"He knows very little; she made sure of that. He's not involved with the lab or the CESR either. Although he owns the controlling shares of Downs' Enterprises, he has very little to do with its operation. He is an artist, not a businessman. I would like to keep her name out of all this for as long as possible."

"Agreed," said Kingsley. "I must ask: why haven't you yet released a story on all of this?"

"I have kept this quiet for three reasons: first, I felt that if I released the story, it could do more harm than good; if the Board at Area 51 got wind there was a leak, they might either close down these labs, change their security systems, or go on a witch hunt, thereby rendering much of my information useless. Second, as long as Maria was alive, I did not want to put her in danger. Finally, I knew that if I was patient, I could get this information placed in the proper hands. I wanted to find the most appropriate and effective ally, which is why I am sharing this information with you this evening." She leaned forward slightly to emphasize her next point. "However, please know with—all due respect—that I, along with the International Investigative Reporters Organization, reserve the right of sole authorship if and when this story breaks. This isn't for egotistical purposes, mind you; it's because I wish to help clear the Downs' name, especially Maria's."

"Fair enough, Gwen. I agree, and I'll do my best to adhere to your wishes; I'm certain that we all understand that what's been shared in this regard is strictly confidential."

Megan, Sam, and Gwen all nodded in agreement.

"Now Gwen, I'd like to pause this aspect of our conversation until we can explore it further and give it the attention it deserves; moving along, and making the best use of our time together, I've some further information on some items that Megan, Sam and I were exploring earlier. You are, of course, welcome to stay and participate."

"Thank you, sir," Gwen answered.

Kingsley opened his laptop and pulled up a file. "It appears there are a few illegal seabed mines in operation, not only in our coastal waters, but in those of Canada as well. The Canadian authorities have been notified by our Navy, and your Coast

Guard is in the process of finding and closing them down. I've withheld the information on the one off San Francisco, as I would like to see if our surveillance team can come up with who is responsible. From what my people tell me, we do not have aircraft with the capability to carry the machinery required, nor do we have the means to operate it, even if we did."

"Therefore, we believe that these Black Ops are alien in origin," said Sam.

Gwen was startled. "Alien?" she said.

"Yes, Gwen," answered Kingsley. "Although we as a government officially claim there are no such things as UFOs, we know there are. We've maintained the cover-up so long that we've tied our own hands."

"The Power Elite? Is this why you wish to have surveillance in certain areas?"

Kingsley nodded. "Now, Gwen, we'll continue with your evidence. In the package from Australia, were there any more genetic codes which originated in the Melbourne Lab?"

Gwen nodded. "The hypothetical concern regarding the security is very real. I've a list of the Black Labs and some of their projects which were underway at the time of the plane crash." Gwen handed him a USB key which had scanned files of paperwork backing up each of the claims. He plugged it into his laptop and pulled up the file.

"Gwen, this is staggering," he said as he reviewed the data. "We knew of the labs in Boston, Area 51, and Melbourne, but as far as the rest goes, we suspected only one of these—that being the one in Russia. The ones in India, Japan, and China are a surprise. May I have my staff look into these three? I've an excellent group I trust. Also, I'll tell them to see if they are currently functioning, nothing more."

"That would be fine," answered Gwen.

"Now, these labs, according to Maria, were built within two years of one another, and they all were of the same design," Gwen continued. "The items denoted in red in the walls of the lowest levels are explosive devices. Apparently, they'll not bring down the walls; their sole purpose is to knock out a piece of the wall and eject canisters containing highly-flammable fluid and detonators. These are designed to destroy the contents of the offices and labs, leaving the basic structure intact. It creates very short blasts of fire and heat only. The sprinkler system is shut off when these bombs are detonated by remote control."

"Are we sure these systems haven't been updated or altered in any way?" asked Sam.

"According to Maria, they've not. They know they were state-of-the-art when they were installed. Because of the fire in the Boston Lab, they know this system works extremely well."

"What about the remote detonating devices?" Megan asked.

"It's actually quite impressive what they did here; each lab has its own unique device which can be deactivated by another special device housed in the security office, which is located on the floor above. This device is controlled by a code which is unique to each lab. The code is the name of the city spelled backwards. The one for Boston is: n, o, t, s, o, b which is entered twice with a space between each letter. If you can deactivate this master switch, then the lower levels cannot be torched."

"Gwen, I see why you feel you need protection. Is there anything more?" asked Kingsley.

"Oh, yes. I've the list of the directors of the Black Ops Lab in Area 51 as of the time of the plane crash. You'll note there are six plus two serving as co-chairs. Maria said that one of the co-chairs is an alien by the name of Anin. This Board not only controls the laboratories we've already talked about—it controls many other facilities as well, which are funded by Black Budgets. She also enclosed a list of some of the projects of which she was aware, and noted that there were many others which she could not verify." Gwen paused to allow everyone in the room a moment to process the information before she moved on; she knew that the next revelation could be alarming. "One more thing," she added. "Maria said she heard two rumours which she suspected were true: the first was that the US was building military bases on both Mars and the moon, and the second was that they were going to arm space with nuclear weapons."

"My God, Gwen—they can't do either of those things, can they?" Megan was shocked and angry.

"I don't see why not," Sam said. "They certainly have the knowledge."

Gwen, having poured herself another coffee, turned to Kingsley and said, "I hope this information is of some help. I imagine you may already be aware of certain parts of it."

"I knew only bits and pieces of what you have. Thank you, Gwen. This is very important material. I agree that you should be involved with certain discussions. As Maria is no longer with us, this evidence is not as strong as if she were alive."

"She enclosed one more thing," added Gwen. "It is an affidavit and a video explaining everything she put in the box. She also enclosed her diary and photos of her progress through her plastic surgeries. There are also photographs of various documents she had signed and witnessed. I think you will find these helpful."

"This is what we have been looking for," Kingsley, said gathering up the material. "Before we go any further, all three of you have given me a great deal of help. I can't tell you everything we have in place; however, I can say that we have two agents placed in deep cover within labs on your list, along with an additional three in various top secret military bases around the world. All five can be activated on short notice.

"The main problems we currently face are the following three: first, there are so many moles in our various agencies who answer to the Secret Government that it's going to be very difficult to find law enforcement agents whom we can trust; second, if any of these facilities become aware that we're onto them, they'll close up shop and destroy any evidence—or hide the evidence so deep we'll never find it; finally, they may simply decide to unleash the bacteria, which will kill large numbers of people."

"Could there also be a threat of civil war breaking out here between the 'Dark Forces' and the legitimate Armed Forces?" asked Sam.

"Yes, and in such a scenario, the world could lose a very high percentage of its citizens."

"If you try to raid any of the labs in question, how could it be done without them finding out in advance?" Sam asked Kingsley.

"That would require meticulous strategizing; fortunately, we have a highly-specialized team that we keep on call for such an occasion. With the information that you've brought forth, I would like to take it under consideration. If all of you could stay here for another few days, it would be greatly appreciated; your respective contributions are going to be a critical part of any plan that is developed. I'll leave for a bit, and let you discuss this amongst yourselves."

As the door to the study closed behind the president and his aide, Megan, Gwen and Sam sat still in astonishment.

"Wow!" exclaimed Megan. "I never dreamt it would go this far!"

"It's probably Maria's information that did it," said Gwen.

"Well, Gwen, what do you think?" asked Sam.

Gwen was quiet for several moments. "Let's have a show of hands," she said. "If you wish to move forward, put your hand up."

All three raised their right hands simultaneously.

"Let's do this!" said Sam.

* * *

Megan was resting on the sofa in the library when she heard Gwen calling her.

"Come and see this; it appears there's been another major outbreak of illness in China."

Megan drew closer to the television, and covered her mouth in horror as she listened and watched CNN.

"Over 500,000 people have already died, with the crisis spreading rapidly through the city of Beijing," said the announcer. "The World Health Organization has been called in. Though the origin is unknown at this time, it appears to be similar to the bacterial disease which cost hundreds of thousands of lives in India last year. Authorities are cordoning off a large, circular area in an attempt to stop it from spreading. We're currently trying to contact our reporters in the region. No aircraft are allowed anywhere near the affected area. We'll bring you further reports as we receive them."

"I'm trying to contact our reporter in Beijing, but so far no luck," Gwen said.

"If you do, could you try to get a description of the symptoms? Also, it would be ideal if we could get a sample of the bacterial DNA."

"Right—I'll do my best. Could it be the same one that occurred in India?"

"It is a distinct possibility."

"You think this disease is going to pop up elsewhere, don't you?"

"I hope not, Gwen, but I've got a gut feeling it will."

Gwen had left the TV on mute. The news ticker at the bottom of the screen showed that the death toll was climbing steadily.

Megan left CNN on as she brought up her file on the Indian outbreak, adding new information as she received it. Two hours later, the death toll was approaching one million, and there was still no definite word on the cause, or if it had emerged elsewhere.

After eight hours, the death toll was approaching one and a half million.

"I was able to talk to my contact there," said Gwen. "There's still no definite word on the cause however, it appears to be the same bacteria which occurred in India. My contact has heard rumours that it has also broken out in Shanghai, but there is no official confirmation yet. I've also talked to the epidemiology section of the World Health Organization; they currently have a few swabs. It's definitely a form of E. coli."

Late the next day, the death rate from Beijing was decreasing; it had reached a projected death toll of three million, which was almost a third of the population of the city. The rumour of a similar outbreak in Shanghai had proven false. The entire world had been put on alert. At ten o'clock that night, CNN had another news flash:

"Similar outbreaks are occurring in Moscow and in Tokyo, and it appears we may have an outbreak in New York City."

Megan shook her head. "This can't be happening. How is it spreading over such great distances when it has such a short life span? It could mean that separate individuals released the bacteria in Moscow, Tokyo and in New York City."

"It looks like we may have a worldwide epidemic on our hands." Gwen commented.

"Only if they can show it's the same E. coli strain as the one in Beijing. We'll have to get samples from each area for comparison. I don't think these are linked—it's just a gut feeling. I think we're seeing a bit of panic setting in."

By ten pm, pictures were beginning to come out of China. They were horrific. The cordoned-off area was completely surrounded by the Chinese army. There was very little moving in the streets, except for military picking up the dead. There were thousands of corpses, and the trucks were taking bodies to a mass cremation area. A full curfew was in place, and the authorities were hoping against hope that it was now under control. It appeared it had started at one central point and spread. Once this was determined, the authorities had put in place three concentric circles of police with the Army around it, and cleared two blocks in either direction as a barrier. People were not allowed out of their homes or businesses. Those who appeared to have contracted the disease were quickly isolated. Healthy ones were given masks and gloves to wear. If these precautions had not been taken, a few more million may have died. The death toll at eleven pm stood at 3.25 million. All communications from the affected area have stopped. The rumours of outbreaks in Tokyo and New York City had been confirmed to be just that—rumours. However, those rumours were proven to be effective, as signs of panic had occurred; there had been a rush to emergency rooms by those with benign symptoms. By morning, the world seemed to have calmed down, as China was reporting only a scattering of new cases. Still, the death toll in Beijing was horrific, as it came to about 3.3 million.

"I've received confirmation from my sources," said Gwen over breakfast. "This is definitely a mutated strain of *E. coli*, which produced exactly the same symptoms during the outbreak in Delhi."

"Would I ever like to get my hands on a sample," said Megan.

"I know one of the researchers in the lab in Atlanta, and I told her about you. I've already requested that she send you a copy of the genotypes."

Two days later, Megan was looking at what she was positive to be a different bioengineered strain of E. coli.

* * *

The President had been extremely busy for a day and a half after the breakout of the epidemic in Beijing. Megan, Sam, and Gwen didn't meet with him during that time.

An artificially-induced quake in the South Pacific occurred the day after the E. coli breakout in China; the resulting tsunamis had claimed hundreds of thousands of lives.

"I don't believe that the timing of these two disasters is a coincidence," said Gwen.

"I agree," Megan said. "What are your thoughts?"

"If they are connected in any way, and if they were both created by humans and/or aliens, then the question is, why? I mean, if these are creations of the Power Elite and The Company, then why did they unleash this in China and Polynesia? An even bigger question may be this: are they just testing, or are they trying to distract us from something bigger?"

"Have you any reports of anything else that's suspicious?" Sam asked, keeping an eye on his computer.

"I've put the word out to each of our worldwide investigative reporters that I wish to have information on any strange occurrences in their region, no matter how small—especially in China and Polynesia. So far I've received very little."

"So, for the moment, these two disasters appear to be ongoing tests. If this is so, then the next ones may be even larger, resulting in a much higher death toll!" Megan said; she was very upset. "We need to meet with Kingsley immediately to keep him as up-to-date as possible."

Together, they formulated and wrote a short report of their findings and comments, and had it hand-delivered to the President. Two hours later, they received word that he would be with them shortly, and that they were not to plan to go anywhere.

He appeared in the library within the hour. He looked haggard and exhausted, but he was still impeccably-groomed.

"It has been a hectic forty-eight hours," he said. "Activity in those two regions seem to be calming down—but my God, the combined death toll is staggering! It's much higher than we originally thought; it's in the neighbourhood of five and a half million. China has closed all her borders, which is making it very difficult to access information. I just pray that we don't receive reports of further disasters. Sam, are you certain this is an artificially-induced quake?"

"I'm certain of it!" said Sam. "It was not a case of simultaneous quakes being sent off—it was a sequence of quakes, one after another, which I'm positive set off the 8.5 quake. This was clearly done intentionally."

"But why, Sam?"

"We believe, sir, that this was done in conjunction with the outbreak of E. coli in Beijing," Megan interjected. "We suspect this is the same E. coli strain, or at least a very close copy of the one which caused the outbreak in India. At the moment, we have no actual proof. I was promised a genetic map of it from Atlanta; however, I never received it. They apologized, saying they had orders not to release such information at this time."

"You need this genetic map of E. coli?"

"Yes—if I'm to confirm my suspicions, Mr. President."

"Then you shall have it," Kingsley said. He picked up his cellphone and made a quick call.

"I believe you will have it within the hour," he said as he hung up. "If it's as you think, Megan, what do you think is going on?"

"Gwen, I would like you to answer," said Megan.

"Mr. President, we've been discussing that very point. We agree—those behind this are the Power Elite and The Company. The question is, what are their motives? They've done this for at least one of three reasons: first, the E. coli outbreak in China and the violent artificially-induced quake in Polynesia are continuing tests of the series we were talking about a few days ago. Both are much stronger and deadlier. Second: both of these disasters were created to draw attention away from something they didn't wish us to know about. Third: they're creating fear amongst Earth's people in order to maintain their control over us." She paused for a sip of water. "I've contacted every member in our group of investigative reporters with directions to inform me of any strange occurrences of any kind in their respective regions. So far, I've not received anything which would be considered out of the ordinary."

"We'll assume these were tests for now," Kingsley said. His expression was grave. "If this is the case, then they're getting ready for something even more destructive, which would take many more lives, creating a worldwide panic."

"Yes. I believe it would," said Gwen.

"Well then, we'll have to do whatever it takes to stop them," Kingsley said, pacing around the room. "Do you, Megan, have any suggestions on how to prevent the further use of these deadly bacterial strains? How can we prevent their further production?"

"The three of us have been struggling with this. The only way to stop them is in the labs where they're being created."

"I agree with you. With the information that Gwen has, I'm sure the special forces which Interpol put together a few years back will be able to infiltrate and execute a plan to apprehend these labs quietly and efficiently."

"Is it possible for you to tell us a bit more about this Interpol force?" Gwen asked.

"Off the record, I can only give you generalities."

"We understand," replied Gwen.

"Several years ago, many countries became concerned with the increasing funds being put into these Black Budgets for top secret facilities and operations. Some of the elected leaders quietly got together about five years ago, and we approached Interpol for their help. They organized a group of people from each of the interested governments. In certain facilities around the world, there are undercover agents who'll assist us. We're working under the umbrella of Interpol. These two interconnected groups, along with additional personnel, will successfully resolve the bioengineered bacteria problem."

"What is going to done about the artificially-induced quakes?" Sam asked.

"Those may be more difficult to stop; we are, however, in the process of quiet investigation. Here again, we may have some inside help. I can promise you and Sam that we are taking the artificially-induced quakes and E. coli problems very seriously.

"Gwen, this brings me to you. We'll continue to protect all of you. Sam and Megan, when you return to Canada, we have arranged for the RCMP to keep you safe until this is all over. However, if at all possible, I would like to have you both stay here; that way, if you get any more information, we would be able to act immediately. However, I also understand if you feel you need to go home. Gwen, I would like you to stay here also. If any of you need anything, and I mean absolutely anything at all, I insist you call me immediately."

There was a knock on the library door. "Enter," Kingsley said.

A young aide appeared with an envelope and a stack of files. "I'm sorry to interrupt, Mr. President, but these need to be taken care of as soon as possible." The aide placed the files on the table, and then turned and left the room.

"Megan, this envelope is for you. It's from Atlanta."

Megan thanked him, and opened it. It was the genetic map of the Hs $E.$ $coli$ strain suspected of causing so many deaths in China. Megan was busy entering it into her computer and then performed a comparison against the Hs 1031.

"I knew it!" she exclaimed.

President Kingsley finished signing the papers that the aide had delivered. He looked up at Megan's exclamation.

"What is it? Megan, what have you found?" he asked, closing the file in front of him.

"This is not $E.$ $coli$ 1031 but it's a very close relative of it. I'll give it the notation of 1041. I'll have to send this genetic code to my lab in Halifax in order to get confirmation and to determine what the exact differences are. Is there any safe way I can get this to my lab?"

"Yes, I'll take care of it for you, along with any future requirements," said Kingsley.

He turned to Gwen. "Gwen, because you have been so gracious in allowing us to access your information, I guarantee you'll be the first reporter to have the rights of publication."

"Thank you, Mr. President."

"The three of you may stay here as long as you wish. You'll be very safe here. Whenever you wish to leave to go shopping or whatever please notify security. Also, if there is anything you require, let the staff know and they'll oblige. From time to time I'll be back here and meet with you. You'll also be kept up to date as much as I can. Please keep me informed of any new findings or news pertinent to the situation."

Kingsley picked up his cell and spoke to an aide. "Would you please ask Colonel Ashton to come in?" he requested.

Colonel Sean Ashton entered the room. Introductions were made and the President rose to leave. "Sean is the head of your security detail. He'll go over certain protocols with you. This is a very unusual scenario, both for you and for me." He turned to Sean. "Sean, you've been briefed?"

"Yes sir. Thank you," he said.

With a brief nod, Kingsley left the library as an aide came in with refreshments.

"Please call me Sean. I understand the three of you will be here for a few days. Any requests are to be made through me. By that I mean trips to town, or anything you need in terms of personal effects; communications to and from the President in any from will be through me. I and my people are at your service twenty-four hours a day. Please be assured that I'm not privy to any aspect of the work you are involved in. Our purpose is to keep you safe and secure and to make you as comfortable as possible at the same time. Any questions?"

"Yes," Megan said. "Do we still use our current burn phones, and are we free to speak to our families?"

"Yes. Once the covert operation gets underway, we'll be taking the extra precaution of changing each of your burn phones frequently. We hope it'll not be too much of an inconvenience—however, we feel it's necessary."

Sam nodded. "You understand about Megan's doctor's appointments?"

"They'll be kept on schedule," said Sean. He glanced at his file. "Megan, I see you have one with Dr. Burton at ten am tomorrow. This will not be a problem unless you are in conference with the President; if that happens, the doctor's appointment will be changed. We'll be responsible for getting you there and back safely.

"Whenever you wish to leave the immediate premises, call me or one of the staff and let them know where you wish to go, whether it be on Camp David grounds, or into the city. Whatever you're working on is extremely sensitive, and President Kingsley has ordered the highest level of security for you all. I've been informed that one, two, or all three of you may be called on a moment's notice at any time of the day or night. It may be for a meeting here, or you may be required to go into Washington. Whatever the case may be, we'll be with you whether you see us or not." Sean reached into the large briefcase beside him and pulled out a box of red envelopes. "If you have material or information coming to you from the President or vice-versa, use these envelopes. They'll be delivered by hand. It's much safer than using the computer."

Gwen was looking at Megan.

"Megan, you look puzzled, what is it?" she asked.

"Is there any way I can be in constant and secure contact with my colleague Dr. Sandy Johnson? Quick transfer of classified information may be required over the next while."

"You trust her?"

"With my life."

"Is it photography, video, or text?"

"It could be all of those, but it would be mostly text messages and a few coloured photos."

Sean took note. "I'm sure we can work something out," he answered.

"I'll probably require a similar system of communication with a Dr. Alan Croft of Nevada," said Sam.

"Why don't I work out something for each of you. Write down what each of you require and I'll look into it immediately. Write down anything you'd like to have taken care of, such as preferred foods, snacks, etc. I suggest we meet again here in an hour unless we get a call to meet sooner."

After lunch, Megan, Gwen, and Sam sat outside; it was a beautiful early spring day. They enjoyed the warmth of the sun and the gentle breeze caressing them. The air carried the wonderful softness of spring; birds, squirrels, and chipmunks were busy looking for food.

"I talked to Gram this morning. Their combined lecture series has been was very successful so far. They may go to Europe," said Megan, enjoying a cold drink of lemonade: "They wish to go to Glasgow, Dublin, London, Paris, and a couple of other places. They may be away for almost three weeks. Andrew says it'll be a long and tiring trip, but both Fred and Gram appear to be gaining energy as they go rather than getting tired. Gram says she will keep the burn cell with her at all times. I'm so pleased that she's happy. She emailed me and told me that one of the speaking events was recorded on video and put on Youtube, and she sent me the link.

"Did she ask when we will be home?"

"Yes. I told her we may be here for a while yet."

"I wonder how much longer we'll be here. It's rather exciting being on the front lines, so to speak." Gwen said as she was tidying up. She glanced at the clock. "I guess it's time to go to our afternoon conference."

Sean was about ten minutes late arriving.

"My apologies; I was waiting for this package to be prepared. Megan, this is for you. I believe it's imperative you look at it immediately. We've decided to give you a new burn phone to be used only for contacting your colleague Sandy Johnson. I'll get it set up, so it'll be ready shortly."

Megan opened the envelope and emptied its contents on the glass-top desk she was using in the library. A few seconds later, she had found the results on her computer.

"This is astonishing!" she exclaimed. "It's basically what I initially expected. This bacterium is E. coli 1041. It is a derivative of E. coli 1031. I must talk with Sandy right away."

Sean handed her the burn phone and excused himself.

"I'll be out in the hall; when you're finished, please let me know."

"Sandy, I just got the information you sent me," said Megan. "How are things going there?"

"Great, Megan! We miss you. Hope your arm and leg are on the mend."

"Thank you, Sandy, they are. We have an upgraded version of E. coli 1031 which I'm calling E. coli 1041. The modification is most interesting."

"Isn't it just! Why do you think they did it?"

"The lifespan has been shortened to just over an hour, and it is spread only by contact, which increases the ability to control the spread of the disease. It is a very dangerous weapon which could be used in a confined space—a building with closed air circulation, a stadium, or any sized crowd, just as long as it's isolated. I also have some news for you about our bioengineering of an antiserum for MMB 69: we are getting close to being able to test it. The one for E. coli 1031 is coming along, and we hope to have it ready for testing in a day or two. I've got the staff working on the computer model for the new bacteria." said Sandy. "Anything else?"

"Yes—use this cellphone number from now on. I hate to cut this short, but there's a great deal going on here. I'll talk with you soon. Take care."

Sam called Sean back to the library, and Megan gave him a red envelope. "Sean, please deliver this asap to President Kingsley. It's very important."

Sean took the envelope and left, and Megan finished making some notes. Both Sam and Gwen were working at their respective computers when Sean re-entered the room.

While waiting for the president, they watched a Youtube video of Nona and Fred's speech.

"When my eighty-two-year-old mother heard I would be traveling the world on a speaking tour, her advice was, 'Fred, be well informed, be honest, and for heaven's sake, be brief.' I'll try."

"Nona Teal and I will be speaking to you about what may seem, from our respective titles, to be two separate topics; however, they're connected in many ways. I'll be giving you some insights as to UFOs and ETs or aliens. I've changed what UFO and ET stand for, to give what I feel is a better understanding of who and what are out there in space. UFO to me means 'United Federation Outlanders—that is, space explorers; ET means 'Extraordinary Technology.'"

"There's no doubt that spacecraft and aliens exist. There'll always be skeptics whatever their reasons may be, and I respect that. Our governments and other powers try to manipulate our thinking, but we don't have to believe everything they tell us. In fact, we must question it. I'm referring to the Roswell events and the subsequent cover-up. More people are asking questions and demanding that our government come clean." At this statement, there was a roar and applause from the audience.

"Polls taken in February of 2015 show that sixty-seven percent of US citizens believe there is extraterrestrial life. This probably happened due to pictures of a face on Mars, a sphinx, and a complex of pyramids, and huge domes on the moon which were—or are—cities; the discovery of water on Mars, and a piece of metal of unknown origin found on the moon have also contributed to our belief in extraterrestrial life. Many books have been published showing this evidence and more.

"For years, our government in the US has outright denied the existence of spacecraft, and yet there is evidence they have been designing, testing, and yes, using spacecraft without the public's knowledge.

"Many years ago, a government official gave a briefing to a select group based on reliable sources. It stated that aliens have been visiting Earth over thousands of years and were probably involved in helping to create the human race.

"There was a collision of two alien crafts near Roswell. One alien survived. Actual contact with the other aliens occurred in the late 1940s. There were ensuing crashes of alien craft, along with contacts with aliens. Military, NASA officials, and astronauts who have first-hand knowledge of certain projects and sightings are now speaking out. A former NASA expert has stated that the Apollo and Gemini flights were followed by alien craft. Various astronauts have seen these craft, but were ordered to remain silent.

"Shortly after the A bombs were dropped on Japan, the number of alien craft sightings increased dramatically. Can you imagine being an Alien Outlander exploring and being near Earth when this happened—watching in horror as humans slaughtered other humans? To top it off, their detection equipment picked up two clouds of radioactivity heading out into space, polluting it. These aliens probably thought humans had gone crazy. Why were they killing each other, and why did they create a means whereby they could cause their own extinction along with virtually killing all living matter on their beautiful blue planet?

"Aliens did contact Earthlings after this disaster and offered their help. It was refused!" There was a loud groan from the audience.

"Why? Hindsight is twenty-twenty. When we look back, it's easy to say maybe that decision was incorrect. But let's try to put ourselves in the position of the powers that be at that time. This is not an excuse. This is not condoning or agreeing with it. It just might give you a better understanding of the times. It's post-World War II. Millions of people died as a result of five to six years of fighting. The allied countries were recovering, as were those in Germany and Japan. Everyone in every country was physically and psychologically damaged. At the same time, the victorious ones were celebrating and feeling rather invincible. Then the Cold War began. For those of you who remember, it was very intense. Not only did the US have the atom bomb—so did Russia. These two countries did not trust one another. So as the US increased their nuclear arsenal, so did the Russians. If one of these nuclear warheads was ever fired, either by accident or by intent, the ensuing array of nuclear bombs detonated in the Northern Hemisphere would produce enough radioactivity to exterminate every living entity on Earth."

Many heads nodded in agreement.

Fred paused and drank some ice water, and then continued.

"The threat of a nuclear war was so prominent that bomb shelters were being built, even in people's backyards. So it does not surprise me now—nor should it surprise anyone—that we've been and still are being very closely watched and monitored by aliens from afar. I believe they have every right to be concerned.

"Here, I would like to return to Roswell. There was one surviving alien from that crash, and there were probably additional crashes and survivors. We know there has been reverse engineering of component metals and equipment from these crashed space vehicles. Putting all this together, can you imagine what has been developed using Black Budgets in certain top secret locations? In the US alone, trillions upon trillions of our tax dollars have funded these projects, and we see very little in return."

The audience applauded loudly.

"Our government has for years officially denied the existence of UFOs. I'm talking about the Stealth Bomber. The B2 aircraft cost billions of dollars to make. They finally showed us a fake. There is a very different aircraft. It is a US spacecraft with a form of antigravity propulsion, and maneuvers like an alien spacecraft. The UFO sightings at Hudson Valley back in 1983-84 were not UFOs, but B2 stealth bombers. Why? Because the powers that be are trying to confuse us. They can now say, if necessary, 'No, you didn't see an alien craft—you saw one of our new experimental crafts.'

"If a very select few received this type of technology from aliens, what else were they given? Perhaps they were given cloaking devices, new metals for space travel, the location of worm holes and Stargates, space travel, and time travel, just to name a few.

"There is also another aspect which I find particularly distasteful and frightening in many ways: experiments into mind control. It's believed that during the Cold War years, Russia and the USA were working separately on this. Now, they're more than likely working together on using telepathy in psychological warfare. Early forms were used in the Gulf War. Experiments of the CIA in the US were used routinely to block nerve transmissions by the use of electrical devices in order to wipe out long-term memory in individuals, especially if they were former CIA operatives. They also seeded multiple personalities by combining memory-changing drugs and hypnosis. Many of these experiments were stopped, but were they really?

"Who may these aliens be, and where are they from? They're from various planets and stars. Some are from within our own galaxy system and others from beyond it. The Greys are from Zeta Reticulii, Anunnaki are from Nibiru, Sirians from Sirius, and the Pleiadeans from Pleiades. The first two are considered interventionists, being members of the Dark Federation which interfere with humans for their own purpose. The latter two are trying to help us. They are noninterventionists and require our permission. In other words, if we seek help, we need to ask for it. There are two opposing forces.

"In the distant past, Earth did, in fact, experience a gross intervention and disruption by the aliens called Anunnaki from Nibiru (now referred to as the Red Planet or Planet X). These aliens were and are very advanced. Hundreds of thousands of years ago, they discovered Earth, and without invitation, they interfered by bioengineering our DNA so we would be under their control. Humans became their slaves and to a certain degree, we still are. They are here currently and are mixed up with and part of the Power Elite and Secret Governments.

"We are now entering an era of enlightenment; we are seeing worldwide awakening to the presence of aliens and; we're far from being alone or having separate entities. Now I'll ask my very dear friend, world-renowned scientist and speaker Dr. Nona Teal, to speak on this very subject.

A tremendous applause arose from the audience.

"Thank you, Fred. You did very well in packing a lot into a brief period of time. Your mother will be most proud, I'm sure."

Laughter rose from the audience. "I hope I can do the same," she added.

"I agree with Fred," she began. "We're definitely approaching a very critical point in Earth's history. You are all very aware of the problems that the Earth as a whole is facing: overpopulation, lack of food, droughts and diseases, pollution on a massive scale, and our unsustainable resources which are running out at an ever increasing rate. Everything seems to be out of control. It is a massive problem. Our governments seem to be unable to fix it. It appears that about two to three thousand people are in control of the rest of us, and they don't want to take the steps necessary to save our planet. These are what a dear friend calls

The Power Elite, which are made up of wealthy families, so-called Secret Governments, and militaries who want to keep the earth's riches, monies, and power in order to control the rest of the seven billion of us who call Earth home.

"As most of you are well aware the only way for the seven billion of us to do anything to help is to band together to help save Earth. It has to be a grassroots movement—a non-selfish and peaceful movement. We already have several of these, and we're beginning to work together. It is amazing how rapidly these groups and the movement to help heal Earth are growing.

"Many of you know my favourite topic is Universal Harmony. Is not a new concept by any means. It is probably one of the oldest pieces of wisdom we possess. It still exists within the cultures of many of the indigenous peoples of the world, and is very much a part of many of the Eastern religions. However, for many societies, it has been lost.

"The basic principle of harmony is very simple: oneness does not mean isolation or disconnection; it means just the opposite. Humans as individual entities are not separate from one another. We are very much interconnected. Imagine living totally isolated from one another. There would be no one with whom to share life, and no one to love. Come to think of it, how would our species survive?"

Laughter rose from the audience.

"Wouldn't life be boring? You know, one of the worst punishments they give prisoners is to put them in isolation. As humans, we depend on one another; however, on the whole, we do not seem to get along very well do we? We fight within families, within communities, between religions and beliefs, between societies, and between countries. Look at the twentieth century. Earth has lost millions and millions of humans due to World War I and World War II. We seem to be bent on killing one another.

"There are several reasons for this, but all of them generally come down to jealousy, hatred, greed, competition, and the feeling that one belief system is better than another. Wars and competition all arise from a feeling each is separate; one way is better or superior. Some would say it's all based on the ego.

"Stop and think for a moment: doesn't this all come down to a lack of respect, a lack of understanding, and a lack of trust? All of these lead to a feeling or belief that we're separate. Expand this further, if you will. Many humans, especially in what we refer to as Western philosophies, believe we are the superior beings on Earth and can take whatever we want —be it animals, plants, minerals, water, whatever, regardless of the reason. If we want it, we take it. We abuse Earth at will. Look at where this belief and attitude has brought us. We've even polluted our land, our air, and our oceans and lakes to the point where, in many regions of the world, our oceans may never recover. Yes, there have been positive signs that we realize what we've done, and that we are trying to correct it, but it is not enough."

"Imagine what Earth would be like if every human being not only respected every other human being, but also every animal, plant, and our natural resources. Stop and think for a moment. It sounds like it would be impossible, doesn't it? But you know, it's not—not really. You have to start with yourself. Take a deep breath, then another. As you do so, imagine what is happening inside you. The air you breathe in goes into your lungs where poisonous carbon dioxide is removed from your blood; fresh oxygen is taken up by the bloodstream which then carries it to every single one of the billions of cells making up your body. Let's take a minute and just breathe.

"Now, realize that virtually every living thing needs oxygen—except plants, which recycle our carbon dioxide for us. Is there an interconnection between plants and animals? Yes. One can't live without the other. Plants in turn require sunlight and nutrients to grow and survive. As you can see, everything on earth, air, and sea are interconnected. Thus, if Earth is to survive, if we're to survive, we must learn to respect not only one another, but every living entity on our planet. We must also learn to use sustainable resources responsibly, and cease the rape of Earth and her unsustainable resources. We have to choose this in order to achieve peace, to achieve joy, and to leave our descendants a place to live in harmony.

"We communicate mainly through sight and sound. It's sound I would like to explore with you. How awful would this world be if there was no sound! No birds singing, no waves breaking on the shore, no music, no ability to talk or sing. Sound is made up of vibrations, and the number of vibrations per second, or frequency, determines whether the sound is high or low. Vibrations exist as wavelengths, and energy moves in waves. These waves occur in various intensities, or amplitudes, and speeds or frequencies which gives them unique qualities. Modern science has shown that everything, be it animal, vegetable, or mineral vibrates. Therefore, every single entity on Earth has its own unique frequency, even the Earth itself. Light is a good example; when it passes through a prism, it breaks up into its component wavelengths or colours.

"Quantum physics proved that every entity vibrates. How? Scientists were able to investigate the atom at a sub-atomic level. Remember your periodic table from chemistry; carbon, hydrogen and oxygen, etc., and their atomic structures? Each element had a nucleus and its own unique set of electrons and protons. Each had their own orbits in which they moved, hence frequencies. Everything consists of atoms in different combinations; various rocks and minerals, bacteria and viruses, plants, and animals each have their own specific frequencies. Every living thing contains DNA, which in turn is made up of long strings of tiny proteins. As you know, each of our DNA is absolutely unique, except in twins. We each have a unique frequency.

"Now, back to sound: there are pleasant sounds, such as music, and then there is noise, such as an airplane taking off. Music is balanced or harmonious, whereas noise is not. When I first started to give talks, I didn't put the same stress on the importance of sound until fairly recently. It was my granddaughter Megan who suggested I should look into the importance of sound. Sound is everywhere—we are surrounded by it. The universe is entirely made up of vibrations. Relationships between its components are vibrational, and they perfectly correspond to the laws of music and harmonics. Harmony is when sound is in balance. Disharmony is an imbalance of frequencies.

"Another way to look at this is to look at our own bodies. If the various cells, tissues, or organs—all of which have their own frequencies—are not in balance or in harmony with each other, then the body is not totally in balance, resulting in illness or a disease. The same thing is true in relationships; if they are not in balance, they are not in harmony. Remember, we're all interconnected with every entity and thing on Earth; if a part of an ecosystem is ill or out of balance, it will throw the rest of the ecosystem into disharmony and will affect other ecosystems in turn. Of course, there are varying degrees of disharmony: Earth, unfortunately, is very much out of balance. She is very ill, and we humans are the cause of it, though we're now trying to heal her—and heal her we will!

"Sound is a very important aspect of healing. First of all, we use sound to communicate, to teach, and discuss ideas; this, along with music, are our most familiar uses of sound. We are just beginning to realize other important uses of sound frequencies, such as ultrasound and lasers in medicine. Other aspects of sound are currently being used in healing. Sound, being multidimensional, can heal on several levels of the body: the emotional, spiritual, and physical and mental components of the body.

"Sound was extremely important to the ancients. Tibetan monks for centuries have used special bowls made of a particular combination of metals to vibrate such sounds or chants of sacred tones as 'ah' and 'om' to aid in their prayers and meditations. These sounds help them to concentrate on prayers of intent.

"As many of you already know, in areas of high crime or a conflict, if a small number of individuals pray and meditate with the intent of love and peace, the level of crime or conflict in the area is greatly reduced. It is a result of collective consciousness by those persons meditating. In fact, it has been shown on the as few as 1%—some even say 0.1%— can create a difference. What if such a number or even greater numbers of people simultaneously and collectively made sacred sounds while meditating and praying with the intent of peace and love? What would be the result? I believe this would help to heal Earth. We must work together as one. We can do this; we *will* do this; we *must* do this!"

There was a standing ovation and tremendous applause with shouts of "Yes! Yes!" and "Hear, Hear!" Nona and Fred stood side-by-side on the stage with the microphone between them. As the applause died down, it was Fred who began to speak:

"Nona has shown you that we as humans must act as one; we must respect one another—every rock, our water, be it fresh or salt, and our air; all is interconnected."

Fred handed the microphone to Nona.

"Fred has shown you there are other planets which support aliens, some of them with dark intentions, and others of the light. The dark ones have caused serious problems, interfering with our development. Because of that, Earth has become separated from the rest of the universe. Who would ever want to have anything to do with a planet with a humanoid presence which appears to be bent on destroying their home? Not only that—we appear to be a murderous lot. Not all of us, of course, but enough to give an outsider from space the impression that we seem to be intent on killing one another.

"Fred also pointed out that some of the noninterventionist light aliens have offered to help us to prevent the total destruction of Earth."

"What if there was a means whereby we could acquire peace on Earth?" said Fred. "At the same time, we could make contact with the noninterventionist aliens who have very advanced technologies, and agree to accept their help." He gave the microphone back to Nona.

"We feel that everyone can begin a major healing of the Earth by combining these two ideas: we are all one and must work together with the concept of initiating sacred sounds while meditating and focusing our collective intent on peace and love on Earth. We must, through a collective intent, and in a loving and peaceful manner, ask for help from any or all of the peace-loving aliens.

"Every aspect of our universe is vibrating. I think we would all agree that Earth is in a serious state of imbalance. It is in such a state of disharmony that it'll take a miracle to fix it."

"Our planet is over seventy percent saltwater," added Fred. The seventy percent is by surface area only. If you add the volume, then you will note that the percentage would be much higher. The whales and dolphins are the predominant mammals in the Earth's oceans. These cetaceans are the most evolved mammals, while on land humans occupy that place. Whales have been here, in their present form, for about forty million years. The current estimates put Homo sapiens, in our present form, arriving here only about 200,000 years ago. Whales and dolphins have had a much longer time to adapt to their watery environments than we have to being on land. Also—and this may shock some people—the brains of whales are, relative to their total size, greater than in humans. The whales and dolphins, with their sounds and songs, are designed not only for intercommunication, but also to keep the oceans in a balanced and therefore healthy state. <u>Homo sapiens</u> have the same responsibility on land. But we've managed to screw things up!"

Nona joined in. "We propose an experiment. In the near future, all the grassroots groups have agreed to get together and simultaneously meditate and pray, making harmonious sounds with the intent and desire for Earth to be healed and peace to come forever. We'll gather in groups interconnected by the Internet, and everyone can join in."

Fred added, "Some of us will be out in boats in areas where there are whales and dolphins. We believe when they hear humans making a sacred sound, they too will join in."

"All we ask," said Nona, "is that if you believe in all of us working together, please, feel free to join us. We currently are in the process of getting the word out. In June or July we'll attempt to do this. If you're interested, please spread the word, and you'll see on the bottom of your programs a list of related websites for you to visit."

Together they said, "Thank you, and Namaste to all."

* * *

George Dean had been pacing in his office, which was a very unusual for him. He'd been desperately trying to get in touch with Anin to find out why the Chinese and the Polynesian incidents had occurred so close together. There was to be a minimum of two to three weeks between such incidences. Three hours had passed since his first attempt at contacting Anin. His mind was in a whirl; he began fret, trying to make sense of it all.

Is Anin purposely making me wait? Is he making me pay for questioning him about his loyalty to The Contract? he wondered.

Just then, the yellow phone on his desk flashed.

"Anin here—sorry. There's so much going on here, and I've just now had a chance to call you."

"What happened? Why have both of these incidents occurred virtually simultaneously and without warning?"

"We are trying to get an answer. The antimatter bomb explosions in Polynesia was planned to explode as they did. The epidemic of E. coli in Beijing was planned for four weeks from now. I've been trying to get in touch with Chang to find out if he knows anything about what happened but no one can find him or his family. They own the lab in Beijing, and it could easily have been the source of the infection. As a precautionary move, it has been destroyed."

"Do you think Chang had anything to do with it?"

"We are currently investigating that. I'll keep you posted."

The line went dead.

* * *

While Megan was dealing with the news from Sandy regarding the E. coli, President Kingsley was meeting with a select group of experts at the White House. Each person in the room had expertise in specific areas. All were related to the planning of the upcoming raids and seizures of the E. coli strains, plus all related documents from all the covert laboratories. Kingsley was about to try to answer questions regarding the bacteria when a red envelope arrived.

"Excuse me a moment," he said. He read it quietly to himself, and then spoke. "These are the most recent findings from our microbiologist on the E. coli strains. I'll ask her to come here; she'll be able to answer your questions."

Megan was enthralled when entering the White House. She'd seen pictures of it in the movies, but seeing it in person was an entirely different story. It was intimidating, yet majestic. She would love to have been able to take a really good look at her surroundings; however, Sean had his orders, and before she knew it, she was being wheeled into a room where President Kingsley and several others were seated around a long table.

"Welcome to the White House, Megan," said Kingsley. He took the wheelchair from Sean as they entered the room. He placed her next to him, and introductions were made. "I took the liberty of giving some of your background to everyone here before you arrived. I explained why you were here and also why you are currently in this wheelchair. I would like you to give us a brief history about these strains. Then, if you would, spend some time on the specific characteristics of MMB 79, E. coli 1031 and E. coli 1041."

Megan did so by using the computer and projector that they had set up in anticipation of their meeting. She carefully went through the history of each of the bacteria in question—how they were bioengineered, and the qualities of each one: lifespans, mode of infection and what each one did that caused death in humans so quickly.

"I know you have questions," she said. "Please feel free to ask—but please note that I cannot disclose how I obtained this data."

The question and answer period went as follows:

"Are these the only ones out there?"

"As far as we know, these are the only ones. There may be more."

"Why are the whales being targeted?"

"We don't have a definitive answer. It could be that MMB 79 is an earlier form or a sport of the 1031 series."

"Are there any antibiotics or serums to counteract these bacteria?"

"These bacterial strains are totally resistant to all known antibiotics; our lab in Halifax is bioengineering antibiotic serums for E. coli 1031 and 1041. We are doing the final tests on serum 1031and we we working around the clock on the 1041 serum. It'll be ready in a few days."

"What sort of rate of production can you expect once the serum is positively tested?"

"We'll have enough of the 1031 serum to supply each member involved in the collection process of the bacteria stored in each facility. Also, if you are wearing the new lightweight hazmat suits, you will be fine."

"How are these bacteria to be handled once we get our hands on them?"

I've almost finished a list of precautions as to how we'll handle them. My understanding is that those actually handling these bacteria will undergo special training. The necessary number of swabs will be placed in special vials containing growth medium. These in turn will be placed in specialized aluminum tubes for transporting to my lab. We only need a few from each lab in order to confirm which labs are making which bacteria, and to see if there are any other strains out there. These will be destroyed along with any information as to their production."

There were no further questions.

* * *

Sam was busy working on the Polynesian quakes. Kingsley had cleared him for access to the legitimate top secret resources regarding information on the current status of the production of antimatter, plus all the equipment available which could handle it. After several hours of manipulating all the data in many ways, he came to the following conclusions:

1. No current man-made flying device was capable of lifting the amount of material required. Nor was there anything that could create a strong enough burst of focused energy to the depth within the Earth's mantle required to cause the result in what they'd seen in the artificially-induced quakes.

2. There was one possible scenario: all of the artificially-induced earthquakes to date were created by the use of carefully placed antimatter bombs at a specific depth in the Earth's crust. The holes would have been drilled by specialized submarines. He had not been given any description of such a submarine.

His overall conclusion was that either the Black Ops had such equipment, or that these artificially-induced quakes were a result of alien technology of which he had no knowledge. He decided he would send in his report to Kingsley.

Three hours later he received a reply by email:

> I agree with your assessment, Sam; I'll be in touch soon
>
> —Kingsley.

Sam turned to Gwen.

"Gwen, have you received any information about unusual sightings of UFOs in the area around the quake's epicentre?"

"I think I found something. Look at this," she said as she projected the data up on the big screen. They were looking at a report from her colleague in Port Moresby, New Guinea. He'd learned from some very reliable sources that several fishermen from different boats had seen several UFOs going in and out of the ocean in the area of the quake.

"I'll summarize this and send it to the President as well," said Sam.

Later, Sam told Megan what Gwen had found. Megan was very tired and decided to have a short rest. Lying on the sofa and thinking of what Sam had just told her, she contacted Lacuna to see if she knew anything about this. Lacuna appeared in her vision knowing already why Megan had called to her. In their usual way of communicating, mind to mind, Megan asked about these artificially-induced quakes. Immediately, Megan saw images of UFOs; they resembled a cereal bowl upside down with three large legs sitting on the ocean floor. From its centre, a cylindrical-looking device protruded into the ocean floor, and debris was heaped around it. She saw two others close by doing the same thing; they were drilling into the ocean floor. That image was replaced with another. The three saucers had left, and a cap of some sort was covering each hole. Megan wanted to know if this was an underwater mining operation. The lids were lifted, and similar UFOs were lowering a cylinder-shaped device into each of the three holes. The next vision was a huge explosion which jolted her awake.

Trembling, she called Sam.

"Sam, those explosions which set off the sequential artificially-induced quakes in Polynesia—could each one have been set off by three or more antimatter bombs rather than one large one?"

"Where did you get that idea? I'll feed that data into the simulation and see what we get. I think you might be on to something, Meg. It certainly would explain certain things."

Megan sat beside Sam as he worked.

"I divided the explosive force required to cause an earthquake of that magnitude by three. Oh my God, Megan, look at this! That is exactly what happened. I'd better contact Kingsley with this information!"

That evening, Kingsley requested a meeting of the four of them for the next morning. Megan, Gwen, and Sam sat down after dinner and summarized what they had discovered to date, and came up with a series of conclusions and possibilities.

"Gwen, you're a reporter and a non-scientist looking in on this whole scenario. Why is this happening?" Megan asked.

"First, I'd ask the question: are Megan's and Sam's findings interrelated in any way? The answer is both yes and no. Yes, I believe they're both funded by the Power Elite; are they the only one? Is it commanded by one person, a tribunal, or a group such as a Board of Directors? Whatever or whoever is in total control of the Power Elite also controls the funding for the various projects. Strong circumstantial evidence says your respective research findings are related.

"Let's try a couple of 'what ifs'," she continued. "What if two completely separate entities are behind all of these disasters? Could it be a splinter group from an original single entity, which, for whatever reason, is competing with the original one for world domination? Or could it be two or more powers which have been separate from the start? What if a single group of aliens is behind the whole thing—aliens who have successfully infiltrated the human race and the human psyche?

"It would be a great help if we had a stronger and clearer sense of who's behind this and why. Hopefully our meeting with President Kingsley will clear up some of these questions."

Megan woke up at two in the morning and couldn't get back to sleep. Her mind was racing. It was something Gwen had said about who was behind all these disasters.

I wonder if Ortho knows.

She reached out with her mind, and he was there.

"You have a question or two for me?" he asked.

"Yes Ortho, I do. Who's behind all the horrendous disasters we're having on Earth?"

"You wouldn't like the answer. Humans have allowed this to happen."

"What do you mean?"

"Earth was a very peaceful and beautiful place at one time—so beautiful that many different alien societies visited it eons ago. Not all aliens were there to help the humans to advance, however; some were there for their own greed and purposes."

"You mean the Anunnaki?"

"Yes. They decided that all its resources and its peoples were theirs to do with whatever they pleased. Through bioengineering, they disrupted your natural evolution to keep you, as a race, controlled by fear so that they could mine your precious metals.

There is another way, though, through the Ascended Masters. Many have listened and practiced their ways of peace, love, and harmony. Until recently, their numbers were overpowered by other humans who lived their lives through war, hatred, and greed. You now call them The Power Elite. Megan, I honestly don't believe most humans would choose to live on the Earth of today with all its problems.

"The power and control of the Power Elite and the Anunnaki are weakening day by day. There is a massive awakening—or should I say a re-awakening—of humans to hope, and to an understanding that things are changing quickly. The result will be a very positive one. Earth and its people will be fine. There is much to be done before we get there."

"Ortho, you are saying that behind these disasters are a combined force of the humans and aliens?"

"Yes."

"Can they be stopped?"

"Yes. But it must be done in a peaceful manner. If enough of the Earth's people believe in this, it will happen!"

"Will there be more disasters?"

"Yes; the Power Elite and aliens involved are losing ground. They fear they're losing control. They are like caged animals; they will fight to the end. All you have to do is ask. If enough humans ask, through peace and love it will happen."

"Ortho, do you mean that if humans worldwide—say, even one percent or so—can actually do this, we can begin to turn things around?"

"Yes. Certain humans have taught this belief over the ages. There were never enough at one time, who by peaceful meditations and prayers worldwide to change the path of total destruction of Earth and its people. Nona's and Fred's speech, along with many other similar groups, are currently on the right path, and are coming together. We are thrilled to see this happening. It may be hard for many of their respective members to keep that belief strong over the next while; there will be more disasters."

"Are Sam, Gwen and I doing the right thing by helping President Kingsley and his group?"

"Yes. You can trust Kingsley completely. Now Megan, you must go. I will definitely be with you; call on me anytime. I'll speak to you again soon."

"Thank you, Ortho."

"I've a message for Nona and Fred," added Ortho. "Thank them for us, and let them know that June 21 will be a good day."

Megan awoke in the morning feeling very refreshed and positive.

"You're very bright today, my love."

"That I am, Sam. I've a powerful feeling that everything is going to work out just fine."

"Another vision?"

"Yes. We are going to go through another rough spell, but in the long run, everything should be fine."

The meeting with the president started at ten-fifteen am.

"Good morning, everyone," he said.

Kingsley handed each one of them a folder, with a copy of Megan's portion of the meeting at the White House the previous day. In turn, Gwen had given him a summary. "This is a brief working summary of what we've collected recently," she said.

"We were brainstorming and asked Gwen what she thought was behind all these artificially-induced quakes and outbreaks of E. coli 1031 and 1041. This was her reply, which we all agree on," said Sam.

"You're right, Gwen, in saying that any of these scenarios you've mentioned here could be the case. Most of the evidence you have before you is circumstantial but very strong. The three of you have given us much information; I in turn will give you some entirely off-the-record information on a confidential basis. Certain aliens are directly and indirectly involved. We and other governments have been in contact with many alien civilizations. I'm not at liberty to tell you the specifics, but I can give you some general aspects as I've been told. Contacts have been going on for years."

Kingsley confirmed what they knew about Roswell and the subsequent cover-up.

"After ten years, the lone alien survivor returned to Zeta Reticula. Over the years, various aliens have made contact with us. Some we made deals with; that is, an exchange for a certain amount of Earth's resources in turn for their technical expertise. Everything was to be top secret; because of the necessity for secrecy, parts of the budgets supporting the secret complexes became known as the Black Budgets which have grown enormously. Some of the wealthiest people in the world began to pour billions of dollars into these Black Budgets. When this started, we don't really know, as it was done without our government knowing. Therefore, certain aspects of our legitimate governments became involved mainly through greed. As a result, parts of the Black Ops are legal, and some are illegal.

"For years, a group of people in our respective legitimate governments and militaries have been quietly trying to figure it all out. Today, we know the following: there were originally six top secret labs around the world bioengineering lethal bacteria and viruses: Boston, Area 51, Tokyo, Moscow, Beijing and Melbourne. Boston and Beijing are gone, leaving four that we still must deal with, and all are concentrating on bacteria.

"Sam, your information regarding the artificially-induced quakes is not quite as clear; however, the information you've given us has revealed the following: they are definitely caused by antimatter bombs. You were right; we have no craft capable of handling the equipment required to perform such a feat. We've been actively watching the cluster of five off of San Francisco, and the one north of the Aleutian Islands. We have some results to share with you: both were illegal attempts at mining the ocean floor. There were sightings of UFOs leading up to the actual artificially-induced quakes. The area is being heavily patrolled, both by air and sea. There will definitely be no mining the sea floor in either case. The 8.0 quake in the Polynesian area wasn't the result of mining—it was artificially-induced to produce the fatal tsunami in the area to increase the fear level. It was definitely aliens who caused it. We are currently attempting to find out whether aliens did this on their own or if they in collusion with the Power Elite.

"Thanks to the material Gwen gave us, we are formulating plans to simultaneously take down the four remaining Black Labs. It is a complex project. It'll take a few more days of preparation and coordination through Interpol for it to be complete. I guarantee you, we'll move quickly and decisively as soon as we feel it's safe to do so. Gwen, you'll get the exclusive rights to publish the story."

Megan was agitated.

"Megan, something is bothering you. What is it?" asked Kingsley.

"Mr. President, I know these things can't be rushed; however, I have a strong premonition that things are going to get worse before they get better."

"I believe you may be correct. If we rush things, we could be in a much worse state than we're in now. The four remaining labs are under constant surveillance. I'll let you know if we pick up anything unusual. If there are no more questions or comments, I'll be heading back to the White House."

* * *

Megan remained uneasy for the rest of the day and that night; she was homesick for Grand Manan. As she lay awake, tears streamed down her face. She yearned for the peace, calm, and quiet of the days when she was young. Back then, she was without a care in the world; she would run the length of Seal Cove Beach racing the seagulls as the sand softly gave way under her feet. Her face covered with sea spray as she stood up on the bow of Serendipity, she would watch and wait for Lacuna to join them; she recalled the simple joy of sitting on a log, watching the waves being carried in and out by the tide as she dreamed of soaring above with the seagulls.

She dozed off with her face wet with tears, asking herself, *Will I ever return? Will I ever see my home again?* Once she was asleep, she dreamt she was home, and all was well. It was the first taste of fall, and the air was so fresh and clear she could see forever. The clear blue sea was so calm that the Cape Island boats mirrored their twin. The next thing she knew, she was surfing along this sea of blue, laughing and filled with a feeling of joy and freedom; she was with her beloved dolphins and swimming through the water feeling as if she was born anew. There was no more pain or stiffness—it was gone.

When she awoke, the sun was on the rise; the sky was a gorgeous combination of yellows, oranges, and mauves. She had only slept for an hour or so.

Megan knew she'd been swimming with the dolphins. Not wanting to break this spell, she slowly got into her wheelchair, thinking, *Oh, it'll be so great when I can walk on my own again!*

"Good morning darling; you look fantastic!" Sam said as he kissed her. "You've had a vision—dolphins, I'll bet!"

"Yes, I did, and it was fantastic," said Megan.

At eight am, Sean called to remind her that she had an appointment with Dr. Margaret Burton. He would pick her up in time so that they would not be rushed.

Megan was sitting in the examination room, looking at the x-rays of her arm and her leg.

"Megan, I've never seen anything like this," said Dr. Burton. "It appears that the fracture in your leg has completely healed!"

"Does that mean no more cast?" Megan asked hopefully.

"It does; however, you'll have to be very careful for the next while. If you do your therapy consistently, that leg will be as good as new."

"Thank you!" said Megan. "I almost can't believe it myself."

"Now let's have a look at your left arm. Megan, I think we're looking at a miracle—the arm is healing very rapidly. You don't require a full cast any longer. I've never seen anything like this! Your bones have healed much faster than I've ever seen—they're virtually perfect!"

I wonder, thought Megan, recalling her dreams of swimming with the dolphins.

After the cast was completely removed, Megan tried to stand up, with assistance. She very tentatively put a bit of weight on her leg and was surprised that it held as much as it did. The physiotherapist was also amazed. She slowly put more weight on it. The leg was fine, as far as the bones were concerned, but the muscles were quite weak. Because her left arm was not yet completely healed, it ruled out the use of a crutch. Although she was free of the casts, she would still require a wheelchair for a while. Megan didn't care; in her mind she was free.

Sean could not believe his eyes as he helped her into the SUV.

"Wow, Megan! You must feel terrific!" he marvelled.

"I certainly feel a lot lighter!" she said, smiling.

"Wait 'til Sam and Gwen see you!"

"Thanks, Sean."

Megan's thoughts, however, were consumed with Sam and the night they could anticipate being together without casts hindering their closeness.

Sean flashed his lights as he pulled up to the main lodge at Camp David. His agents, followed closely by Gwen, Sam, and some of the staff, ran out to meet them. The SUV had come to a stop and Sean was out like a flash.

"Wait 'til you see this!" he said.

Sam was the first one to the car. "Excuse me, Sam, please allow me," he said. He was smiling ear to ear as he opened the car door.

Sam had gone to get the wheelchair out of the back, but as he came back around, he saw Sean helping Megan get out of the car. Easing herself around and with the steadying hand of Sean, Megan very slowly and cautiously planted her right foot on the ground, and slid out of the car by lifting her left leg with her right arm, letting it drop to the ground. Placing her right hand in Sean's, and looking up at him, she smiled and whispered, "Now."

Megan stood up, turned, and looked at Sam. Everyone stopped and stared. After a moment of stunned silence, everyone present started speaking at once.

"Wow!"

"What?"

"Where's your cast?"

"Way to go, Meg!"

"Congratulations!"

"Fantastic!"

Sam simply stared at her in disbelief, then rushed forward and took her in his arms, just as she took a step towards him.

"Oh, Meg! I love you so!" he exclaimed.

Everyone crowded around them as Sam lowered Meg into the wheelchair, and they all went inside.

The TV was on silenced to mute as they had lunch; everyone celebrated Megan's freedom from her leg cast. They were drinking coffee a short while later when Sam decided it was time to pay attention to the news once again.

"This just in!" The announcer said; despite his polished professionalism, he was slightly frowning as he read the report. "Another breakout of some sort of disease or a mass poisoning has occurred once again in Calcutta, India, which has a population of over five million people. As of early this morning, Eastern Standard Time, eyewitness reports from the outskirts of the city claim that thousands are dead already. They fear this outbreak may be the same deadly bacteria that Beijing recently experienced."

"Oh my God, no! I pray it's not E. coli 1041!" cried Megan.

The room fell into a shocked silence.

There were no additional updates for over an hour; then, the announcer returned.

"The outbreak in Calcutta is a regular outbreak of the flu," he said. The Indian authorities claim it's not the Beijing bacteria."

Everyone breathed a sigh of relief, but only moments later, another news bulletin flashed on the screen.

"There has been an 8.5 earthquake near the islands of Guadalupe off the north-central part of Baja California. There is a tsunami warning out for the coasts of Southwest USA, Mexico, and Central America. In areas near the epicentre, the tsunamis may reach as high as twenty to thirty feet. The Southwest USA, especially the Los Angeles area, will experience waves in the ten to twenty-foot range. Because of its closeness to the shoreline, there is very little time for a complete evacuation."

"Is this one real, or is it an artificially-induced quake?" Sam said. He turned on his computer to see the seismograph in real time. "Here it is," he said as he projected it up on the screen. "Just as I thought—it's almost a carbon copy of the one in Polynesia. It's definitely an artificially-induced quake created by aliens to raise the fear and confusion up and down the west coast of the Americas."

Before he finished speaking, his cell phone rang; it was the president.

"Yes, sir, the two quakes are virtually identical," he confirmed. After listening to instructions on the other end of the line, he ended the call and said, "Kingsley has ordered the Navy to begin a full investigation of that area."

For the rest of the afternoon, Sam followed the advancement of the tsunami as it made landfall. A twenty-foot wave hit San Diego first, then San Francisco was hit with a twelve-foot wave a few hours later. It was feared the loss of life may be high. It would be a disaster. By the next day over 500 were reported dead; over 700 were missing.

After dinner, everyone sat around reading or working on their computer. It was the quietest evening they had since coming to Washington.

Megan sent Sam an email, even though they were in the same room.

I'm tired; I'm going to bed—with you, please.

Sam immediately turned off his computer, and went over to Megan.

"I agree," he whispered.

At the door of their cabin, Sam tenderly carried Megan over the threshold. Once they were inside, Sam built a roaring fire in the fireplace, and they held each other tight.

"It's hard to believe this old world is in such turmoil," said Megan. "Will it never end? Sam, I'm really homesick for my island. I always felt so at home there—it was safe and secure. Maybe soon we can go home."

"I know, darling; Grand Manan is such a spiritual place. I miss it too."

It started to rain, and the raindrops on the roof sounded like drums in the distance. The crackling fire cast dancing shadows around the cabin.

Megan turned to Sam and said, "Please take me to White Head Island."

Sam swept her up and gently lowered her on the bed. Their bodies were consumed with desire; he wanted to be gentle, but passion engulfed them. They gave themselves to one other, over and over, until finally they lay spent in each other's arms.

The next morning, Sam was up early; he made coffee and breakfast, and brought it to Megan so she could have it in bed.

Wednesday brought word of a new outbreak: <u>E. coli</u> 1041 had reared its ugly head in Delhi, India, and had spread out from different areas of the city. Five planes, two trains, and several buses were turned back. Some travellers appeared to have found their way through the blockades as it was spreading towards Pakistan, which was forced to close its borders. By morning, estimates of the death toll ranged from two million to five million. Later reports of possible outbreaks came in from New York, Mexico City, Toronto, and London, England.

Megan was sure that not all of these were caused by <u>E. coli</u> 1041. It appeared as if a pandemic was starting. Samples were flown to Megan's lab in Halifax, and she was flown home in order to see firsthand what was happening. If it was a pandemic, it could take thirty to forty-five percent of the world's population. By the time she got to the lab, they had received over twenty swabs, and more were coming in constantly.

"Sandy, I think we should split the lab staff into three shifts in order to keep up. You take the first watch, I'll take the next one," said Megan. She called Sam and told him to tell Kingsley that all swabs so far were testing positive for 1041. The antiserum was in full production.

* * *

"I thought we were to meet prior to *this* meeting," Dean said to Anin as they walked towards the conference room on the lowest level of the lab complex near Area 51. He was really annoyed. "Anin, this is unacceptable!"

"Unacceptable or not, George, it could not be helped. I've been occupied with trying to figure out exactly what's been going on, so back off!"

The last sentence was said quietly as they entered the conference room. Igor, Wolfgang and Worthington were already waiting, and they didn't look happy.

"We've called you here on very short notice; we need to review some recent developments and make some critical decisions," Dean said, taking his chair.

Anin rose from his place. "I apologize for my late arrival. We've been endeavouring to get to the bottom of the various incidents which have occurred recently. The outbreak of the epidemic in India was definitely caused by our own bioengineered bacteria E. coli; however, it was not ordered by us."

There were gasps of disbelief from the floor. Anin raised his hands to indicate that he wished to continue speaking.

"However, the outbreaks in New York, San Francisco, Mexico City, Toronto, and London, England were test areas for another newer version of 1041; this newer version is identified as 1051. The main difference or advance of this strain it that it self-destructs after twenty minutes whether it has successfully infected a human or not. You'll see that these urban outbreaks stop as fast as they start."

Seeing that Igor and Worthington looked a bit puzzled, he continued to explain.

"All three strains of <u>E</u>. <u>coli</u> were developed to cover a broad set of circumstances. 1031 and 1041 were designed to wipe out very large numbers of humans, whereas 1051 kills small numbers or groupings of designated human beings. Combined, we can create a worldwide pandemic."

"Who infected the citizens in Delhi, if we are the only ones producing 1051?" asked Wolfgang.

Anin cut Wolfgang off before he could continue.

"I'm trying to get an answer for you. We had a similar situation in Beijing. I've questioned every one of our labs involved. No one knows anything or is admitting to anything. There are two possibilities: Either there's been a leak from one of our labs, or another lab facility that no one knows about is making a strain of <u>E</u>. <u>coli</u> very similar to ours, and is using it."

"Is it possible Chang could be responsible?" Worthington asked.

"Anything is possible," Dean said. "Our investigations into what has occurred in Beijing are ongoing. Both Chang and his son have mysteriously disappeared. We were aware that Chang was not happy with the way we were moving forward. Could he have sent us a message? Maybe his son was involved. Were one or both of them in the city? If so, have they died as a result? These are but some of the questions to which we are seeking answers."

"The recent two earthquakes were both caused by the Anunnaki," Dean continued. "During this time, we did three test landings of the giant space crafts which will transport you and your families to planet E2. They have landed in Siberia, the Sahara desert, and the middle of the Atlantic Ocean. These were all done while the world was distracted by the tsunamis. We now know we can land them anywhere in the world, no matter the climate."

"How close are we to being able to evacuate Earth when necessary?" Worthington asked with a sly smile.

"As far as the proven capabilities of our spacecraft are concerned, we can evacuate at any time—but E2 is not ready yet. The earliest we can go is probably during fall of this year."

"Well, that's good news," Wolfgang said. "So, all we have to do is keep whoever has been causing epidemics with 1041 and 1051 from causing any more. After we're gone, it really doesn't matter. Humans are bound to destroy themselves, anyway."

* * *

Sam was packing up when he heard an alert come from his computer.

"Gwen, come and see this; turn on CNN on the television."

"What the...is that *another* earthquake?" she asked, bewildered.

"Either that or a huge explosion; look at the location!"

"Good Lord! That's in the vicinity of Las Vegas—just west of Las Vegas, actually."

"How close is it to Area 51?" Sam asked, zooming in on his computer.

"It's adjacent to a small mountainous area near Nellis Air Force Base."

"It's registering at about a magnitude of 6.0," said Sam. "It's not directly on a fault. This is very strange. The epicentre is quite close to the surface, if not *at* the surface, and it's causing deeper aftershocks."

"Sam, listen to this on CNN's breaking news," she said as she turned up the volume on the television.

"There's been a major explosion in the area of a large underground military installation west of Las Vegas," said the announcer.

"What do you think happened, Sam?" she asked.

"Whatever caused that explosion was either a nuclear device, or it was an antimatter explosion. We know they've been manufacturing antimatter somewhere in the Southwest. Hold on for just a moment, Meg—I'm in the process of sending a message to the president."

Within minutes, Sam's phone rang.

"Yes sir. From what I can make out from here, I believe that it was antimatter or nuclear in nature."

"Sam, I just received word; it was a massive explosion in a lab, actually one inside a mountain near the Nevada and California border," said Kingsley. "It was most likely an accident related to antimatter. We've no idea as to the amount of damage. I'm afraid the death toll may be quite high."

"I agree, sir. If it was an antimatter explosion inside the mountain, it would be catastrophic."

More news was beginning to emerge on CNN. The Air Force had immediately launched some planes; reports and aerial photographs were slowly but steadily coming in. An aircraft flying into Las Vegas from San Francisco had been damaged by flying debris. The pilot reported the loss of one engine. Several people on board were injured, some quite badly, and the pilot had requested ambulances to meet them when they landed.

A young man was being interviewed on CNN.

"I was looking out my window when it happened," he said. "The whole side of the mountain was blowing apart. There were rocks flying everywhere, and the plane began to bounce violently. Something hit one of the wings. I noticed that the pilot had just lowered the landing gear, and he assured us that all was okay. The landing was a bit on the rough side, and several passengers were injured; I'm pretty sure that a stewardess and a passenger have been seriously hurt."

The report was cut short as the news anchor interjected.

"We've just been informed that the explosion was a massive one; the cause of the explosion is unknown."

"I can sense another military cover-up resulting from this," said Gwen. "If it was an antimatter explosion, the public will never know."

"Probably," Sam agreed. "I wonder if it was even an accident!"

* * *

The explosion was a huge disaster. Local police, ambulances, and fire trucks were on their way. The first responders could only get their vehicles within a quarter of a mile of the entrance to the facility. Checking their hazmat suits and gear, some started to walk in, proceeding with great care. Some had almost reached the main entrance when they were ordered back.

* * *

About seven miles from the now-ruined top secret lab, there was a large building which housed some of the lab staff. There were five individuals sitting around a table having a snack when they heard the blast. They quickly kicked into gear, and as per their plan, they immediately put on their hazmat suits. As they were doing so, they were hit with the first shock waves coming from the explosion. One of them unlocked the main door and panicked. He ran as fast as he could down the road. Once the initial shock was over, the four remaining began to fill their backpacks with water and food; they quietly left the building and headed towards a range of mountains to the west.

"They'll be too busy at the main site to worry about us; however, they'll come looking. We'll need to find a secure hiding place for the night," said one of them. By evening, the four had safely arrived at the foothills and had found a cave in which to hide.

"We must be on the go by sunrise. They'll come looking for us."

Megan had been following the explosion closely. Her lab had received some more samples. Sandy brought her the results, knowing Megan would be most interested in them.

"I'll put these on the screen," said Megan.

"It looks a lot like 1041. How does it compare?" asked Sandy.

"It's another variety!" Exclaimed Megan. "It's 1051. We need to get samples from the rest of the contaminated areas. I must see if our assumptions are correct."

As soon as Sandy left, Megan phoned a report to Kingsley. By seven that evening, they had received swabs from all of the cities affected. Every result pointed to E. coli 1051.

"This new strain of E. coli 1051 appears to be a strange one. It seems to be a very specialized weapon; it is very restrictive in its use, killing a select few at any one time," said Megan. "Whoever is behind it can now selectively release it into any city or building; because it acts like 1041, it will cause fear and panic without killing thousands of people. We're currently waiting for information from each of the infected sites as to how many have died and the extent of the respective infected areas."

"Excellent work, Megan," said Kingsley. "I know that Atlanta is actively collecting that data. I will personally see that they send it to you as soon as they get it."

***

The four escapees managed to make it through the night in the cave; they packed their gear and moved further into the hills, using a GPS.

Initially, there were five of them; they had survived the crash of their craft, and were rescued by the US Air Force. They had subsequently been taken to Nellis Air Force Base. Since then, they were forced to work against their will in the covert sites within the place called Area 51. JJ, Al's older brother, was assigned to work with the scientists involved with antimatter research. Whenever JJ could, he would do something to a piece of equipment or a computer program to slow them down. At the same time, he would do something brilliant to advance a less dangerous area of their work. As a result, JJ moved up the ladder, and he got closer and closer to the lead scientists and their superiors. During these times, he would be quietly collecting their thoughts rather than listening to their words. He had a brain like an encyclopedia; he was able to remember in great detail their thoughts, along with all he heard and saw.

About two months before the explosion, JJ had put it all together. He knew the antimatter and the machines they were designing and building were not going to be used for peaceful purposes; they were going to be placed in space. They said they were to be there to protect Earth. The truth was that many of these would be aimed at Earth to control the civilian population. From that moment on, JJ acted alone, and planned to stop the arming of space. Timing would be everything. Because he was so well-respected, no one questioned his loyalty to their projects.

Thus, JJ had devised a plan to escape; when the day came, he would be ready. With his cohorts out of the way, he would put his plan in motion. He put a signal into the computer program that would cause the cyclotron to malfunction; the cyclotron would then explode and destroy the entire complex. He also placed a tiny explosive capsule beneath the two main alarm systems which would set off all the alarms in the complex. JJ had no desire to kill anyone; he waited until there were the fewest number of people on duty.

His plan worked. He set off two alarms in sequence, and everyone safely evacuated the building, including himself. When he felt all were in the clear, he used his cell phone to trigger his computer; two seconds later, there was a deafening explosion. Everyone ran for cover. JJ hid behind a building at a safe distance, and then slowly moved away from the area. At the end of the path, he left the scooter and, picking his small backpack, he moved west, checking the GPS on his watch.

* * *

When the military arrived; they were stunned by the amount of damage. Heavy equipment was brought in to clear the road of debris. Several men in hazmat suits approached the mountain. The main entrance was blocked and unsafe; they started to clear the other exits, and soon it was obvious that all were impassable. There was nothing they could do; all retreated.

Those who evacuated had been taken by bus to a safe location.

"Does anyone have a list of the personnel who were inside at the time of the explosion?" asked the team leader.

"We've accounted for all but two," a young officer said. "We are missing the scientist in charge and an individual by the name of JJ; they would've been in the antimatter section when it happened, and they would have been vaporized."

* * *

"Gwen Ross—this is John Gray, Las Vegas, Nevada," said the voice on the other end of the line."

"John, hello—thanks for calling. What's happening?" answered Gwen.

"I've something of interest. I received a message a week ago from someone who would not identify himself. It said, 'Keep a close eye on Area 51, Southwest sector.' I didn't pay much attention to it as I get a lot of UFO-related messages. Then, two days ago, the same person called and told me that he and four others were being held against their will, and if they could escape, they would have some very valuable information for me. They said they would be in touch. I tried tracing the message, but it was sent on a burn phone."

"John, what do you think it is?" Gwen asked.

"I don't need to think—I *know*. I just heard from them. They've escaped and are on the run. Gwen, I got the call within minutes of the explosion in Area 51!"

Gwen was stunned.

"Oh my God, John, this could be huge!" she exclaimed.

She turned on the television in time for a newsflash on CNN.

"All but two persons have survived the explosion in Area 51; names to be released later," said the news anchor. This was followed by discussions from experts on every possible aspect, but despite speculation, no one knew what had actually happened.

* * *

President Kingsley was furious.

"Why wasn't I told about a production site for antimatter in Nevada?" he said angrily to the military officer he had summoned.

"That facility is funded by the Black Budget. We couldn't get an answer."

"I don't care; if I don't get some clear and honest answers from them, I'll make certain that their next budget will be cut drastically. I want the truth about this explosion!"

"Yes sir." The officer said as he left the room. He knew this message was going to cause big trouble.

Kingsley looked around at those present.

"Okay—what do we *really* know so far?" he asked.

The room was tense, as those who were close to the President knew just what he had done. By uttering this threat, he challenged the very foundation of the Black Budget. He was threatening to take back some of its control, and that would not sit well with some of the top military officers —and others.

"We're positive it was an antimatter explosion; two men are unaccounted for. They're clearing the site. Everything in the vicinity would have been vaporized," offered one staff member.

"Has my order to close down whole area of the Nellis Air Forces Base been carried out?"

"Yes sir."

"Good. Now please leave, I wish to have some time to think."

He had about ten minutes before his next meeting, and he needed to prepare himself.

* * *

Anin had encountered George Dean shortly after the explosion. "Were you or your agents responsible for this?" he asked.

"No way," George answered. "I thought maybe you might know something about it."

"No, I don't. It must have been an accident," Anin said. "The results of our tests in the cities have proven positive so far. I still have nothing new regarding the Delhi, India episode."

* * *

"I feel we should activate our plan to take over and stabilize the remaining four Black Labs, asap." Kingsley said, addressing the commanders of his secret force. "Can we be ready in three days?" He knew the US and Australian and Japanese forces were ready. The one he was worried about was Russia.

The Russian commander confirmed they were now ready to go ahead. They had gone over the plan in meticulous detail, and had each of their forces trained and ready.

While Kingsley had been waiting for this meeting, he had called Megan.

"Could you have the 1041 and 1051 antiserums here tomorrow?" he'd asked.

"Yes, I'll send all 500 ready to you. We're manufacturing more if needed."

"Thank you," he said. "What does the Delhi situation look like?"

"Some are 1041, and a few are 1051. The good news is that the spread is under control."

With this in mind, Kingsley looked down at his iPad while listening to his commanders conversing among themselves. "The antiserum will be here in a few hours," he told them. "We've more than enough for each of your troops involved. We'll meet again tomorrow morning for a final briefing."

* * *

"There's a white SUV approaching," Al said to Rad.

Rad checked. "All clear—it's for us," he responded.

When he last called John Gray to arrange a meeting, John had described his vehicle, including the license plate.

John stopped the vehicle and opened the door. He had a gun hidden in the small of his back.

"Hello, there...Rad?" he said as casually as he could.

Rad stepped forward and assured him that none of them were armed. John walked over to Rad, and they shook hands. The remaining three stepped out from their hiding place.

"When did you escape?"

"Yesterday afternoon, right after the explosion; our guard ran away and left the door open, so we took off."

"Why were you being held captive by the Air Force?"

They looked at one another. "Our spacecraft crashed during a very severe thunderstorm several months ago; five of us survived. The Air Force found us."

"So...you're aliens?"

"We're from a planet well beyond your galaxy, and are part of a universal watch group that has been keeping an eye on military developments by your country and others. We're non-interventionists; we are a peaceful civilization. Those in command here assured us that if we helped them with our technological expertise, they would let us go so we could be rescued."

"Do they know you've escaped?"

"Everyone was so busy after the explosion; I imagine they'll come looking for us soon."

"Let's get out of here immediately. We can talk while I drive. We must find you a safe place to hide. Have you food and water?"

"We've enough for a couple of more days."

John began to drive west. "Rad try to find the police band. Everyone keep your eyes open for any suspicious vehicles," he said.

"Where are we going?"

"I'm heading west to California, I've friends there who will hide you. I have a feeling we may have to go over some pretty rough roads to get there."

John had contacted his Shoshone friends in California. He told them to meet him at the GPS coordinates he'd given them with supplies to hide four adult men. He turned off on a narrow road and started driving into the hills. They'd heard on the radio that roadblocks were going up for miles around Area 51, and that they were looking for four suspects wanted for questioning in regards to the explosion.

"That'll be us," said Rad.

"I'm going to let you guys out up here. My friends will take very good care of you. You'll probably be moving around a bit; you'll be safe. Here are two new burn phones and my cell number. Send me a message to confirm that you've connected with my friends, but after that, use these only if absolutely necessary. I'll call you when I can."

As Rad got out, he handed John a USB drive. "I think you'll find this very interesting," he said.

"John, thank you very much," he said. The four got out and made their way to a nearby small cave.

"No problem—good luck, and wipe out your footprints as you go," said John. He turned his vehicle around and slowly moved down the hill. Instead of going back the way he came, he turned down another path to a small lake. He always had his fishing gear in the trunk, along with a tent. He built himself a fire, pitched the tent, and began to fish.

About a half-hour later, he got a message on his burn phone.

We found them, it said.

John smiled.

A short while later, a police car stopped close by.

"Hey there," said the officer.

"Hi," answered John with a casual tone.

"Have you seen any other vehicles along this way recently?"

"Nope, only mine."

"Thanks," the officer responded. After casting his eyes around the area briefly, he continued driving.

John plugged the memory stick in, and when he looked at the images, he just about jumped out of his skin. He was looking at an enormous lab facility and what looked like a cyclotron. It wasn't like anything he'd ever seen. Beyond a thick glass wall was a bank of computers. Everyone was wearing a full white bodysuit. Not being a scientist, he wasn't sure what he had. There were pages of scientific notes, diagrams and photos.

I wonder if these are of the lab that just blew up? I must get this copied. I'll hide it and make one for myself.

He tried to contact Gwen, but he'd used up the battery. He picked up his cell, but the service was too weak. It was too dangerous to make his way out of the hills at night, so he camped out until sunrise and drove home. He plugged in his phone to charge it as he drove, knowing that it wouldn't take long. He'd driven east for about twenty minutes when he pulled off to the side of the road and phoned Gwen.

"Did you just say aliens?" asked Gwen after John updated her.

"Yes, I did. I picked them up just west of Area 51. They escaped."

"Escaped!"

"Yes, they were taken prisoners by the Air Force after their spacecraft crashed in a storm."

"It's Roswell all over again. It makes you wonder how often this has happened over the years. Where are they now?"

"I left them with some Shoshone Indian friends of mine. They are safe."

"Did they say which planet they were from, or anything about the explosion?" Gwen asked.

"They were able to escape because of the explosion. They also said they were from a planet beyond our galaxy. They were keeping an eye on what was going on in Area 51."

"Do they know what caused the explosion?"

"They didn't say so, but I believe they've a good idea. We were too busy trying to get to the meeting site with the Shoshone. However, as their leader got out of my SUV, he handed me a USB key. Gwen, there are photos of the inside of the mountain facility, some equations, diagrams, etc. If you have secure access, I'll send it to you."

"My access is pretty secure. I've been using some pretty solid encryption software for some time now," she said.

"Great—I'll send this as soon as I can," he said. He decided not to go straight home; instead he went to the home of a trusted friend who was also a computer geek. If anyone had a secure system, it would be him.

"Andy, can you email this info for me?" John asked. "It's really sensitive material, so there must be no trace left on your computer or in your email's sent folder or server after you've sent it."

"Got it, John—I'll do it right away."

When Gwen received it, she was very excited, and called Sam over immediately.

"Sam, is your computer secure and encrypted?" she asked. "I want you to have this on your laptop as well."

"Yes, it is. What's up?"

"I don't know for sure. My contact in Nevada has some incredibly sensitive information about the mountain in Area 51, and I want to forward you what he sent me."

"It's safe to send; I've got all of my encryption software up to date. We're good to go."

Once he received the data, Sam was shocked. The very first photo was of a giant cyclotron.

"This machine is more sophisticated than anything I've ever seen," he said.

"What do you think it's been used for?" Gwen asked.

"Probably to make antimatter. This'll confirm the theory that it was antimatter that caused yesterday's explosion."

"Do you think we should notify Kingsley right away?"

"Let's look at what else is on it first to make sure it's not a hoax."

"Good idea, Sam."

Over the next couple of hours, Sam and Gwen studied this information. "Some of these equations are used in atomic physics. I can't say what," said Sam. "Others describe certain chemical reactions. The photos are of various parts of the complex. That complex was enormous!" He quickly flipped through some of the files and photos one more time. "Gwen, I believe this information is legitimate; Kingsley must see this asap."

"I'll get hold of him right away," said Gwen. She quickly called Sean.

"Is the President in the White House?" she asked, once she'd reached him.

"I believe he's on his way here."

"We've some extremely important information which he should see as soon as he arrives," she said. "We'll wait for him here in the library. Tell him he'll probably need a chemist and a quantum physicist to look at the data we have for him."

President Kingsley looked exhausted when he walked into the library half an hour later.

"I heard from Sean; what have you got for me?" he said, sitting down. He poured himself a fresh cup of coffee.

Gwen put the data up on the big screen. The first picture was the huge cyclotron. Sam explained to him what he thought it was.

"You mean to say, this is the lab which blew up in Nevada yesterday?"

"Yes sir."

Sam then turned to some of the formulas and notes.

"Where did this come from?" Kingsley asked.

"John Gray is a reporter in Nevada," she began, and described all that he'd imparted to her.

"Where are these four aliens now?"

"They are in the safe company of certain Shoshones in the mountains of California. Apparently, there are people who would rather find them dead than alive, and those people are looking for them."

"They'll never find them if the Shoshone Indians have them," Kingsley commented.

They were each pouring a second cup of coffee when Sean came in with a man and a woman. He introduced them as Dr. Pamela West, a specialist in quantum physics, and Dr. Anthony Wilberforce, a specialist in chemistry.

"I've called you here to look at some information we can't decipher," Kingsley said. He gestured towards the screen where the information was displayed. "Can you please tell me if you recognize any of this material?"

"Some of the equations are very advanced on a quantum physics level, but they are recognizable," said Dr. West. "However, the last few are unfamiliar; I need time to study them closer in order to determine what they mean."

"We'll provide you with what you need; please be aware that this information must stay here."

"I quite expected that, Mr. President, and I respect it."

"What do you think of those chemical equations, Dr. Wilberforce?"

"It appears to be a formulation of a new metal alloy. If it's what I think it is, it will be a major advancement in the manufacturing of military and domestic vehicles. I think this other one is of a similar nature, but like my colleague, Dr. West, I'll require more time for analysis. I also understand the delicate nature of this data, and I agree to stay here to work on it."

* * *

The Nellis Air Force investigators were dumbfounded as to how the cyclotron along with the stored antimatter could possibly have blown up. Ultimately, they decided to spin it as a very unfortunate accident, and placed the blame on the missing scientists.

"Have we any idea as to where our missing aliens are?" asked the head of security for Area 51.

"No sir. There's no sign of them. Could they also have been in the lab facility at that time?"

"If we can't track them down, that'll be what we will put in the official record."

"We're still searching in the hills and mountains to the west. We sent specialized teams; if they are there, I guarantee we'll track them down."

* * *

The Shoshone Indians had their charges well and truly hidden. Rad spoke to the others quietly. "I gave John one of the sticks of memory as a sign of good faith. He is a man of his word, I am sure."

"How long must we remain in hiding?" one of the others asked.

"Soon, my friends, we'll hopefully be on our way home. First we must carry out JJ's plan," Rad answered.

"I'm sure he is still alive and simply unable to communicate with us," said one of the others.

As it turned out, JJ had escaped and was hiding out in an old abandoned barn. He moved by night and slept by day. He'd wait another day or so before contacting John Gray.

* * *

Early the next morning, the final decisions were under way for the raids on the labs. The antiserum had arrived and was distributed to the various commanders. By late morning, each leader was on their way to their respective staging areas. The raids were to occur simultaneously.

All Kingsley could do was hope all went according to plan. He knew very well the official word coming out of Nevada was not trustworthy. He'd seen too many spins and cover-ups to believe anything they said. Unless he had the complete and true story, there would be no way to regain the trust of the American people, not to mention the people of the world. He was pulling out all the stops. If he failed, he would be finished as far as politics were concerned, but he didn't care about that. The world was facing disaster—he had to do whatever he could to prevent it from occurring. He already was walking on thin ice. He knew his life was in danger. His personal Secret Service detail had been fortified. As he contemplated all of these details, a message was delivered to him by Sean.

"Mr. President, Gwen Ross needs to see you right away."

"Thank you, Sean. I'll be down in a couple of minutes."

"Sorry to disturb you, sir, but I've just received another call from John Gray. He's heard from the fifth alien. He's alive and well and hiding in the mountains of Nevada. He caused the explosion. He wants to share some very valuable information; he'll only give it to you."

"If this is true, we need to get him out of there safely and quickly."

"I agree—but how? What about the other four? My understanding is that one of them is this alien's brother."

"I'll call in a couple of Seal extraction teams. As soon as we get a plan together, I'll see that they get out safely and to a secure location; we will go from there."

Gwen turned on the news channels. There was nothing new; all the reports covered the Delhi epidemic, which was now showing signs of being well under control. The death toll was in the millions. The much smaller outbreaks of bacterial disease were definitely under control. The final total death toll resulting from the tsunamis in the Pacific was in the 600,000s.

"My God," Gwen sighed. "When is this carnage going to end? It seems Earth has gone crazy." The rest of the day was amazingly calm and quiet. She helped Sam pack up his equipment.

Afterwards, the two of them had gone for a walk along one of the paths.

"This certainly has been some adventure, hasn't it?"

"Yes, and I'm afraid it is not over yet," Sam said, watching some squirrels playing in the trees above them. "What are your plans?"

Gwen shrugged her shoulders. "Right now, I'll go with the flow. Hopefully they'll be able to extract the aliens and bring them to safety, and I'll go from there."

"You certainly will have quite a story to tell, won't you?"

"Yes, Sam, I will, especially if we finally get to the truth regarding this whole mess."

"That's a good way to put it —a quest for the truth."

"I think so, too," Gwen said, smiling. "When this is over, I'm going to Grand Manan to just sit on the deck and watch the world go by for a while."

"What a wonderful idea!"

Sean had been walking a few paces behind them, and as they entered the library, they noticed the two scientists were packing up and getting ready to leave.

"You're on your way?" asked Gwen.

"Yes. We've done as much as we can, and have sent our reports off to the President. It was a real honour to be asked to help." Each of them said their goodbyes, and the two scientists departed.

Sean came back with an envelope for Sam.

"Here are your plane tickets. I'll be taking you to the airport tomorrow," he said. "Also, the President sends his gratitude for all you've done. He really wanted to have dinner with you tonight, but he simply could not be present."

"Sean, I totally understand. Thank you—for everything."

The next morning, Sam was up at the crack of dawn. He was so excited about going home. He had breakfast with Gwen, and as they were having their coffee, Sean came by to say they'd be leaving in about ten minutes. He had already put Sam's luggage in the black SUV.

Sam rose from the table and gave Gwen a big hug.

"Be careful, Gwen. I sure hope to see you soon." With a big smile, Sam was gone.

It's going to feel rather lonely here now, she thought as she returned to the library.

She logged on to her computer, opened a new window, and began to type. 'The Truth'— *that'll be the lead for my story,* she decided.

After lunch, she received a call from Kingsley's office requesting her presence at the White House at two-thirty pm. When she entered the Oval Office, two officers stood up, and she was introduced to them.

"We are sending two Seal teams, and these officers are in charge," Kingsley said. "Would you please phone Gray so plans can be arranged?"

Gwen nodded, and dialled immediately.

"John, I'm at the White House with two Navy Seals who are heading up the extraction teams. I'll put you on speakerphone, okay?"

"Okay, but I want you to stay there as a witness," he said.

Once he was on speakerphone, John explained the situation. "As to their exact locations, I don't know, as they were on the move during our last communication; however, I do know their general location."

After the phone call was complete, a plan was set: they'd be in touch, and John would get the aliens' respective locations and relay them to the Seals.

* * *

"George, I've some information for you. It was my superior who ordered the release of E. coli in Beijing. He knew Chang and his son were getting ready to split away from the Board. He had to act quickly. Having lured Chang into the city of Beijing, he had Chang's lab release the bacteria; the lab was then destroyed, and Chang was killed in the process as a message to Chang's son to back off. Chang's son got hold of several vials of 1041, and in revenge, he took them to India and infected several different areas of Delhi, knowing we would be blamed."

"Perhaps we shouldn't release any 1041s ourselves until the Delhi situation calms down. I'll take care of it," George said. He ended the call and sent out the order.

* * *

Megan was in the waiting room at her doctor's office, waiting for a checkup. She had finally been able to get some well-earned rest, as the E. coli 1041 and 1051 appeared to be under control. She didn't know when the raids were to occur. If they were successful, she'd be very busy once again testing swabs.

Of the utmost importance to her was that Sam was coming home. She wanted to spend some quality time with him and leave all of the world's problems behind for a while, and she knew Sam felt the same way. They hoped to go to the island for a few days, but she knew with the upcoming raids it was not possible.

Will this never end? she thought. Just then, the receptionist called her name, and led her into her doctor's examination room.

Her x-rays were great, and her doctor was impressed.

"I think you can now begin to confidently walk on your own, Megan. We'll give you a special arm brace. Walk as much as you feel comfortable with, and continue at home with the wheelchair as necessary. I must say, though, that I've never seen anyone heal as quickly as you have!"

Megan smiled at her doctor.

Wait 'til Sam hears this, she thought.

She could hardly contain herself; she was so happy.

* * *

By late afternoon, the Seal teams arrived as a training exercise in Death Valley, California. Their first attempt would be under the cover of darkness. They figured that the extraction of the four currently with the Shoshone would be relatively easy as long as the Nellis search parties were not in the area. They were using state-of-the-art helicopters, which were faster and quieter.

However, they couldn't attempt an extraction of JJ that night, as there were search teams nearby. They had to wait.

The next day, Gwen received the call from John Gray.

"Gwen, the four have been successfully extracted, but the leader has yet to be found."

"John, this is fantastic news!"

"It really is. Now, in speaking with them, they've related that they'll only talk with you before they'll deal with authority figures. I assured them they can trust you."

"Thank you, John."

She no sooner ended the call when her burn phone rang. It was Kingsley.

"Mr. President."

"Gwen, we've the group of four, and they'll be arriving shortly. They'll only talk to you. They're being taken to a secure location."

"I shall await further instructions. Thank you, Mr. President," Gwen answered.

She was genuinely excited. This would be her first contact with aliens. She relished the idea of being in the presence of such beings.

Two hours later, Gwen was being taken by Sean to an unknown location where she would have a private conversation with four beings who would give her first-hand confirmation of some of what was going on in Area 51.

"We're heading for the Walter Read National Medical Center and the Navy lodge. You'll meet with Commander Sheila Lang; she's in charge of protecting the aliens."

"Thank you, Sean."

A half hour later, she was introduced to Sheila and the four aliens. She was a bit surprised; they looked very much like anyone else. She noted their heads were larger and there was an expression in their eyes she couldn't read. They all had blonde hair and blue eyes. The one called Rad seemed to be the spokesperson. Al was shorter than Rad, who was quite tall. Ben and Art were quite tall as well. All were striking figures with well-proportioned, muscular bodies.

Gwen tried to put them at ease by calling John and letting them speak with him for a few moments. Al wanted to know if there had been any word about his brother, JJ.

"JJ escaped the explosion; hopefully he'll be joining you in the next day or so," said John. Al gave the phone back to Gwen.

To relax them a bit further, she asked them to talk about their escape. For the next half hour she just let them talk. She wanted to get to know them and they her.

"Would you fellas like something to eat and drink?" Gwen asked; they all nodded. Drinks and sandwiches were delivered. They continued chatting about their experience over lunch. When they finished, Sheila stood up.

"I think you've some rather more important things to discuss amongst yourselves," she said. "There is a guard outside, and if you need me, he'll come and get me."

Gwen walked out with her; as she did so, she turned and said, "I'll be right back."

"I think they'll be more forthcoming if I was not in the room," said Sheila.

"I agree; thank you."

Gwen returned to the room and immediately noticed a more relaxed atmosphere.

"Has everyone had enough to eat and drink?" Gwen asked. She sat down and began talking. "You probably know I'm a reporter." She waited for their reaction. They nodded. "For now, your story, and anything else you wish to tell me, will be strictly off the record."

"What about the authorities?" Art asked.

"President Kingsley will wish to speak with you, but only if you agree. I guarantee you'll not be forced to talk."

"I wish JJ were here. He knows much more than we do!" explained Al.

"Hopefully he'll be with us in the near future."

"Where do you want us to start?"

"How about from the beginning," suggested Gwen.

She listened quietly while they described their home planet, located way beyond the solar system. They were flying a spacecraft near Area 51 where they crashed. Gwen was totally mesmerized as they described Astestus.

"It's a planet very similar to Earth in many ways," said Al. "It's a bit smaller, with over eighty percent of the planet covered by oceans which are so full of life that no one would ever go hungry. We have whales that are almost identical to yours. The whales and dolphins are revered by one and all, for they are responsible for keeping the oceans of Astestus balanced and bountiful. They're considered to be the original inhabitants; therefore, Astestus truly belongs to them. We humanoids are newcomers—much like the situation here on earth. They are the wise ones.

"We have mountains reaching even higher into the atmosphere than Earth's. Only the highest of the high get snow on them. If you could only see the valleys...they're greener than green, and are lush year-round. The streams running through them are pure. There're no diseases such as we see here. On your timescale, we have an average lifespan measured in hundreds of years, not decades."

"Do you have conflicts and wars?" Gwen asked quietly.

"No, Gwen, not anymore. They're a thing of the distant past. We have many races, and we all get along," Al said, feeling very homesick.

"Al, you said you used to have wars. What happened to stop them?"

Rad explained. "Gwen, we've no such thing as time where we come from, so it's hard to say when it happened; we learned about it from our elders. Many generations ago, our planet was in a very serious situation, much like Earth is today, with the same disastrous future which you are currently experiencing. We experienced food shortages, droughts, and wars, and our natural resources were running out; even our freshwater was dangerously contaminated, and most importantly, our oceans were dying. We were desperate.

"We received help from another astral civilization, and we recovered through peaceful means, regaining our beautiful home. It was originally called something else. Our ancestors renamed it 'Astestus,' which stands for 'as a testament to us.'"

Tears began to flow from Gwen's eyes and slowly ran down her cheeks.

"Astestus is a beautiful name, and what a wonderful history you have. Thank you so much for sharing it with me. I'm truly honoured." Gwen dabbed her eyes, then continued. "Tell me, Rad, are there other planets out there similar to Astestus?"

"Yes, there are many planets and stars supporting humanoid life," he said. "However, only three have more freshwater and saltwater than land."

"Including Astestus and Earth?" asked Gwen.

"Yes."

"How many other planets are involved?"

"Several; most of us are noninterventionists, but there are a few who want to control Earth and keep it for themselves."

"Why are aliens so interested in Earth?"

"There are three major reasons," Rad answered. "One, we don't want to see you destroy your planet and most of the life on it; two, we would like to build up trade with you; and three,

Earth has been told not to contaminate space by putting nuclear weapons into orbit. Unfortunately, you are in the process of doing so."

"Can aliens prevent this from happening?"

"We are capable of disarming nuclear weapons without touching them."

"Fascinating—I want to explore that further, but I do have a more specific question that is rather time-sensitive, given recent events. Please know that you are free to answer only if you wish: what was going on inside the mountain lab?"

Al shook his head. "I am not prepared to answer that question at the moment; we would rather wait to see if JJ makes it; if he does, he knows a lot more of the details about the newly-designed cyclotron and the production of antimatter. He is very advanced in technology and participated in the design of several machines. He's also accomplished in what you call chemistry and physics. If he does not make it here, we will do our best and tell you what we know."

"Well, hopefully they'll be able to extract him tonight," Gwen said.

"I've a question for you," asked Rad. "Why are humans so intent on killing one another?"

"I wish I knew the answer," answered Gwen. "We're not all that way. Battles and wars seem to arise from human attitudes, usually on the part of one or group of individuals, through greed, opposing beliefs, or misunderstanding. If we don't soon get our collective and individual acts together and learn to live in compassion, mindfulness and care towards our environment, and mutual respect, wars and killing will continue."

"Do you think you can do this in time to save Earth?" asked Art.

"That is a huge question. There are definite signs, especially among our young people, that things have to change, and quickly. We've what has been called The New Age Movement, which is increasingly bringing spirituality to the foreground. Attitudes of many humans are changing for the better; for example, the Harmony idea which says that we're all interconnected with each other and our environment. As to whether we can change our attitudes in time to save Earth is very debatable, but many of us are trying."

"From what we've seen in and around Area 51, it seems virtually impossible," said Rad.

"The vast majority of the world's human population would love to live in peace and harmony. However, there is a small percentage of very wealthy and powerful humans who control the rest of us."

"Could you not defeat them?"

"We're trying to. The New Age Movement is a very peaceful one," Gwen said as she poured coffee and tea for everyone. "You say the peaceful aliens are noninterventionists. Does that mean humans must ask for their help? And if so, how?"

"The request is one of a welcome. They are waiting to be asked, but it must be sincere, and conveyed through peaceful prayer and meditation. If this is done, you'll be welcomed back into the universe as an active and peaceful planet. You have no idea of the technology and understanding that awaits you."

There was a knock on the door; Sean came in with their meals, and they sat around the table and chatted as they ate. No serious questions arose during this time, and everyone relaxed. As they finished dessert, Al asked, "Gwen, do you know if after we've answered all your questions we'll be able to go home?"

"You're not prisoners. You're being held in protective custody, which means you'll be protected from the people who were trying to find you and take you back. You'll be able to negotiate something," she said. "It has been a long day for you. I'm going to return to my place. Here is a burn phone; if there is anything you need, or if you just want to talk, please do call. You'll be very safe here. I'll see you tomorrow."

* * *

The second Seal team got word that the search by the military had stopped. They were on their way to Washington, DC just after eleven pm with a very thankful and quiet JJ.

The next day, Gwen was back in Baltimore. She was very anxious to meet JJ. His colouring and features were very similar to Al's—only he was quite tall, at approximately six foot ten, and he was very quiet spoken. His four companions were overjoyed to see him.

"The authorities are going to wish to talk with you," said Gwen.

"I've had a long chat with my brother and friends. They tell me I can trust you. So, I'm only going to talk to you."

"I'm honoured, JJ; as I said yesterday, anything and everything you say will be held in strict confidence."

"Thank you, Gwen. To begin with: the people that found us were nice enough, initially, I was led to believe that what we were doing was helping and benefiting all humans. However, I found out later that they were developing weapons for their own use."

Rad spoke up. "JJ has a photographic memory, as well as a few other talents," he said. With that, Gwen watched in awe as a pitcher of iced water moved independently. It poured water into a glass, and quietly slid across the table towards her.

"Thank you, JJ—you knew I was thirsty," she said. They all laughed.

"It was JJ's skills and technical expertise that captivated the scientists. We all have specialized skills, but not to the extent of JJ's abilities."

"Were the people at Area 51 aware of all your gifts?"

"No, Gwen, they were not. They only knew of my technological skills; I only let them know what I felt was necessary. My ability to telecommunicate has decreased over my time here on Earth."

"How did you trigger the explosion—in non-scientific terms, please."

"I helped design the new cyclotron and computer systems to run it," JJ told her. "It was easy for me to change the program to disrupt the proper functioning of the machine so it would self-destruct."

"Your companions gave John a USB memory stick, which they in turn gave us. On it were some very interesting diagrams and equations. Can you explain them to us?"

"I am willing, yes," answered JJ.

"Do I have your permission to see if I can arrange a meeting with the President of the United States?"

"Yes—but only if you're present, Gwen."

Gwen nodded. Then she quietly got up, shook hands with JJ, and said, "You'll hear from me soon; thank you, JJ."

As she left the room, she was so exhilarated that she thought she'd be overcome with excitement. Then her cool, clear mind kicked into gear, bringing her into focus.

"Sean, I must speak with Kingsley right away."

"Of course; I'll contact him immediately, and will let you know when he can communicate directly with you."

Within ten minutes, Sean connected Gwen with Kingsley on the phone. She briefed him on her latest meeting with JJ, and he agreed to have Sean facilitate a private and secure meeting immediately. Sean was told that JJ and Gwen were to come to the White House; the President would meet them privately.

At one-thirty pm, Gwen, JJ, and his companions were safely ushered into a small office.

"The President will be with you momentarily," said Sean. He left the room and closed the door quietly behind him. Shortly after, Kingsley entered.

For the next hour and a half, Kingsley and Gwen sat and listened in awe as JJ told his story, covering everything from the time they had come to Earth to the time he caused the explosion in the lab. He explained his reasons why he blew it up. Then, President Kingsley had several questions for him. JJ gave precise details on what he'd accomplished, and what the real purpose of their research was.

"I knew they were illegal, but now I have proof," said Kingsley. "I'm not saying that all top secret facilities are—however, we now have proof that some of them are. JJ, is there any way we can assist you and your companions in your return to Astestus?"

"I'm certain there is. In return, I'll give you everything I know about Area 51, especially the mountain facility. I'll also give your scientists more formulas for metal alloys," JJ said, shaking hands with Kingsley.

"JJ, would you consider sitting down with some of our top physicists and chemists? They are trustworthy, and any meeting will be conducted entirely on your terms."

"Yes, I am willing—providing Gwen can be there as a witness."

* * *

Megan was making notes in her computer when her phone rang.

"Megan, this is Kingsley speaking. I've just heard from the commander who led the raid on the lab in Area 51. They had a few small problems, but on the whole, it was successful. You'll be receiving swabs by special delivery in the next few hours.

May I presume upon you to come back to Camp David to work on your analysis here?"

"No problem; I'll stay here until the samples arrive at the Centre. I'll fly out immediately afterwards. Were they able to arrest all the scientists involved?"

"All but one; George Dean committed suicide."

Shortly after his conversation with Megan, Kingsley received two more calls. In Tokyo, partway through the raid; there was a fire in one area of the lab, and some of the documents were destroyed. One scientist had died of smoke inhalation, and two members of the assault team had been slightly injured. The swabs were sent to Megan; all of the recovered documents were secure and on their way to Washington. He no sooner hung up when his phone rang again.

"This is Commander Riley, reporting from Melbourne. The raid was very successful; all scientific staff are safely in custody. I'll be arriving in Washington tomorrow with a full report. The swabs are on their way to Canada."

Kingsley was fully expecting another call to come in from Moscow; however, it didn't come in until almost an hour later. It had been a disaster. The entire building aboveground was ablaze when the raiding team arrived. There was a major explosion just seconds before they were to enter the building. Everything inside was destroyed, including the labs containing the *E. coli* strains and all the records. They were, however, able to arrest some of the scientists.

He phoned Megan again and told her what had happened.

While Megan was waiting for her flight to Washington, she called Gwen.

"I'm coming back to Camp David."

"What? You just got home! What's up?"

"The raids on the four covert bioengineering labs have just occurred. The samples are coming to Halifax for analysis;

however, the data and computers are all going to Washington. As a result; so am I."

"It'll be so wonderful to have you back! When do you arrive?"

"Sometime mid-afternoon today; Sean will be picking me up. Gwen, can you get a hold of your young friend, the cryptographer, and ask him to meet us there?"

"Jamie? Sure I can. He's still in Australia, but I'm sure he'll come. Do you need him here or in Halifax?"

"I need him there in Washington; I have a feeling there is going to be a ton of data to analyze."

"I'll get him here as soon as possible."

* * *

With the death of George Dean, Anin realized he was now in sole charge of The Company. The loss of all their covert labs was a disaster. However, with what he wanted to do next, they were not really necessary. He felt he knew just how to fix the whole problem. It would take a while, but it could be done.

* * *

It was late afternoon when Megan arrived back at Camp David. Gwen was there to meet her with big hugs.

"You're walking on your own now! That is fantastic!"

"It sure feels good to be free. Is there anything new to report here?"

"Yes, but I'll tell you about it later. It has to do with the Nevada explosion."

"When does Jamie arrive?"

"Late tomorrow; he was staying with Shelley and David."

"How is David taking the news of his lab being raided? Is there any word of Margo?"

"He is honestly relieved and thankful that the covert part of his lab complex will no longer exist. Margo is in protective custody, along with the others. David is going to see what he can do to help her."

Megan nodded in understanding. "How is Kingsley doing?"

"He is very tired; he's had so many things to deal with recently; I don't think he's had much sleep over the last week or ten days. Right now he really has the most demanding job in the world. Let's get you settled, and then we'll get some dinner."

* * *

For the first time in days, Kingsley had a relatively quiet evening, and he caught up on some much-needed sleep. He awoke at seven am and was in the Oval Office at eight-fifteen am.

Commander Jones, who was in charge of overseeing the Area 51 operation after the explosion, entered the Oval Office to bring Kingsley up to date.

"Good morning, Commander, and congratulations on a job well done. You've the laboratory documents and computers with you?"

"I have, sir; they are in a secure, armoured vehicle; we are awaiting your next orders."

"We'll take responsibility of them here," said Kingsley. He called Sean and gave him instructions to take the material to Megan.

Kingsley turned back to Jones.

"Commander, tell me—what's the status on the scientists we have in custody?" he asked.

"Some of them were relieved to be arrested; a few of them demanded lawyers," answered Jones. "As it was a national security issue, they lost the right to counsel for the moment. Two or three wanted to talk right away, so we let them. Their recordings are in this sealed envelope. They're still being questioned, and their answers are being recorded. A summary of the findings will be delivered to you promptly. Be assured: they are being treated with dignity, and will remain where they are until we hear more from you."

In a similar manner, Kingsley personally received the computers, documents, and any other relevant material from Australia and Tokyo. Later that day, he would speak to the other commanders in turn as they arrived in Washington with comparable reports.

* * *

The amount of material and information that JJ had put on the memory sticks was astounding. He started off by giving a very detailed layout of the set-up inside the mountain. The complex was huge, and virtually all of it was enclosed inside the mountain or underground. He was only able to give descriptions for the areas he worked in; he didn't know what was in the other facilities—however, he heard that one area was developing some form of chemical weaponry. The name Saxitoxin had come up a couple of times.

Having described the facility as best he could, he began to work through some of the formulae he'd helped develop or had found out about. There was the formula for the clear piece of metal he had with him. He further explained its properties, along with other formulae for metal alloys.

"Regrettably, you humans are not quite ready for some of the information I possess. We believe that if I gave you that knowledge now; it would be misused. However, if Earthlings would welcome us to your planet, we would be able to set up some trade agreements as a way to establish mutual trust and an eventual alliance," he said.

When Gwen returned to Camp David the next day, she went into the library and saw a man standing beside the fireplace.

"Jamie, you're here! How are you?" she said enthusiastically. She went over and gave him a big hug. "You look fantastic; Australia agrees with you."

Megan joined them. "You and I are going to be working together on codes relating to DNA," she said. "I'm afraid there is going to be a lot of it, and of course, it's extremely sensitive and classified as top secret. We are getting some translating programs, as some of it'll be in Japanese and maybe Russian."

"Perfect," said Jamie. "I'll set up my systems and get my cryptography software running."

"How about we have our dinner and exchange stories this evening? We'll start first thing in the morning."

Megan had just put her head back on her pillow that night when she heard a voice calling her.

"Megan..."

It was Ortho. "What are you doing here?" she asked, surprised.

"I'm here to see how you are doing," he said.

"I'm doing fine; I just wish this business of these E. coli strains was over with. I'm exhausted, and I don't see an end in sight."

"That's why I'm here. You should know that three of the four raids have been successful. Someone tipped off the Russian one, which was totally destroyed by fire. Someone got out with the E. coli 1051."

"Who got out?" Megan asked. She felt afraid.

"The mole was a junior member of the Russian team. One of the scientists is now missing. You must get Kingsley to investigate quickly and push until he gets the name; once they find him, they'll find the missing bacteria before he gets to use it. Once that is done, there'll be no more E. coli 1041 or 1051 on Earth."

"I will do my best."

"Be encouraged; a certain measure of peace is coming, Megan. Hopefully humans will take the upcoming relatively quiet time and put it to good use. If you don't, there will be more disasters."

"I understand, Ortho" said Megan. "I share your hope. I truly long for lasting peace."

"Megan, how would you like to go for a trip with me and Lacuna?" said Ortho. His tone was kind and uplifting.

"Oh, I would dearly love to!"

"Come along, then," he said gently.

Through astral projection, Megan felt herself rise from the sofa; as she did so, she felt lighter and lighter until she was just floating weightless through space. They weren't on a ship of any kind; they were just floating.

"Lacuna has been spreading the word of how humans are really beginning to change, and how they are awakening to their spiritual side throughout the oceans of Earth," said Ortho.

"She's like Gram and Fred!" Megan exclaimed.

"Yes. We've always known Earth would survive if whales and humans could work in cooperation; together they could solve almost all of Earth's problems. Look over there, Megan. I see Lacuna and Shadow."

There was a great reunion taking place, and it was full of joy and unconditional love.

"Come, follow me," Ortho said.

"Where are we going?" Megan asked. Shadow had approached and was swimming circles around them.

"You'll see. It's far away from Earth. You and Lacuna joined us through a portal—a type of wormhole. This is a very special day for you, Megan. Something you've wished for over the years is about to happen."

Megan was getting very excited as they were beginning to slow down. A figure was slowly moving towards them—a beautiful woman dressed all in white. She was humming very softly and very low. In her own deep, resonating voice, Lacuna joined in. Megan, without realizing it, also began to hum. Suddenly, Megan stopped; tears streamed down her face—tears of joy at the realization of who it was that appeared before her.

"Mom...Mom...it's really you!" she cried. She stretched her arms out towards the figure in white who immediately took her in her arms.

"Yes, Megan; it's me. I too have longed for this moment for a long time," said Mary. She continued to hold Megan, rocking her gently back and forth as she kissed Megan's tears away.

Megan pulled back a bit and looked up into Mary's eyes; they were filled with such love and tenderness. "Mom, I've seen you in my dreams many times, but I could never see your face."

"I have visited you often, and now, darling, I get to hold you. I'm so proud of everything you've done and are doing."

"Thank you, Mom...that means the world to me," said Megan. She had a thought, and pulled back a bit further. "Does this mean I've died?" she asked.

Mary laughed. "No, no, dear; you're very much alive. You've been allowed to visit another dimension, the one I'm currently in. Your angels arranged it; however, you can't stay much longer. I have a message for you: you're on the right track, and you're to continue to help Kingsley for a while; then you must return home. You, Gwen, and Sam are to go to our home and turn all your energies into helping arrange the plans for June 21. Meg, please give Nona a hug, and tell her I'll visit her in her dreams. I love you."

Mary slowly faded away as Megan said, "I love you, Mom, and I'll do as you say."

"Come Megan, we must go," said Ortho, who gently guided her back.

Megan slowly opened her eyes; she was stretched out on the sofa. She pulled the blanket up around her and drifted off into a very sound sleep.

Megan awoke the next morning feeling refreshed and peaceful. She quickly showered, and went over to the main building, hoping to have breakfast with Gwen.

"You look almost radiant, Megan. What's happened?"

Very quietly, Megan told her about her vision.

"Meg, that's absolutely wonderful! No wonder you are so happy!"

"Gwen, Ortho told me something very important, and I'm going to tell you about it, because, somehow we have to get this message to Kingsley; he must not only believe it—he must act on it."

"Okay, tell me."

Megan described the foiled raid on the Moscow lab and the missing scientist who took some of the E. coli 1051.

"He must be stopped!" said Gwen. "If we tell him you got this through a vision, though, he probably won't believe it. I'll tell him I got a tip from one of my colleagues in Moscow."

"Gwen, I can't have you lie."

"It won't really be a lie, because I did get some e-mails from Moscow saying there was a rumour that confirms what you've just told me."

Gwen immediately called Kingsley. "Have you interviewed the Russian commander yet?"

"No. He'll be here in my office within the hour...why?"

"I've some evidence which may throw some light on what happened there. I've four independent sources of a very strong rumour that there was a leak. One scientist is unaccounted for, and he may have escaped with some of the E. coli 1051. Unfortunately, no name was given."

"How did you receive this information?"

"Mainly through e-mails from reporters in Moscow; I received this late last night. The other came this morning. The last is very reliable; I received it just before I called you."

"What is your overall sense of the validity of this information?"

"This is entirely valid; additionally, a warning came up with the last one: we must act quickly or we may have another outbreak on our hands."

"Thank you very much, Gwen. I'll respond to this accordingly."

Kingsley sat in deep thought for a moment, then reached for a folder marked *Top Secret Intelligence Report*. He found what he was looking for: the name of a visiting scientist to the Russian lab from Germany.

This might be the one, he thought.

He was interrupted by his secretary informing him that Commander Ivanov was there to see him.

As Ivanov entered, he bowed; he looked totally exhausted.

"What happened?" Kingsley demanded.

"No problems were encountered until after we had the lab surrounded," Ivanov began. "Our electronic and computer experts were in the process of disarming the lab security when suddenly there was an explosion. The entire surface structure just crumpled inwards, and a fire ensued. Rescue crews are still working and trying to get to the lower levels of the underground lab. They've recovered five bodies so far; all five were security personnel. We're carrying on a full investigation. I apologize."

"Who is the mole on your team?" Kingsley said with an edge to his voice.

"A young intelligence officer; he's since been arrested."

"The damage has been done," Kingsley said, looking down at a folder on his desk. "There appears to be one scientist missing from the list of those you were supposed to have captured. What do you know about a Dr. Felix Schultz?"

"He's a German, and had been working with our scientists over the past two months. We think he was in the lab the night of the raid. He may have been responsible for the explosion."

"That's impossible," Kingsley said in a quiet voice, restraining his anger. "What if I told you that a man matching his description was seen on camera leaving Heathrow airport, and is currently on a plane to Frankfurt?"

The Russian was in shock. "I don't believe it!" he exclaimed.

Kingsley stared directly at his visitor. "I would like you to stay here until I get word from Interpol, who are waiting for Schultz to land at Frankfurt."

"I would be happy to remain here as your guest. I too wish to know the truth," answered Ivanov.

"By all means; I appreciate your cooperation in this matter," said Kingsley. He rang the buzzer on his desk and his secretary came into his office, accompanied by two Secret Service agents.

"Please take the commander to the outer office. Provide him with refreshments; however, he is not allowed to use any form of communication," he said sternly.

Three quarters of an hour later, Kingsley was on the phone with Interpol.

"We have your man in custody," they reported. "We confiscated a small package, and as per your directions, a bacteriologist took a swab and sent it by air express to the address in Canada. His papers and computer are on their way to you as I speak. We'll hold Schultz until we receive further word from you."

"Thank you very much; job well done."

Ivanov was escorted back to the Oval Office.

"Schultz is in custody," said Kingsley. "I expect a full, unabridged copy of the results of your investigations in Moscow."

"Understood," the Russian said as he left the office.

He called Gwen. "Your information was correct, and I thank you. Please tell Megan that the Tokyo packages will arrive later today."

When Gwen relayed the information, Megan was elated. "So far as we know, there'll be no more mass murders resulting from the covert strains of E. coli!" Megan exclaimed, pumping her fist in jubilation.

Gwen sat down and wrote on a pad of paper. *Man-Made Epidemics: Fake Quakes Gone: Black Future For Black Budgets: Aliens Do Exist.*

"Wow, I've a funny feeling we're on the crest of a huge wave bringing us the truth, and hopefully a better way of life!" she said.

Megan and Gwen laughed together. "Okay, guys, let's get rolling," said Megan. "We've work to do."

By mid-afternoon, a definite picture was beginning to emerge from the Area 51 lab. The bioengineering on the E. coli had begun over three decades earlier, but early attempts had failed. The first tests by The Company occurred about one year prior to Matthew's and Mary's deaths. The Russian and Japanese labs were developing some viruses as well. They skipped up to the first recorded large test.

"Gwen, come and see this," said Megan.

They looked at notes of the mass murder of over 600,000 people in Bombay, India.

"Here's our proof. Could you make a hard copy of anything to do with any of the epidemics?" Gwen asked, getting excited. "I think I feel a huge story coming on!

***

Kingsley was a Democrat and held the majority in both houses; he was also Commander-in-Chief of the US military forces—therefore, he felt fairly safe in what he was about to do. He called the heads of each military service to the Oval Office. They had no idea what they were in for. The president entered, and they all stood and saluted. Behind the president stood the speaker of the house and the senate majority leader.

"I want each of you to review the part of the Black Budget that is under your control. By noon the day after tomorrow, I want a complete breakdown, along with a full description of each project listed here, as well as the rationale behind each project."

"But, sir, there is no way we can do that. A lot of this is top secret."

"Top-secret or not, it's your job to know every aspect of how and why these monies are spent. I'm your Commander-in-Chief, and I've just given you an order. I expect it to be carried out. If anyone disobeys or tries to interfere or hide anything, I expect you to arrest them on the spot, and charge them with treason. Do I make myself perfectly clear?"

All who were present nodded.

"Good. We'll meet here again at noon the day after tomorrow." He glanced around. "Remember, you may not discuss anything that's been said here today. You're dismissed."

The two House leaders remained behind.

"Gentlemen, what do you have to say?"

"Do you have good reasons for what you just did?" one of them asked.

"I have, Richard. If the two of you have a few minutes, I'll explain. I have absolute proof that some of the Black Budgets were used to create the bacteria which were used to murder millions of people to date."

"What? I don't believe it."

"By our next meeting, we'll know if the military will cover this up or not. I'm tired of being lied to," said Kingsley. He was getting angry. "I promised the people of the United States of America that I would run an honest and open government. I intend to do just that. If I don't have the complete breakdown of every Black Budgeted facility in this country, both military and civilian, by our next meeting, I'll be forced to declare a limited state of emergency, which will cover each and every one of these projects currently being funded by the Black Budgets. You know what that will entail."

Kingsley felt this was the only means whereby he could really shake up the government within in his government. He was making enemies of certain government and military officials, but it had to be done.

Gwen had been very busy all day getting her story ready. She had checked with reporters around the world, and they all had told her to go for it. They would have their own twists after her story hit the press—and hit the press it did. Instantly, word spread around the world.

By noon the following day, the world was in an uproar; people were demanding that their respective governments come clean. They wanted answers. There were demonstrations in virtually every major city in the world and politicians were scrambling to find answers. Promises were made for prompt and quick action.

Megan, Sean, Gwen, and Jamie were watching the various newscasts from around the planet. "Well, Gwen, your articles have certainly got the world's attention. Do you think that we'll get to the bottom of all this or not?"

"I honestly think we will," she said. She smiled at Megan.

Megan looked over at Jamie and Sean. "With their help, it won't be much longer. The samples from Japan were very similar to those of Area 51. The Australian lab was the first to successfully make E. coli 1041. They were also the first to bioengineer lethal viruses; however, they were never developed into biological weapons. We're still awaiting the results from the Russian strain. My guess it will be the same as the others. I should have a complete analysis done by tomorrow night. Hopefully I can go home soon."

* * *

The meeting with the joint Chiefs of Staff had been moved to one-thirty pm, as Kingsley had been called away to an emergency conference of unknown content.

When he entered the Oval Office, he was even more certain that he was doing the right thing. He was pleased to see some very thick files on his desk, and he glanced at them.

"I assume I now have all that I requested," he said. The two chiefs of staff nodded in agreement. "Did you encounter any problems or any refusals to comply?" He asked. He listened to each one in turn and made notes. He left Area 51 to the last.

"Well, Ian—you had a very serious situation to handle. How did it turn out?"

"The head of the mountain facility continued to refuse; he is now in prison. We got the information you requested. We had some problems with certain civilian contractors; however, they were convinced to comply. There are several questions arising from the raid on the CESR."

"Well, maybe I can help you there. The reason for the delay today was that I was talking to a man who can explain a great deal." Kingsley said as he pressed an intercom button. The door opened, and a tall blond man with unusually piercing blue eyes entered the Oval Office.

"Gentlemen, this man has stepped forward to help clarify what was really going on at the CESR. May I introduce Anin; he has no last name, as he is an alien. He was co-chair with Dr. George Dean of the Board of Directors of what we have learned was called The Company. This board is the head of the entire illegal aspect of the facilities around the world, funded by the Black Budgets. Anin, please tell them what you have told me."

"My real name is Mesda. I was kidnapped as a child by the Anunnaki and grew up in their ways. In my early upbringing, I discovered who I really was. I came originally from a peace-loving star and I never forgot my roots. But three decades ago, in your time, I was chosen by the Anunnaki to become a leader in their forces. I did so gladly, as I knew this was the best way to serve my own planet. I became a spy for the non-interventionists who wish more than anything to help Earth heal."

He talked for over an hour, and told them all about the Board and their members.

"Why didn't you come forward before this?"

"I couldn't—not as long as Dean was alive. Now that he's dead, everything to do with that Board is in shambles."

"Are the Anunnaki after you now?"

"They are far too busy trying to regain their balance and power after the Beijing and Delhi catastrophes," Anin said. He more comprehensively described the truth of what had happened. "I knew the truth; however, they did not. I managed to muddy the waters, in order to make it even more difficult for them to discover what really happened. They have no time or desire to come after me."

"Were you responsible for that?"

"The blowing up of those labs? No, I wasn't." He looked at Kingsley, who nodded and encouraged him to continue.

"I'm responsible for many of the artificially-induced quakes; however, I never caused any that were greater than 5.0. Anything over 5.0 that was unnatural were caused by my superiors. The Annunaki were very annoyed with us at the CESR. for not moving along faster and being more destructive."

"How do we know that you are who you say you are?"

"I guess you'll just have to take my word for it," Mesda said.

"Mr. President, what really is going on here?" asked one chief of staff. "It seems as if Earth is falling apart; what about the ones Mesda called the Anunnaki? Do they really exist?"

Kingsley looked up. "Yes, they do," he said. He told them what Mesda related to him earlier—how the Anunnaki had made humans their slaves; how over hundreds of thousands of years they robbed Earth of many of her natural resources. He described how they made alliances with some of Earth's most powerful families by promising to take these families to another planet when Earth reached the point of extinction.

"They never were going to carry this plan through; in reality, they planned to kill off most of Earth's human population," said Kingsley. "They would only leave enough to develop our natural resources for their benefit. With the coming of the New Age, they are slowly losing their grip on us Earthlings. They're trying to keep us in a state of fear so that they may control us forever."

"That seems to me to be a bunch of hogwash," said the other chief of staff.

"Is it? Just recently I met five aliens who had been on a spacecraft which crashed near Nellis Air Force Base. They were held prisoners there; through lies and empty promises, they were convinced they were helping mankind. They found out the truth. They escaped when the mountain lab blew up a few days ago. Gentlemen, that facility was destroyed by a massive antimatter bomb. Our own forces were sent out to hunt these aliens down and kill them. They didn't succeed; they are very much alive and telling their story as I speak; and you wonder why I'm angry?"

* * *

JJ and his five friends were filming an interview with Gwen in a room at Navy Lodge. This film would be released to the public in the next couple of days; once they had made contact with one of their space vehicles.

* * *

Megan was putting the final touches on her report and had just received word that Kingsley was coming out to Camp David to say goodbye to her personally that night. The next day she would be flying home. She and Sam were planning to take a long holiday on Grand Manan.

Dinner at Camp David was stuffed meatloaf and gravy cooked from Kingsley's grandmother's recipe, with a medley of root vegetables, accompanied by a prize-winning California red wine, followed by a sorbet to cleanse the palate. Fresh strawberry shortcake rounded out a superb meal. There was no shop talk while they ate; they were simply three friends telling stories, relaxing and enjoying each other's company. After dinner they retired to a cosy sitting room; a lovely fire had been laid to welcome them. It was spring and there was a chill in the air. On a round oak table, a selection of liqueurs were arranged in a circle. Megan chose her favourite, Grand Marnier; Gwen chose Drambuie, while Kingsley poured himself a glass of brandy. They relaxed and were all in a very introspective mood.

It was Kingsley who finally broke the silence. "Let's raise our glasses to friendship and peace," he said.

"To friendship and peace," Gwen and Megan answered. As they put the glasses down, Megan spoke.

"Wouldn't it be wonderful if this was the end of all disasters and the beginning of an era of a peaceful world?"

"I have a feeling it is the beginning, Megan. It may take a few more years, but it will happen. I honestly feel we've put the worst behind us," Kingsley said as he raised his glass again. "To truth!" he toasted.

Kingsley took another drink of his brandy, and looked at the two women.

"A lot of what we have achieved is the result of the dedication and work of you two and of Sam. I cannot thank you enough for all of your help," he said. He raised his glass again in a salute to them.

"What do you think will happen next?" Megan asked.

"Let me tell you a story," Kingsley said, smiling. "The strangest thing happened to me today. I was on my way to a meeting with my joint chiefs of staff when I looked up from my desk. Standing there was the tallest man I've ever seen. He had very piercing blue eyes, with golden hair that went down to his shoulders."

"'Robert Charles Kingsley, I come in peace,' he said to me. His voice was almost musical. 'I have been known as Anin, but my true name is Mesda. I mean you no harm.'"

"I asked him where he came from, and why he was here. I knew instantly he was an alien."

Both Gwen and Megan were leaning forward in anticipation. Kingsley went on to tell them Mesda's, story and why he had come to Earth as a spy.

"So, we know who's behind the epidemics and the earthquakes, but who was behind the stronger ones that caused deadly tsunamis off the West Coast of the Americas and the other one in Polynesia?" Gwen asked.

"He said it was his superiors, the Anunnaki. He warned they may cause similar disasters in the near future to try to regain control."

"Mr. President, did he give any hints as to when and where?"

"No, Megan; he couldn't, as they have been doing this without his knowledge," Kingsley said. He turned to Gwen. "How did the interview go with the five aliens this afternoon?"

"It went extremely well. They've made contact and will be on their way home in the next few days."

Megan was surprised at this news.

"Sorry Meg, I'll have to tell you all about it later."

Kingsley poured them each another glass and said once more, "To truth."

Megan and Gwen echoed his words as they too raised their glasses.

"To truth!"

After he'd finished his drink, Kingsley looked at his watch. "I've had a very long day, and I wish to watch the DVD that Gwen gave me earlier today. I believe, Megan, it's a recording of the speeches your grandmother and my dear friend Fred have become so famous for." He got up, went over to Megan and shook her hand.

"Megan, you are a very talented, wise, and beautiful woman. You've helped me, my country, and our world more than you'll ever know. I consider you a personal friend. Thank you. I'll never forget what you and Sam have done."

"It has been my pleasure, Mr. President, to know you and have you as a friend." She reached up and kissed him on the cheek. "Namaste."

Megan had tears in her eyes as he left.

***

JJ and his four alien companions were secretly transported out of Washington into the blue Mountains in an SUV, driven by Sean with Gwen at his side. It was a beautiful spring evening. As they got out of the vehicle at their destination, Gwen thought she had never seen so many stars. A few of them seem to be particularly bright. She commented on this, and as she did so, Al leaned over and whispered, "They're not stars!"

"You mean...?"

"Yes, those extra bright objects are spacecraft which have come to welcome us and take us home."

The five brilliant stars began to move, and then in a flash, one of them descended and landed no more than two hundred feet away from them. A large door opened slowly as the seven of them walked towards it. Gwen and Sean were spellbound. As they approached the craft, the five aliens began to glow more and more.

"I think this is where we'll say our goodbyes. With the energy radiating out from the ship, you may not be safe to go any closer."

Gwen began to weep. She had become very close to these five wonderful beings and was very sad to see them leave.

Each alien came over to Gwen and hugged, thanking her for her friendship before they walked towards their ship. The last one, the one they called Al, came over and warmly embraced her.

"You'll see us again, my friend," he said. He drew back, leaned over, and kissed her cheek.

"Thank you," he said.

Then, with the joy of a child, he ran to catch up with the others. They entered the craft and turned and waved. The door slowly closed and they were gone.

Gwen stood as still as can be. She did not want to move. She couldn't believe that they were gone.

"Gwen...." Sean said, calling her softly. "We have to go."

He put his hands on her shoulders and turned her towards him. He took her in his arms and held her tightly, stroking her hair: "It'll be okay."

"I know," she answered softly.

Something had happened to her when Al kissed her cheek. It was like an electric shock, and yet it wasn't. Whatever it was, it had left her with a sense of peace, calm, and a sense that all was going to be okay. All was well.

As she turned to go to the car; Gwen turned and looked into Sean's eyes.

"Now that all of this is over, I can say this: I...I love you Sean; I love you."

He smiled, and swept her off her feet. "Gwen Ross, I've loved you since the very first time I saw you."

* * *

Megan returned to Halifax, and two days later, Sam and Megan packed their vehicle and were headed for Grand Manan. Nona and Andrew had just returned from their speaking tour and were very happy that Megan and Sam were coming for a visit. There would be lots to talk about.

* * *

Kingsley, with the help of his staff, was going through each report and budget given to him by the commanders of the various US military forces. There were boxes of material to go through. He was determined to know everything the Black Budget was funding and who really was benefiting from it. He also had his legal staff looking for anything illegal.

The military, and those in the government connected to the World Power Elite, started to threaten legal action; however, they were silenced when they realized how angry and vocal the citizens of their respective countries were. Many of them had quickly tried to divorce themselves from the WPE. Some even feared for their lives. All the directors had either committed suicide or had been arrested. They panicked and tried to draw out all the monies from their various offshore accounts; they had been frozen. Additionally, they were being investigated. How did they find out about their involvement? Who had ratted them out? The WPE were rapidly losing whatever powers they had. Within a few days, many had been arrested and there were more arrests every day.

Throughout this period of time, Anin/Mesda had been quietly leaking information and documents showing who and what the connection was to the WPE. Kingsley now held the entire list of the names of the upper-levels of those who were wielding their power and making decisions as to who and where the monies in the Black Budgets went. It was no wonder their assets were frozen immediately. Interpol had organized their arrests to happen simultaneously.

A large number of the Black Ops were found not to be corrupt, and their designation of top secret was very necessary. However; many were not necessary, and Kingsley requested they be declassified. Some, in fact, looked extremely suspicious. Two of these were located on or near Area 51. One was the now-destroyed mountain lab; the other was the lower raided levels of the CESR. When Kingsley saw the truth of what was being developed in these facilities, he demanded a full investigation into both of them. This also made him extremely suspicious of some of the other operations—not only in Area 51, but also several other military bases. Once these were fully investigated, he ordered the same scrutiny on any suspicious activities by contractors hired by the military. If he did nothing more during his first term of office other than destroy the WPE, his term would be widely regarded as a great success.

Kingsley also wished to address and clarify the whole Roswell cover-up. He wanted to be the president who told the world the truth. He felt now was the time to do so, and he summoned the leaders of the two houses to get their opinions.

"Gentlemen, I feel with everything that has happened, along with what we have learned, that it is now time to reveal what really happened at Roswell."

Senator Watson from Missouri tentatively agreed. "I think before you do so, you should decide how far you wish to go into some of the technology. I fear some of it is just too far advanced to release at this moment."

"I agree, Mr. President," Representative Billings from Montana added. "If we put free energy out into the marketplace all at once, the oil and gas industries will be in ruins. Our economy, and the world's economy, would collapse."

"I'm well aware of what you're saying. That is why I think the various aspects of the advanced technology must be looked at closely. A way must be worked out whereby we can bring forth this incredible technology incrementally. If we phase it in slowly and work with industries, it should work. I know it will take quite a while, but that is why we need expert support. Can you two come up with names of people who we know we can trust to give us some suggestions quickly? Meanwhile, I think I should stand up and reveal the truth about Roswell; it is time that the US government acknowledges that UFOs and aliens do exist.

* * *

"Sam, Gwen here. I'm thinking of publishing an article on the artificially-induced earthquakes and I would like very much if you would co-author it with me."

"Gwen, this is a surprise, and an excellent idea. Have you received clearance from Kingsley?"

"Actually, Sam, it was he who suggested it."

"Fantastic! How would you like to proceed with this?"

"I was hoping to come up there. I know you and Meg are at Nona's place, and I don't wish to interrupt your time with them. Sean and I just got engaged, so if you could suggest a quiet place for us to stay, it would be much appreciated."

"Gwen, this is fantastic news! Yes, I know of a lovely little cabin which sits up on a cliff looking southward over the Bay of Fundy. Let me get Meg—she'll love to hear your news."

Sam called Megan to the phone.

"Meg, I'm so incredibly happy. Sean and I are engaged!" said Gwen.

Megan was so excited, she was laughing with joy. "Gwen, this is wonderful news. I had a feeling something was going on between you two. Have you picked a wedding date yet?"

"We're still talking about that, hopefully this summer. Sam has some news for you. Must go—I'll talk to you later."

Megan found Sam out on the deck standing looking out at the sea. "Wonderful news about Gwen and Sean; Gwen said you have some news for me."

Sam sat and told her of Gwen's plan.

* * *

On their flight home from Europe, Nona and Fred began to analyze why their tours had been so successful, especially of late. There was the outbreak in Beijing and India, and also the earthquake near Australia. Earth seemed to be in utter turmoil with tsunamis, floods, and new outbreaks of a particularly deadly disease. They were sure their tour would have to be discontinued due to the level of fear and panic that seemed to be gripping the world—yet the opposite had occurred. The halls were packed to standing room only; many places had additional rooms or locations set up with TV monitors to take in the overflow. They soon found out they were not unique. Virtually all spiritually-orientated websites worldwide were growing in numbers and creating community. Many who had not been promoting the use of vibration and sound were now doing so. People were searching for an answer as how to save the planet, and sought an answer as to how to stop the chaos that was going on around them. They began to realize the world's population must work together if there was to be any hope for Earth's survival.

The easiest way humans around the world could communicate with one another in a trusting and calm manner was through pure sound which came from their hearts and souls. Ancient sounds such as *um, oh,* and *ah* were proven to be effective, especially when used in concert with meditations and prayers of love and peace. This technique, in various formats, was shown to work over thousands of years with confirmed, positive results scattered around the globe. Virtually all spiritual groups and individuals around the world decided this idea was worth a try.

There was an agreement in the works: every human on Earth was welcome to become a part of this experiment. All that was necessary was to be sincere on praying or meditating for love and peace to come to Earth. Any method could be used—whatever each individual was most comfortable with. Many had already begun to experiment with various techniques ranging from total silence to intoning certain sounds and notes. People were becoming kinder and more helpful to one another.

The main issue to be overcome, however, was how these groups and individuals were going to coordinate their efforts to provide a worldwide unified call for peace and love. Suggestions as how to do this had been solicited from the public; they were collected, summarized, and voted on.

It was early May when the results were in. They aimed for the next solstice; June 21 would be the date. Several suggestions regarding the importance of the number three had also been made. Because of the huge success of the "Nona/Fred" speeches, they were asked to help coordinate what was tentatively called "Earth's Meditation for Peace." After analyzing suggestions as to how to coordinate it, Nona, Megan, Fred, Andrew, and Sam had come up with an idea:

The emphasis was to be put on the freedom of choice. There would not be any hard and fast rules; they recognized the varying belief systems and customs of the world's population were so varied that many would have their own way of how they wanted to participate. Of paramount importance was the timing. Throughout Earth's history, the sun was of prime importance; therefore, as the sun rose around the world on the mornings of June 19, 20, and 21, meditations and prayers focused on peace and love would begin, and hopefully continue for at least two hours or longer. This way, a wave of positive energy would sweep around the globe.

An invitation went out from all of the interested groups over the Internet; it read:

> PLEASE JOIN US IN A THREE-DAY EVENT TO SAVE OUR PLANET.
>
> Let sounds and voices of all nature, every aspect of heaven and earth, sound your notes of joy, love, and peace. Come, one and all, all as one,

from above and below, below and above, and all that is between. Join us in one continuous symphony: a peaceful and harmonious energy as we create sacred sounds rising from fearless thoughts of peace and unconditional love. Let our Earth's chorus be heard by all—the heavens above and throughout our galaxy, the universe, and through eternity. Let it be known that Earth and all that's part of her are free.

With love, join the 'All that was, the All that is, and the All that ever will be.'

The announcement went on to give the dates; the event was to start with the sunrise wherever one would be on the planet.

Word of agreement spread far and wide. By mid-June, the numbers of those who wished to participate had risen into the millions and was still rising, when another 8.5 earthquake occurred off the west coast of the United States, west of San Francisco.

Sam immediately confirmed that it was indeed an artificially-induced quake. Within hours, a second one at the magnitude of 8.0 occurred off of Japan. It too was of unnatural origin. Sam immediately contacted Kingsley with his findings. Minutes later, Mesda let the president know it was produced by the aliens, the Anunnaki.

"They know they are losing their grip on earth and have panicked. This is probably their last stand. They are trying to interfere with the upcoming three-day event to help save Earth."

"Do you think they'll succeed?" a worried Kingsley asked.

"No, I think that they've left it too late and have overdone it," answered Mesda.

Kingsley called Gwen.

"How close are you and Sam to publishing the article on artificially-induced quakes?"

"I've just sent it to the editors at the Washington Post, and was about to send it to the world wire service when we got the news of these two new ones. I'm in the process of updating it; I'll send this corrected version asap. CNN, etc. will be showing it within the hour."

"Thank you, Gwen. I'll contact our news outlet here and fully endorse your report. I'll make it very clear these are isolated cases and that things are under control."

He paused before continuing.

"This is for your ears only, Gwen: Mesda tells me there will be no more artificially-induced quakes in the near future."

Gwen turned on CNN; ten minutes later, she saw the piece on artificially-induced quakes. Shortly after that, Kingsley spoke reassuringly to the American people and to the world.

Neither of these two quakes caused much of a tsunami. Most of the damage was in the coastal areas of Southern California and northern Japan. It would be a while before the death toll would be known; however, San Francisco sustained a fair bit of damage to its buildings.

Nona and Andrew were watching the various websites concerning the effect on the numbers of people who had volunteered to join the three-day event. It was too early to tell what the impact of these quakes would have. For the moment, they were holding steady. After an hour or so, when they expected a decrease, the numbers slowly increased. Sam watched over their shoulders and smiled.

Well, that sure backfired, he thought.

Megan turned to Sam and quietly said, "I want to go for a walk on the beach; please, let's try to forget all this, just for a while."

It was late afternoon, and the cool breeze was coming in from the ocean. Sam grabbed his jacket and Meg's sweater. Meg was quiet; as they started to walk the beach, she was doing her favourite thing: picking up sea glass.

"I wonder if we'll ever get back to a normal life, or if this is our new normal," Megan said as she picked up small, smooth pink and white stone.

"Kingsley is assuring us that there will probably be no more artificially-induced quakes," said Sam.

"How does he know that?"

"He has a very reliable alien source. But Megan...something else is bothering you; what is it?"

"I was just wondering if it's safe to bring children into this world."

Sam stopped and spun around, facing her, and looking straight into her eyes. "Meg, you're thinking about having children, aren't you?"

"Well, kind of," she admitted. She couldn't help smiling. "I'm not thinking about it."

Sam just stood there and stared at her like a deer looking at headlights of a car; he was stunned. "Meg, are you sure?"

"Yes, darling, you are going to be a father!"

Sam was ecstatic. He picked her up off the ground and slowly swung her around.

"Oh Meg! I'm so happy!"

"I'm so glad you are darling, because, we're having twins."

"When?"

"Sometime in January. Let's go and tell our folks!"

Everyone was blown away with the news, and they were all so happy.

"Gram, you're going to be a great-grandmother!"

"I'm so thrilled for you both. Now off you go—Roger will jump out of his boots when he hears your news!"

That evening, they all sat down after dinner, discussing what they were going to for the three-day event.

"Seeing that today is June 10th, we'd best start making plans," Andrew said, looking at his calendar. "Meg, what would you like to do?"

"I thought how wonderful it would be to go out on Serendipity, if the weather is good."

"What a fantastic idea!" Gwen said. "I like it."

Everyone agreed it was what they would do. Gram smiled and added, "Roger was telling me this morning they've spotted humpbacks in the Gulf of Maine headed our way.

"Oh, Gram—I knew it! Lacuna will be here, too!"

"Who's Lacuna?" Sean asked; everyone laughed. "You'll soon find out!" Gwen told him.

"Papa Joe is arriving in a couple of days; he'll be with us also," said Nona.

"I'm so looking forward to seeing him again," Megan said.

"I've had another thought," said Andrew. "There are a lot of folks here on the island who would like to take part in the event. Why don't we invite them to bring their families and friends to come out on their boats and join us? That way we would have a flotilla of boats from virtually every community on the island."

"What a great idea! I'll help to make some calls," Megan said, taking her cell phone out of her purse.

* * *

June 19 was rapidly approaching. They had done all the planning they could; now it was time to wait and pray that all was going to go well. On Grand Manan alone they had over fifty boats that were going out on the bay. They planned on forming four large circles, one off each main harbour: North Head, Ingalls Head, Seal Cove and White Head Island. Everyone who was going out on a boat was up very early and on their way well before sunrise. Word had spread all up and down the East Coast of New Brunswick, Nova Scotia, Prince Edward Island, Newfoundland, and the coast of Maine and New England. Boats of all sizes and descriptions were moving out to sea. They formed circles as the weather was calm and clear. They started singing hymns and down east songs, waiting for the sun to rise.

Just before sunrise, they all went quiet, preparing and clearing their minds to get ready to start their meditation. Those on Serendipity chose the sacred sound of 'um' to intone as they meditated on peace and unconditional love.

People all over the world were either getting ready or were well into the process. Those on land gathered outdoors where they could; others were indoors in groups; thousands had stayed home and used the Internet for the signal to start. Many formed circles, and some even formed circles within circles. Thousands upon thousands had gathered at the various sacred sites around the world. Many had camped there for a few days beforehand.

It began spreading from the British Isles, Western Africa, the Mediterranean Sea, across the Atlantic through Iceland, Greenland, Newfoundland, and Brazil; the wave swept over the Americas to the Pacific, the Hawaiian islands, Polynesia, the Philippines, New Zealand, Russia, Japan, China, Australia, India, Asia, Africa and Europe. This huge wave of unconditional love spread over the planet. As it went, the peaceful energy began slowly to spread outwards beyond Earth's atmosphere and into space.

The patrolling alien spacecraft circling and monitoring Earth could not believe what their instruments were telling them. They had picked up these extraordinary vibrations, and were astounded by their strength and the speed with which they encircled the planet. They had been waiting for years for something like this to happen, but they had no idea it could be this powerful. By the end of the day, they had contacted their mother ships, who in turn contacted their home planets. It was decided they would wait another day. Were the Earthlings really sincere?

The next day, the same thing happened, only the signals were even stronger. They formed a stronger energy network which extended far out into space. The aliens took this is a very positive response and prepared themselves to answer.

By the morning of June 21, even more humans had joined. Before the sun rose over the east coast of the Americas, submarines were reporting and recording underwater sounds from whales and dolphins. Each day, they were clearer and clearer, and were very harmonious across all the oceans.

As the sun rose over the Bay of Fundy, the group on Serendipity was ready. As they began to chant, Papa Joe began to hum. Megan joined in immediately, and one by one, so did the others. The adjacent boats did the same. Nona leaned over, giving Megan a hug, and pointed out to sea. Megan began to weep with joy. Sam came over with Gwen, and soon all of them were humming Joe's tune as loud as they could.

The other boats in their circle picked up on whatever it was Megan was looking at. They had carefully lifted Megan up on top of the wheelhouse. Through her tears, she shouted, "Lacuna! Lacuna! Lacuna!"

With that, the huge humpback whale dove, only to come flying straight up out of the water; as she cleared the surface, she did a 360° spin and landed with a huge splash. Then, several other whales did the same thing in sequence behind her. Everyone was spellbound. Papa Joe began to hum again as everyone joined in. The breaching had occurred just over hundred feet from the boat.

The whales slowly glided towards the circle from all directions. There were not just humpbacks—there were also finbacks, and a few right whales in the group. They took turns swimming under the boats and coming up inside the circle, and then out again. It was like a dance. The last time they did this, five humpbacks resting on the surface and dove simultaneously, leaving large, calm circles on the surface. These circles, called footprints, formed a beautiful star design.

Lacuna had returned and came up to rest alongside Serendipity; she sent Megan a message:

Not now, Megan—you and I will swim together later.

Within a half an hour, white-sided and white-beaked dolphins appeared and put on quite a show. Shortly after they all left, Lacuna left Megan with the message she'd be back. She was needed elsewhere.

The aliens had made their decision; they were going to land a few of their scout ships to attempt peaceful contact with humans at various locations around the world. While they awaited their signal to land, they listened and watched what was happening below. One special cloaked spaceship was hovering in the Nova Scotia/New Brunswick area. It had just come from observing similar scenes up and down the east coast of North America. They had witnessed the display of the whales around the boats below.

Earth was alive and vibrating with unconditional love and peace. Everyone, every being, every plant, right down to the molecules forming the rocks were vibrating in unison. The oceans around the world had never been in such harmony—not for millions of years. Earth was encompassed by the most beautiful symphony of vibrations. The sound which humans could hear was an enormous choir of pure sounds—millions of them: birds, people, whales, crickets, elephants, wolves, cats, dolphins, seals, and so many more were blended into a silky harmonious symphony which rolled over them in a series of waves. Tears were streaming down the cheeks of virtually every human who was partaking in this event; they were tears of joy and relief.

Lacuna, keeping her promise, came back to Serendipity, and to Megan. A spacecraft was slowly landing on the water, about 200 feet away.

Suddenly, all the humming stopped, and everyone stared at the craft.

Megan shouted, "Please, please—do not be afraid. They will not harm us; I'll show you."

She untied the zodiac, and Joe started the engine. Together, they headed for the spacecraft; Lacuna swimming beside her. They slowly approached the huge circular vessel ahead. As they did so, a small door opened, and two figures came out onto the platform. Behind them, they could hear the same piece they had been humming on their boats.—only now there were more parts to the music. Immediately, a sense of peace and serenity spread forth from the spacecraft; everyone felt secure and very peaceful, and all the people began to wave both arms over their heads as they shouted, "Welcome; welcome to Earth!"

Megan and Joe climbed out of the zodiac onto the platform, and stood beside the two aliens. Megan was smiling ear to ear.

"Ortho...Saron—I knew you would come to meet us!"

This same scene was repeated in many places in the world. Those on land were initially greeted in the same fashion; many of the children between the ages of five and twelve rushed forward as a group. Their parents were about to rush after them when they realized that youngsters of similar ages were running out of the spacecraft's to greet them. Before their eyes, the children intermixed and were kicking around a soccer ball, thoroughly enjoying themselves. Slowly, the older and younger kids joined in. Next, some of the children ran back to take their parents' hands, and took them to join in the fun. The same happened with the aliens. Before they knew it, there were impromptu soccer matches springing up all over the world.

In one such landing area, there was a young disabled boy in a wheelchair. One of the young aliens came over and took the wheelchair and, with the boy's parents following him, he pushed it over to an alien couple who walked towards the wheelchair. With each kneeling on either side of the boy's wheelchair, and without touching him, they moved their hands about six inches away from his body; the whole time they were humming quietly. After several minutes, they stopped. Standing in front of the young lad, each of the two aliens extended a hand out to him. The boy reached out tentatively, and placed each hand in the hands of the aliens. A couple of the young aliens approached from either side and placed their hands under his elbows, and slowly started to lift the paralyzed boy out of his wheelchair. His parents moved towards them; a few of their fellow humans said, "Wait; let's see what is about to happen. We are right here; he'll be okay."

Everyone watched in amazement; the boy stood up. The aliens withdrew their support. One of the adult aliens stepped back about six feet and motioned for the lad to come to him. For a few seconds, he stood frozen, afraid to move. Again, he was motioned to move forward.

"Come on, Ron—you can do it!"

Several shouts of encouragement rang out. What seemed like minutes went by; then Ron slid his right leg forward about six inches; it held. He moved his left leg forward. The huge cheer went up as Ron was standing on his own. His mother was in tears. One of the young aliens brought him a soccer ball. The crowd fell silent.

"Come on Ron; let's play!"

Ron dropped the ball and gave it a kick; he started to play. It took him a few minutes to gain confidence, and then he began to run.

Similar scenarios were occurring everywhere the hundreds of spacecraft landed. These peaceful exchanges heralded a promising future for one and all as Earth began to heal.

Printed in Canada